ONE

DARK

THRONE

KENDARE BLAKE

HARPER TEEN
An imprint of HarperCollinsPublishers

HarperTeen is an imprint of HarperCollins Publishers.

One Dark Throne
Text copyright © 2017 by Kendare Blake
Map of Fennbirn by Virginia Allyn

Library of Congress Control Number: 2017943441
ISBN 978-0-06-238546-8 (trade bdg.)
ISBN 978-0-06-269045-6 (int.)
ISBN 978-0-06-269935-0 (special edition)
ISBN 978-0-06-269730-1 (special edition)
ISBN 978-0-06-274764-8 (special edition)
ISBN 978-0-06-279729-2 (special edition)

Typography by Aurora Parlagreco
17 18 19 20 21   PC/LSCH   10 9 8 7 6 5 4 3 2 1
❖
First Edition

CAST OF CHARACTERS

INDRID DOWN
Capital City, Home of Queen Katharine

THE ARRONS

Natalia Arron
Matriarch of the Arron family. Head of the Black Council.

Genevieve Arron
Younger sister to Natalia

Antonin Arron
Younger brother to Natalia

Pietyr Renard
Natalia's nephew by her brother Christophe

ROLANTH
Home of Queen Mirabella

THE WESTWOODS

Sara Westwood
Matriarch of the Westwood family. Affinity: water

Bree Westwood
Daughter of Sara Westwood, friend to the queen. Affinity: fire

WOLF SPRING

Home of Queen Arsinoe

THE MILONES

Cait Milone
Matriarch of the Milone family. Familiar: Eva, a crow

Ellis Milone
Husband to Cait and father to her children. Familiar: Jake, a white spaniel

Caragh Milone
Elder daughter of Cait, banished to the Black Cottage. Familiar: Juniper, a brown hound

Madrigal Milone
Younger daughter of Cait. Familiar: Aria, a crow

Juillenne "Jules" Milone
Daughter of Madrigal. The strongest naturalist in decades and friend to the queen. Familiar: Camden, a mountain cat

THE SANDRINS

Matthew Sandrin
Eldest of the Sandrin sons. Former betrothed of Caragh Milone

Joseph Sandrin
Middle Sandrin son. Friend of Arsinoe. Banished to the mainland for five years

OTHERS

Luke Gillespie

Proprietor of Gillespie's Bookshop. Friend of Arsinoe. Familiar: Hank, a black-and-green rooster

William "Billy" Chatworth Jr.

Foster brother to Joseph Sandrin. Suitor to the queens.

THE TEMPLE

High Priestess Luca

Priestess Rho Murtra

Elizabeth

Initiate and friend to Queen Mirabella

THE BLACK COUNCIL

Natalia Arron, *poisoner*

Genevieve Arron, *poisoner*

Lucian Arron, *poisoner*

Antonin Arron, *poisoner*

Allegra Arron, *poisoner*

Paola Vend, *poisoner*

Lucian Marlowe, *poisoner*

Margaret Beaulin, *war-gifted*

Renata Hargrove, *giftless*

GREAVESDRAKE MANOR

❧

*N*atalia Arron oversees her younger sister's move back to Greavesdrake with a critical eye. Genevieve was banished from the house for only a few months. If one were to judge by the endless line of trunks the footmen carry through the front door, you would think she had been gone for years.

"It will be good to sleep in my own bed again," Genevieve says. She inhales deeply. The air at Greavesdrake smells of oiled wood, and books, and savory, poisoned stew bubbling in the kitchen.

"Your bed in town is also your own," says Natalia. "Do not act as though it were a hardship."

Natalia studies Genevieve from the corner of her eye. Genevieve's cheeks are rosy pink, and her lilac irises sparkle. Long, blond hair tumbles past her shoulder. People say she is the beautiful Arron sister. If they only knew what wicked thoughts whirled inside that pretty head.

"Now that you are home," says Natalia. "Prove yourself useful. What is the Council whispering?"

"The story has been told as you instructed," Genevieve replies. "That Queen Katharine survived Queen Arsinoe's attack with the bear and cleverly went into hiding until all was deemed safe. But they have still heard the stories."

"What stories?"

"Nonsense, mostly." Genevieve waves her hand. But Natalia frowns. Nonsense becomes truth if enough mouths repeat it.

"What sort of nonsense?"

"That Katharine did not survive at all. Some actually claim to have seen her die, and some say that they saw her as she made her way home: gray-skinned and covered in mud, with blood running from her mouth. They have been calling her Katharine the Undead. Can you imagine?"

Natalia barks laughter. She crosses her arms. It is ridiculous. But she still does not like it.

"But what did happen to her, in the days that she was missing?" Genevieve asks. "Do even you not know?"

Natalia thinks back to that night, when Katharine returned, covered in dirt and bleeding from a dozen cuts. Mute in the foyer with filthy black hair hanging over her face. She had looked like a monster.

"I know enough," Natalia says, and turns on her heel.

"They say she has changed. How has she changed? Is she strong enough yet to return to her poison training?"

Natalia swallows. Poison training will not be necessary. But she says nothing. She inclines her head and leads Genevieve down the hall, looking for Kat so that Genevieve might see for herself.

They walk together deeper into the manor, where the light is softened by drawn curtains and the sounds of the footmen laboring beneath Genevieve's trunks fade.

Genevieve tucks her traveling gloves into the pocket of her breeches. She looks very smart in her soft, brushed carnelian jacket. She claps at imagined dust on her thigh.

"So much to do," she says. "The suitors will arrive any day."

Natalia's mouth twists up at the corner. *Suitors.* But only one requested first court with Katharine. The golden-blond boy, Nicolas Martel. Despite Katharine's strong showing during her Beltane poison feast, both of the other suitors had elected to pursue Arsinoe.

Arsinoe, with her scarred face, trousers with frayed cuffs, and shorn, unkempt hair. No one could be attracted to that. They must be curious about her bear.

"Who would have thought our queen would have only one request?" Genevieve says, reading Natalia's sour expression.

"It does not matter. Nicolas Martel is the finest of the bunch. Were it not for our long alliance with Billy Chatworth's father, he would be my top choice."

"Billy Chatworth has been lost to the Bear Queen," Genevieve mutters. "The whole island knows that."

"Billy Chatworth will do as his father commands," Natalia

snaps. "And do not call Arsinoe the Bear Queen. We do not want that to stick."

They turn the corner past Katharine's staircase.

"She is not in her rooms?" Genevieve asks as they pass by.

"You can never tell where she is anymore."

A maid carrying a vase of white oleander blooms pauses to drop a curtsy.

"Where is the queen?" Natalia asks.

"In the solarium," the girl replies.

"Thank you," says Genevieve. Then she yanks the girl's cap off her head to reveal dark brown roots beneath fading Arron-blond dye. "Now go and tend to your hair."

The solarium is bright and open, with many uncovered windows. White paint on the walls, and multicolored pillows on the sofa. It hardly belongs in the Arron house and is usually empty, unless they are entertaining guests. But Natalia and Genevieve find Katharine inside humming, surrounded by wrapped packages.

"Look who is home," Natalia says.

Katharine presses a lid onto a pretty purple box. Then she turns to face them, smiling broadly.

"Genevieve," Katharine says. "It is good to have you and Antonin at Greavesdrake again."

Genevieve's mouth hangs open. She has not seen Katharine since the day after she returned. And Katharine was such a mess then. Still filthy, and with so many fingernails missing.

As she stares at Katharine now, it is not difficult for Natalia to guess what she is thinking. Where is the little girl with her large foolish eyes and tightly braided bun? The skinny girl who bows her head and only laughs after someone else laughs first?

But wherever that Katharine is, it is not here.

"Antonin," Genevieve murmurs once she finds her voice. "He is already here?"

"Of course," Natalia replies. "I asked him back first."

Shocked as Genevieve is by the sight of the queen, she does not even pout. Katharine sweeps forward and takes her by the wrists, and if she notices the way Genevieve recoils at the sudden, uncharacteristic gesture, she does not show it. She simply smiles and drags her farther into the room.

"Do you like my presents?" Katharine asks, gesturing to the packages. They are all beautiful, wrapped in colored paper and tied with satin ribbon or large white velvet bows.

"Who are they from?" asks Genevieve. "The suitors?"

"Not 'from,'" Katharine says. "But for. As soon as I have put on the last loving touches, they will be dispatched to Rolanth, for my dear sister Mirabella."

Katharine caresses the nearest bit of ribbon with a black-gloved finger.

"Will you tell us what is inside them," Natalia asks, "or must we guess?"

Katharine tosses a tendril of hair over her shoulder. "Inside she will find many things. Poisoned gloves. Tainted jewels. A dried chrysanthemum bulb painted with toxin, to bloom into poisoned tea."

"This will never work," Genevieve says. "They will be checked. You cannot kill Mirabella with prettily wrapped poison presents."

"We nearly killed that naturalist with a prettily wrapped poison present," Katharine counters in a low voice. She sighs. "But you are probably right. These are only a bit of fun."

Natalia looks over the boxes. There are more than a dozen, of various sizes and colors. Each will likely be transported individually, by separate courier. Those couriers will be changed several times, in different cities, before arriving in Rolanth. It seems a lot of trouble to go to for just a bit of fun.

Katharine finishes inking a gift tag with dark stars and swirls. Then she sits on the gold-and-white brocade sofa and reaches for a plate of belladonna berries. She eats a handful, filling her cheeks, mashing them with her teeth until the poison juice shows at the corners of her lips. Genevieve gasps. She turns toward Natalia, but there is no explanation to give. When Katharine recovered from her wounds, she turned to the poisons and began to devour them.

"There is still no word from Pietyr?" Katharine asks, wiping juice from her chin.

"No. And I do not know what to tell you. I wrote him immediately after you returned, to summon him back. I have also written to my brother inquiring about what is keeping him. But there has been no response from Christophe either."

"I will write to Pietyr myself, then," says Katharine. She presses a gloved hand to her stomach as the belladonna berries take effect. If Katharine's gift had come, the poison should not cause her pain. Yet she seems able to bear more than she ever could before, taking in so much that every meal is like a *Gave Noir*. Katharine smiles brightly. "I will have a letter ready before I leave for the temple this evening."

"That is a good idea," Natalia says. "I am sure you will be able to persuade him."

She motions to Genevieve so they might leave the solarium. Poor Genevieve. She does not know how to behave. No doubt she would like to be mean, to pinch the queen, or slap her, but the queen before them looks like she might slap right back. Genevieve frowns, and drops a lazy curtsy.

"Has her gift come, then?" Genevieve whispers once she and Natalia have mounted the stairs. "The way she ate those berries. But I could feel that her hands were swollen through the gloves. . . ."

"I do not know," Natalia replies quietly.

"Could it be the gift developing?"

"If it is, I have never seen any gift develop similarly."

"If her gift has not come, she must take care. Too much poison . . . she could harm herself. Damage herself."

Natalia stops walking.

"I know that. But I cannot seem to stop her."

"What happened to her?" Genevieve asks. "Where was she for those days?"

Natalia thinks back to the shadow of a girl who walked through her front door, gray-skinned and cold. Sometimes she sees the figure in her dreams, lurching toward her bed on the stiffened limbs of a corpse. Natalia shivers. Despite the warmth of the summer air, she craves a fire and a blanket around her shoulders.

"Perhaps it is better not to know."

Katharine's letter to Pietyr consists of only three lines.

Dearest Pietyr,

Return to me now. Do not be afraid. Do not delay.

Your Queen Katharine

Poor Pietyr. She likes to imagine him hiding somewhere. Or running through scratchy brambles and twigs that sting like lashes, just as she did the night he met her beside the Breccia Domain. The night he threw her down into it.

"I must take care with my words, Sweetheart," she says softly to the snake coiled around her arm. "So he will still think me his gentle little queen." She smiles. "I must not scare him."

He probably thinks that he will be put into the cells beneath the Volroy when he returns. That she will allow some war-gifted guard to beat his head against the walls until his brains run out. But Katharine has not told anyone about his role in her fall that night. And she has no plans to. She told Natalia that she stumbled into the Breccia Domain on her own as she fled in a

8

panic from Arsinoe's bear.

Katharine looks out her window from where she sits at her writing desk. To the east, below the last of the Stonegall hills, the capital city of Indrid Down glitters in the late-afternoon sun. In the center, the twin black spires of the Volroy jut up into the sky, the great castle fortress dwarfing everything else. Even the mountains seem hunched in comparison, backing off like trolls brought down by a shining light.

The belladonna berries roll in Katharine's stomach, but she does not wince. It has been more than a month since she had to claw her way up and out of the heart of the island, and now Katharine can withstand anything.

She leans over and pushes the window open. These days her rooms smell slightly of sickness and whatever animals she is testing her poisons on. Many small cages of birds and rodents litter the room, on top of her tables and lined along the walls. A few lie inside dead, waiting to be cleared out.

She taps the cage on the corner of her desk to rouse the small gray mouse inside. It is blind in one eye, and mostly bald from Katharine's rubbed poisons. She offers it a cracker through the bars of its cage, and it creeps forward, sniffing, afraid to eat it.

"Once, I was a mouse," she says, and strips off her glove. She reaches into the cage to stroke the rodent's tiny bald haunches.

"But I am not anymore."

WOLF SPRING

---　❧　---

*A*rsinoe and Jules are at the kitchen table slicing small red potatoes when Jules's Grandpa Ellis bursts through the side door with his white spaniel familiar. He arches his graying brow at them and holds up a small black envelope bearing the wax seal of the Black Council.

Grandma Cait pauses just long enough in her herb-chopping to blow loose hair out of her face. Then all three women go back to the tasks at hand.

"Doesn't anybody want to read it?" Ellis asks. He sets the letter on the tabletop and lifts his spaniel, Jake, to sniff at the potatoes.

"Why?" Cait snorts. "We can all guess what it says." She gestures with her head to the other side of the kitchen. "Now would you crack me four egg yolks into that bowl?"

Ellis sets Jake down and tears the letter open.

"They make a point of noting that the suitors all requested

first court with Queen Katharine," he says as he reads.

"That is a lie," Jules mutters.

"Maybe so. But it hardly matters. It says here that we are to welcome the suitors Thomas 'Tommy' Stratford and Michael Percy."

"Two?" Arsinoe scrunches her face in distaste. "Why both of them? Why any?"

Jules, Cait, and Ellis trade glances. More than one suitor at the same time is a great compliment. Before the show of the bear at the Beltane Festival, no one expected that Arsinoe would receive any requests for first suit, let alone two.

"They are to arrive any day," Ellis says. "And who knows how long they might stay on if they like you."

"They'll be gone by week's end," Arsinoe says, and chops a potato in half.

Jules takes the letter from Ellis.

"Tommy Stratford and Michael Percy." So much of the Beltane Festival is a blur, but they were the two who came ashore on a barge together the night of the Disembarking. It seemed that they could not stop laughing. Billy had wanted to throttle them.

Arsinoe tosses her knife onto the table and piles the last of the potato slices onto a wooden platter.

"That's done, Cait," she says. "What's next?"

"What's next is you getting out of this house," Cait replies. "You cannot hide in my kitchen forever."

Arsinoe sinks in her chair. The people of Wolf Spring

cannot get enough of their Bear Queen. They gather around her in the market and ask for tales of her great brown. They buy him huge silver fish and expect her to tear into it, too. Raw, right before their eyes. They do not know that the bear was a ruse, called onto the stage during the Quickening Ceremony to dance as if on a string. They do not know that it was Jules controlling it and a low magic spell. Only the family and Joseph and Billy know that. And still fewer know of Arsinoe's biggest secret: that she is no naturalist at all but a poisoner, her gift discovered when she and Jules both ingested poisoned sweets from Katharine. Jules had sickened to near death, and the damage to her body gave her constant pain and a limp. But Arsinoe had not sickened at all.

That secret only she, Jules, and Joseph know.

"Come on," Jules says. She claps Arsinoe on the shoulder and rises, stiffly. Beside her, her mountain cat, Camden, favors the shoulder that was broken by Arsinoe's first false familiar, the diseased bear that scarred Arsinoe's face. Not even two months passed between the crippling of Camden in that attack and the crippling of Jules by poison. It is as if the Goddess cruelly intended for them to match.

"Where're we going?" Arsinoe asks.

"Out from underfoot," Cait says as she tosses scraps of food up onto the cupboards for the crow familiars, Aria and Eva. The birds bob their heads appreciatively, and Cait lowers her voice. "Do you need some willowbark tea brewed before you go, Jules?"

"No, Grandma. I'm fine."

Outside in the yard, Arsinoe follows Jules past the chicken coops as she and Camden stretch their sore limbs in the sun. Then she darts off into the woodpile.

"What are you digging for?" Jules asks.

"Nothing." But Arsinoe returns with a book, brushing bits of bark off the soft green cover. She holds it up and Jules frowns. It is a book of poison plants, lifted discreetly from one of the shelves in Luke's bookshop.

"You shouldn't be messing about with that," Jules says. "And what if someone sees you with it?"

"Then they'll think I'm trying to get revenge, for what was done to you."

"That won't work. Reading a book to out-poison the poisoners? You can't even poison a poisoner, can you?"

"Say 'poison' one more time, Jules."

"I'm serious, Arsinoe." She drops her voice to a hissing whisper even though they are alone in the yard. "If anyone finds out what you really are, we lose the only advantage that we have. Is that what you want?"

"No," Arsinoe says quietly. She does not argue further, tired of listening to Jules talk of advantages and strategies. Jules has been considering their options since before she was even able to get out of bed from the poison.

"You sound hesitant," Jules says.

"I am hesitant. I don't want to kill them. And I don't think they really want to kill me."

"But they will."

"How do you know?"

"Because every queen we have ever had has done the same. Since the beginning."

Arsinoe's jaw tightens. Since the beginning. That old parable, that the Goddess sent gifts through the sacrifice of queens, triplets sent to the island when the people were still wild tribes. The strongest slew her sisters and their blood fed the island. And she ruled as queen until the Goddess sent new triplets, who grew, and killed, and fed the island. They say it was an instinct once. The drive to kill one another as natural as stags locking horns in the autumn. But that is only a story.

"Arsinoe? You know they will. You know they'll kill you whether they want to or not. Even Mirabella."

"You only think that because of Joseph," Arsinoe says. "But she didn't know and . . . she couldn't help it." *I did it*, she almost says, but she still cannot, even after all that her botched spell has cost them. She is still too much a coward.

"That's not why," Jules says. "And besides, what happened with Joseph . . . it was a mistake. He doesn't love her. He never left my side during the poison."

Arsinoe looks away. She knows that Jules has tried hard to believe that. And to forgive him.

"Maybe we should just run," Jules goes on. "Go to ground and hide until one destroys the other. They wouldn't hunt for you too hard with each other there to choose from. Why bother searching the scrub brush for a grouse when there's a deer standing in the clearing? I've been squirreling away food, just in case. Supplies. We could take horses for distance and trade them for provisions when we go on foot. We'll circle around the capital, where no one will look. And where we'll be sure to hear of it when one of them dies." Jules looks at her from the side of her eye. "And for the record, I hope it's Katharine who dies first. It will make Mirabella easier to poison if she's not on the lookout for it anymore."

"What if Mirabella dies first?" Arsinoe asks, and Jules shrugs.

"Walk up and stab Katharine in the throat, I suppose. She can't hurt you."

Arsinoe sighs. There is so much risk, no matter which queen falls first. Mirabella might kill her outright, without a bear to defend her, but if Katharine were to cut her with a poisoned blade, her poisoner secret would come out. Then even if she won, the Arrons would claim her, and she would be yet another poisoner queen seated on the throne.

There must be a way, she thinks, a way out of this for all of us.

If she could only talk to them. Even if it was forced. If she could force a stalemate and they were locked together in the tower. If they could only talk, she knew it could be different.

"You have to get rid of that book," Jules says stubbornly. "I can't stand the sight of it."

Arsinoe slips the book guiltily into her vest.

"How would you feel if I told you to hide Camden?" she

asks. "If you hate the poisoners, you hate me."

"That's not true," Jules says. "You are ours. Haven't you been raised a naturalist all this time? Aren't you truly a naturalist, at heart?"

"I am a Milone," she says. "At heart."

Arsinoe bends down and parts the foliage and longer grasses in the meadow north of Dogwood Pond. She sent Jules into town, to the Lion's Head to look for Joseph and Billy. She said she would follow as soon as she hid the poison book. But she lied. Crouching, she combs through the grasses, and it does not take long for her to locate what she seeks: a stalk of white-flowered hemlock.

The poison sent by Katharine, meant for Arsinoe but swallowed by Jules as well, was thought to have contained a measure of hemlock. According to her book, it causes a peaceful death as it paralyzes the body from the feet up.

"A peaceful death," Arsinoe mutters. But it was not merciful, combined with whatever other poisons Katharine mixed it with. It was terrible. Slow, and damaging, and Jules suffered cruelly.

"Why did you do it, little sister?" Arsinoe wonders aloud. "Is it because you were angry? Because you thought I tried to have that bear slice you open?"

But in her mind, Katharine offers no reply.

Little Katharine. When they were children, her hair was the longest. And the shiniest. Her face had the sharpest little features. She would float on her back in the stream behind the cottage, with her hair clouded around her like black widgeon grass. Mirabella would send currents through it, and Katharine would laugh and laugh.

Arsinoe thinks of Jules's face, contorted in pain. Little Katharine is not to be trifled with.

Impulsively, she reaches forward and tears the hemlock out by the root. She should not have those fond memories anyway. She would not, if not for Mirabella and her cursed sentimentality, making her remember things that might never have been true.

"And even if they are," Arsinoe mutters, "Jules is right." Before the year is over, two of them will be dead. And no matter how hesitant she is to kill, she does not want to be one of the fallen.

She sniffs the hemlock blossom. It smells terrible, but she jams it into her mouth. The rancid smell takes on a new note as her chewing brings out the juices.

The hemlock does not taste good. Yet it tastes . . . satisfying. What she feels chewing poison must be something like Jules feels when she ripens an apple, or Mirabella feels when she calls the wind.

"Later I'll go take a nap in a bed of poison ivy," Arsinoe says, and chuckles as she eats the last of the flowers. "Or perhaps that is going too far."

"What's going too far?"

Arsinoe steps quickly away from the hemlock plant. She

drops the last of the stems and kicks them about to be lost in the grass.

"Good Goddess, Junior," she barks. "You sure know how to sneak up on somebody."

Billy grins and shrugs. Somehow he never seems to have enough to do. And he always manages to find her. She wonders if that is some mainlander gift. The gift of being a busybody.

"What are you doing?" he asks. "Not more low magic?"

"Cait sent me out after blackberries," she lies. Blackberries are not even in season yet.

Billy cranes his neck and looks over the shrubbery.

"I don't see any berries. Or a basket to carry them."

"You're a pain in the arse," Arsinoe mutters.

He laughs. "No bigger one than you."

She walks past him, leading them away from the hemlock.

"All right, I'm sorry," she says. "What are you doing here? I thought you would be with Joseph and Jules, at the Lion's Head."

"They need their time alone together." Billy plucks a fat blade of grass and puts it between his thumbs to whistle. "And Jules says you've had news of your suitors."

"So that's why you've come running." She grins, and the grin pushes up the side of the black lacquered mask she wears to cover her facial scars.

"I didn't 'come running,'" he insists. "I've always known this would happen. I knew they'd be after you once they saw that bear. Once they saw you up on that cliff at the Disembarking.

"And everyone else knew too. Down at the pier, we have

boats lined up to have their hulls scraped and repainted. No one in Wolf Spring wants to seem like they care what the rest of the island thinks. But they are lying."

Wolf Spring. A hard, farming, seafaring town full of hard, farming, brutal people. They value their land, and their waters, and the swing of their axes.

Arsinoe puts her hands on her hips and looks out over the meadow. It is beautiful. Wolf Spring is beautiful just as it is. She does not like to think of it changing to please some so-called illustrious guests.

"Tommy Stratford and Michael . . . something or other," she says. "Are you worried I'll like them better than I like you?"

"That's just not possible."

"Why? Because you're so irresistible?"

"No. Because you don't like anyone."

Arsinoe snorts.

"I do like you, Junior."

"Oh?"

"But I have more important things to think about right now."

Billy has let his hair grow since coming to the island, and it is long enough now to almost move a little in the wind. Arsinoe catches herself wondering what it would be like to run her fingers through it and promptly stuffs her hands into her pockets.

"I agree," Billy says, and turns to face her. "I want you to know that I've refused to go to your sisters."

"But your father. He will be furious! We'll stop the letter. Did you send it by bird or by horse? Do not say by boat. Jules can't call one of those back."

"It's too late, Arsinoe. It's done." He steps closer and touches the cheek of her black-and-red mask. He was there that day, when she had foolishly led them into a bear attack. He had tried to save her.

"You said you didn't want to marry me," she whispers.

"I say a lot of things."

He leans toward her. No matter what she says about putting off thoughts of the future, she has imagined this moment many times. Watching him from the corner of her eye and wondering what his kisses would be like. Gentle? Or clumsy? Or would they be the way his laughter is, confident and full of mischief?

Arsinoe's heart beats faster. She leans into him, and then she remembers the hemlock that still coats her lips.

"Don't touch me!"

She shoves him, and he lands on his hip in the grass.

"Ow," he says.

"Sorry," she responds sheepishly, and helps him up. "I didn't mean to do that."

"The near kiss or the shove?" He brushes himself off without looking at her, his cheeks red with embarrassment. "Did I do something wrong? Did you want to be the one to kiss me? Is that how it is here? Because I would be fine with that—"

"No." Arsinoe can still taste the hemlock, in the back of her throat. She almost forgot. She almost killed him, and the thought takes her breath away. "I'm sorry. I just don't want to. Not right now."

* * *

Jules and Joseph finish two mugs of ale before acknowledging that Billy is not coming back with Arsinoe.

"Probably for the best," Joseph says. "It's grown late. Drunk folk might start demanding to see her bear."

Jules frowns. Their phantom bear is becoming a problem. Arsinoe has not been seen with him since the night of the Quickening, saying that he is too violent and must be kept far off in the woods. But that will not satisfy the people of Wolf Spring for much longer.

"Well," Joseph says, and pushes back from the table. "Shall we go? Or do you want another order of fried clams?"

Jules shakes her head, and they walk together out into the street. The early-evening light is softening, and the water of Sealhead Cove glitters cobalt and orange, visible between the buildings. As they make their way down toward it, Joseph slips his fingers into hers.

His touch still gives her a pleasurable jolt, even if it is tainted by what happened between him and Mirabella.

"Joseph," she says, and holds his hand up. "Your knuckles."

He lets go of her to make a fist. His knuckles are split and scabbed from working the boats. "I always said I would never work in the shipyard with my father and Matthew. Though I don't know what else I thought I would be doing." He sighs. "It's not a bad life, I suppose. If it's good enough for them, who am I to think any different? As long as you don't mind me smelling like a barnacle."

Jules hates to see his brave face. And how trapped he seems.

"I don't mind," she says. "And anyhow it's not forever."

"It's not?"

"Of course not. It's only until Arsinoe is crowned, remember? You on her council and me on her guard."

"Ah," he says, and slips his arm about her shoulders. "Our happy ending. I did say something like that, didn't I?"

They walk companionably through the alley between the Heath and Stone and the Wolverton Inn, Camden hopping up and down on stacks of wooden crates full of empty bottles.

"Where did Arsinoe go off to tonight?" Joseph asks.

"To the bent-over tree, probably. To find Madrigal and do more low magic."

"Madrigal is with Matthew. She met him on the docks, the moment he came in off *The Whistler.*"

Madrigal and Matthew. Their names together make her wince. Her mother's fling with Joseph's older brother should be over by now. Matthew at least should have come to his senses. He should realize how flighty and fickle Madrigal is. He should remember that he still loves her Aunt Caragh, banished to the Black Cottage or not.

"They ought to end that," she says.

"Maybe. But they won't. He says he loves her, Jules."

"Only with his eyes," she spits. "Not with his heart." Joseph nearly flinches when she says that, and she glances sideways at his handsome profile. Perhaps that is how all men love. More with their eyes than with their hearts. So maybe it was not the storm and the circumstances. The delirium. Queen Mirabella is certainly more to look at than she is, and maybe it was nothing more complicated than that.

Jules pulls away.

"What?" Joseph asks. They round the corner at the end of the alley, and a small group spills out from the doors of the Heath and Stone. When they see Joseph, they stop short.

Joseph wraps an arm about Jules's shoulders.

"Just keep walking."

But as they pass, the nearest girl, brave on too much whiskey, cuffs Joseph in the back of the head. When he turns, she spits on the chest of his shirt.

Joseph exhales in disgust, but does his best to smile.

Jules's temper flares.

"It's all right, Jules," he says.

"It's not all right," the girl snarls. "I saw what you did at the Beltane Festival. How you protected that elemental queen. Traitor!" She spits again. "Mainlander!" She turns to walk away but warns him over her shoulder, "Next time it won't be spit. Next time it'll be a knife between your ribs."

"That tears it," Jules says, and Camden leaps. She knocks the girl to the ground and pins her to the worn stones of the street with her one good paw.

Underneath the cougar, the girl trembles. The whiskey-courage is gone now, but she manages to curl her lip.

"What are you going to do?" she challenges.

"Anyone who touches Joseph will answer to me," Jules says. "Or maybe to the queen. And her bear."

Jules motions with her head, and Camden backs off.

"You shouldn't protect him," one of the girl's friends says as they help her up.

"Disloyal," says another as they back away and turn down the street toward their homes.

"You shouldn't have done that, Jules," Joseph says when they are alone.

"Don't tell me what I should and shouldn't do. No one's going to touch you as long as I'm around. No one's going to so much as look at you wrong."

"And here you were worried that you and Camden would seem weak with your matching limps. I think they give you a wider berth even than before."

"They must sense that we're more ill-tempered now," Jules says wryly.

Joseph steps close and tucks a lock of wavy brown hair behind her ear. He kisses her softly.

"You don't seem so ill-tempered to me."

ROLANTH

"*A*re the preparations made?" Mirabella asks.

"Your guards and the decoy carriage will be ready tonight," replies High Priestess Luca. "Though the people would have you wait until morning for a proper send-off."

Queen Mirabella's heart thumps. She is seated on one of Luca's small sofas, elbow-deep in striped silk pillows, and looks for all the world to be a queen at ease. But she has been waiting for this night ever since Arsinoe betrayed her by sending the bear across the Quickening stages.

The door of Luca's chamber opens, and Elizabeth enters. She closes the door quickly behind her to shut out the ruckus from the rest of the temple. There is no peace to be found in Rolanth Temple anymore, except for the quiet space of Luca's personal rooms. Everywhere else is busy from sunrise to after dark. The apse bustles with visitors lighting candles for their elemental queen or leaving offerings of scented water dyed to a bright blue or dark black. The priestesses are constantly occupied with sorting the gifts and crates of supplies arriving in the city daily: all they will need to lavishly entertain the coming suitors.

Luca tells the queen that they are sorting the supplies. But everyone knows that since Katharine has returned, they are checking each parcel for poison.

"Elizabeth," Luca says. "What kept you? The tea is nearly cold."

"Forgive me, High Priestess. I wanted to bring some honey from the apiary." She sets a small clear jar on Luca's table, half-filled with fresh honey still leaking from a piece of comb. Luca dips a spoon into the jar and sweetens their cups as Elizabeth brushes dirt from her initiate robes and takes a seat. Her cheeks are rosy from hurrying, and a fine glow of sweat sits on her deeply tanned forehead.

"You smell like the garden and hot summer air," Mirabella says. "What is that in your pocket?"

Elizabeth reaches into the skirt of her robes and pulls out a small spade fitted with a leather cup and bracelet.

"I had it made in the central district. It affixes directly to my stump." She holds her arm up so Mirabella can see the scarred end of her left wrist where the priestesses cut her hand off as punishment for aiding Mirabella's escape from the city. "I can buckle it one-handed, and it makes tending the vegetables much easier."

"That is wonderful," Mirabella says, but her eyes linger on the scars.

Luca sets their teacups before them.

"So," Elizabeth says. "We are leaving in the morning, then?" She sips her tea and studies the High Priestess over the rim of her cup. "Don't be worried, High Priestess. Bree and I will keep her safe until we find Queen Arsinoe in her woods."

Mirabella tenses.

"I do not need to be kept safe. I need to find my sister and to do my duty by her. And I would not wait for morning, Luca. I would leave tonight."

Luca takes a sip of tea, using the cup to hide her smile.

"For so long I waited for you to find the heart to kill your sisters," she says. "And now I worry that you are too rash."

"I am not rash. I am ready. Arsinoe sent her bear for me, and it killed our people and our priestesses. It cannot go unanswered."

"But the Ascension Year has barely begun. We could make opportunities for you. Just as the Arrons are sure to arrange for Katharine."

Mirabella's mouth tightens. Luca practically raised her. Mirabella knows the tone in her voice, and she knows when she is being tested.

"I will not waver in this," she says. "And this Ascension will be over far sooner than any anticipated."

"Well then." Luca nods. "Take my mare at least."

"Crackle?" Elizabeth asks.

"I know she is not as fine as the white horses of the temple," Luca says, "nor as beautiful as the black horses who will draw your decoy carriage to Indrid Down, but she is tough and fast and has been my trusted mount for many years."

"Tough and fast," Mirabella muses. "You think I will need to run."

"No," Luca replies softly. "But I must still try to protect you where I can." She reaches across the table to lay her hand atop the queen's, when a shriek cuts through the walls of the chamber. All three quickly stand.

"What was that?" Elizabeth asks.

"Stay here," Luca orders, but Mirabella and Elizabeth follow her, down the stairs and through the door to the long east hall and the upper storerooms.

"The main storeroom!" Elizabeth points.

The scream tears through the hall again. It is so full of panic and pain. Priestesses are shouting, barking frightened orders. When Mirabella bursts through the door it is chaos, white robes flashing as priestesses run back and forth.

In the corner of the room, a young initiate jerks and cries, held still by four shouting novices. She is practically a child, perhaps fourteen at most, and Mirabella's stomach goes cold at the sound of her screams. It goes colder when Rho, the war-gifted priestess with the bloodred hair, takes the initiate by the shoulder.

"You little fool!" Rho shouts. Baskets of goods topple; voices grow louder, talking over one another to soothe and question the girl.

Mirabella's voice rings out over the erupting room.

"What has happened? Is she all right?"

"Stay back, Mirabella, stay back!" Luca says, and rushes to the corner. "Rho, what is it?"

Rho grasps the novice by the neck and jerks her arm upright. It is bloody to the wrist. Blisters rise and burst as they watch, traveling farther down the arm as the poison makes its way deeper into her body. Toward her heart.

"She has put her hand into a poisoned glove," Rho says. "Stop squirming, girl!"

"Stop it!" the initiate begs. "Please, make it stop!"

Rho grimaces in frustration. There is no saving the girl's hand. She holds up her serrated knife, considers it a moment, then tosses it clattering to the floor.

"Someone bring me an axe!" She bends the girl down across a table. "Hold out your arm, child. Quickly. We can take it at the elbow now. Do not make it worse."

More priestesses join Rho to hold the girl and shush her gently. A priestess runs past Mirabella with a small silver hatchet.

"It was all I could find," she says.

Rho grips it and flips it over, testing its weight.

"Turn her face away." She raises the blade to strike.

"Turn yours as well, Elizabeth," Mirabella says, and pulls her trembling friend close to hide her eyes and tuck the edge of her hood closed so the tiny, tufted woodpecker nestled in Elizabeth's collar cannot fly out and be seen.

The hatchet comes down, one hard, chopping thud into the table. It is a testament to Rho's war gift that she did not need to strike twice. The surrounding priestesses wrap the poor girl's bleeding arm and steal her away to be tended. Perhaps they have saved her. Perhaps the poison, meant for Mirabella, has been stopped.

Mirabella clenches her teeth to keep from screaming. It was Katharine who did this. Sweet little Katharine, who Mirabella knows not at all. But Mirabella is smarter now. She made the mistake of sentimentality with Arsinoe. She will not make it again.

"When she is healed, I will have a spade fashioned for her. Just like mine. We will tend the gardens together. She will not miss her arm at all," Elizabeth says tearfully.

"That is kind of you, Elizabeth." Mirabella says. "And when I am finished with Arsinoe, I will silence Katharine so no one will have to fear poisoned gloves out of the capital ever again."

That night, Mirabella and Bree and Sara Westwood meet Luca and the priestesses before the temple courtyard. Mirabella's black dress is covered in a soft, brown cloak, and her riding boots are laced up tight. Bree, Elizabeth, and her escort of guards and scouts are all similarly outfitted. Anyone who sees them pass might mistake them for traveling merchants.

Mirabella strokes the muzzle of one of the long-legged black horses who will pull the decoy carriage toward Katharine and Indrid Down. The carriage is a beautiful, empty shell, lacquered and trimmed in silver, the horses so dark they would be shadows if not for the shine off their bits and buckles. They will be enough of a distraction for Katharine and the Arrons. Just enough to keep them from interfering with her in Wolf Spring.

"Here is Crackle," Luca says, and places her stout brown mare's reins into Mirabella's palm. "She will not fail you."

"I have no doubt." Mirabella scratches the horse beneath the forelock. Then she moves to Crackle's side and swings into the saddle.

"What are these?"

Mirabella turns. Her party is mounted, but one of the priestesses is tugging on Bree's saddlebags.

"Leave off!" Bree nudges her horse a step forward. "They are pears."

"We have not inspected any pears," the priestess says.

"That is because I picked them myself, from the orchard at the edge of Moorgate Park."

"They should not go," the priestess says to Luca.

"And yet they are going," Bree insists. "Queen Katharine is not so devious as to poison these three particular pears from one particular tree in one particular orchard in one of the many parks in Rolanth. And if she is," she says to Mirabella through the side of her mouth, "then she deserves to win."

Mirabella and Elizabeth suppress their smiles. But there is not much light; the moon is waning, and what slice is left is obscured by clouds. So perhaps the priestesses will not see how their sides shake.

"Ride fast," says Rho. She has taken down her hood, and dark red hair spills over her shoulder. "And quietly. We have heard reports of another bear mauling near Wolf Spring. A man and his boy, disemboweled and necks broken. Your sister does not have control of her familiar. Or she does and is wicked. Either way there is no time to waste."

Mirabella takes up her reins and whirls Crackle onto the road.

"For the first time, Rho, you and I are in agreement."

INDRID DOWN

❧

*K*atharine's horse's hooves slide on the cobblestones on the way toward Indrid Down Temple, and she pulls his head up sharply. She loves to ride fast through the capital, through the middle of the streets as people jump out of her way, her black hair and Half Moon's tail streaming behind like flags. Half Moon is the gamest, most agile horse in Greavesdrake's stables. Bertrand Roman, the boorish guard that Natalia appointed on Genevieve's recommendation, cannot hope to keep up.

She reaches the temple and signals to an initiate priestess standing in the shadows, earning her black bracelets by serving at the temple door. The initiate comes forward immediately as Half Moon comes to a hopping stop and Katharine dismounts.

"Shall I take him to the stable, Queen Katharine?"

"No thank you. I won't be long. Just walk him, and he would not mind some sugar if you have some handy." She turns away and smiles as she hears Bertrand Roman approaching, huffing and puffing on the back of his black mare.

Katharine does not wait. She walks through the doors, out of the bright heat of Indrid Down June and into the nave, which always smells of smoky incense and wood polish. The exterior of Indrid Down Temple may be as dramatic as the rest of the city, a facade of black marble and spitting gargoyles, but the interior is surprisingly austere: only a scant path of well-worn black mosaic on the floor, wooden benches for the devotees, and bright white light streaming from the upper-level windows.

Katharine waves to Cora, the head priestess, and loosens the collar of her black riding jacket.

"Some cool water for the queen," Cora calls, and a novice scurries for a pitcher.

"You should not ride so far ahead of your guard," Cora says, and bows.

"Do not worry about me, Priestess," Katharine replies. "Natalia has eyes and ears in every corner of the island. If there had been any movement out of Wolf Spring or Rolanth, you can be sure I would be locked up tight."

Cora smiles nervously. They are all so afraid. As if Mirabella will appear out of nowhere and shake the temple to the ground, or Arsinoe will storm the city astride her bear. As if they would dare.

Katharine walks between the aisles, squeezing the hands of temple visitors in her black-gloved fingers. The temple is nearly full, even at this odd hour. Perhaps it is as Natalia says and the Ascension brings people back to the Goddess. Or perhaps they are there for a glimpse of their Undead Queen.

"We will have a suitor here in the capital soon, is that not so?" Cora asks.

"Yes," Katharine replies. "Nicolas Martel. Natalia is preparing the banquet to welcome him, to be held at the Highbern Hotel."

"We will be honored to receive him at the temple. Can you recommend any decoration?"

"Indrid Down Temple is elegant enough as it is," Katharine says distractedly. "Though Natalia likes poison flowers. Something pretty, but nothing that can be absorbed through the skin."

Cora nods, and walks with Katharine as they approach the apse and the altar. There, behind a silver chain, lies the Goddess Stone, a great, curved circle of obsidian set into the floor. It shines brightly even in the low light. Looking into its depths feels to Katharine like looking into the blackness of the Breccia Domain.

"It is very beautiful," Katharine whispers.

"Yes. It is. Very beautiful, and very sacred."

They say it was taken from the eastern side of Mount Horn. That the mountain opened up one day, like an eye, for them to claim it. Katharine does not know if that is true. But it is a good story.

She reaches down and takes Cora by the wrist. The head priestess's tattooed black bracelets are old and faded, though Cora cannot be more than forty. She must have come to the temple so young.

"Such devotion," Katharine says, and rubs the tattoo with her leather-clad thumb.

In the back of the temple, the doors open and close around Bertrand Roman's clomping boots. Katharine purses her lips.

"A moment alone with her, perhaps," she says.

"Of course." The head priestess bows and turns to clear the room. "Everyone, please, quickly," she says. Clothes rustle and footsteps hurry along the aisles. Katharine is still until the door thuds closed and all is silent.

"You too, Bertrand," she says, irritated. "Wait for me outside."

The door opens and closes again.

Katharine smiles and slips quietly beneath the silver chain. She can feel the Goddess Stone watching as she approaches.

"Do you know us?" Katharine whispers to it. "Do we still smell of the rock and the deep, damp earth that you threw us down into?"

She kneels and places her hands on the marble floor. She leans across. The Goddess Stone lays before her curved and black, showing her pale reflection.

"You will not have your way this time," Katharine says, her lips close enough to the obsidian to kiss it. "We are coming for you."

Katharine strips off her glove and places her hand against the cold, hard surface. Perhaps it is only her imagination, but she could swear that she feels the Goddess Stone shudder.

WOLF SPRING

───────────── ❧ ─────────────

*A*rsinoe, Jules, and Joseph arrive at Luke's bookshop to find a service of tea and fried fish sandwiches already set out on his oval table on the landing overlooking the main floor. Luke sent his black-and-green rooster, Hank, up the twisting hill road to the Milone house to collect them early that afternoon. Jules still has the bird tucked under her arm (he demanded to be carried back), and drops him to the floor in a puff of feathers.

"What's all this?" Arsinoe asks. "Why the official rooster summons?"

Before Luke can answer, Joseph nudges her in the ribs and nods toward the dress hanging in the shop window: the gown that Luke is making for Arsinoe to wear at her crowning. A bit of lace has been added to the bodice, and Arsinoe winces. Luke will have to take it off again if he ever wants to see her in it.

"Come," Luke says. "Sit. Eat."

The three share a heavy look. Even Camden seems suspicious, her tail swishing nervously against the rug. But they climb the stairs and take their seats, and stuff fish sandwiches into their mouths.

"Mirabella is planning a strike," Luke says.

Arsinoe feels their eyes upon her and is glad the black mask hides so much of her expression.

"How do you know?" Joseph asks.

"A tailor friend traveling from Rolanth. He saw them readying two caravans. One is a decoy. To drive toward Indrid Down and ensure that Katharine stays put."

"How would he know that?" Jules objects. "The decoy could be for us."

"He saw scouts on the road and followed them as they curved around the capital toward Highgate. He lost them then, but it isn't far from there to disperse into the wood. Our wood."

Luke continues to serve, sliding biscuits onto each of their plates.

"I'll be relieved to have one done, to be honest," he says. "I wouldn't have thought her brave enough to come here after the way she ran from the bear onstage."

Joseph lowers his head.

"What luck to have the drop on her," Luke goes on, and smiles. "The Goddess is with you, like I've always said."

"Yes. It's grand to have the upper hand," Arsinoe says quietly. Luke does not know that the bear was a ruse. That she would have to walk into the fight alone. He will be so disappointed in her when she and Jules run away, to hide until Katharine is dead.

"We don't have long," Luke says. "If we are right, she could be in our forests in a day or two, just behind the scouts."

The room falls silent. Hank pecks at the biscuit in Arsinoe's limp fingers.

"We . . . ," Jules says hesitantly. "We should go. Prepare."

"Of course," Luke says as they stand. "Take some biscuits with you. And some fish. I . . . I'm just so glad that I could give you this news. I almost wish I could go with you and fight."

He hugs her, so unafraid. Confident that she will win, and Arsinoe hugs him back tightly.

"We'll have to go," Jules whispers as they go down the stairs. "If Mirabella is coming, we have no choice but to run."

"I can bring the horses around after dusk," Joseph says.

"No, I ought to bring the horses. My gift will keep them calm."

Arsinoe walks through the shop on wooden legs as they assure her it will not be for long. That Mirabella will turn straight around when she finds Wolf Spring empty and go for Katharine. They might be able to come back within a week.

"I didn't think she would attack," Arsinoe says, dazed.

"I told you," Jules growls, her eyes narrowed. "I told you that she would."

They step out of the shop, ready to separate and race off to gather supplies, but instead run face-first into a gathered crowd. The shock is such that Camden hisses and paws the air at them.

"What . . . uh . . . what are you doing here?" Arsinoe asks. But she knows. They have come to see her off. Luke was never very good at keeping a secret.

"Will you bring the bear into the square before you go?" someone shouts.

"Go?" says Jules.

"Well, you can't stay! You can't let the elemental come to Wolf Spring! She's a nightmare."

"They've had lightning strikes as far west as Kenora," someone else calls out. "Cows burned up in their pastures."

"She'll burn our boats into the harbor, looking for you!"

Joseph shakes his head. He should have stayed still. Too many still hate him for saving Mirabella at Beltane. Some hate him just because he has lived too long on the mainland.

"Burned-up cows in Kenora," he mutters, looking past Jules right at Arsinoe. "As if she can command storms across the island while she sits at home in Rolanth."

"It doesn't matter, does it?" Jules asks sharply. "If she's coming here? They are right to be afraid."

"They are," says Arsinoe. "If she really means to kill me, I can't let her do it here."

"Right. So we run."

"No. I can't let her burn down houses looking for me. I have to find her first."

"Arsinoe, what are you saying?" Jules asks, but Arsinoe can barely hear her over the growing noise of the crowd. Finally, Jules shouts at the people, loud enough that Arsinoe swears the planks beneath their feet quiver at the sound.

"You're not ready," Jules says, and Joseph slides his hand onto her shoulder. "Your bear . . . isn't ready!"

"He seemed ready enough at Beltane!" someone shouts, and the crowd cheers.

Jules grasps Arsinoe by the arm.

"Let me slow her down. Let me be your decoy."

"No, Jules. You know you can't interfere." She turns to Joseph. "Where is Billy? He should have been here. He should know."

"His father sent a boat and he sailed for home. He said he wouldn't be gone more than a couple of days. I . . ." He pauses helplessly. "If you go before he comes back, he'll never forgive himself."

"He'll be fine," Arsinoe says. "You'll tell him I asked about him?"

Joseph nods.

"I'm going to go out and meet her," Arsinoe says loudly. "I'm going to keep her out of our city so she can't do any harm."

The people smile and cheer. They clap their hands. Someone demands that she bring Mirabella's body back strapped to the bear for them all to see. Something flies through the air and she catches it: a bag packed with supplies.

"A change of shirt and some food," Madge says, and winks. "Bandages, though you won't likely need them."

Arsinoe swallows, and steps down into the square.

Jules tries to pull her back, and Camden cuts in front of her to curl around her legs.

"You can't. You're not ready."

"It doesn't matter, Jules. I don't have any other choice."

Beneath the bent-over tree, Arsinoe sits on a small log, edging her knife with poisonous nightshade. But though the poison on the blade practically sings through her blood, she does not want to use it. She does not want to hurt Mirabella.

But nor does she want to die.

"It won't come to that," she says to herself. "She'll see me, and I'll see her, and we'll figure this out. It'll be just like before." She looks around beneath the tree, searching for agreement from the Goddess. For some sign.

The ancient, sunken stones are covered over with moss, and the tree has sprouted long, strange leaves, but that is only a disguise. Here in the sacred space, where the Goddess's eye is always open, the tree does not care for summer, or winter, or time at all. Arsinoe listens to the utter silence, and wonders how much of her will be trapped here forever after she has sunk all that blood into the soil.

She gets back to work, rubbing and squeezing the nightshade along the blade. The scars of her face begin to itch, and she nudges the mask onto her crown. A twig snaps behind her and she tugs the mask quickly back down again.

"You don't have to wear that thing on my account," Madrigal says, dipping prettily below the bent branches in a bright green dress. "It can't be that comfortable in the heat."

"It's fine," Arsinoe says.

"You like the way that people look at you in it, you mean," Madrigal says, and Arsinoe purses her lips. "I heard about Mirabella's attack. I thought I might catch up with you here. I hoped that I would."

"Why?"

"Because it would mean you are doing something more than walking out to face your death. Jules is going out of her mind. Not even Joseph can calm her."

Arsinoe looks down. She hates to think of Jules that way. Panicked. Afraid.

"Is there anything?" she asks. "Anything that might help? Bring me luck? Make her attacks miss?"

"What a spell that would be. There is something, though, but we will need to work fast." Madrigal raises her brow and looks at Arsinoe's knife, and Arsinoe discreetly tucks the nightshade up into her sleeve. Madrigal will have brought her own knife anyway.

"What are we doing?" Arsinoe asks.

"Calling your bear," Madrigal replies. "The same bear that we enchanted with low magic onto the stage at the Quickening. He is the only one you can hope for, and that's only if the spell we cast was strong enough to still bind you together."

"Even if it was, he will never get here in time."

"Perhaps not," Madrigal says. "But it is worth it to try."

"Very well, then. Let's have your knife."

"What's wrong with the one in your hand?"

"I'm saving that one for my sister," she says, and Madrigal tosses hers over.

Arsinoe walks to the bent-over tree, ready to reopen the cuts in her palm, to paint the bear's rune in blood and press it to the bark.

"He might only cause more problems. He certainly did before."

"He did just what he should have."

"Tell that to Jules. She still holds on to that, you know. Those people he killed. Even though I was the one who got her into it. Even though she didn't do it on purpose."

"Who says she didn't do it on purpose?" Madrigal asks. "I saw the way that bear went straight for Queen Mirabella. You shouldn't underestimate the depth of my Jules's temper. It grows worse and worse. But when this Ascension is over, she will calm again, and we can all relax. So I'm doing this for her, and all of us, as much as for you."

Arsinoe touches the knife to her skin and then pulls back.

"Maybe I shouldn't. The low magic could go wrong again."

Madrigal rolls her eyes.

"It's our fault, you know," Arsinoe says. "What happened to Jules and Joseph. It was the spell that we did, that I ruined. That's what pushed him and Mirabella together."

"You don't know that."

But she does. She feels it, deep down.

"Joseph is a man," Madrigal says, "and men are changeable.

Put off their wits, they cannot resist a pretty girl on a storm-struck beach. There did not need to be low magic to cause what happened. And besides, he and Jules are back together now, and all is well. So what does it matter?" She stomps her foot, and her long, chestnut hair ripples in a sudden gust of wind. "Now make the cuts."

"Madrigal," Arsinoe asks, "how did you find this place?"

"It was a long time ago. I had to be about . . . fourteen. I was with Connor Howard. We'd gotten turned around in the woods and ended up under this tree. When I lay with him here, something inside me woke up. And I've been coming back ever since."

"Connor Howard? Mr. Howard? The baker? But he's so old."

Madrigal laughs.

"He wasn't back then. Well, not that old, anyway." She cocks her head. "If you do not want to make the cuts, it does not always have to be blood. Sometimes you can use spit."

"Spit?" Arsinoe grimaces. "Yuck. That's worse."

"As you like."

Madrigal smiles, and Arsinoe slices into her palm. The moment her blood touches the ancient bark she feels her link to the bear pull taut and knows that he will come running.

THE STONEGALL HILLS

———————— 🔥 ————————

*T*he road through the Stonegall Hills is quiet. The queen's party has not passed anyone in half a day. Scouts were sent ahead; they have been sent more and more often now that Wolf Spring is so near. The quiet makes Mirabella nervous as she sits with Bree and Elizabeth, resting against an oak tree. The only bird sound is from Pepper, Elizabeth's black-and-white tufted woodpecker, happily drilling into the wood.

"It is too quiet," Mirabella says. "As if the birds are silenced. Will they do that, Elizabeth, when a naturalist queen is nearby?"

"I don't think so. They certainly don't do it for me." Elizabeth tilts her head to look up fondly at her familiar. "She could ask them for quiet. But they wouldn't do it on their own."

"A flock of birds with bowed heads," Bree muses. "That would be some sad processional." She sits behind Mirabella, separating the queen's long, black hair into sections for a braid. "I wonder what fanfare she does have. I wonder what it is like when other queens leave their cities."

"All swords clashing and shields for a war queen in Bastian," Elizabeth offers. "And maybe some arrows shot into the sky or hurled with their minds."

Mirabella chuckles.

"They cannot do that anymore, Elizabeth. The gift has weakened."

"I don't know. Sometimes it seems that the plates hover in the air when Rho slams her fists onto the table at mealtimes." Elizabeth wrinkles her nose and giggles. Mirabella grins as she bites into one of Bree's forbidden pears.

Not long ago, she was the Chosen Queen and thought that she would leave Rolanth beneath banners flying. Instead, it was in the dead of night, and no one in the towns they passed has stepped out into the road to wish her well. She is in hiding, in secret, and even if she was not, Arsinoe and Katharine had such strong showings at the Quickening. There is no Chosen Queen anymore.

"I cannot wait for this to be over," Bree mutters, eyeing the sweet yellow pear. "When we can eat what we want and go where we want again. I am looking forward to the suitors' arrival, when perhaps Queen Katharine will be too busy entertaining to send many poisons."

Bree stops short and Elizabeth looks at her sharply.

"It is all right," Mirabella says. It is not as if she does not know that none of the suitors requested first court.

"It does not matter anyway," Bree says, her chin high. "We know who you really want. That handsome naturalist boy. Perhaps you can keep him as a lover after you are married."

Mirabella smiles. But she cannot imagine Joseph as a lover. He would demand all of her. He would deserve all of her, and that can never be.

"That naturalist boy will never speak to me again," she says softly, "after I have killed Arsinoe."

"The scout returns." Elizabeth nods up the road and gets to her feet. They are not far now from Wolf Spring and the meadows and streams where the spies say Arsinoe is often alone. "It's a wonder they let her out by herself so often during an Ascension Year."

"Naturalists are not accustomed to raising a queen with a true chance," Bree says. "They do not know how to take proper care."

"Perhaps they do not need to," Mirabella says, rising. "With a great brown bear as their queen's familiar."

The scout slows his mount and gives his report to the head of her guard, who nods. They are safe to advance again.

"This close to Wolf Spring I hoped for actual news," Mirabella says, patting Crackle on the neck and mounting. "A sighting. There have been no firm reports of the bear, and that makes me nervous."

"Not the bear, but the mountain cat is often with her," Bree says. "And the Milone girl. Often"—Bree hesitates—"Joseph as well."

Mirabella's eyes flash to her, and Bree drops her gaze. Mirabella will not harm Joseph. She has no wish to harm Juillenne. But if Juillenne interferes, if she sends her cougar, then she and the cat will have to die with the queen.

WOLF SPRING

Arsinoe leaves Wolf Spring by way of the Valleywood
Road. It is the most common route to the capital, a
nice, wide road covered over with trees that passes through
Ashburn and Highgate on its way through the Stonegall Hills.
If Luke's spy is right, she should run into Mirabella somewhere
in the Ashburn Woods.

Perhaps Luke and his tailor friend were wrong and she will
walk the Valleywood all the way to Indrid Down.

But somehow she does not think so. It is as if she can sense
Mirabella advancing through the hills. She can almost smell
her, like the coming of summer rain.

"You can't go after her! You can't interfere!"

"I'm not going to interfere," Jules says. It is difficult to
pack with her mother in the room. Everything Jules tries to
pack, Madrigal takes back out. Her scarf. An apple. A roll of

bandage. Madrigal takes them and holds them behind her back. As if that will stop Jules. As if she will not go anyway, even empty-handed.

"If you're not going to try to save her, then why go? Stay here. Wait with us. You are not the only one who's worried!"

"She's my best friend," Jules says quietly. The image of Arsinoe walking away that afternoon haunts her. It was so hard to let her go, even knowing that she intended to follow.

"You've been practically in my shadow since Beltane," Jules says. "Why? Because you want me to forgive you for being with Matthew?"

"No," Madrigal says, her face full of hurt. But Madrigal can twist her face in an instant, into any expression that she thinks will earn her the most sympathy.

"Don't bother playing the concerned mother now. And don't tell me not to help. You helped plenty, teaching Arsinoe low magic. And you assisted with the spell to charm the bear onto the stage at the Quickening."

"That was different. That was a show. That was not the Ascension. Now it is up to her."

"Now our role ends," Jules says, her lip curled. "I know you haven't been here, Madrigal, but even you should have seen. Arsinoe lives or we both die, and that is always the way it was going to be."

The boards in the hall creak. Cait appears outside the door to Jules and Arsinoe's bedroom, her gray hair tied tight at the nape of her neck and her eyes wary.

"I'm sorry for the noise, Grandma. Everything is all right."

"She's going to go after the queens," Madrigal mutters. "You should never have kept her here, so close to all this."

"You weren't around to give an opinion," Cait replies in her calm, deep voice. "But maybe we shouldn't have. We knew it meant heartbreak when Arsinoe would die. But that's what comes of fostering a queen."

"Don't talk about her like that," Jules growls. "Like she's finished."

"You should have sent Jules away," Madrigal says.

"'Away.' Not 'to you.'" Jules nods. "I suppose I'm glad you're not lying and pretending you wanted me then." She edges past her grandmother and runs down the stairs, with Camden grumbling at her heels.

Cait and Madrigal wait until the front door slams before they speak again.

"We should have told her," Madrigal says.

"No."

"She will find out anyway. You're not blind. You've seen what's happened since the Ascension Year began. How her temper grows. The bear she killed by the bent-over tree . . . the one she killed without touching! And how many broken plates have there been? How many vases knocked off tables? You tried to bind it, but it didn't work."

"Madrigal," Cait says, her voice weary. "Be calm."

Madrigal laughs.

"How many times have you said that to her? Be calm.

Don't worry. Control your temper. The oracle said that she was cursed. That she would bring about the fall of the island. And you *believed* her."

Cait stares at her daughter quietly. It has been a long time since anyone spoke such words aloud. But it was true. When Jules was born a blessed, Beltane Begot, and a girl, the first girl of a new generation of Milones, Cait sent for a seer, as was the old custom. But the moment the seer took one look at Jules, she spat upon the ground.

"Drown her," she said. "She carries the legion curse. Her naturalist gift will be touched with war. Drown her now, before she goes mad with it."

When Madrigal refused, the seer tried to take Jules from her arms, and when she touched the baby, fell into a trance, babbling about things to come.

"It must be drowned. It must not live. She is ruin, and the fall . . ." She went on and on, eyes rolled back to the whites, and Madrigal screamed, and the baby wailed, until Cait and Ellis ordered the oracle out.

They could not drown little Jules. They would not. So they bound her legion curse with low magic, a binding in her mother's blood. What they did to the fleeing seer, Cait cannot bear to think about. But after it was over, they all agreed to forget.

Cait blinks at Madrigal and shakes her head.

"That is not why. You know why we bound it. Not because she would destroy Fennbirn. Because she would destroy herself."

"But she hasn't destroyed herself. She's ready now."

"You are never ready. The legion curse drives people mad. More than one gift is too much for a mind to bear."

"So they say," Madrigal counters. "But they also say that the gifts under a legion curse are weak. And my Jules is the strongest naturalist anyone has ever seen. Just think what her war gift might be beside it."

On the banister, Cait's crow familiar croaks and shifts angrily from foot to foot. Madrigal was always ambitious. No doubt some part of her was excited that a child of hers had received such a prophecy.

"Is that what this is about?" Cait asks. "Your daughter. *Your* daughter. Being a part of this. Having a great destiny. But it is still really about you, Madrigal. *You* being a part of this. Hoping for your own great destiny."

"What an ugly thing to say, Mother." For an almost imperceptible moment, Madrigal's eyes narrow. Anyone who knew her any less would have missed it completely. And then her eyes are wide again, and imploring.

"I know we had to bind it," she says gently. "Sufferers of the legion curse were burned once. They were drowned. The Council would have demanded I leave her in the woods to die." She touches her mother on the shoulder. "But she has grown up. Strong. And sane."

"We bound Jules's war gift for her own good," Cait says. "And"—she hesitates to say what she has never wanted to believe—"as the seer was right about the legion curse, it must

54

have occurred to you that she could also be right about the rest of it."

"That Jules will bring about the fall of the island?" Madrigal scoffs. "That oracle was mad, like so many oracles before her."

"Perhaps. But, Madrigal, the binding will stay."

"Stay. But it will not hold. It weakens even now. I could release it if I chose. Her blood is my blood. I am her mother. And I will do what I think is best."

THE ASHBURN WOODS

W hen Arsinoe gets tired of walking, she stops and builds a sizable campfire by the side of the road. Mirabella's scout comes upon her as she lies beside it, her head resting on her sack of clothes.

She or he is fairly good at stealth. Arsinoe does not hear them until they are so close that she does not need to shout to be heard. Of course, a truly stealthy scout would not have come so close in the first place.

"Tell my sister I'm here," Arsinoe says without moving. "Tell her I'm waiting."

"Mirabella." Elizabeth shakes her shoulder gently. "Mira, wake up. The scout has returned."

It is still too dark in the deep woods to see anything but a shape. Mirabella thought she had fallen asleep against the trunk of a tree, but as she dozed, she must have fallen over into the dirt. Her cheek is gritty with it.

Somewhere to her right, Bree grumbles, and then her face is illuminated by orange flames as she lights a small pile of sticks on fire.

"Well," Bree says, her eyes puffy. She flicks her wrist and the fire grows. "What's so important that we must wake from our spots on the hard ground?"

The scout dismounts and takes a knee. He seems nervous. Confused.

"What is it?" Mirabella asks. "Is the way through to Wolf Spring barred?"

"That is unlikely." Bree yawns.

"It is Queen Arsinoe," the scout says. "She is waiting for you on the main road."

No one reacts, except for Bree, who comes fully awake and inadvertently sends her small flames rushing into the air.

"How did she know we were coming?" Elizabeth wonders. "She must have better spies than we thought."

"Did you see the bear?" asks Mirabella.

"I did not. I looked for it everywhere, but not even my horse ever seemed to catch its scent."

Mirabella looks eastward. Dawn is beginning to gray through the trees. The thought of the bear is like ice in her stomach. She remembers claws and roars and screams, and swallows hard.

"I will leave as soon as it is light enough to keep from tripping over roots," she says. "Do I need Crackle, or is it walkable?"

"Mira!" Bree and Elizabeth exclaim together.

"You cannot go if we do not know where the bear is," says Bree.

"Let us scout ahead more, in the daylight."

"No," Mirabella says. "If she has hidden her bear, then she has hidden it. I will be ready." She looks at her friends' faces in the firelight and is careful not to show her own fear. "She is here. It is time."

Joseph travels as fast as he can along the dark, tree-covered stretch of the Valleywood Road. He is exhausted after a long day working the boats and had barely closed his eyes to sleep when Madrigal started throwing pebbles at his bedroom window.

He thought she was looking for his brother Matthew, but when he opened the sash, she called to him and waved her arms. So now he is running through the dark, hoping that he has gone the right way after Jules and Camden. They do not have much of a head start, and the pain in Jules's legs may slow her down after a while.

But what Madrigal told him about Jules cannot be true. That Jules is legion cursed and touched with war. Joseph saw a legion-cursed child once, and the poor boy was half mad, holding his hands over his ears and dashing his shoulder against a wall. Joseph and Matthew had come across them in Highgate as the boy's family was traveling to Indrid Down Temple, where the boy would be mercifully poisoned and put out of his misery.

That is not Jules. To hear Madrigal tell it, the low magic

spell that bound Jules's curse is weakening, and the war gift may show itself any time she loses her temper. But Jules has lost her temper often, and he has seen no evidence of that.

He does not know what Madrigal is up to, telling him such lies. But he went after Jules anyway, to keep her out of the queens' business. Because if she intervenes, the Council will have her hide, legion cursed or not.

Arsinoe screams when Mirabella brings her dying campfire roaring back to life. She cannot help it. The flames are so hot. The wood is charred to embers in seconds, and when she rolls away, she smells burned hair, and her mask is so hot for a moment she fears it melted to her cheek.

"You," Arsinoe sputters. She rolls up against a tree trunk and scrambles to her feet. Mirabella is barely on the other side of the road. Arsinoe did not hear so much as a footstep or a snapped twig. "You've gotten quieter."

"Perhaps you just sleep harder."

Arsinoe glances down at her makeshift pillow, singed black now and full of lumpy clothes and hard cheese.

"That's not likely."

"Where is your bear?" Mirabella asks.

"I left him behind."

"You are lying."

Arsinoe swallows. The poisoned knife is a comforting weight in her vest, but she does not want to use it. She will have a hard time getting close enough to use it, anyway. That blast of fire was no trifle. Mirabella has found her nerve.

"You had better bring him out," Mirabella warns, and a strange pulse settles over Arsinoe's skin. She looks down. The hair on her arms is standing straight up.

The bolt of lightning shines bright white in the foggy morning, and the tree behind Arsinoe erupts in sparks. The jolt goes through the bottoms of her feet, and she drops into a tight crouch as it slams her teeth together. Pain rushes from her toes to the roots of her hair.

Talk, she thinks, but she can barely force her jaw apart. So she runs instead, one leg dragging as she makes for the cover of the trees. She hurls herself over a low shrub, and Mirabella's fire eats it away behind her in an explosion of orange and hissing steam.

"Stop, stop!" Arsinoe shouts.

"You had your chance to stop," Mirabella shouts back. "And you sent a bear for me instead."

The wind changes direction, circling around Arsinoe's collar, tossing her hair into her eyes. Mirabella is gathering a great storm overhead. The first gust shoves Arsinoe against a tree. A branch whips into her eyes, and a section of the burning shrub cracks loose and strikes her in the side, singing a hole through her vest and shirt. She winces, and looks down into the carved rune of low magic in her hand. She can feel the bear is on his way. She should have called him long ago.

The next bolt of lightning knocks Arsinoe off her feet. Pain, then stars, then blackness before her eyes, and she rolls bonelessly back into the road.

* * *

Jules is not far away when the first lightning strikes. The ground shakes, and the wind follows soon after.

Jules and Camden start to run.

"Jules, wait!"

She turns. Joseph hurries toward her in a wrinkled shirt.

"I can't," Jules calls. She points to the rising smoke. Arsinoe needs them.

Mirabella walks cautiously toward Arsinoe lying in the road. She holds the storm at the ready, to lash out on command, and keeps one eye on the woods. Her heart hammers in her chest, but so far, no great brown bear has come rushing out, roaring, and slashing its claws.

It must be there. Arsinoe said that she left it behind. A lie. It is only waiting until Mirabella drops her guard.

Arsinoe lies on her back in the road, one arm extended past her head. She is not moving. She looks like a dirty pile of twigs and rags. Mirabella nudges her with a toe.

"Get up."

Arsinoe is completely still. Mirabella edges closer. Could it really be as easy as that?

"Arsinoe?"

She thinks she hears a mumble and flinches, looking about wildly for the bear. But still it does not come.

"What did you say?" Mirabella asks, and Arsinoe rolls over.

"I said, 'one.' Fire, lightning, wind . . . It would be nice if you would just choose *one*."

Mirabella straightens. "Just because you have only one trick does not mean I must."

"You don't know anything about my tricks." Arsinoe stares up at her from behind that infuriating mask. Her nostrils are ringed with blood. Her hand twitches toward the interior of her vest. There are old cuts on her palm. "You look different." She glances at Mirabella's brown cloak and her black hair held tight in a long braid. "All dressed up for your crown." Arsinoe coughs and her eyes wobble. It is a wonder she is still conscious.

"Why did you come here?" Mirabella asks. "Are you giving up? Do you want me to turn you into a lump of charcoal?"

"Maybe? I'm not sure. I wasn't raised like you were. We never made any plans. So now I just do things."

"Is that right?" Mirabella says through her teeth. "You just do things. Like what you did at the Quickening, when you sent your beast to slice me open?"

Arsinoe swallows and grimaces, her teeth tinged pink with blood. Then, to Mirabella's astonishment, she actually chuckles, and her hand slides away from her vest to fall in the dirt.

"You thought I sent him for you." She chuckles again. "Of course you would."

"You did."

"Did or didn't, I haven't sent him at you today, now have I?"

"You tried to kill me not two days after I saved you. You ungrateful brat!" Mirabella clenches her fists, careful to keep control of her elements. She wants to throttle her sister. Box her ears. Beat every last chuckle out of her. She could strike her with lightning now and be done with it. Arsinoe is an easy, immobile target.

"What are you doing here?" Mirabella shouts. "Why did you come out here?"

"To keep you out of Wolf Spring," Arsinoe replies. "Away from the people I love."

"I would never harm them."

"They're not so sure. Ascensions turn ugly. Ascensions *are* ugly." Arsinoe pauses. "We could walk away. Let Katharine and the Arrons win. The poisoners have won three times before. Nothing much will change with a fourth, no matter what the temple lackeys say."

"Abdicate?" Mirabella barks a sad laugh. "They would never let us. Stop trying to bargain when you have been beaten. You are the one who said it was the way things are. We kill or we are killed."

Arsinoe breathes in slowly. She looks at the trees, and the light streaming through the clouds.

Mirabella's mouth twists downward. Her eyes blur. She does not want to talk anymore. One fast bolt of lightning is all it will take, and if she looks away, maybe she will not be haunted by it afterward.

"Mirabella," Arsinoe whispers.

"Yes?"

"When you go after Katharine, don't hesitate. I know she was our little girl whose hair we braided full of daisies, but she isn't anymore."

* * *

"Jules, stop!" Joseph grabs Jules by the arm.

"We can't stop! Can't you see that storm? Didn't you see the lightning?"

"Arsinoe is clever," Joseph reasons. "She would never walk into this fight without a plan. Let her do it."

"Let her do it. You would let her kill your Mirabella? Or are you hoping that she'll lose?"

Jules jerks free, and Joseph does the only thing he can think of. He tackles her to the ground.

Her response is immediate and fierce. She elbows him in the temple and Joseph's vision swims. But he does not let go. Not even when Camden's formidable weight crashes into him and sends them all rolling.

"Joseph, let me go! Let go!"

"No, Jules, I can't!"

She screams and strikes out with everything she has. The sound of their struggle has to be loud enough to reach the queens. If Arsinoe falls, at least she will know that Jules was there.

Camden's teeth sink into Joseph's shoulder and she jerks hard, trying to wrench him off.

"Ah!" he yelps. "Jules, please!"

"No!" she screams. "NO!"

It is so hard to keep his grip on her that he does not notice the quaking of the trees. He does not hear the branches rattling, not until the first one snaps and flies toward the ground to embed itself deep into the dirt.

Joseph ducks his head as more branches rain down, stabbing into the ground like knives. He lets go of Jules and covers his head with his arms.

At once, the branches stop. The trees stop quaking, and the only sound is of their frightened breath, and Camden's nervous groans.

"What was that?" Jules asks. She struggles to her knees and gathers her mountain cat close, feeling all over her coat to make sure she was not cut or stabbed.

"I think," Joseph pants, "that was you."

"What was that?" Mirabella asks. "Did you hear that?" But of course Arsinoe heard it. And she knows those screams.

"That was Jules," Arsinoe says, and struggles up onto her elbow, spitting blood. "Something's happened to her! Did your priestesses do something?"

Arsinoe reaches into her vest, and her hand wraps around the handle of the poisoned knife. She does not want to do it. Mirabella saved her at Beltane. Mirabella loves her. But if Jules was hurt, they will *all* be hurt.

"No," Mirabella says quickly. "They would not! And they are not that way. They are there," she turns and points toward Highgate. Then she scowls. "Is this meant as distraction? It will not work!"

The storm grows dark again overhead, and Arsinoe considers her options. Perhaps she could still throw the knife, slide it into Mirabella's heart. Poisoners are naturally good at those arts, or so she has heard. But even if they are, she has never practiced.

The rune in her hand begins to burn.

A tingling rune is not much of a warning, and Arsinoe screams right along with her sister when the bear crashes through the trees onto the road. He bellows, louder even than the thunder, and his strides are as long as a horse's and just as fast.

"Wait!" Arsinoe shouts, and the bear hesitates just enough to keep him from slashing his claws across Mirabella's chest.

Mirabella falls back on her haunches, her courage broken. She scrambles away, cheeks wet with panicked tears, no doubt reliving the last moments on the Quickening stage, when she watched as the bear tore apart priestesses on his way to kill her.

"Wait, wait, come to me," Arsinoe says urgently, and holds her rune hand out.

The bear is not her familiar. The charm that binds them together is only low magic. But Arsinoe is a queen. Her low magic is strong, and the bear does as she asks. She smears blood from her nose onto her palm and presses it to the great beast's forehead, and he licks her face.

"Let's go," she says. She holds on to the bear's fur as he takes her burned shirt in his teeth and drags her down the ditch and into the cover of the trees. He is fast, and shockingly quiet, and they are deep into the woodland before Mirabella recovers.

"Arsinoe!" her sister screams. "Where did you go? Where are you hiding?"

"She doesn't really expect me to tell her, does she?" Arsinoe whispers, and she and the bear sink low and silent, hoping that Mirabella will not be able to find them.

GREAVESDRAKE MANOR

❧

*N*atalia stares down at the letter in her hand. Now and then she sips brandy tainted with foxglove and taps her teeth against the glass. The letter is from her brother, Christophe. It arrived that morning, and in it he says that his son, Pietyr, returned home only briefly before departing for Prynn on a business errand. What that business entailed, he could not say. He had assumed it was some errand requested by her. But (and she could envision the carefree shrug of his shoulders) he sends greetings and well-wishes from his wife, Marguerite, who extends an invitation to their country estate as soon as Natalia's affairs with the Ascension are finished.

Natalia crumples the letter in her fist. How nice it must be to live so far removed from the capital, and from the Council, able to speak of the Ascension with such flippancy. Lucky Christophe, who had married and escaped. But she had not, and his son, Pietyr, had not, and the boy had best turn up on her doorstep soon. Katharine must still be crowned. They still have work.

Genevieve knocks once and enters without waiting for permission. It seems that everyone in her family is determined to make Natalia's head ache.

"I have been at the Highbern all morning," Genevieve says, referring to the hotel in the city where they will hold their welcome banquet for the suitor Nicolas Martel.

"And?"

"All is well. The silver is polished, the menu selected, and the flowers ordered from the hothouses."

"Good," says Natalia.

They will not need to impress the boy much. Natalia remembers how he watched Katharine the night of the Disembarking and at the feast afterward. And he apparently has not been dissuaded by the unsavory rumors surrounding her return. She and Pietyr had hoped that Katharine would have her choice of suitors, but all they really need is one, for show, until Katharine is crowned and selects Billy Chatworth to be her king-consort as she ultimately must.

"What is that noise?" Genevieve asks. She turns and cocks her ear to the hall. Natalia does not hear anything, but when Genevieve wrenches the door open, the sound of clapping echoes up the stairs.

Natalia sets down her brandy, and she and Genevieve follow the applause, past the foyer and the gallery hall and into the billiard room, where a small crowd of servants has gathered.

They slip in quietly, and when they see what has them so enraptured, Genevieve gasps.

Katharine has erected a target on the far side of the tables. Her maid, Giselle, is tied to it. And as Natalia and Genevieve watch, Katharine throws five small knives. Each lands with an audible thud, mere inches from Giselle's arms, hips, and head.

The servants applaud, and Katharine bows. She walks gaily to Giselle and kisses her cheek before ordering other servants to untie her.

"What is this?" Natalia asks, and Katharine whirls.

"Natalia," she exclaims, and the servants hunch their shoulders, preparing to be caught in the middle of a great argument.

Natalia arches her brow at them. Since when has Katharine ever argued with Natalia, or with anyone?

"Do you like it?" Katharine asks. "I needed a diversion, kept inside for so many days, hiding from the elemental queen. And I thought the suitors might be impressed by a little sport."

"A little sport," Natalia says. "They will be impressed by your riding prowess and your skill with a bow. But I think you will find their mainland stomachs less at ease with a bride who excels at knife throwing."

"Is that so?" Katharine laughs. "Are they really so frail?"

"I hope not all of them," Genevieve says quietly.

Katharine fixes upon her with black eyes. Since she returned, Genevieve has not dared to say much to the queen. She has only watched, and reported to the Council so they might whisper.

About how the queen is endangering herself. About how she takes in too much poison without a gift, and someday will take in the wrong one.

Katharine inclines her head toward the target.

"Would you care to take a turn, Genevieve? Give the servants a little thrill?"

Genevieve looks at Natalia, as if hoping she will forbid it, and smiles brightly at the queen when she does not.

"Of course."

She steps out of the crowd and allows Giselle and another maid to secure her wrists to the target. The mood in the room cools. All are hushed. Katharine fans out her silver knives and slides them between her fingers.

She throws the first one. It strikes solidly beside Genevieve's waist, and she jerks away.

"Be careful," Katharine scolds. "Do not move. What if I throw another too quickly, and you twitch into its path?"

She throws again. This one hits so close to Genevieve's cheek that it slices off a curl of light gold hair.

"I think that is enough, Kat," Natalia says. "Giselle, Lucy, untie my sister if you please. I am sure we will all enjoy more of the queen's sport at some other time."

Giselle and Lucy quickly free Genevieve's wrists. Genevieve is silent as she and the servants quit the room, but she gives Natalia a betrayed glare.

"You think me cruel," Katharine says, once she and Natalia are alone.

"No," Natalia replies. "A little reckless. I know that Genevieve has taken a firm hand with you, Kat. But it was always in your best interests."

Katharine sighs. "I suppose I should forgive her, then."

"I did not know you were harboring ill will. You never have before. What has changed, Kat? What really happened to you, the night of the Quickening?"

Katharine wanders through the darkened room and draws the red drape away from the windows. She squints into the daylight. Her face has lost its hollows, despite her ingestion of extra poison. Katharine looks different. She looks new.

"Only what I have told you," she says. "I ran away and was lost. I fell and the Goddess saved me. If I am out of sorts now, it is only that I have been inside for too long." She turns to Natalia. "Mirabella's carriage was only a decoy, was it not?"

"It was. And it has departed. So perhaps that means one of your sisters is now dead."

Katharine rides Half Moon high into the hills beside Greavesdrake. She rides fast, her heels to his sides, hoping to make it to the summit and see her sister's decoy making its retreat. But when she arrives, the road is empty.

"It is all right, Half Moon," she says, and pats the gelding's sweaty neck. She knows what it must have looked like: a gaudy, overdone black carriage with silver fastenings and blue velvet cushions, the horses groomed to high polish, and every one of their white hairs covered with dye.

"I wish it had not been a decoy," she says to her horse. "I wish she had blown the doors off Greavesdrake and found me huddled in my bedsheets. I would have thrown a knife into her pretty white throat, and she would have been so surprised."

Katharine turns Half Moon and rides him back down from the summit. As they enter the cover of the trees, her senses prick, and she realizes they are being followed.

It must be Bertrand Roman, her near-constant shadow. Natalia has sent him out after her, and it has taken him this long to catch up. She pulls Half Moon to a halt. But the hoof-beats behind them are too light to come from Bertrand's long-suffering black mare.

Katharine urges Half Moon to a canter. Behind her, the pursuing rider does the same. She glances back discreetly, peeking beneath her arm, and sees a light bay horse and a male rider with a flash of blond hair.

Pietyr? She sends Half Moon flying down the path. He will not sneak up on her, and he will not overtake her. No one on the estate is a better rider than she is, and no mount in the Arron stable can twist and cut through the trees the way Half Moon can.

She loses him easily and doubles back, circling to his left. She kicks Half Moon into his path, so suddenly that his mount rears up and veers off sharply, and Katharine smirks when Pietyr is thrown rolling across the ground.

She rides to where he lies groaning in the ferns. Her mouth drops open.

"You are not Pietyr!"

The boy, who does have blond hair but not the pale blond of Pietyr and Natalia, gets slowly to his feet.

"No, I am not," he says, and shakes dead leaves from the cuff of his shirt. "Do you not remember me? I am Nicolas Martel."

"My suitor!" Katharine blurts, and for once she does not need to use the tricks Pietyr taught her in order to blush. She does remember him now, but he looks different than he did far below the cliffs on the beach of the Disembarking, or even across the firelight of the feast. His face in the sunlight is softened angles, and there is a pleasing curve to his lower lip. Golden blond hair brushes against his shirt collar and curls over his temples.

Katharine searches for words. She drops one side of her reins and puts her hand on her hip.

"That was a stupid thing to do! Sneaking up on me like that during an Ascension Year! I have poisoned knives; I could have killed you!"

She should not be so shrill. According to Pietyr, mainland boys do not like it. But Nicolas smiles.

"I did not mean to sneak," he says. His accent is lilting; his voice is soft and low. She likes it immediately. "I've only just arrived. They told me to wait at the manor house, but I'm afraid I was too curious."

"That is . . . sweet. Someone should have stopped you."

"Once I have made up my mind, I am not easy to stop." He

cocks his head as though intrigued. "You would have killed me? I thought the queens were only lethal to one another."

"Then you have much to learn," Katharine says. She sighs. "Though you are right that my sisters are my favorite quarry."

"Forgive me," he says. "It seems that I've ruined our meeting. Me, facedown in the dirt was not the way I wanted to introduce myself."

Katharine turns in the saddle.

"Let us go and find your horse. If she was from our stables, she would have been trained and would not wander far. But as it is, I do not know where she has gone to." She holds out her hand. Nicolas accepts it along with one of her stirrups and climbs onto Half Moon behind her. He slides his arms around her waist.

"I thank you," he says into her ear. "Perhaps this was not so bad a first meeting after all."

WOLF SPRING

鸿

Arsinoe, Jules, and Joseph leave the Valleywood Road and cut west, following the stream that joins eventually with Dogwood Pond. They sneak onto the Milone property as the sun sinks below the trees, and manage to avoid the eyes and questions of people in town.

Cait, Madrigal, and Ellis burst through the front door before anyone can call out. Jake the spaniel jumps into Jules's arms and the crow familiars flap soft, worried wings against their heads.

"My Goddess." Ellis walks up and takes Arsinoe by the hand. "We'll send for a healer."

"No," Arsinoe says. "I'm fine. Look."

As if she needed to tell them. The great brown bear is hard to miss.

"He's called Braddock," Arsinoe says. She places her hand atop the bear's large furred head.

Madrigal extends her arm like she might touch him, then reconsiders. "Is Mirabella dead, then?" she asks.

The door slams, and a moment later, Cait returns with a bowl of water, already hot. She sponges off Arsinoe's face and arms, which are crusted with blood and blistering burns. Cait looks almost like she might cry, but when she speaks her voice is like it always is.

"You look like a propped-up corpse. She had better be dead." She prods Arsinoe's bruised ribs. "You won't survive another fight like this."

"She's not dead. Braddock, he . . . I don't think she had the stomach to face him again."

"She will soon," says Jules in a low, tired voice.

"Did you get to her at least?" Madrigal asks Joseph.

Joseph tightens his arm around Jules's waist and puts his chin protectively atop her head.

"I got to her," he says. "And I told her what you told me."

"Come inside," Cait says gravely. "Those burns need tending. Braddock, I'm afraid, will have to stay out here. He's not a familiar, and even if he was, he wouldn't fit through any of the doors."

The next morning, Arsinoe wakes with her mask askew. She had been so exhausted that she fell asleep without taking it off. She straightens it and turns to Jules, who is rolled on her side facing the wall. But Camden is sitting up, her black tail-tip curling up and down. Jules is awake.

It is hard to believe the things that Cait and Madrigal said last night. Even though Joseph said he saw the branches break off the trees and stab into the ground. Jules, her strong Jules, is legion cursed. Touched with war. The Milones had known and hidden it all this time, with not one word of warning. They had bound the war gift with low magic, they said. But the binding is beginning to fail. And what would happen if it tore loose completely? The legion curse is an abomination, and the legion cursed go mad. Everyone knows that.

"Stop staring at me, Arsinoe," Jules says. She turns over and blinks her two-colored eyes. Arsinoe has always thought them pretty, one blue and one green, but Cait said the oracle had wanted to drown Jules as soon as she saw them.

"You'll be all right, Jules. You've been all right so far."

"Of course I'll be all right." Jules turns and stares up at the ceiling, dark wood beams and one pretty spiderweb left in the east corner. "Now we both have secrets." She looks at Arsinoe again. "Why didn't you tell me that you'd called the bear?"

"I did it after I'd left. I never thought he'd make it in time. He must've been looking for me already." She sits up in bed and peers out the window. Braddock spent the night in the yard, probably trying to figure a way into the chicken coop. Arsinoe grins.

"I can't wait for Billy to come back so I can show him."

Jules smiles softly. She stares down at her hands and squeezes them into fists.

"Will you let Madrigal do the unbinding?" Arsinoe asks.

"Do you think I should?"

"I don't know."

"Joseph doesn't think so. He says it's too dangerous. That the binding might be the only thing holding back the curse. But I keep on thinking of something that Luke said . . . that there must be a reason why the Goddess put me near you. Like I could be strong. Like I could help you win."

"You don't need the war gift to make you strong," Arsinoe says. "You already are. Is there anything else that Cait and Madrigal aren't telling us? Anything else that the oracle said, something that might help?"

"No. She said I was legion cursed with war, and they paid her to keep the secret. I think it was fairly simple."

They smile at each other, a bit uncomfortably. Arsinoe does not know what Jules will decide. But she does wish that it was someone other than Madrigal who held the key to the binding.

Ellis knocks and pokes his head in with Jake, who gives a bright bark.

"Up and dressed," he says. "We have suitors to prepare for."

"Suitors," Jules says, and grins.

Arsinoe pulls her light summer quilt up over her head. She had been so focused on Mirabella that she completely forgot about Tommy Stratford and Michael Percy.

"Wake me when it's over," she says with a moan.

"Well, if that won't get you up, how about the fact that on the way back from the southern field I ran into Madge and she said that Billy's mainland boat put in this morning?"

* * *

Billy arrives at the Milone house just after noon, as Arsinoe is walking her bear in the far west part of the yard.

"Well, well," says Billy. "Joseph told me it was true. I almost didn't believe him."

Arsinoe grins. He is such a welcome sight. She had not realized how much she had been waiting for him, how much she missed him while he was away.

"His name is Braddock," she says.

"Braddock the bear. Seems fitting enough. Is he safe?"

Arsinoe strokes Braddock's large forehead. She has been with him since the morning, getting him used to the smells and sounds of people. The Milones are naturalists, and their gift puts the bear at ease. But giftless folk will see him at the feast as well, and clueless mainland suitors besides. No matter how docile the bear seems she must take extra care. With his sweet face shoved into her hip, it is easy to forget that theirs is a bond of low magic, not of familiars.

"He is safe for now," she says. "He's stuffed full of ripened apples and striped bass. Plus one of the children who came round to spy on him."

Billy cautiously slides his fingers into the bear's brown fur.

"He's . . . ," Billy says, and swallows. "Softer than I thought. And he doesn't smell like the last one."

"The last one was old. Diseased. It was a mistake. Or maybe it was the price for this one."

"Low magic, right? You never know the price until you've paid it."

Arsinoe shoves him playfully, and Braddock raises his head. "What would you know about it, mainlander?"

"Less than nothing," Billy says. Then his eyes lose focus on the ground. "I have some news."

"News. I'm beginning to hate that word. It is never anything good anymore."

Billy does not smile or tell her to stop being so glum. But it cannot be so bad when he has just returned.

"I'm afraid I've been sold to the Westwoods," he says.

"What?"

"I've been appointed Queen Mirabella's royal taster. My father's punishment for refusing to take part in the courting. I'm leaving for Rolanth tonight on pain of disinheritance." He smiles ruefully. "Always on pain of disinheritance. But he let me come back here to tell you. He gave me that, at least."

"But," Arsinoe sputters. "You can't!"

"I must."

At her anxious tone, Braddock bobs his head and wanders away.

"Junior! Don't be an idiot. You can't be her taster! Doesn't your father understand the danger? She . . . Katharine is already sending poison to Rolanth. One of Mirabella's maids has already died in a poisoned dress!"

"It was not a poisoned dress," Billy says. "It was a poisoned glove. And she did not die. They cut off her hand in time. They don't even know if it would have killed her or if Katharine is only playing."

"The Arrons do not play," Arsinoe insists. "And how do you know all that?"

"My father discussed it with the Westwoods at length."

Her brow furrows, and he smiles charmingly and slips his hand onto the back of her neck, beneath the fall of her hair. That stupid, mainland bluster, but she cannot seem to move away.

"Do all mainlanders think themselves immortal, or is it just you?"

"I will be perfectly safe! My father wouldn't put me at risk. And when he's done being angry, I'll come back to you, I promise. In the meantime, I can be your eyes and ears on Mirabella." He caresses her mask with his thumb. "I heard what happened in the woods. You shouldn't have gone up against her like that. You great half-wit."

She pushes his hand away from her mask.

"Are you sure that your father wouldn't make some other bargain? He is always in Indrid Down, with the Arrons."

"He likes Indrid Down. It's more like home. Civilized. He's looking forward to ousting the Arrons when you are queen."

She rolls her eyes and he laughs, trying to cheer her.

"Don't be so worried! I'm his only son. And where I come from, that means something."

"Can't anyone change your mind?"

"No one," he says. "Not even you."

"So you'll leave. When?"

"We're sailing for Rolanth today."

"But you've only just returned." Everything inside her is suddenly heavy. She takes a clumsy, half step forward and throws her arms around Billy's neck. After an initial "oof" of surprise, he holds her tight.

"Don't be daft," he says into her hair. "No matter how far I go, I'm still your person. We stand together now. We *are* together now, aren't we?"

"Are we?" she asks.

He kisses her forehead, and her cheek. He kisses her shoulder, still too nervous to kiss her properly, and that is her fault. Then he gently removes her arms and turns to walk away.

"Billy!" she calls out, and he stops. "Why did you choose me? Instead of one of my sisters?"

"Because I saw you first," he says, and winks. "I'll be back soon. But . . . just in case I die, I want you to remember that you could have kissed me that day in the meadow."

Jules and Joseph load barrels of ale onto the back of an oxcart. It will be driven over the hill to the apple orchard northeast of the Milone house, where the feast to welcome the suitors will be held.

"You're strong for someone so small," Joseph says as they load the last one. He wipes sweat from his brow.

"What is that," she asks, "a compliment wrapped in an insult?"

He laughs, and they move into the shade on the back steps of the Lion's Head. Camden stretches out at their feet on the cool stone pavement, and Jules leans forward to scratch her belly.

"I can't believe that Billy's father is sending him to be a taster," Jules says. "It feels like we shouldn't let him go. Or that he should refuse."

"He never refuses his father," says Joseph, and cocks his head thoughtfully. "*No one* ever refuses his father. All that time I lived with them, I only saw folk kiss his arse and tell him what he wanted to hear. He's used to getting the things that he wants." He shrugs. "I wonder what that's like."

"It doesn't sound like much to me," says Jules. "Sounds like arse-kissing and lies. One of us ought to go with Billy. To ease Arsinoe's mind, if nothing else."

"I'm going with him, Jules," he says, and she looks at him in shock.

"I didn't mean you! And I was really only saying it to be kind!"

"I'm not staying," he says, half-smiling at her outburst. "Just going to get him settled in. Make sure everything is on the up and up, like you said. So Arsinoe won't worry."

"She'll worry anyway." Jules crosses her arms. "Will you see Mirabella? Climb into her bed, maybe?"

"That's part of the reason I'm going. To see her! Not the bed part!" he adds when Jules's fists come up.

"Why do you need to see her?"

"To tell her that it's over. To make sure she knows."

"She doesn't need to know, does she?" Jules asks, knowing how mean it sounds but unable to keep quiet. "It was never anything to start with. Mirabella will die or marry a suitor. You were never an option."

"Jules." Joseph takes her face in his hands and kisses her. "I love you. What I did was wrong, but I wronged her, too. This was my fault. She didn't know about you until it was too late."

Jules sighs.

"Go, then."

"So you trust me?"

She turns and looks squarely into his handsome, storm-blue eyes.

"Not one bit."

THE SUITORS ARRIVE

INDRID DOWN

*T*he Highbern Hotel is the finest in the capital, a tall, imposing rectangle of gray brick and gold-gilded rainspouts fashioned into the likenesses of falcon heads, close enough to the Volroy to cast its morning shadow into the western gardens. The black-and-white flags above the doors have been replaced with pure black ones embossed with coiled snakes and poisonous flowers. A clear announcement that the poisoner queen is in attendance.

In the grand ballroom, Katharine sits restlessly between Natalia and Nicolas Martel as he oohs and aahs at the finery. It is nothing new for her. She has been to the Highbern many times, with Natalia for tea and for other banquets through the years. Personally, she has always thought the place smelled too old, as if it were rotting beneath its carpets. But today they have opened the doors and windows, so at least she can enjoy the lilac wafting from the Volroy's courtyard fences.

"Have you heard the news from Highgate?" Renata Hargrove asks.

Natalia arranged the seating differently for the suitor's feast, more intimately, around curving tables covered in deep red cloth. To Katharine's great delight, it meant she was able to place Genevieve nearly all the way across the room.

"What news is that?" Natalia asks.

"Apparently, the elemental called not one but two storms. With fierce lightning and fires with smoke that was visible for miles."

"Yet the naturalist lives," says Lucian Marlowe, the only non-Arron male on the Black Council.

"A pity her carriage was only a decoy. We could have used the rain." Natalia sips her tainted wine, and the guests chuckle. "Though with any luck, she will kill the naturalist, and we will never have to close our windows against the smell of bear."

"But what fun is that for our Queen Katharine?" Lucian says, and laughs.

Katharine ignores them and leans toward Nicolas.

"You must think us awful with all this talk of death."

"Not at all," he says in his soft accent. "I have been educated in the ways of the queens. And I have seen death, and dying, on the battlefield. Coups in my country cost tens of thousands of lives. Your Ascension Year seems civilized in comparison."

"You sound very certain," Katharine says. "But your eyes are nervous. Perhaps even afraid."

"Only of accidentally eating something that was not meant

for my plate." Nicolas smiles and looks down as though to guard it.

The feast is a *Gave Noir* but not of the scope of the Quickening. Each dish is served as a separate course, and all of the poisoners in attendance partake, not only the queen.

Katharine pushes her fork into a green salad dotted with poisonous mushrooms, and adjusts the itchy gloves on her hands. Underneath, her skin is healing from a rubbing of dwarf nettle. The combination of healing scabs and sweat is making her want to scratch her skin off.

"Before the Beltane Festival, I thought watching a *Gave Noir* would be vulgar. But afterward"—he looks up at her from beneath his fall of gold hair—"there is something alluring about it. That you may eat something that I will never be able to taste."

"Shall I describe it to you?"

"Do you think you could?"

"I do not know." She looks down at the mushrooms: their bright red caps spotted with white. "Much of what we eat is bitter or has little taste. But there is something in the sensation of it. It is like eating power." She stabs a bit onto her fork and pops it into her mouth. "And it does not hurt that our cooks drown everything in butter."

Nicolas laughs. His voice is not deep—indeed, Natalia's voice is deeper—but it is pleasant.

"It must be more than that," he says. "Every poisoner here has turned their nose up as my dishes go by." He glances about the room, and Katharine raises her eyebrows at his plate: a shallow bowl of chilled summer soup. Only he, giftless Renata Hargrove, and war-gifted Margaret Beaulin are eating that, and they all have the sense to pretend they are not hungry.

"Do not pay them any attention," Katharine says. "Poisoners are always that way about untainted food." She reaches up and touches the flowers of the centerpiece and the towers of shining fruit. "They see it as inelegant, no matter how much silver they pile it upon or how much spun sugar they hide it under."

Nicolas reaches out as well, and their fingers touch. He seizes the opportunity and takes her hand to press it firmly to his lips, so firmly that she is sure to feel it even through the gloves.

Katharine does feel it. It shocks her just how much, and for a moment, Pietyr flashes into her mind, the memory of him suddenly strong enough to make her heart pound. She clenches her teeth and takes a breath. She refuses to think of Pietyr that way. Pietyr, who tried to murder her. She touches her face. Her cheeks are flushed. But Nicolas will think it is because of his kiss.

"There is such finery here," Nicolas says. "But less of a heartbeat than at the Beltane Festival. Those nights beside the fires were so exciting. Watching you through the flames. Looking up at you from the sand. Will there be other festivals like that?"

"The next festival is for Midsummer," Katharine says, and

coughs when her voice trembles. "Celebrated across the island, of course, but really it is a naturalist affair, of harvest and bounty. Then there is the Reaping Moon in autumn, though the elementals claim that through fires and chilled winds."

"Which festival is the poisoners' festival?" Nicolas asks.

"*Every* festival," Natalia answers from Katharine's other side. She should have known that Natalia would be listening.

"At every festival there is a feast," Natalia explains. "And every feast is for the poisoners."

The main course is served: a poisoned hog with a bright spring pear stuffed into its mouth after roasting. The servers bring it first to Katharine and Natalia's table, to carve her the choicest bits along with spoonfuls of orange squash sweetened with molasses and arsenic. The hog is delicious, juicy and robust. The seared bird on Nicolas's plate looks shrunken and sad in comparison.

After the meal, Katharine leads her suitor onto the floor to dance.

"I can't believe how well you are," Nicolas whispers, gazing at her in awe. "There was so much poison . . . enough to kill a man twice your size."

"Enough to kill twenty," Katharine corrects him, smiling. "But do not worry, Nicolas. I have been eating poison since I was a child. Now I am practically made of it."

ROLANTH

*M*irabella turns back and forth in front of the mirror with a pained expression as Sara and the priestesses adjust the fall of her dress.

"It is so thin in places," Mirabella says, studying a transparent spot near her hip.

The gown is fashioned from gauzy material overlaid and wrapped around itself. It is light as air and moves in the breeze.

"It is beautiful," Elizabeth assures her.

"Just the thing to welcome a suitor in," says Bree.

"William Chatworth Junior is not here as a suitor. He is here as a prisoner. Everyone knows he has already chosen Arsinoe. This feast is a farce."

Sara fastens a necklace around Mirabella's throat: it is the one she selected for Beltane, with the obsidian beads and gems that burn like fire. "Boys' minds are changeable," she says, and taps the gems. "This will remind him of your dance. His eye was on you then, no matter what he says about the naturalist."

With an impish grin, Bree bumps Mirabella aside and turns before the mirror.

"I cannot wait for the feast. Stewed apples and pork . . . berry tartlets . . . All this business of poison and tasters. I'm so afraid of my plate most days that I barely manage a mouthful." She points to a gap between her dress and her armpit. "Look at this bodice! My breasts have shrunk!"

"Bree," Elizabeth says, and giggles. "They have not."

"Easy for you to say, with the pair that you have. If they were not trapped under temple robes, no one would look at me twice." She swishes her skirt back and forth. Despite her words, the dress is very becoming, embroidered with bright blue hydrangeas.

"And what young man do you have your eye on now, daughter?" Sara asks.

"Mrs. Warren's glassmaking apprentice," Bree replies. "The tawny-headed one. With good shoulders and freckles." She turns. "Mira, if we fall in love, you must promise to appoint him to your royal guard. And then you must promise to get rid of him when we fall out of it."

"Bree," Elizabeth objects. "She can't dismiss someone just because you've finished with them! If you turn around one day and find that Mira's guard is filled with your old lovers . . . then that will be your own fault."

Mirabella tries to smile. They have worked hard to cheer her since Arsinoe and her bear escaped in the Ashburn Woods.

Mirabella had searched and searched, but it was as if her sister and the bear had vanished.

"There will be whispers," Mirabella murmurs. "They are saying I ran home with my tail tucked between my legs."

"But we know the truth," Elizabeth protests. "It was Arsinoe who ran, not you."

Arsinoe had run. But why? The bear had caught Mirabella completely by surprise. It could have torn her wide open. She does not understand why it did not. Why Arsinoe did not fight back.

The pavilion in Moorgate Park has been decorated with wreaths of flowers and long, trailing white and blue ribbons. The temple means to present William Chatworth Jr. to her there. As though he is a gift.

"So many people have come," Mirabella whispers as their coach draws to a halt. All of Rolanth must have emptied, from the sheep farms in the south to the northern stalls at Penman Market.

Mirabella takes a deep breath. The air smells of baked apple pies and fragrant spiced smoke from the roasting fires.

"Mirabella! Queen Mirabella has arrived!"

Those near to the coach rush toward it. Mirabella, Bree, and Elizabeth get out and are quickly jostled into the center of nine guardian priestesses. Some in the crowd are into their cups and push too close.

"Get back!" Bree shouts as the priestesses grasp the handles of their serrated knives.

"We should have brought Rho," Elizabeth says.

"Rho is with Luca," Mirabella replies.

"And besides," Bree adds, "who likes to bring Rho any-where?" But Elizabeth is right. If Rho were there, they would not have to worry about trouble from the crowd.

"Do you hear that?" Elizabeth mutters. Mirabella does not hear anything except the noise of the people, and the music from the players beside the pavilion.

"Hear what, Elizabeth?"

Elizabeth cranes her neck toward the green-leafed branches casting shade onto the path.

"It is Pepper," she whispers. "He's agitated. He recognizes someone."

"I think I know who," Bree says. Beside the fountain, Luca and Rho stand at the head of a band of priestesses. Kneeling at their feet, his head down so she can see only the top of his sandy hair, is the suitor, William Chatworth Jr.

And to his right is Joseph Sandrin.

Mirabella wants to shout but she does not react. She has been raised a queen and feels every eye on her. She cannot ask what Joseph is doing there. She cannot even reach out to squeeze her friends' hands.

"Queen Mirabella," William says. "I have come to serve."

"You are most welcome," comes her distant reply.

William raises his eyes, and she forces herself to smile. Has Joseph come to stay? Is this the way he has found to be near her?

"Come, Mira," Bree whispers, and escorts her to the banquet

table. Elizabeth bows, and leaves to dine with her fellow priest-esses.

They seat Joseph on the other side of William Chatworth, who is seated to Mirabella's left. At her right, High Priestess Luca signals the musicians to play, and dancers and jugglers fill the space in the grass before the table.

When a novice priestess brings Mirabella the first cut from the haunch of a roasted boar, Chatworth takes her knife and fork before she can even touch them.

"Not yet, my queen," he says. "This is my lot. To chew and swallow and see if I will die so you won't." He takes a little of the meat and a section of apple pastry. Then he washes it all down with wine from her goblet.

Mirabella waits. He drums his fingers.

"No cramps. No burning. No blood from my eyes."

"Do you think it safe, then, William?"

"Call me Billy," he says. "And yes, I think it's safe. Safer anyway than what you did to Arsinoe in the forest."

Mirabella's eyes flash to his. They are squinted at the corners as though smiling, but that is not real. Underneath, they are hard as stone.

"There is no suitable apology for that," she says. "So I will make none."

"Good. I would have spat it back in your face."

"May I have my fork now, Billy?"

"No." He nods out, toward the crowd, where people eat roasted boar and smoked fish off trenchers of bread. Dancing and laughing, and watching the royal table from the sides of their eyes. "We ought to give them a proper show. Isn't that what they expect? A love story for their queen?"

He cuts a bit of meat and skewers it onto her fork. He offers it to her with his hand on the back of her chair, doting, as though feeding her sweets with his fingers.

When she eats it, the people cheer.

"There now," Billy says. "That's better. Even though you were hesitant. Did you think I might push the fork into your throat? Every one of these barbaric priestesses would be on me the moment I did."

"But your death would serve Arsinoe. So perhaps you will still risk it."

"Things aren't that bad yet, Queen Mirabella."

She tries to see around him, to Joseph, but he has turned away, conversing with Rho of all people. No one seems to be listening; no one is hearing the things that Billy is saying to her. Sara is talking with Luca. Even Bree is distracted, calling out to a boy with tawny hair.

"This is how it will be," Billy says, his voice low. "I will taste for you, and I will smile. I will appease my father." He feeds her another bite of sweet apples. "And I will be back with my Arsinoe before she can even miss me."

WOLF SPRING

--- ❧ ---

"*J*'m not wearing that," Arsinoe says.

Madrigal sighs, and drops the long black dress onto Arsinoe's bed.

"It's their first time meeting you. You could wear a dress. Just once."

Arsinoe turns to her mirror and adjusts the cuffs on her black shirt. She straightens the mask on her face.

"I haven't worn a dress since I was six years old. It was half the reason I was crying when they came to take us from the Black Cottage." She holds her hands out. "Well? How do I look?"

Madrigal raises her eyebrows.

"Oh, who cares, anyway?" Arsinoe snaps.

"You're in a foul mood. And you haven't even seen them yet."

"Tommy Stratford and Michael Percy," Arsinoe grumbles

as she strips off her vest and throws it aside. Perhaps another. The pinstriped one that Luke made. She looks at her frowning reflection, at the bit of her soft pink scar peeking out from beneath the red and black of the mask.

"Just what is the punishment," she asks, "if Braddock accidentally eats them both?"

"It's not wise to joke about such things."

"I wish Billy was here."

"If he was, there would be a fight," Madrigal says, and Arsinoe hides a smile. "Well, if you will not wear this, maybe I can get it onto Jules. It will be longer—"

She bends to pick up the dress, and something small and dark falls out of the green sash at her waist.

"What is that?" Arsinoe asks.

Madrigal picks it up quickly and tucks it away. "It's nothing," she says. But Arsinoe has done enough low magic to recognize the cords they use to collect blood.

"It's not your blood," Madrigal assures her. "Not even I would dare to use that. Besides, for this kind of spell, it's better to use your own."

"What type is that?" But Arsinoe already knows. The length of cord was tied around a familiar gold ring. She hopes she is wrong, but it looked just like a ring that Matthew gave to Caragh, a long time ago.

"Only a charm," Madrigal replies, and avoids her eyes.

"How did you even get it? Did you go through her things? I thought she'd have taken it with her to the Black Cottage."

"Well, she didn't. She gave it back to him. And what does it matter?"

Madrigal goes to the window and looks out, where down in the yard Braddock is bonding with Camden and Jules. "It is almost time to go."

"Don't change the subject," Arsinoe says, and Madrigal whirls.

"Caragh isn't here," she hisses. "So why should he still love her? Why shouldn't he love me?"

"Because it's ugly, what you've done. Have you done it all along? Is that why he came to you in the first place?"

"No. He wanted me. He still wants me, but—"

"But he doesn't love you."

"Of course he does. Just . . ." Madrigal pauses. "Not like he loves her."

"Well, so what? If he still cares for you?"

Madrigal shakes her head. "You don't understand." She lays her palm flat against her stomach.

"You are pregnant."

"Yes." She looks down at her belly and smiles a little sadly. "Another Beltane Begot, I think. It seems I have a way with them. Only this time, I will not tell anyone that is what it is."

"Because you want it to have a father," says Arsinoe. "You want it to have Matthew." She purses her lips. All this time using low magic, and still Madrigal does this. Knowing the risks. Knowing that there is always a price.

"This will not go well for you," Arsinoe says.

"It will be fine. It will. But you can't tell Jules. Not until I'm ready. She will be happy, eventually. Jules loves babies."

"She's not going to raise it for you, if that's what you're thinking," Arsinoe says, and Madrigal draws back as though slapped. It was a cruel thing to say. But it was not without cause. She looks at Madrigal's sash, where the charm hides.

"You should throw that away before it's too late. It is less a charm than a curse."

The bear is staring at the chickens when Arsinoe comes out. When he sees her, he rolls his head back and flaps his lower lip, and Camden tucks her tail and flattens her ears.

"Do not do that," says Jules, and touches her head. "He's a friend now."

"Camden, Camden," Arsinoe scolds. "You won't forgive my bear for being a bear, but you forgive everyone else? I've seen the way you nuzzle Joseph, you furry little pushover."

Jules laughs and rubs the cat's back.

They walk together to the orchard: two girls, a bear, and a cougar. Arsinoe's stomach is tight as a fist. The mask on her face is a comfort and so is the poisoned blade in her vest, but she would still like to crawl into a hole and hide until morning.

"Are they there yet?" Arsinoe asks.

"Yes."

"How do they seem?"

"Rather like buffoons," Jules replies honestly. "But remember that you thought the same of Billy when he first arrived."

"Aye, but what are the chances of me being wrong twice?" She kicks at pebbles in the road, and Braddock swats at them like it is a game. It is hard to imagine that he is the same bear who tore apart those people on the Quickening beach. But he is, and someday she will see those claws again, tearing someone open.

"How are you, Jules? Are you all right?"

"I'm not going mad, if that's what you mean," Jules says.

"That's not what I mean. It's just . . ."

"I'm fine. I don't feel strange. Or sick. Nothing's different."

"Well," Arsinoe reasons, "that's not exactly true."

Jules has started to push her war gift. Arsinoe knows she has. Jules has been spending too much time off by herself for it to mean anything else.

"Will you show me?"

"I don't like it," Jules says.

"Please? I can understand having a gift that is a mystery to everyone around me. Sometimes I wonder what a poisoner I would be if I'd had the Arrons at my back. You must wonder what you might have been like if you had been sent to the warriors in Bastian City."

"I would only ever be a naturalist," Jules mutters. But she takes a deep breath and tenses her jaw, raising her arm toward the nearby trees. As Arsinoe watches, the branches of a maple begin to shake, as if from rowdy squirrels. Then the shaking stops.

"That was you?" Arsinoe asks.

"I'm working on breaking off branches. Save us time cutting wood for winter," Jules replies bitterly.

"Well, that will come in handy."

"They say the war gifted can't float things anymore. That the mind-mover part of the gift is gone."

"I guess they were wrong. The gifts grow strong all across the island. Before you know it, we'll be seeing great oracles again, and nothing will ever be a surprise." Arsinoe squints. "I wonder what it all means."

"Maybe that a great queen is coming," says Jules. "Maybe you."

ROLANTH

The day after the banquet, Joseph comes to Mirabella at Westwood House. Bree lets him into the drawing room in secret.

"You earned an audience with her," Bree says. "Saving her like you did. But if you try something on behalf of the naturalist queen, I will skin you and your handsome suitor friend and send your bodies back on a barge."

"Uh, thank you," Joseph says, and Bree bows to Mirabella and leaves.

"On a barge?" he asks when they are alone.

"A river barge, most likely." Mirabella's smile is tight lipped. Nervous. This meeting is not like before. Joseph is well-dressed and composed, and the day is bright.

"Then at least our bodies would enjoy some fine scenery on the way back to our families," he says, and she laughs.

"What are you doing here?" she asks.

"In this house? Or in Rolanth?"

"Both."

When he does not reply, she steps farther into the room, toward the windows.

"Did you come to tell me to stay away from Arsinoe? To spare her?"

"But that would be a wasted trip, wouldn't it?"

"Then why?" Mirabella holds her hands out to her sides. "This is not what I imagined when I imagined seeing you again. It is not the way we left things that night on the beach, when you saved me from her bear and all I could think of was being parted from you. Has it been so long, since Beltane?"

"No," he says softly. "It hasn't."

"When I saw you with William Chatworth—with Billy—I wanted to run to you. I lay awake last night, thinking you might find a way to come. I waited." She looks at him and he looks away. "But I suppose you were with him. Not so far from my room, but with many locked doors and watchful Westwoods in between."

"Mirabella—"

"I keep talking because I know that when I stop, it will be over. That is what you have come to tell me."

"I came to say good-bye."

Mirabella's throat tightens. Her eyes sting. But she is a queen. A broken heart must not show.

"You chose her. Because you could not have me?" She would take that back the moment it leaves her lips. She hates the tone of it. The foolish hope.

"I chose her because I love her. I have always loved her."

He is not lying. But it is not the whole truth. It is plain in the way he refuses to meet her eyes.

"Words," she says. "You said you loved me as well once. You still . . . want me, Joseph."

He does look at her finally, but what she sees in him is not lust. But guilt.

"Part of me may always," he says. "And I will always care, about what happens to you. But I choose Jules."

"As if there were a choice to make," she says.

"If there were, if there truly were, my choice would be the same. What happened between us was a mistake. I wasn't thinking. I didn't know where I was, or who you were."

"And the night of the Hunt? We both knew better then. Are you still going to tell me it was a mistake? An accident?"

Joseph lowers his head. "That night was . . ."

Ecstasy. Passion. A moment of peace amid the chaos of the festival.

". . . desperation," he says. "I wanted to be with Jules, but she refused me. I thought I'd lost her."

Bitterness rises in her throat. Jules wants him and has him, and now she gloats. She cannot even leave Mirabella her memories. *But that is not fair*, Mirabella thinks, and closes her eyes. *I have always known that I was the trespasser into their story.*

"Why have you come to tell me this?" she asks, and in her ears her voice sounds even and faraway.

"I suppose I didn't want you to hope. I owed you that, didn't

I? I couldn't just disappear, not after what happened."

"Very well," she says. "I will not hope. If I ever did."

"I'm sorry, Mirabella."

"Do not apologize. I do not need it. When do you sail back for Wolf Spring?"

"Tonight."

She turns to him and smiles, her hands folded atop her skirt.

"Good. Sail safely, Joseph."

He swallows. He has much more to say. But she will hear none of it. He takes his leave, and the textured wallpaper of the drawing room wavers before her eyes.

As his footsteps fade, Bree slips into the room and comes to take her in her arms.

"He chose her," Mirabella says. "I knew that he would. He was hers before he was mine."

"I heard," Bree says softly.

"You were listening."

"Of course I was. Are you all right, Mira?"

Mirabella turns her head. If she went to the southward-facing windows, she could watch as he left. She could know if he ever looked back.

"I am fine, Bree. It is over."

Bree sighs. "No," she says. "I saw the way he held you that night, Mira. And how he jumped in front of that bear. Half the island saw that. You are right: as a queen it must be over for you. But anyone with eyes can see that for him, it never will be."

WOLF SPRING

❧

*T*he orchard is full when they arrive and so bustling with activity that no one even notices the arrival of a great brown bear.

"There they are." Jules points. Two boys, both with red-gold hair, stand talking with Ellis and Madrigal. Madrigal flirts with them mercilessly.

"I hope they don't expect me to giggle like that," Arsinoe says.

"No one expects anyone to giggle like that," Jules replies, watching her mother with a sour expression.

"Which one is Tommy and which is Michael?"

"Tommy is the bigger of the two. Michael, the more handsome."

"Jules," Arsinoe scolds. "When Joseph gets back, I'm telling him."

She squares her shoulders. The unpleasantness can no

longer be put off. She reaches out to Braddock and pats him. He is calm, blinking curiously at the activity and the food piled high on the tables.

Arsinoe takes a step toward the suitors and raises an arm in greeting, just as children come streaming out from between the trees. She falls in the midst of them, bowled over in the dirt as they squeal, caught up in a game of tag. Braddock grunts and joins in the fun. He rolls her back and forth on the ground. She rolls into chairs and upends them. Apples rain down like hail, and she covers her head as the bear lies down on top of her legs.

Someone shouts, and Arsinoe quickly holds her palms up.

"No, no, Braddock, back now," she says. She rolls onto her knees just in time to see Jules twist a knife out of Tommy Stratford's hands.

"Enough, Braddock, enough." Arsinoe laughs, and shoves his large brown head.

"I'm sorry," Tommy says. "I thought . . . I thought she was being attacked."

Michael Percy works up his courage and moves past Tommy to offer her his hand.

"The bear's a lot to handle," he says as he helps her to her feet. "How do you manage?"

"Sometimes I don't. As you've seen." She smiles at him, and his expression flickers. No doubt he remembers the carnage on the Quickening stages. But the bear was not Braddock then. He was only a bear under a low magic spell. Angry and frightened.

Arsinoe slips her hand loose from Michael's. There is

nothing wrong with accepting a suitor's helping hand. Only she cannot help wondering what Billy would say, and what he is doing in Rolanth, with her sister.

Tommy approaches from her other side.

"Are you all right?" he asks, speaking fast as if to cut off Michael's questions. If they keep up like that she will be tired of them by the end of the day.

"Why have you chosen to pay court together?" Arsinoe asks them. "Sharing a barge for the Disembarking was odd, but this is truly uncommon."

"Competitiveness," Tommy says simply. He grins and shows bright white teeth in a pleasantly handsome face. He is more sturdily built than Michael, but with their shared red-gold hair and similar features, looking at them is like viewing one through open air and another through a magnifying glass.

"It's true. We've always been this way," Michael cuts in. He bends to help Luke right an upended table. Arsinoe smiles apologetically, but Luke only winks. No one seems to mind the cleaning up. As long as she has her bear, she can do no wrong.

"We're cousins, you see," Michael goes on. "Go to the same schools, spend summers on each other's estates. When you spend so much time together, it's hard not to engage in one-upmanship."

"You must feel the same about the other queens," Tommy says.

"It's not exactly the same when you have to kill them," says Arsinoe, and cranes her neck to look for Jules. Maybe she can take one of these boys off her hands. They were nearly as impressed by the sight of Camden as they were by Braddock.

She looks back at Tommy, and he glances away. It takes her a moment to realize why: he had been trying to peek at what is underneath her mask. Arsinoe cannot decide whether to laugh or punch him.

"Why did you request first suit with me?" she asks. "Did you think I would die first?"

Michael shakes his head emphatically.

"Not at all," he says. "We just had to see the bear up close. We couldn't wait." He gestures, rather shyly, toward Braddock lumbering ahead of them. "May I?" he asks. "I mean, is he safe?"

"If you feed him a fish he will be perfectly safe."

As the sun sets over the orchard and the braziers are lit for evening, Arsinoe and Jules stand back from the crowd. It is a good night. The children of Wolf Spring chase one another from hot brazier to hot brazier, fearless. Folk sit at tables playing games and nibbling on leftover pie. Camden leans against Jules's legs, and Braddock lies somewhere in the dark, finally stuffed full of fish and apples and tired of the children's shrieks.

"They aren't really so bad," Jules says. "They could be much worse."

"I suppose so." Arsinoe cocks her head wearily. Tommy and Michael are at a table near the roasted suckling pigs, nodding and chuckling at something Luke is saying.

"Luke seems to like them."

"Don't be fooled," says Jules. "He finds them tolerable. You know his heart is pledged to Billy nearly as solidly as yours is."

"As mine is? I don't remember making any pledges."

"Well. As soon as he gets back from Rolanth, maybe."

"Maybe." Arsinoe snorts, and crosses her arms. Her heart skips. Her knife is no longer in her vest.

"Jules, my knife is gone." She pats herself all over, as if it might have moved to another pocket by itself.

"It probably fell out when you were tussling with Braddock," Jules says. "We can find it tomorrow, in the daylight."

"No, you don't understand." Arsinoe looks quickly over the people in attendance. Her people, talking and drinking. Luke calls to Tommy and Michael from the edge of the nearest row of apple trees and they get up to play a shadow game with the children. Before he goes, Tommy slices another serving of meat and eats it, and Arsinoe's heart stops at the sight.

He used her knife. The whole table had. Her knife, with the poisoned edge.

"Oh, Goddess," she whispers, and runs to the table to pick it up.

"Arsinoe? What's wrong?" Jules asks, running up behind her.

"They used my knife! The knife I dropped!"

It takes Jules a moment to understand. To her, Arsinoe is still not a poisoner.

"Who was eating here?" she asks.

"Both of the suitors . . . I don't know who else! We have to send for a healer, Jules, now!" Arsinoe moves to bolt, but Jules holds her fast.

"Send for a healer and say what? That our poisoner in disguise accidentally poisoned her own suitors? You can't!"

Arsinoe blinks.

"What are you saying? That doesn't matter now. They need help!"

"Arsinoe, no."

She has grasped on to Arsinoe's arm with a grip like iron when they hear the first cry.

"Poison!" Luke shouts. "Poison! Send for the healers! The suitors have been poisoned!"

"No," Arsinoe whispers miserably, but Jules holds her fast and takes the knife to slide into her back pocket.

"You did not mean to do this," Jules hisses fiercely. "This is not your fault! And it's too late to help them now."

GREAVESDRAKE MANOR

❧

"Poison the suitors? I did no such thing!" Katharine declares. "Why would I poison them before I even got to meet them?" She crosses her arms and turns her back to the tall windows in Natalia's study.

"Because they chose your sister," Genevieve says. "Because she had two to your one. Because you could!" Genevieve crosses her arms as well, and Natalia rubs her temples with tired fingers.

"Stop sniping at each other like spoiled children," she mutters.

"Well, she has truly made a mess of this," Genevieve halfshouts. "Returning from the dead is one thing. But murdering mainland suitors?" She throws up her hands.

"I did not do it, I said!" Katharine shouts back. "Natalia, I did not!"

"Whether you did or did not does not matter. They are dead,

and if you did not do it, then someone did it on your behalf. So what do we do now?" Natalia steadies her nerves with another sip of brandy tainted with yew. Except that she has already had too much, and her mind is sluggish when it should be sharp. She looks at her glass and then drains it anyway.

"It could be worse," she says. "The suitors will have families to appease, but once we would have had whole countries. We will not go to war over this."

"Think of the money it will take," Genevieve grumbles. "The resources and favors. She will bankrupt the crown before she even wears it!"

"At least they were cousins, so it is only one family to appease and not two," Katharine mutters, and Natalia reprimands her with an arched brow.

"The island will not like this." Genevieve paces. When she stops, her whole body bounces with the motion of her tapping foot. "Word is spreading. The suitors were not the only ones to die. An old man and a little girl in Wolf Spring also fell to the poison. And this amid the talk of farmers dying in wildfires and lightning-struck cattle. This Ascension is going out of control!" She points at Katharine. "If you would just poison like Queen Camille did or Queen Nicola. Fast and clean. Poisons that found their targets and no one else!"

"Genevieve, be quiet," Natalia says. "How a queen poisons is a queen's business. Issue a statement from the Council. Remind the people that the greatest Ascensions are bloody and turbulent. That it is when the strongest queens rise. Suitors die.

It is known. If they had still been alive for the Beltane crowning, they may have died in the Innisfuil woods during the Hunt of the Stags."

"It is still a mess," Genevieve says. But she says so more softly.

"Natalia," Katharine says. "I really did not—"

Natalia waves her hand.

"Whether you did or did not, we must find a way out of it." She stands up and walks from behind her desk to look out the windows, at the great city of Indrid Down across the hills.

"Those suitors did not matter anyway. Our alliance with the Chatworth boy's father still holds. Chatworth has gone to great lengths to insinuate himself into the trust of the Westwoods, in case we have need of him, and the boy will make a fine king-consort when the time comes."

"Can we not get him away from my sister?" Katharine asks. "I do not like him standing between us. I want to go to her. I would look her in the eye when I carve up her pretty face with a poisoned blade." She walks to Natalia's decanter of brandy and pours herself a measure, then drinks it in one large gulp.

"You take poison now at every meal," Genevieve says.

"How do you know?"

"The servants talk. They say that you sicken long into the night. That you take too much and will do yourself harm."

But Katharine only laughs.

"Have they not heard?" she asks. "You cannot kill what is already dead."

Natalia frowns. Rumors of the Undead Queen have not

faded as they hoped. Instead they grow stronger, and Katharine is not helping the people to forget.

"Kat," Natalia asks thoughtfully. "Would you really like to go to Mirabella?"

Katharine and Genevieve look at her curiously.

"With the temple inspecting everything, it would be easier if you are face-to-face," Natalia says. "So what if we put you together? Put you all together, for the Midsummer Festival. It is barely two weeks away. We could descend upon Wolf Spring."

"Perfect," says Genevieve. "Whatever damage is done to Wolf Spring from the queens' business will be penance for failing to protect the suitors. But High Priestess Luca will not like it."

"Who cares what she likes and does not like?" Katharine says. "If it were up to you, I would do nothing until Beltane was over, and the three of us would end up locked in the tower. I do not like to think of how I would fare trapped in close quarters with a bear."

"Besides," Natalia says, "I think the High Priestess would force her queen's hand as well. None were happy when Mirabella returned from the Ashburn Woods with Arsinoe still alive. If we offer to hold the festival of the Reaping Moon in Rolanth afterward, I do not think she will object to Midsummer."

"I will discuss it with the Council at once." Genevieve half-curtsies and then walks toward the door.

"Wait," says Natalia. "Let me send a letter to Luca first. Perhaps we can save ourselves an argument."

ROLANTH

*B*illy has ordered a table set for two in the sunlit grounds behind Westwood House. It is a pretty table, with a bright white tablecloth and silver platters. But as Mirabella sits, the sun glints off one and nearly blinds her. So she calls some clouds, and soon the sky is filled with thunderheads.

"What's the point of dining outside?" Billy asks. "If you wanted shade, I could have had the table moved underneath the trees."

"I will not let them rain," Mirabella says as he presses his lips together crossly. He has warmed to Bree and to Sara. And of course he could not resist Elizabeth. But when Mirabella speaks, he barely listens. Much of his time is spent in the city with Bree and her glassmaking apprentice, and when he is not there, he is with Elizabeth at the temple, fascinated by the white-robed priestesses and their black tattooed bracelets.

Mirabella clears her throat and turns toward the cart of

food. Fortunately, he is a good taster, taking complete control of the kitchen. Unfortunately, he is a horrible cook.

"What have you brought for us today?"

"Pork stew," he says, "with spoon bread for dipping and, for dessert, a baked strawberry tart with cream."

"You are becoming quite skilled," she says, and smiles.

"Lying is a waste when you know I have to taste it." He serves them both. The stew looks thin and strangely pale. A sheen of grease has collected on the surface. He uses her fork and knife to sample everything on her plate and waits in silence to see if he will fall over or froth at the mouth.

"I don't know why I bother," he says. "The priestesses there"—he gestures into the shadows of the house—"they watched me prepare it and insisted on tasting it themselves."

"They do not trust you?"

"Of course not. My father gave his word that I would do as I was told, but everyone knows how I feel about Arsinoe." He clears his throat. "But regardless, I don't want you eating anything except what I prepare, do you understand?"

"Why not?"

"Because I've been assured that if you die on my watch, Rho will saw off my head and send it back to my father on a barge."

Mirabella laughs. "We send many grisly things back on barges, it seems."

"Yes." Billy arches his brow. "Joseph told me what Bree said to him before he sailed."

The cloth overlay of Billy's cart clucks, and a brown chicken pokes her head out from under the covering, stepping out of the basket she was riding in.

"There is a chicken in your cart."

"I know," Billy snaps, and slaps his napkin across his lap.

"Why is there a chicken in your cart?"

"Because this was supposed to be chicken stew," he says. "I've been hand-feeding this bird for days to be sure it was not poisoned before the fact. And now . . ." He pours Mirabella some water and drinks from her cup. The hen clucks, and Billy tosses down a chunk of bread.

"Now her name is Harriet," he says quietly.

Mirabella laughs.

"No doubt you think I've been spending too much time with lowly naturalists," he says.

"I would never say that. The naturalists are the island's life-blood. They feed us. They ensure good hunts."

"A very queenly answer. One you have been groomed to say?"

"You think because I was raised for the crown I do not know how to think for myself."

Billy shrugs. He takes a spoonful of greasy stew and swallows it down hard before turning to the bread.

"I've known girls like you before. Not queens, of course, but very rich, very spoiled girls who have grown up hearing nothing but praise. Nothing but talk of their family's important place in the world. And I never liked any of them more than just to look at."

Mirabella takes a bite of pork. It is terrible. If all she has to eat between now and the crowning is food that Billy has cooked, she will be nearly as thin as Katharine.

"Those are unkind words," she says. "Your family is not poor, or you would not be here."

"True enough. Or it would be were my father not reminding me daily that he will take it all, that he will give it away if I don't earn it."

"How must you earn it?" she asks.

"By accomplishing whatever benchmark gets into his head that day. Being accepted into the right school, impressing the governor, winning a cricket match. Becoming king-consort of a secret, mystical island."

"But you ran away from the island," Mirabella says. "With Arsinoe. You would give up your fortune for her?"

Billy chuckles around a mouthful of bread.

"Don't be ridiculous. I always planned on coming back."

Mirabella lowers her head and smiles. His words say one thing, but the truth lies in the color that rises to his cheeks.

"Besides," he says, "I hardly believe he means it anymore. The same threat used daily loses its shine, you know? Why are you smiling?"

"No reason." She stabs a piece of potato with her fork and drops it into the grass for the chicken. "It is tragic what has happened to Arsinoe's suitors in Wolf Spring. But some part of you must be glad that they are not there with her anymore."

"'Glad' is not the word I would use when discussing it. Those lads are dead, and Katharine is insane. It could have just as easily been me who was killed. I don't know whether you're truly the 'chosen queen' like everyone around here seems to believe, but for Fennbirn's sake, you had best hope that it's not Katharine. She'll be ruinous."

"The queen who is crowned is the queen who was meant to be."

Billy sighs.

"My God. Isn't it exhausting to parrot back temple rhetoric? Do you ever think for yourself?"

"I thought for myself when I saved Arsinoe," Mirabella says sharply, and the clouds overhead darken. "At Innisfuil, when they tried to cut her to pieces. And two days later, she sent a bear after me. So do not tell me she would be better for the island. She is just as heartless as Katharine."

He stabs at a chunk of pork like he wishes it was Mirabella's eye.

"She didn't send that bear after you, you great idiot," he says.

"What?"

"Nothing. Never mind."

"No. What did you mean by that? Of course she sent it!" Mirabella glances at the priestesses near the house and lowers her voice. "Who else could control her familiar?"

"Who else do you think?" Billy asks, his voice equally low. "Another strong naturalist, perhaps? One who would have just as much motivation to hurt you after you stole the boy she loved?

"Perhaps someone who Arsinoe would always lie for?" Billy adds, but when Mirabella opens her mouth, he stops her. "Don't say her name out loud. I shouldn't have told you. Arsinoe's going to kill me."

"Then," Mirabella says as Billy goes back to prodding at his horrible meal, "Arsinoe never meant to hurt me."

"No. She didn't. Arsinoe grew up believing that she would die. She just didn't count on having so much to live for. Jules and Joseph and the Milones." He smiles slightly. "Me. But what good is knowing any of this? This is the way of the island, isn't it? The natural order. So what does it change?"

Mirabella's fingers dig into her napkin. She wants to scream or cry, but if she does, the priestesses will come running.

"I almost killed her that day in the road," she whispers. "Why did she let me do that?"

"Maybe because she knew you had to. Maybe she wanted to make it easier on you."

Mirabella's eyes fill with tears, and Billy quickly wipes his mouth. He scoops strawberry tart onto his fork and holds it out.

"Here," he says. "You must try this." As she takes the bite, he uses his thumb to discreetly wipe the tear that falls down her cheek.

"I'm sorry," he says softly. "I suppose I haven't even tried to consider your point of view. It was thoughtless of me."

"It is all right," Mirabella says. "Does she know that you love her?"

Billy raises his eyebrows.

"Why would she when I didn't? It wasn't like I read in books. A thunderclap. Eyes meeting. Tortured glances. With Arsinoe it was more like . . . having cold water poured down your back and learning to enjoy it."

"And does she love you?"

"I don't know. I think she might." He smiles. "I hope she does."

"I hope so too." Another tear slides down her cheek, and Billy darts forward to discreetly hide it.

"It is all right," she says. "They will think I am only crying because of how terrible this strawberry tart is."

Billy sets down his fork, insulted. Then they both begin to laugh.

WOLF SPRING

❧

*T*hey put the suitors in long wooden boxes to sail them home, as is the mainland tradition. The boxes seem small, and are so still that Arsinoe's throat squeezes shut. She knew Tommy and Michael so briefly. Two boys who thought they might be king. Who perhaps thought it was all just a great game.

The Black Council sent the poisoners Lucian Arron and Lucian Marlowe to examine the bodies, hoping to find evidence that they did not die from poison. But of course, they had.

"Let them start as many rumors as they want," Joseph says. "Everyone will know now that they've lost control of their queen." He slips one arm about Jules's waist and the other around Arsinoe's, but she slides out of it. She killed those boys, not Katharine. She was careless, and she killed them.

Arsinoe steps closer to the edge of the dock and watches as the ship bearing Tommy's and Michael's bodies casts off into the cove.

"I can't breathe, Jules," she says, and gulps air. She feels Camden press warm fur against her legs, and then Jules is there, to hold her up. "You were right. I shouldn't have played with it. I didn't know how to be careful."

"Hush, Arsinoe," Jules whispers. There are too many people gathered on the dock. Too many ears.

Arsinoe waits until the boat is out of sight and turns back toward shore, her feet hammering the wooden planks. The faster she gets back to the Milone house, the faster this day will be over.

"Queen Arsinoe!" someone shouts as she crosses the docks toward the hill road. "Where is your bear?"

"Well, he's not in my pocket," she snaps without pausing. "So he must be in the woods."

ROLANTH

§

*T*he letter from Natalia is addressed to the High Priestess and not the queen, but Rho insists that it be opened by gloved novices in a windless room. She will not allow Luca to touch it before it is thoroughly examined.

"You are being ridiculous," Luca says. The priestesses have been with the letter for most of the morning, and none of them have fallen ill with so much as a paper cut.

"There is nothing to be gained by poisoning me." Luca paces across her room indignantly. "And if there were, Natalia would have done it by now. Goddess knows, she has had many chances."

She goes to her eastern window and throws the shutters open for the breeze. As far north as it is, Rolanth does not get terribly hot, but in summer, her rooms in the temple can still feel stifling. Her old quarters in the capital were much better. When her legs were young, she walked off tension on the many stairs of the east tower of the Volroy. She sighs. She is so old. If Mirabella is crowned and they return to Indrid Down, she will have to be carried up and down in a litter.

Finally, her chamber door opens, and Rho enters with the letter in hand. From the look on her face, Luca knows that she has ignored the order not to read it.

"Well?" Luca asks. "What does it say?" She snatches the letter angrily, but Rho does not flinch. Rho never flinches. Her toughness is as much a comfort as it is annoying.

"See for yourself," Rho says.

Luca's eyes skim over it so greedily the first time that she barely comprehends a word and must start again.

It opens with only her name, "Luca," as if she and Natalia are old friends. No "High Priestess." No other greeting. The corner of Luca's mouth twists upward.

"She wants to push the queens together for the high festivals. With Midsummer in Wolf Spring and the Reaping Moon to be held here."

"They are plotting something," Rho says.

Luca purses her lips and reads the letter again. It is short, and for Natalia, almost conversational.

Luca reads aloud. "'Surely you would welcome the chance for your Mirabella to make good on her promises.'" She puts the letter down and scoffs. "Surely."

"She fears a stalemate. She does not want the Ascension to end with queens locked in the tower," says Rho. "She knows that poisoners do not fare well there."

"Mirabella may not either if Arsinoe is still alive with her great brown bear." Luca taps her chin.

"You know that by sending this letter she is lulling you with courtesy. She knows that we could stop it if we chose. The Black Council does not have the final word when it comes to the high festivals."

Luca kicks at embroidered pillows that have fallen onto the floor.

"I think we should do it," she says. "Mirabella is strong. And whatever action the Arrons have planned to take, at least it will not come as a surprise."

"We will take care," Rho says. "But with the three queens face-to-face, I like our chances. She is strong, like you said." Rho's eyes sparkle. Despite her cautious words, she craves bloodshed.

Luca lowers her head and asks the Goddess for guidance. But the only answer that hums into her bones is the one she has known all along: that if the crown is meant to be Mirabella's, then she will rise up and take it.

"Luca?" Rho asks, always impatient. "Shall we begin preparations for an envoy to Wolf Spring?"

Luca takes a breath.

"Do it. Get started right away. I am going to take some air."

Rho nods, and Luca leaves to wander down the steps and through the temple, keeping clear of the gathered worshippers who flock to the altar daily.

As she passes one of the lower storerooms, she reaches

out to close a door that is slightly ajar and glimpses someone inside. It is the suitor, Billy Chatworth, searching through the temple stores with a large brown chicken perched beside him on a few crates of dresses.

"High Priestess," he says when he sees her, and bends a shallow bow. "I was after some fruit, to attempt a pie with."

"To add to your chicken?" she asks, and chuckles. "You do not need to do all of this. The priestesses will prepare meals for you."

"And leave me with so little to do? Besides, I'm not in the habit of having my life in anyone's hands but my own."

Luca nods. He is a handsome lad, with sandy hair and an easy smile, and despite his devotion to Queen Arsinoe, Luca has come to like him. She does not trust him, and priestesses watch his every move, but to Luca, his fondness for Arsinoe is only evidence of a good heart. Once she is dead, he will learn to love Mirabella in the same way.

"Will you take a walk with me, Billy?" she asks. "These old legs need to stretch."

"Of course, High Priestess."

He takes her arm, and they go out through the courtyard and past the vegetable gardens, toward the roses. It is a fine day. A light, cool breeze races toward the basalt cliffs of Shannon's Blackway, and pink and white roses bounce with bees from the apiary.

"How are you and Mirabella getting along?" she asks.

"Well enough," he says, but there is more fondness in his

voice now than when she asked a few weeks ago. "She's growing thin on my cooking. But I am getting better, I promise."

"Well, you cannot get any worse. She has told me about your stews."

They pass Elizabeth and she waves, with netting around her face from gathering honey.

"Could I get a measure of that?" Billy asks.

"I will bring some to the house later," Elizabeth calls. "And some grain for your chicken."

Luca turns to look behind them. She had not noticed that the brown hen was following from the storeroom.

"You have found a familiar, it seems," Luca says. "Will you bring her back to Wolf Spring when you go?"

"I suppose I will. But who knows when that may be."

"Sooner than you think." Luca stops, and turns to face him. "Have you heard much of the Midsummer Festival?"

"The next high festival," he says. "I have heard Sara and the priestesses discussing preparations."

"Here in Rolanth, the elementals sacrifice a small barge of vegetables and rabbit meat. They set it alight in the river and push it out to sea." Luca turns south, toward the city, remembering all the past festivals she has presided over. Sometimes Mirabella would put on beautiful displays of water spouts. Luca had felt so close to the Goddess in those moments. She knew then that she was precisely where she was meant to be, doing precisely what she was meant to do.

"In Wolf Spring," she goes on, "they set lanterns on their

boats, and take to the harbor at twilight. They throw grain into the water to feed the fish. It is more rustic, perhaps, but quite lovely. I went there for the festival many times as a girl." She sighs. "It will be nice to see it again."

"Why would you go to the Wolf Spring Festival?" Billy asks suspiciously.

"We will all go. You, and I, and Mirabella, and the West-woods. The Black Council and Queen Katharine. I am about to send word to Indrid Down that the queens will spend the remaining High Festivals together. Midsummer in Wolf Spring and the Reaping Moon here, in Rolanth."

"You're putting them together. So that one will die."

"Yes," she says. "That is the way things work in an Ascension Year."

GREAVESDRAKE MANOR

❖

Nicolas has targets set on the long, level swath of grass past the rear courtyard. He nocks an arrow and fires it near the center of the target, just to the left of the one he fired before that.

"Beautifully done," Katharine says, and claps. Nicolas sets down his bow and lets her take her turn. To his credit, the smile on his face flags only slightly when hers strikes right dead center.

"Not as beautiful as that." Nicolas bends and kisses the back of her gloved hand. "Not as beautiful as you."

Katharine blushes and nods downfield toward the targets.

"It will not be long until it is a true contest. You are becoming quite good. I cannot believe you have never practiced archery before."

Nicolas shrugs. He is nearly as handsome as Pietyr, even dressed strangely in a white mainland shirt and white shoes.

His shoulders stretch the fabric when he takes position with his bow, and the underside of the gold hair against his collar is darkened with sweat.

"I had no interest in it," he says, and lets another arrow fly. It goes slightly wide. "Not as good. You must have distracted me."

"My apologies."

"Do not apologize. It is a welcome distraction."

Katharine reaches for another arrow. Her bow is newly fashioned, longer, and harder to draw than her old one. But then, her arms have never been stronger.

She nocks an arrow and fires it. Then another. And another after that. The sound the arrows make when they hit is solid, and satisfying. She wonders if they would sound the same catching Mirabella in the back.

"I do not have to inspect the target to know that those were better shots than mine," says Nicolas as they set down their bows and move toward a small stone table beneath the shade of a tall, leafy alder tree.

"I have been practicing archery since I was a small girl. Though I must admit, I was never that skilled at it. A few months ago, those arrows might have been lost in the hedge."

On the table are two silver pitchers and two goblets. One is filled with Katharine's drink: straw-colored May wine, sweetened with honey and fresh berries, both poison and not. The other holds wine for Nicolas: dark red and cooled with water. Impossible to mistake for the other.

"They tell me we are to depart soon, for Wolf Spring,"

Nicolas says. "And I was just becoming accustomed to Greavesdrake Manor."

"We will not be away long. And their Midsummer ritual is said to be beautiful: floating lamps flickering in the harbor. I always hoped I would see it. I just assumed I would have to wait until after I was crowned."

Nicolas takes a large gulp of wine. He looks at her slant-ways and his eyes narrow with mischief.

"I will long to return to your home and the capital. But I truly cannot wait to see you face-to-face with your sisters. I hope," he says, and reaches for her gloved hand, "that you will not leave me back when it happens."

"Leave you back?" she asks.

"When you kill them. You will, of course." He gestures toward the bows, toward the targets full of arrows. "And the servants have told me of your skill with a knife. Throwing them near to a target? I would very much like to see that."

Katharine's stomach tightens with pleasure, and a tingle rolls up and down her back as if touched by unseen fingers.

"Would you indeed," she whispers. "Perhaps you only think so. You might feel different when you saw your future queen slide a knife into her pretty sister's breast."

Nicolas smiles.

"I come from a family of soldiers, Queen Katharine. I have seen much of that. And worse." He takes another swallow of wine. It gathers at the corners of his mouth, bright red. "And I do not like to be back from the action."

Katharine's pulse quickens until her heart beats so fast it seems there is more than one in her chest. The look in his eyes brings blood to her cheeks. She has seen that look before, on Pietyr, right before he would pull her to him and take her to bed.

"Natalia prefers that I poison from the safety of her bosom," she says. "That is how the Arrons like to do it. Quiet and refined. Nothing pleases them more than pleasant dinner conversation that ends when someone's face falls dead to their plate."

Nicolas lets his eyes move over her body.

"There is charm in that," he says. "But I would see your hands around their throats. A memory to take with me on the night of our marriage."

Giselle clears her throat.

"Ahem, pardon me, my queen."

"Giselle," Katharine says. "Forgive me. We were so . . . engrossed . . . that we did not hear you."

Giselle looks from Katharine to Nicolas, and flushes slightly at their expressions.

"Natalia sent for you," the maid says. "She says you have a guest."

"But I am already entertaining a guest."

"She says you must come."

Katharine sighs.

"Please, you must go," Nicolas says. "You don't want to keep the lady of the manor waiting."

Katharine trudges up the stairs and down the hall to Natalia's study.

"Natalia," she says, "you sent for—" The rest of the words do not leave her mouth. Because standing in the middle of the room, his back straight and eyes bright as a frightened rabbit's, is Pietyr.

"I knew you would want to see him right away," Natalia says, smiling. "Do not be too hard on him, Katharine. I have already given him a stern lecture about leaving us for so long."

But of course he would want to. Out of fear that she would send him to the cells beneath the Volroy, down so deep that he would never again see the sun. Out of terror that she would order Bertrand Roman to batter his brains out against the stones of the long, oval drive. Or that she would do it herself.

"No doubt you two would like to be alone," Natalia says.

"No doubt," Katharine agrees.

The cages of dead birds and rodents were cleared out of Katharine's rooms when Nicolas arrived, but though her windows are kept open daily to combat the smell, it still lingers, and she hopes that Pietyr can detect it when he walks inside. The smell of death. Of pain. And not of hers, anymore.

He enters the room ahead of her, so he does not see it when she takes up the short-bladed knife from one of her tables. He walks into her bedchamber unaware. So bold. As if he still has the right to be there.

He taps the glass sides of Sweetheart's cage, and the snake lifts her pretty head.

"I see Sweetheart is well," he says, and Katharine leaps upon him.

She drags him to the bed and twists her body around his, kneeling on the mattress to grip him from the back. One arm wraps around the crown of his head as the other drags the knife lightly across his throat.

"Kat," he says, and gasps.

"This will be messy." She presses the knife harder into his skin. It will not take much. The edge is sharp, and his vein is close. "Giselle will have to fetch me a new coverlet. But it is true what Natalia says. You cannot poison a poisoner."

"Kat, please."

"Please what?" she growls, and squeezes his head tighter. His pulse races under her hands. But even as she wants to carve into his neck, she remembers what it was like, pressed against him like this. Her Pietyr, who she loved and who said he loved her. The scent of him, vanilla and ambergris, brings angry tears to the corners of her eyes.

"How could you, Pietyr!"

"I am sorry," he says as the knife cuts into his throat.

"I will give you sorry," she hisses.

"I had to!" he shouts quickly to stop her from cutting more. "Kat, please. I thought I had to."

Her grip on his head does not loosen.

"Why?"

"There was a plot. Natalia told me of it in the days before Beltane. The priestesses, they had devised a scheme. To make Mirabella a White-Handed Queen. After your poor showing at the Quickening, they planned to charge the stages. They planned to cut you into pieces and feed you into the fires."

"But I did not *have* a poor showing," Katharine says, pressing the knife down again.

"I did not know that! When you came to me that night, beside the Breccia Domain, I thought that you were running from them! And I could not stand to see them touch you." His hand strays up to her arm and she steels herself, but he does not try to draw the knife from his neck. He only touches her softly.

"I thought they were coming to kill you. And I could not let them. I would rather it be me."

"So you pushed me down that hole!" Katharine screeches through her teeth. Her whole body trembles with the rage of it. The shock and confusion when he shoved her.

It was a crime what he did. It was betrayal. She should slash his throat and watch his blood pool around her legs.

Instead, she draws back and throws the knife into the wall.

Pietyr crumples forward, his hand pressed to the shallow wound on his neck.

"You cut me," he says softly in disbelief.

"I should have done worse." He turns to look at her, and she relishes the fear in his eyes. "I still might. I have not decided yet."

Clever, calculating Pietyr. He has dressed just so, in his dove-gray shirt and dark jacket, and he has kept his hair a little longer, the way she likes it best. Looking at him on her bed, she hates him, and is angry in so many ways. But he is still her Pietyr.

"I would not blame you. But I am sorry, Kat." He looks at her full, round shoulders. "You look different."

"What did you expect? One does not get pushed into the Breccia Domain and crawl out again unchanged."

"I have wanted to come back to you for so long."

"Of course you have. Back to the seat of Arron power."

"Back to you." His fingers twitch with wanting. He lifts his hand to caress her cheek.

Katharine slaps it away.

"You do not know what you have come back to," she says. She grasps the sides of his head and kisses him forcefully, her lips hard enough to make it a punishment. She bites along his jaw. She licks the blood from the cut on his throat.

He wraps his arms around her waist and pulls her to him.

"Katharine," he says, and sighs. "How I love you."

"How indeed." She shoves him hard. "How you must love me, Pietyr," she says, and leaves to return to Nicolas. "But you will never have me again."

WOLF SPRING

The house is quiet. An odd thing for a naturalist house to be. Usually, it is filled with barks and caws and someone in the kitchen or Cait talking to the flock as they cluck and honk through the yard. Jules takes a deep breath and listens to the air move in and out. She sips a hot cup of willowbark tea and strokes Camden's head where it rests on her leg.

She and the cat have been even closer than usual since Jules's legion curse became known. They cling to each other, unsure what it might mean for their bond. The thought that one day she could wake and find that Camden is not a part of her anymore—it is more terrifying than anything she could do with the war gift.

Madrigal walks in, back from the market with her arms full of baskets. Breaking the peace.

"Will you help me?" she asks. "I'm making chowder with fresh cream, and biscuits with that soft white cheese that you like."

"What's the occasion?" Jules asks suspiciously. She takes the basket of clams and dumps them into the sink to wash.

"No occasion." Madrigal sets the rest of her shopping on the countertop. "But when it's ready, you could float the bowls onto the table for us."

Jules scowls.

"That isn't how it works."

"How do you know?" Madrigal asks. "The war gift has been weak for so long that nobody knows how it works."

That is true enough. Everything Jules has ever heard about the war gift has been the stuff of long-ago legends. Of the recent there are only rumors. Folk in Bastian City who have uncanny accuracy with knives and bows. Near-impossible shots made so clean that it is almost as if the weapon were pulled on a string.

But it is not pull so much as push. Jules has worked at it, alone and mostly in secret, aghast and amazed at what she is able to do.

At the sink, Madrigal begins scrubbing clams, nearly managing to look like she has done it before. She wipes her forehead. Sallow circles mar the undersides of her eyes. And she is still breathless from the walk.

"Are you all right?" Jules asks.

"I'm fine. How are you? Is that willowbark tea? Is your leg paining you?"

"Madrigal, what's going on?"

"Nothing," she says. "Only that . . ." She pauses and heaps washed clams into a pot. "Only that I'm pregnant." She twists at the waist and flashes a fast smile, then looks back down at her hands. "Matthew and I are going to have a baby."

Aria flies nervously onto the table. Her wing feathers shift in the quiet.

"You," Jules says, "and Aunt Caragh's Matthew are going to have a baby?"

"Don't call him that. He is not *her* Matthew."

"That's how we all think of him. That's how we'll *always* think of him."

"Honestly, Jules," Madrigal says, her tone slightly disgusted. "After what happened between Joseph and Queen Mirabella, I thought you'd have grown up a little."

Jules's temper rises, and on the countertop, Madrigal's knife begins to rattle as if of its own accord.

"Don't, Jules." Madrigal backs away. "Don't do that."

The knife stops.

"I'm not," Jules says quickly. "I mean, I didn't mean to."

"Your war gift is strong. You should let me unbind it."

"Grandma Cait says the binding might be all that's keeping me sane."

"Or all that's holding you back."

Jules looks at the knife. She could make it move. Make it fly. Make it cut. Nothing about her naturalist gift has ever felt so wicked or out of control.

Madrigal picks up the knife, and Jules breathes easier with it safe in her hand.

"I suppose this means you're not happy about the baby. But

you can't hate him, Jules. Just to spite me. You won't, will you?"

"No," Jules says darkly. "I will be a *good* sister."

Madrigal looks at her. Then she rolls potatoes onto the counter and starts to chop them.

"I thought I would be so happy," she mutters. "I thought this baby would make me so happy."

"Pity for you, then," says Jules. "Nothing is ever as good as you want it to be."

A second crow, larger than Aria, flies into the kitchen and lands on the table with a letter in her beak. It is Eva, Grandma Cait's familiar, and the letter bears the seal of the Black Council. Cait comes in behind her and sees the scowl on Jules's face.

"I take it that you've told her about the baby."

"Why does everyone in this family know things before I do?" Jules asks.

"Never mind that, Jules. You'll get over it."

Jules nods toward Eva's letter. "What does it say?"

"That Wolf Spring is about to be crowded. It seems that both of the other queens and their households are coming for Midsummer. Where has Arsinoe gotten off to?"

"The woods, I think, with Braddock."

"You'd better go, then, and tell her."

Jules gets up from the table, and she and Camden head outside. They hurry down the path to the road, stretching the muscles in their bad legs. They meet Joseph as they reach the hilltop fork.

"What's got you in such a hurry?" he asks as she slips her

hand into his and tugs him along.

"News for Arsinoe. I'm glad you're here. It saves us a trip."

"Oh no," Arsinoe says when Jules and Joseph come into the meadow. "What news is there now?" She had been watching Braddock pluck blackberries off a vine, his flapping lips nearly as good as fingers.

"Mirabella and Katharine are coming here," Jules says. "For Midsummer. And they're each bringing an army of supporters besides. The letter from the Council just arrived."

Arsinoe's shoulders slump. The other queens, here. Wolf Spring will be flooded with strangers.

"A lot of good it did, my trying to keep Mirabella out of my city."

"I don't like it," Jules growls, and at her side, Camden snarls. "We won't be able to guard you. It'll be chaos."

"It won't be easy," Joseph agrees. "But at least we'll be here, at home. Where we know how things lie."

"Midsummer is in less than a week," Arsinoe says. "And there was no letter of warning from Billy. What good is having a spy in Rolanth if he can't even tell us about this?"

"Rolanth might not have gotten more notice than we did," says Jules. But that is unlikely. Even if it was an Arron plot, the temple would have needed to agree.

Arsinoe sighs.

"Naturalists. We are always the last to know."

"After you're crowned, there will be naturalists on the

Council," Joseph says. "Wolf Spring will finally have a say again in how Fennbirn is run."

Arsinoe and Jules trade glances. *Joseph*, the look says. *Ever the optimist.*

"Has Billy written?" he asks. "Is he well? Is he safe?"

"He's written twice. He promised to write daily." Arsinoe crosses her arms. Two letters, and both were formal and stilted, containing none of the awful personality that she misses so much.

She looks at her friends standing in the meadow where they have stood so many times before. The summer sun casts their shadows onto the ground, and those shadows seem like the ghosts of their childhood, forever running through these trees.

"Our happy ending," she says quietly.

"Arsinoe," says Jules. "You have to do something. You know why they're coming."

Not to talk. Foolish to have thought that talking would stop Mirabella from searing blisters up and down her back.

Arsinoe watches Braddock foraging in the bushes. She does not want to put him in danger. Or Jules. Or Joseph. But they are all she has. Only her friends and her low magic.

GREAVESDRAKE MANOR

*K*atharine holds Sweetheart carefully as she extracts the snake's venom, pressing the glands. The yellow poison runs down the sides of the glass jar. There is not very much. Sweetheart is a small snake, and even in a small jar, her venom barely coats the bottom.

Nicolas leans across her bed watching, enrapt.

"How strange," he whispers. "That so little of a thing can cause such great harm."

Katharine pries the snake free with a gentle motion and places her back into her cage. Sweetheart writhes crankily and bites at the glass, wriggling as she tries to inject venom that is no longer there.

Nicolas recoils; Katharine giggles. She screws a lid onto the jar.

"What will you use it for?" he asks.

"Perhaps nothing." She tips it back and forth and watches

the poison run. "I just wanted a bit of her with me, since I must leave her behind. Now let us go!" She tugs him playfully off the bed, and he kisses her gloved fingers.

Downstairs, Natalia arches an eyebrow, already waiting at the door. But she does not scold. Indeed, she smiles toothlessly at the sight of their linked hands.

Outside, a dark caravan packed full of Arrons and poisons stretches down the long, horseshoe drive.

"I cannot wait to see the faces on the bumpkins of Wolf Spring when we arrive," Katharine says. "Their bottom teeth will scrape the dirt."

The household servants line up to bid them farewell, and as she passes her maid Giselle, Katharine reaches out and squeezes her shoulder. Giselle jerks back. Her eyes fall to the stone steps.

She is afraid of me, Katharine realizes, and looks down the row. They are all afraid of her. Even Edmund, Natalia's steadfast butler.

Katharine smiles at Giselle and kisses her cheek as if she had not noticed. She turns away when she hears horse hooves clip-clopping in her direction.

She will not ride in a coach like the others. Pietyr rides up on a tall black mare and leads two saddle horses behind him: Katharine's favorite, Half Moon, and the blood bay Nicolas brought from the mainland.

"This will be a good opportunity to let the people see you," Natalia says.

"To see how well and healthy you are," Genevieve adds, and stops talking when Natalia shoots her a look.

The island will see her as she passes, a live queen, not the decaying, animated corpse the rumors would have them believe.

"Whatever the reason, I am glad to ride outside," she says. Loaded as they are, the caravan will move at a snail's pace and still slower when navigating the steep and unkempt roads in the hills.

Pietyr starts to dismount to help Katharine into the saddle.

"Don't trouble yourself, Renard," Nicolas says, using Pietyr's non-Arron name on purpose just to irritate him. "I will assist my queen."

"She is not your queen yet," Pietyr mutters, and Katharine grins at him before Nicolas boosts her onto Half Moon.

"Careful, Pietyr," she whispers after Nicolas has gone to mount his own horse. "Or Natalia and Genevieve will send you away." She takes up her reins, but Pietyr holds fast to Half Moon's bridle.

"They may, but I will not go," he says. "I will be here until the day you tell me to leave."

Katharine's pulse quickens. The look Pietyr gives to Nicolas is so dark that she wonders whether it is a good idea that they both remain at Greavesdrake. If their rivalry goes much further, she will enter the drawing room one day and find Nicolas poisoned or Pietyr slumped across the sofa with a knife in his back.

"May we ride ahead?" Nicolas asks, bringing his horse up beside hers. "We can circle back around to the carriages if we go too far . . . unless your horse will tire?"

"Impossible." Katharine strokes Half Moon's long, sleek neck. "Half Moon can run for days and never tire. He is the finest horse on the whole island."

They trot together down the drive ahead of the caravan but behind the guard and the scouts. The day is hot but with a strong, cool breeze. A true Midsummer day. Perhaps a good omen.

"What is that there?" Nicolas gestures toward the end of the drive.

A cluster of women in white-and-black robes, priestesses from Indrid Down Temple, have gathered to give her a blessing. As they ride closer, Katharine notes that Head Priestess Cora is not among them.

"So many coaches," says one of the priestesses, whose name she does not remember. "Wolf Spring will overflow."

"Indeed," Katharine says. "When I leave, they may be poorer by one queen but much richer in money from the capital. Have you come to give the Goddess's blessing?"

"We have. Tonight we go into the hills to pray and burn oleander."

Half Moon starts to fidget and Katharine takes up an inch of his rein.

"Everyone knows that the temple supports Mirabella," she says. "But you are priestesses of Indrid Down. In service to poisoners since you came."

"All queens are sacred," the priestess responds.

Katharine's jaw tenses. She glances at Nicolas, who moves his horse back.

"I know you do not like me," Katharine whispers. "I know you sense that I am wrong, even if you will not say so."

"All queens are sacred," the priestess says again in her infuriating, even voice.

Katharine would like to ride the white robes into the dirt. Grind them into the mud until they are stained dark red and brown. But the caravan approaches in hoofbeats and jangling harnesses, trunks and wheels rattling. So instead she smiles a smile of bared teeth.

"Yes," she says. "All queens *are* sacred. Even those you threw into a pit."

ROLANTH

A woman and her husband kneel before the temple over an offering of dyed and scented water. The water is a dark, stormy blue, calm inside a beautiful mosaic bowl of white-and-silver glass.

"Blessings upon you, Queen Mirabella," the woman murmurs, and Mirabella extends her hand over her bent head. She recognizes them from the central district. They are merchants who deal in silks and precious stones. And she has seen the woman through her carriage window as they passed, shouting orders to workers restoring the Vaulted Theatre.

Not many from Rolanth will accompany her to Wolf Spring. Since it was announced that the Reaping Moon would be held here in a few months' time, there is simply too much to do.

"Thank you for your offering," Elizabeth says, and picks up the bowl to be brought inside. Bree takes Mirabella by the arm.

Once inside, Mirabella takes a deep breath. The open air

smells of temple roses in full bloom, and beneath that, the salt of the sea and the cold, earthy essence of her beloved basalt cliffs. Today they depart for the long road to Wolf Spring. Wagons have been loaded with supplies, and at Westwood House, coaches stand ready with a portion of her wardrobe folded away in trunks.

"You seem so sad," Bree says as they walk around the southern dome. "Are you not even a little bit excited?"

Mirabella pauses before Queen Shannon's mural, storms and lightning in blue-and-gold paint. The weather queen seems to be gazing down upon her.

"I should not be excited," she says. "I should be ready. No decree from the Black Council is to be trusted so long as the Arrons control it."

Bree rolls her eyes.

"Now you sound like Luca. This is a good thing, do you not see? You will kill Katharine and Arsinoe both, and then we will have nothing but feasting and suitors until your crowning at Beltane."

Everyone in Rolanth seems to agree, indoctrinated by Luca all these years to believe Mirabella's legend.

"It will be hard to protect you in Wolf Spring," Elizabeth says. "The people are wild. And with the temple obligated to be neutral, Rho will not be able to help."

"Her gift will keep her safe," Bree says confidently. "And so will we. That is what foster guardians are for."

She pats Mirabella's hand, but in truth they have always

relied on the priestesses for their security. The Westwoods have had nearly no practice guarding her at all.

"Are you frightened, Mira?" Elizabeth asks.

"My senses are uneasy," she replies. "I do not like leaving Rolanth. And that it was not our idea." And she cannot stop thinking of what Billy told her. That Arsinoe had not sent the bear. And she did not fight back in the Ashburn Woods or use the bear then to harm her . . .

She looks into Elizabeth's wide, dark eyes.

"I am only afraid of what I must do."

Elizabeth slips her arm around the queen. "It will be all right," she says, and Pepper the woodpecker flits from his hiding place in her hood to nibble on Mirabella's earlobe.

"Pepper ought to be in a tree," Bree whispers. "It is risky having him with you in the temple, close to so many watchful eyes."

"I know." Elizabeth rolls her shoulder and Pepper disappears back into her robes. "But it's hard to get him to leave me when he knows I'm nervous or upset."

"So do not be nervous or upset! Mira will not fail us."

As they pass by an open storeroom door, they see Billy bent over in a barrel. Harriet the chicken sees them and clucks. Billy straightens and knocks dust and straw out of his hair.

"Oho! You've caught me."

"What are you doing?" Mirabella asks.

"I'm setting aside things to bring with us to Wolf Spring. I heard there were jarred tomatoes and blackberries. For your favorite of my dishes: warmed jarred tomatoes on toast."

"I thought you would be better at cooking by now," Bree scolds. "Mira has grown so thin, half of her dresses had to be sent to the tailor!"

"Why don't you teach me, then, Bree?" he asks. "If you are any better at it, I'll eat my hat."

Elizabeth giggles.

"Bree can barely slice bread for a sandwich."

"Oh, who needs to slice bread, anyway?" Bree steps into the storage room to help Billy search the crates.

"What happened to buying from town?" she asks, her voice strained as they lift a crate lid. "My mother gave you money, and the priestesses would inspect whatever you bought."

"Yes, well, that money may have found its way into a very fine restaurant on Dale Street. And into a few of the pubs off the marketplace."

"Billy Chatworth," Mirabella exclaims. "You have been feasting, and I have been eating jarred tomatoes on toast."

Billy grins.

"I tried going into the market. But I didn't care for the merchants there. They spat at Harriet like she was a familiar."

Mirabella's smile fades. The resentment between the people will lessen in time. Luca says the island will be united under her once the crown is settled.

"Perhaps I ought to go along—" Bree starts, and then Elizabeth screams.

She shakes her head and covers her mouth with her hand.

Pepper flies from her hood and flaps in noisy circles around the storeroom, his little body striking the walls in panic.

Elizabeth points with the stump of her wrist.

The priestess dead behind the stack of barrels has not been dead long. Her cheeks are still pink, and gold curls fall softly across her forehead. From her neck up, she could be sleeping. But below it is a horror of swollen blood vessels so enflamed that they stand out on her chest like cracks in a vase. The bodice of the poisoned dress is tight and touches so much of her skin. Blue fabric streaked now with blood and the girl's fingernails full of her own flesh, from trying to claw her way out of it.

"There now, there now," Billy says, gathering Elizabeth close and trying to quiet her. "Mirabella, stay back."

Footsteps echo down the corridor: priestesses coming to investigate the screams.

"Get Pepper back into your robes!" Bree hisses.

But the poor bird is panicked. Thinking fast, Mirabella stumbles into the doorway to divert attention so Elizabeth can calm down and collect him.

"What is it?" the first of the priestesses demands. She looks Mirabella over head to toe, and the others push into the storeroom. When they see the fallen girl, a few of them moan miserably. The girl was one of them. One of theirs.

Luca pauses briefly in her pacing to touch Mirabella's hair. Mirabella is on the sofa in Luca's rooms, wedged snugly between Bree and Elizabeth and an embroidered pillow.

The door opens, but it is only an initiate carrying a tray of tea and cookies, which Billy dutifully tastes even though it will all go untouched.

"I do not want you to do that anymore," Mirabella says.

"It's what I'm here for," he says gently. "I knew the risks. As did my father when he sent me."

"You were here to make a point," Luca corrects him. "And so your father could garner favor with us. Personally, I think he is mad to put you in this poisoner's path, even with my priestesses tasting before you."

"No one else must do this," Mirabella says. "No tasters. No more." The dead girl's face floats in her mind, warring with another image locked inside her: little Katharine, sweet and smiling.

The door opens again. This time it is Rho. She has taken down her hood, and red hair blazes past her shoulders.

"Who was it?" Luca asks.

"The novice, Rebecca."

Luca presses her hands to her face. Mirabella did not know her, except for seeing her pass by in the temple.

"She was . . . ambitious," Luca explains, sitting down finally, in one of her overstuffed chairs. "She must have been testing the dress."

"Alone?" Rho asks. "And by putting it on?"

"She was a good priestess. Devoted. From a farm in Waring. I will write to her family and send blessing. We will place the ashes in an urn after she is burned, in case her mother wishes her remains be returned."

Mirabella winces. It is all so fast. So businesslike.

"Did she suffer?" Mirabella asks. "I do not care if you think it a weak question, Rho. I want you to answer."

Rho's jaw unclenches. "I suppose I do not know, my queen. From the skin raked under her fingernails, I would say yes. But the poisoning was fast. No one heard her cry out, and she did not have time to leave the storeroom for help."

"Do we know what it was?" asks Luca.

"Something absorbed through contact with the skin. The wounds are localized near the bodice, where the dress fit the tightest. We will examine it before it is destroyed, to look for hidden pins or razors."

"Katharine," Mirabella whispers. "You are so terrible now."

"Rebecca should never have put on that dress," Rho says.

"But she would not have known," Bree protests. "Do you not see? That dress was blue! It was not sent for the queen. It was sent for one of us!" She glares up at Rho. "Why would she do that?"

"She is clever, this poisoner. If she cannot get to you directly, she will goad you into action by killing those in your household."

"She is not clever." Elizabeth's voice is low as she wipes at her eyes with the back of her hand. Mirabella puts her arms around her. "She is cruel."

WOLF SPRING

$\mathcal{I}$n the clearing, beneath the bent-over tree, Arsinoe lets Madrigal take fresh blood from her arm. Overhead, thin green leaves rustle on the ancient branches.

"There," Madrigal says. "That's enough."

Arsinoe presses a cloth to staunch the bleeding. "Do you have anything to eat?" she asks, and Madrigal tosses her a sack. Inside is a skin of cider and some strips of dried meat.

She eats, but the bloodletting does not really bother her anymore. Her arms and hands are so covered in scars that she has not been able to roll up her sleeves all season.

Madrigal bends slowly down over the small fire she built when they arrived. She is not more than two months pregnant, but already her belly shows.

"Do you hope for a girl?" Arsinoe asks.

"I hope for you to focus," Madrigal says, and blows on the flames.

"But if you had to choose."

Madrigal looks up at her wearily. She has never seemed less enthusiastic about performing low magic. The child saps her strength.

"It doesn't matter." She sits back on a log. "The Milones whelp only girls, but the Sandrins only boys." Her hand passes over her stomach. "So we will have to wait and see whose blood will out."

A wind, cold for this time of year, sweeps through the clearing, and the old tree's leaves hiss like snakes.

"The other queens are coming," Madrigal says, inhaling the breeze. "If you want to curse your sisters, we must do it now."

Arsinoe nods. A memory rises of little Katharine with daisies in her hair. Of Mirabella holding her tight when the priestesses tried to kill her when she washed ashore at Innisfuil. She pushes them away.

She has to concentrate. More than half of a curse is about intent.

"Does Juillenne know you asked me to help you?" Madrigal asks.

"Yes."

"And she didn't try to stop you?"

"For someone who wants me to focus, you sure seem distracted. What will this curse do, anyway?" Arsinoe asks.

"I don't know."

"What do you mean?"

"This is not the same as a rune or a charm," Madrigal

replies. "A curse is a force sent out into the world. And once you set it loose, you can't call it back. Whatever passes through this smoke today will bear your will, and the Goddess's will. But it will also wield its own."

Low magic always wields its own will. Is that why it went out that day into the storm, to cast a net around Joseph and Mirabella? The cuts on her arm throb, and she feels the weight of some price she cannot yet dream of.

Madrigal pours Arsinoe's blood into the fire. The flames seem to jump at it, lapping it up, eating it without sound or sizzle. She pours it all and feeds it higher with cords soaked from past bloodlettings. Her murmurs are the same as murmurs to her unborn child.

Behind her, the bent-over tree creaks, and Arsinoe stiffens, but that is foolish. It cannot move. It will not wake and pull itself free of its roots.

"Think of them," Madrigal says.

Arsinoe does. She thinks of a little girl laughing and splashing in the stream. She remembers Mirabella, stern and ready to wade in if she fell.

I love them, she realizes. *I love them both.*

"Madrigal, stop."

"Stop?" Madrigal asks, and breaks eye contact with the flames.

The fire rises in a wave and reaches for Madrigal. Arsinoe shouts and leaps to press her to the ground, smothering the flames with the sleeves of her shirt. In an instant, it is out, down to only smoke, but the stench of burned hair and skin is thick.

"Madrigal? Madrigal, can you hear me?"

Arsinoe takes Madrigal's shaken face between her hands. Her shoulder was burned down deep, blackened, the red of flesh exposed. But Madrigal does not seem to notice.

"My baby," she murmurs. "My baby . . ."

"What?" Madrigal's stomach is unharmed, and she did not fall hard. The baby is fine. "Madrigal?" She brushes tears away from Madrigal's cheeks.

"My baby . . . my baby . . ." Her cries grow and the corners of her mouth twist down. "My baby!"

"Madrigal!" Arsinoe slaps her. Just a little bit, nowhere near as hard as Cait even when Cait is playing, and Madrigal's eyes jerk left and fix upon her face.

The empty jar of Arsinoe's blood, coated red, falls from Madrigal's hand and rolls across the ground. Arsinoe dares a look back at the bent-over tree. It stands in its place, trying to seem innocent.

"What happened?" Arsinoe asks.

"Nothing," Madrigal says.

"Madrigal, what did you see?"

"I saw nothing!" Madrigal snaps, wiping quickly at her face. "It was not about you! And it wasn't real." She stands up, her arms protectively across her belly. It was about the child, Arsinoe knows that much. And whatever it was, it was awful.

Arsinoe looks again at the tree, at the sacred space. Low magic does not do only what one intends, but nor does it speak in falsehoods. The bent-over tree does not lie, and a spike of fear hits Arsinoe in the gut, for Madrigal and her baby, for Jules and the little sister or brother she will love so well.

"You're right," Arsinoe soothes her. "It was my fault. I couldn't concentrate. I kept seeing images of my sisters . . . memories. We can try again—"

"We can't try again!" Madrigal shakes loose and runs from the clearing. She does not stop when Arsinoe calls after her.

Arsinoe looks down at the ashes of the fire, already cold. She could try again by herself. But somehow she knows that it would do no good. Midsummer is here, and she will have no more advantages than the secrets she has already been given.

"The other queens are coming," Arsinoe says to the tree. "And it seems that you want them here."

MIDSUMMER

THE VALLEYWOOD ROAD

*R*iding near the head of the Indrid Down caravan, Katharine lifts her nose to the breeze and inhales deeply. It is not far to Wolf Spring. She can almost smell the fish market. Theirs is said to be the finest catch on the entire island, and she hopes so, for Natalia has been craving a poison reef fish.

"Will you tell me more about the Midsummer Festival?" Nicolas asks. He and Pietyr ride up on either side of her, so close that Half Moon snorts at the lack of space. "I understand there are to be feasting and lights."

"Lanterns burned into the harbor," Pietyr interjects. "And ample opportunity for poisoning. Wolf Spring is notorious for drunkards; there will be confusion and movement. And Arsinoe will not dare use the bear in the midst of so many of her people." He glares across the saddle at Nicolas, and Katharine has to bite the inside of her cheek to keep from laughing.

"The bear does not frighten me," she says. "I have brought something special for him."

At that, Nicolas smiles. Katharine has brought long, sharp pikes, perfect for skewering through the hide of a bear. He looked over them with great approval before they departed from Greavesdrake.

"Tell me more about the queens, then, whom you will face. A naturalist and an elemental. Is it always so? I had heard of other queens. Oracle queens and war queens."

"There has not been an oracle queen for ages," says Katharine. "Not since one went mad on the throne and ordered the execution of several of the families on her Council. She said they were plotting against her. Or rather, that they would plot against her in the future. She said that she foresaw it. Now when a queen is born with the sight gift, we drown them."

She expects him to pale; instead he nods.

"Madness in a ruler is not to be borne. But what of the war gift? Why is there no war queen?"

"No one knows why the war gift has weakened. The drowned queens explain why the oracle city of Sunpool has nearly emptied but Bastian remains. The war gifted remain. Yet there has not been a queen born with the war gift in generations."

"A shame," says Nicolas. "Though you, sweet Katharine, are warlike enough for me."

He grins. Such a suitor she has attracted. He is refined and charming, but he craves blood. He says she is too bold to poison from a plate. That she is too skilled with knives and arrows to let that skill go to waste. When he said so, she nearly kissed him. She nearly pushed him to the ground. Natalia wants her to take Billy Chatworth as her king-consort to preserve the alliance between their families. But when the suitors engage in The Hunt of the Stags, a sacred hunt open only to them, Billy Chatworth will not stand a chance. Nicolas will hunt him as he hunts the stag. And then Katharine will be free to choose him.

Calls from the lead guard make their way down the line.

"We are nearly there," says Pietyr. "It is just around the next bend."

"Then let us ride to the front." Katharine puts her heels to Half Moon's sides before Pietyr can protest, and Nicolas laughs as he races along behind her. As she crests the gradual curve that leads into Wolf Spring, salty sea air rises like a wall and rushes against her chest.

They do not slow until they reach the outskirts of the town. As expected, it is not much to look at. Buildings of graying wood and signs bearing faded paint. But the people on the streets and in the shop windows stop what they are doing to stare, their gazes slightly hostile and very wary. When the rest of the coaches arrive, most seem relieved to be able to look away.

"You do not even know where we are riding to!" Pietyr says angrily when he catches up.

"Truly, Renard," Nicolas says. "There is the town and there is the sea. How were we supposed to get lost?"

Katharine chuckles. It is true. She does not know why it was necessary to have Cousin Lucian and giftless Renata Hargrove leave a week in advance to select their lodging. In a city this size, there could not have been more than four or five choices.

"Where are we staying, Pietyr?" she asks.

"The Wolverton Inn," he replies. "The lead coach knows the way, if only you will follow it."

Katharine sighs.

"Very well." She slows Half Moon so the rest of their party may catch up, and adjusts the weight of the poisoned knives affixed to her hip. She lifts her chin as they ride through the streets, past the salt-hardened, hateful people. It is not much of a welcome. But she and her knives will have such a lovely time here.

WOLF SPRING

As the queens' arrivals ripple through the town like a current, Wolf Spring comes alive. Workers pound wood and planks as they erect new viewing platforms to overlook the harbor. The Wolverton Inn and the Bay Street Hotel ready accommodations for their guests. Shopkeepers stay open a few hours later and find chores to do outside, hoping to catch a glimpse of the undead poisoner or Mirabella the legendary elemental. According to Ellis—who has been their eyes and ears in town since the other queens arrived—even Luke stayed out late sweeping the walk in front of the bookshop. Though he did take Arsinoe's crowning gown out of the window first.

"We should have refused this," Jules says.

"We couldn't," Arsinoe replies.

Katharine and the Arrons have already made themselves at home in their rooms at the Wolverton Inn, no doubt driving poor Mrs. Casteel and her young Miles half out of their minds with crazy, poisoner demands. And to the west, the temple hill swarms with Rolanth priestesses as they attempt to make the modest quarters of rounded stone fit to house Queen Mirabella.

"It's monstrous. Setting us up this way," Arsinoe says. "Like pieces on a game board. If it's the Goddess, then she is cruel. And if it's the Council and the temple, then we're fools for dancing to their tune."

"Maybe so," Jules says. "But like you said, we couldn't refuse."

"Why can't we just stay here? I want to live our lives here, the way we always have."

From the corner of her eye, Arsinoe sees Jules clench her fists, and glances nervously at the trees to see if they will shake.

"What about our happy ending?" Jules asks. "Isn't that worth fighting for?" But when Arsinoe does not answer, she snaps, "Stop being such a child! If you win, you get to live, and that's better than nothing!"

Arsinoe flinches.

"I wasn't going to hit you," Jules says. "Not any harder than usual. Not because of this curse."

"I'm sorry, Jules. You just startled me is all."

"Sure," Jules says, unconvinced. "Sure."

"Is it getting worse?" Arsinoe asks. But they do not even know what worse is. The war gift growing stronger? Jules's temper? Jules going mad?

"I'm fine." Jules takes a long, slow breath. "I wish it had gone better with you and Madrigal at the tree."

They have helped Madrigal nurse the burns. With Cait's good salve, they will hardly scar. But she refuses to say what she saw in the flames, about her child.

"I guess we'll have the advantages we have," Arsinoe says.

"Why aren't you afraid? Why won't you fight for yourself?"

"Of course I'm afraid! But I can only do what I can do, Jules."

For a long time, Jules is silent, and Arsinoe thinks it is over. But then Camden snarls, and the logs from the woodpile begin to shift and tremble.

"We'll keep you safe just to spite you, Arsinoe," Jules says darkly. "Camden, Joseph, and I."

"You mean to use your war gift? You can't! If they see that they'll . . ." Arsinoe pauses and drops her voice low as if the Council might already be listening. "They'll take you back to Indrid Down and lock you up. They'll kill you. The island doesn't trifle with madness."

"Maybe I won't go mad. Maybe it should be unbound, and this is why I have it, to protect you when you won't protect yourself."

"I don't want you in this, Jules. Please."

"This is your life. Don't tell me to stay out of it." Jules glares at her, hard, and stalks away down the drive.

"Jules!"

"I'm just going to find Joseph," she says over her shoulder. She slows, and her voice softens. "Don't worry. We'll only keep an eye on what the Arrons and the temple are up to."

* * *

Arsinoe escapes for a few moments alone with Braddock beside Dogwood Pond before the chaos begins. But moments alone are not to be. Billy surprises her, returned from Rolanth.

"Arsinoe," he says.

"Junior!" Her whole body jerks toward him. She leaps at him and throws her arms around his neck. His hands press into her back, along with something else that rustles.

"This is a better welcome than I expected," he says.

"Then don't ruin it by talking."

Billy laughs, and they draw apart. He looks unchanged, unscarred by poison. Safe and back home with her where he belongs. Her eyes move over his face, his shoulders and chest. Before she blushes, she looks at his hands.

"Junior," she says. "You have a wreath."

And a lovely one too: whip-smooth vines curled round and round, twisted through with purple butterwort and blue-eyed grass.

"I made it." He holds it out. "For you."

Arsinoe takes it and turns it over between her fingers.

"I mean, I didn't make it," he amends, "but I told the girl from the market what to put in it. It's not meant to be like a bouquet," he adds hastily. "I know you're not the type. Naturalist or not."

"But you brought me a bouquet, once. Remember? Last winter, after we were attacked by the old, sick bear."

"Those were from my father."

Arsinoe smirks. She slides her finger over the bit of pale blue ribbon attached to the wreath, used to hang it on a door in the days before the festival.

"This is . . . very nice," she says with an uncharacteristic lack of sarcasm. "It will be the first one I release onto the water."

Then she laughs when Braddock comes to inspect it, sniffing and sniffing with his large brown nose.

"Will he be with you at the festival?" Billy asks, reaching down to scratch him between the ears.

"Yes. But I'll keep him near the docks, away from most of the crowds."

"Will he be safe, though? So near the other queens? After what happened at Beltane . . ."

"I think it will be fine." She forgets sometimes that Billy witnessed the attack at the Quickening. He is so at ease with Braddock now, ruffling his fur and cooing to him like a kitten.

"You spoiled bear." Arsinoe pats Braddock on the shoulder, and he waddles away, his coat as glossy a great brown's as she has ever seen. Wolf Spring has made him fat and sleek, well-fed on only the best of the catch.

"Tell me you have a plan," says Billy. "Some weapon or action that no one knows about."

"I have a bear. Some would say that's enough." She looks down at her wreath. "Do we have to talk about this? You've only just returned."

"Just returned," he echoes, "as part of Mirabella's entourage."

This stupid festival. His being back is the only good to come out of it. She turns toward him and touches his neck.

"I'm glad to see you're all right. Luke's tailor friends told us horrible stories of poison in Rolanth. Disfigured priestesses . . . poisoned livestock . . . Was any of it true?"

Billy nods. He says no more, but he seems so haunted suddenly that she knows it must have been, and worse.

"I should have written," he says. "But truly there was nothing to tell, and anything I wanted to say, I couldn't get down."

"We are both that way. I can never find words that don't sound stupid on paper. Jules can write for days."

"We must always be sure to come face-to-face, then. So there are never any misunderstandings."

He runs his fingers along the edge of her mask, down to her jawline where the smallest bit of scar shows from behind the lacquered wood.

"I don't know how much I'll get to see you," he says.

"Aren't you staying with the Sandrins?"

"Even in Wolf Spring, I'm still Mirabella's official taster. I will have to stand beside her during the festival ceremonies."

Arsinoe's throat tightens. To see Billy standing behind her sister will hurt, even if it is only for show.

"So you won't do what you did at Beltane. Leave Mirabella and come to me."

"Things are different now," he says quietly.

"How different?"

Billy takes her by the shoulders, and she holds her breath. There is no poison on her lips this time. If he kisses her, she will kiss him back. She will never let him go.

But instead, he crushes her to his chest.

"Arsinoe," he says, and kisses her hair and her shoulder, everywhere but where she wants. "Arsinoe, Arsinoe."

"I hope we can talk once more at least," she says. She buries her nose in his shoulder. "Before one of my sisters gets to me."

"Don't say things like that. For her part, Mirabella has no particular plan here, except to stay alive."

"Or you just don't know of one," Arsinoe counters, drawing back. "Would you tell me, Junior? If you did? Would you tell her if you knew a plan of mine?"

He looks away.

"Don't answer," she says. "They were unfair questions. Mirabella isn't just a name to you now or a face atop a cliff. I don't expect that you would hate her for me."

Billy takes her hand in his and threads their fingers together.

"Perhaps not," he says. "But I will never let anything happen to you. And that will never change."

WOLF SPRING TEMPLE

Luca runs her finger along the windowsill in the temple cottage and holds it up to Rho.

"It is clean at least."

"At least." Rho chuckles. "You have grown soft and spoiled as a cat, High Priestess." Luca chuckles as well. That is true enough. She has been the High Priestess for a long time and enjoyed all the trappings that came with it. If she sets all of that aside, the modest dwellings are perfectly sufficient.

The Rolanth priestesses have done a fine job cleaning and clearing out needed space. They could not say much about the security of the temple grounds, but Rho will take care of that. The difficult thing will be keeping Mirabella close. Already Luca has seen her wandering the edges of the temple garden, eyes cast toward the town and the harbor. Their soft-hearted queen is curious about the life that her sister has led here. And she is yearning to see the boy, Joseph Sandrin.

"I like it here," says Rho, inhaling deeply. "It is harder

than Rolanth. And more honest."

"Such an assessment from one sniff of the air."

"You know me, Luca. It does not take me long to have the measure of a place."

"Nor of a person," Luca says. "What do you make of this little poisoner? I did not think her a threat until she disappeared at Beltane and mysteriously returned."

"So she dragged herself out of a pit." Rho curls her lip dismissively. "She is still weak, propped up by the Arrons."

Luca walks to the eastward-facing window that overlooks the marketplace and the western harbor. It is a sunny, pretty day. Down in the city, people are busy outfitting the town square for their extra guests. Only the queens, their fosters, and the luckiest of the attendees will be able to fit there. The rest will spill out onto the side streets for the feast: Wolf Spring, Rolanth, and Indrid Down mingling together.

"Were we wrong to come here?" Luca asks.

"No."

"Even though we cannot help her?"

Rho places her hand firmly on the older woman's shoulder.

"This *is* helping her. A young queen has only one purpose, and that is the crown."

"I know you are right," Luca replies. "But I still do not like it."

"They celebrate with wreaths," Bree says as she twirls one around her finger. "This was made for you by the Wolf Spring priestesses. They have made one for each of the queens." She hands it to Mirabella. It is beautiful and expertly woven, comprised of some variety of blue wildflower, white lilies, and ivy. "I saw the one they made for Katharine. All dark red roses and thorns."

"What do they do with them?" Mirabella asks, but it is Elizabeth and not Bree who answers.

"We float them onto the water with paper lanterns at their center," she says, her face turned toward the harbor, a little wistful.

"Does this place make you homesick, Elizabeth?" asks Mirabella. "Is it very much like Bernadine's Landing?"

"A little. My home was not so near the sea, but all of that region bears similar scenery and the same traditions."

"I did not see the bear when I was exploring town," Bree says abruptly, and Mirabella stiffens. "Though there was plenty of talk of it. Where is she hiding it, do you think? And why? Perhaps it is not safe. It was so brutal that night. . . . Is it that way for you, Elizabeth? Does Pepper not always do exactly as he is told?"

Elizabeth looks up into a nearby tree, and the tufted woodpecker cocks his head at her.

"Pepper almost never does exactly as he's told," Elizabeth says, and smiles. "Our familiars know what we feel, and we know what they feel. We are joined, but we're each still ourselves. A familiar that strong . . . it may be hard to curb him when he's angry."

"It does not matter," Mirabella says finally. "We will see all of that bear that we want to, and more, during the festival."

Bree stands on tiptoe to look past Mirabella's shoulder.

"What?" Elizabeth asks. "Is there some handsome natural-ist boy?"

Bree's eyebrow raises, but then she pouts.

"No. It is only Billy, coming back from bringing his chicken to his fosters. Not that he is not perfectly handsome. If he were not a suitor—" She stops when Elizabeth throws an acorn at her.

Billy said he was going to bring Harriet to the Sandrins for safekeeping, but Mirabella knows he will have gone to see Arsinoe.

"I will be back," she says to Bree and Elizabeth.

"Do not wander far!"

"I will not." She could not, with so many priestesses watching.

She jogs until she reaches Billy, and falls in step beside him. He glances at her, then back at the ground.

"Is this how it is, then?" she asks after several moments. "One visit to my sister and we are no longer friends?"

He stops at the crest of a hill and squints out at the sun sparkling off the ripples in Sealhead Cove.

"I wish we weren't. When my father sent me to Rolanth, I swore that I would hate you. That I wouldn't be a fool like Joseph and get myself stuck in between." He smiles at her sadly. "Why couldn't you be wretched? Don't you have any manners? You should've had the courtesy to be terrible. So I could despise you."

"I am sorry. Shall I start now? Spit in your eye and kick you?"

"That sounds like something Arsinoe would do, actually. So I would find it endearing."

"Did you tell her that I know the truth?" Mirabella asks. "That I know she did not try to kill me?"

Billy shakes his head, and inwardly, Mirabella's heart aches. She wants Arsinoe to know. She wants to tell her so herself and to shake Arsinoe by the shoulders until her teeth rattle for not telling her the truth about the bear that day in the Ashburn Woods.

"Arsinoe would say that a lack of hatred does not change anything. But I think," Mirabella says slowly, "that I could stand to die. If I knew that the sister who had to do it . . . if I knew that she loved me." She laughs at herself. "Does that make any sense?"

"I don't know," says Billy. "I suppose so. But I resent like hell that you and Arsinoe have to think that way."

He looks at her regretfully.

"I don't want to hate you after this. But I might. I might hate all of you if she dies."

Mirabella gazes out at the sea. It is so pleasant here. In another life, things might have been different. Arsinoe would have greeted her when she rode into town and shown her the marketplace and the spots where she and Jules used to play as children.

"Do not be so quick to say 'after this,'" Mirabella says. "We are here only for a festival. Perhaps nothing will happen at all."

"Mirabella," Billy says softly. "Don't lie to yourself."

THE WOLVERTON INN

*G*enevieve has not stopped glaring in the direction of Wolf Spring Temple since they set foot in their rooms at the inn. She paces and grumbles and crosses and uncrosses her arms. She is upset that Mirabella arrived in Wolf Spring first. Katharine rolls her eyes as Genevieve stalks to the window. She cannot possibly see the temple. The inn is too deep in the heart of the town for that, no matter how hard she presses her nose to the glass.

"Come away from there," Natalia says. "It is better to arrive last than in the middle. There was no arriving first with Arsinoe already here."

Katharine ignores them as they prattle on about appearances and security, like it matters at all. She slides the edge of a short throwing knife against a whetstone and listens to it scrape. Sharper and sharper. She will need them all in perfect condition and a crossbow and plenty of bolts besides.

"Kat," Natalia says, and in the corner of her eye, Katharine sees Genevieve stiffen at the sight of the knives. "What are you doing?"

"Getting ready."

"Ready for what?" Genevieve asks. "You do not need those. You are perfectly safe."

"Natalia," she says, ignoring Genevieve. "What would you edge these with?" She passes the tip of her finger across the blade, paper light. It cuts her skin so quickly that it does not hurt and takes a moment to bleed. "I need something strong enough to take down a bear."

"Do not fear the bear," says Genevieve.

"I am not afraid of it." Katharine smiles. "I have a plan."

THE FESTIVAL OF MIDSUMMER

"**S**he is making a mistake."

"Even so, Jules, it's her mistake to make. You can't push her." Jules and Joseph are in his upstairs bedroom, studying the movements of Wolf Spring through his window using a long black-and-gold spyglass given to him by Billy's father.

"Since when have I done anything *but* push her?" Jules mutters. "Arsinoe has always been mine to protect. I've known that since the moment I set eyes on her when we were children."

She looks through the spyglass. The streets are bustling, filled with people, and the festival is still hours away.

"They'll blanket us from all sides," she says. "Box us in."

"At least we know the streets and the hiding places. We have the advantage."

"This is a trap," Jules says. "I don't think our advantages are going to matter."

Joseph looks down.

"I've never heard you talk like this."

"Then you haven't been listening." She closes her eyes. "I'm sorry. That's unfair. It's just that we are surrounded by poisoners and elementals and no one seems as afraid as they should be."

"I'm afraid," he says, and takes her hand. "I'm afraid for Arsinoe, and I'm afraid for you, Jules. I know you'll say you don't need protecting. But I don't trust Madrigal. I think she might unbind you without your knowing. Maybe she already has."

Jules squeezes his fingers. Poor Joseph. There are circles under his eyes, and he seems thinner. She had not noticed.

"My mother is trouble, but not that kind of trouble." She raises the spyglass back to her eye. "And everybody needs protecting sometimes."

In the market, there are so many white-robed priestesses that it looks like a raid. They are no doubt inspecting the food, though she does not know why. Mirabella will have brought her own. Any poison will have to be slipped into it by hand.

"The poisoners will strike at the feast. We can be sure of that. Arsinoe can't eat or touch a thing . . . and she can't be touched by strangers, in case their skin is poisoned. Then they'll wonder why she doesn't die. . . . Keeping the secret is nearly as bad as worrying about the poison!" She curses and slams the spyglass shut between her hands.

"Where is Arsinoe now?"

"Getting dressed. It'll take longer than usual. Midsummer is the one day out of the year that she lets Madrigal braid a flower into her hair."

Joseph chuckles.

"I should get back. But I'm so tired." She rubs her temples. "I'm so tired, Joseph."

"Jules, this is not only your responsibility."

"Cait will be busy helping with the ceremony. Ellis will help manage Braddock against the crowds. Madrigal is *never* any use."

"Don't forget about Luke," says Joseph. "And me. And Arsinoe herself. She's not helpless. And only one queen here really poses a threat."

"A poisoned knife is still a knife," Jules says. "It can still kill." She lets loose a shaky breath, and Camden comes to the edge of Joseph's bed to nuzzle against her knee.

"You need to rest," he says. "It could be a long night."

"I can't." She shakes her head and turns as if to get up. "What's happening in the square?"

Joseph takes her arms and holds her fast.

"You can see it well enough from here. See? All the tables filling with paper lanterns ready to be released into the harbor. Just like any other year."

But it is not any other year. The blue sky above town is plumed with smoke as every kitchen prepares for the feast. And at the inn and on the west hill of the temple, two other queens are waiting, searching for the chance to kill Arsinoe.

"I said once that it was like you had never come back," Jules says. "That I wished you hadn't. I didn't mean it. I couldn't do this without you."

Joseph reaches out and pushes her hair off her cheek.

"I will always come home to you, Jules." He wraps his arms around her, and Jules holds on tight.

She presses closer, but the tighter she holds him, the more she feels him slipping away. Joseph does not belong here anymore. And she does not know where she belongs.

"Kiss me, Joseph," she says, but she is the one who leans in and pulls him close.

Her arms slide to his back, and she pulls at his shirt until it comes off. He tugs her shirt down off her shoulders, and they laugh when her hands get stuck.

"I love you," Jules says. She allows herself one moment where that is all that matters. Just Joseph, and his hands on her shoulders. Just the touch of his fingers in her hair. She lies back on the bed and draws him down.

"I love you, Jules. I'll love you for as long as I live."

Arsinoe tugs on the edge of her vest. She has worn the same one a hundred times before, but today it feels all wrong, bunchy and ill-fitted. The mask on her face will not sit right either, no matter how she ties and re-ties the ribbon around the back of her head.

It must be the braid. It hangs down the side of her head, itchy with oat stalk and flower petals. They braid something similar into her hair every Midsummer, even if she cuts her hair so short that the braid sticks out like a stiff, tiny arm. But it has never bothered her before. The day is wrong, not the braid.

She finds Madrigal seated in the yard, in the shade with Matthew resting beside her.

"Have you seen Jules?" she asks.

"I haven't," Madrigal replies. "I thought she'd be here by now. We can't hold the processional forever." Her shoulders droop, showing the bandage covering the burn that stretches across her collar and down her arm. She should be playfully putting her wreath of white snowdrops and grapevine atop Matthew's head. Instead, she sits, looking pale and thin everywhere but in the belly.

Matthew reaches out and pulls Arsinoe to him. His Sandrin smile is firmly affixed, charming and handsome enough to make her blush. So Madrigal must not have told him what she saw in the flames either.

"That's a pretty wreath," he says.

Arsinoe swings the temple wreath around her finger.

"I've had prettier." She thinks of the one Billy gave to her. She had to give it to Cait when the temple priestesses arrived with the wreath of the naturalist queen, which is more bouquet than wreath, really. So many sprays of purple and yellow wildflowers that the paper lantern will have to be squeezed into the center.

Back at the house, the side door slams, and Cait walks toward them with Eva perched on her shoulder.

"It's time."

"Already?" Arsinoe asks. "Won't we wait for Jules?"

"We can't wait any longer. As the hosts, we're expected to be first. Jules knows. I'm sure she'll meet us there."

Arsinoe exhales and calls Braddock as Madrigal and Cait step into their places ahead of her, with Matthew to the rear. Ellis walks up and squeezes her shoulder.

"Stop," she says, and smiles at him shakily. "It feels like you're saying good-bye."

"Never," says Ellis. "Just telling you I'm here. So don't worry about Braddock."

Arsinoe nods. The fading Wolf Spring light is gentle and gold.

"Odd," she says, "To feel so in danger on such a fine day."

They begin to walk. All the way down, she cannot feel her legs. She just tries not to trip and keeps her left hand buried in Braddock's warm fur.

By the time they arrive beside the cove, it is already full of people lining the docks and squeezing onto hastily assembled risers. High Priestess Luca stands at the water's edge with three priestesses, including Autumn, head priestess of the temple in Wolf Spring. When Luca sees Arsinoe, she inclines her head. There is no threat in the gesture, but Arsinoe's stomach quivers. She looks around anxiously for Jules, but Jules is nowhere to be seen.

Mirabella walks stiffly with Billy, following behind Sara and Bree. Today the Westwoods ignore that fact that he is only her official taster and treat him like a true suitor. So far, he has gone along with it, though he continually searches through the crowds for his Arsinoe.

Sara slows, and the line bunches together so that Uncle Miles and Nico nearly run into Mirabella's heels. A good thing that her dress is short and has no train, or it would be covered in dirty footprints.

Mirabella cranes her neck. The delay was caused by coming too close behind Katharine's processional, which is much longer and full of members of the Black Council. She cannot see more of Katharine than the back of her head, her hair loose except for one small bun pinned through with dark red blooms. She is arm in arm with her suitor, the handsome boy with the golden-blond hair.

They begin to move again, and Mirabella's stomach hums with something like excitement. She is in Wolf Spring, where Arsinoe grew up. And somewhere near the water, Arsinoe waits. Only she will not be alone. Or smiling. And she will have a bear.

When they reach the shore, it is oddly silent. Mirabella expected glares from poisoners. Perhaps a little spit from naturalists. But there is nothing. No cheers or chatter. It does not feel at all like a festival.

As they take their place, Billy tenses. Arsinoe is there, and when she looks at Billy, a blush creeps across her cheeks from behind her mask.

Mirabella smiles to herself. There is no ill will today.

Nothing will happen, nothing more than pretty lanterns floating on the water and a barge full of fruit and grain to burn into
the sea. Arsinoe's bear is calm, and Katharine seems interested
only in her suitor, whispering in his ear so intimately that it is
almost scandalous.

The Black Council schemed and lobbied hard to bring
them here together. Mirabella is glad that they will be so bitterly disappointed.

Arsinoe looks across the shore at her sisters. It is the first time
since the Black Cottage that she has been this close to both at
once. Little Katharine has been overdone with makeup in the
Arron fashion, but she no longer looks like a doll. Her chin is
high and her cheeks full. The barest hint of a smile plays at the
corner of her lips.

As for Mirabella, she is cold, as always. Her sisters are both
queens and know what they must do.

"This is how it is," Arsinoe whispers. "Someone's going to
die."

"They should have chosen somewhere else to hold the ceremony," says Nicolas. "Somewhere that does not smell like the
inside of a clamshell."

The wind has changed direction, carrying with it the scents
of the Wolf Spring Marketplace. But Katharine does not mind.
What little she has seen of Wolf Spring she likes. The wildness
and the harbor full of rickety-looking fishing boats. They bob

on the water and glow with paper lanterns in the blue light of dusk.

"The queens will come forward," the High Priestess says, and Katharine quiets as Luca holds her hand out to the naturalist. "Queen Arsinoe."

Arsinoe walks to the water's edge, dressed not as a queen but as a farmer, just like she was at Beltane. She receives a lit paper lantern from a Wolf Spring priestess and leans down to awkwardly push her wreath.

"Queen Katharine."

Katharine takes her lantern from an Indrid Down priestess. She places it in the center of her wreath and releases it, then smiles when her red roses bump Arsinoe's wildflowers out of the way.

"They do not mean for the High Priestess to present Mirabella's lantern," someone in the crowd mutters as Katharine returns to her place. But of course they do. Mirabella gets her lantern from Luca herself, along with a kiss on the forehead. The response from the poisoners is so strong that Katharine can nearly hear their teeth grinding.

Mirabella releases her wreath and, in true show-off fashion, uses her gift to push all three out into the harbor. As if it is a sign, the boats drop their cargo of lanterns until the entire cove glows. One of the nearest boats tows a small barge loaded with apples and bushels of wheat. It tows it out before the gathered crowd and cuts it free.

"The people of Rolanth bring an offering to honor the

people of Wolf Spring," Mirabella says. "To thank them for welcoming us into their city."

Katharine pulls close the nearest servant. "Get my bow. Quickly. And the fire arrows." The girl scarcely has time to nod before Katharine shoves her through the crowd.

"In Rolanth," Mirabella goes on, "this is how we celebrate Midsummer. I hope the naturalists will allow us this sacrifice, in theirs and the Goddess's honor."

Heads turn toward a tough-looking, gray-haired woman with a crow on her shoulder. She must be Cait Milone, the head of the Milone family. Arsinoe's fosters. Cait considers Mirabella's request for several long, tense moments before finally giving her permission with a subtle lift of her chin. She is hard, that woman. Perhaps even harder than Natalia.

The people behind Katharine jostle and cluck as the servant girl returns with her long bow, threading it through bodies to get it to the queen.

"Very good." Katharine smiles. "Thank you."

"Kat," Pietyr says out of the corner of his mouth. "What are you up to?" And then someone screams.

"Mira, she has a bow!"

Katharine rolls her eyes. It was that Westwood girl, the one who likes to play with fire.

At the scream, the crowd shudders and collectively ducks. The priestesses drag Luca out of the way, even as the doddering old fool struggles against them, and the stupid Westwood girl runs down the bank.

"Bree, no!" Mirabella cries.

Katharine puts her hand on her hip.

"'Bree, no,' indeed," she says. "I only mean to help." She steps to the center and turns toward the crowd. "My sister has put me to shame. I have brought no offering. But I can help her in the burning of hers."

Katharine nocks the arrow and lights the head in the nearest lantern. The arrow burns prettily as she sights up into the darkening sky. When she draws back and shoots, it arcs out over the cove and strikes the barge dead center. The fire spreads, and the crowd aahs with relief. Many clap softly, and not only poisoners. High Priestess Luca scowls at Natalia, but when Katharine looks back, Natalia nods. Mirabella's moment has been thoroughly stolen.

"This puts me in mind for something else," Katharine says loudly, looking at her bow. "I know there is a great feast awaiting us in the square. But we are in Wolf Spring, are we not? Home of the naturalists?" People in the crowd nod, their eyes filled with reflected flames from the burning barge. Mirabella and the High Priestess shrink backward, but there is nowhere to go but into the sea.

"I have nothing to offer," Katharine half-shouts. "No fine gifts. But I would still honor the naturalist queen." Her eyes settle on Arsinoe, petting her bear. The creature looks confused. Nothing to be afraid of, the poor thing. "Before we sit down to feast together . . . I would have Queen Arsinoe lead her sisters on a hunt."

* * *

Arsinoe's stomach drops into her shoes. Everyone is cheering for Katharine's challenge. Even her Wolf Spring people. The great, wild fools can never resist a hunt. And with her bear, they think she can win. They think the poisoner queen has made a fatal mistake.

Amid the poisoners, a handsome boy with pale blond hair whispers furiously into Katharine's ear, and Natalia Arron and the Black Council shift on their feet. They did not plan this. But they cannot stop it now, and nor can the priestesses or the Westwoods.

It is a challenge from one of the queens. It is why they came.

Arsinoe stares straight ahead. She will not plead and make Cait and Ellis feel guilty when they cannot help. Soon enough, Cait's strong voice cuts through the din.

"The hunt will commence in the northern woods, past the orchard. Make your queens ready."

Out over the sea, the sun is setting. There is too much light left. Too much to be able to wait for cover of dark, when Arsinoe's knowledge of the landscape could help her. She scans the crowd. Billy's eyes are full, as though she is already dead. Luke is praying, probably thanking the Goddess for a sure victory. Arsinoe digs her fingers into Braddock's fur.

"Jules," she whispers. "Where are you?"

THE QUEENS' HUNT

A rsinoe runs from the gathering at the cove. Braddock jogs by her side and butts her with his head, the impact hard enough to send her nearly sprawling. She leans down to quickly kiss his ears. The sweet bear thinks it is only play.

"Arsinoe!"

She turns. Billy lingers at the bottom of the hill. He cannot follow. If only they had a moment to talk, he would try to tell her what to do. He could find Jules and Joseph. Maybe act like a mainlander fool and make her angry enough to have a fighting chance.

"Don't look so sad," she says even though he is too far away to hear. "We both knew one of them would do something like this."

Running probably seemed cowardly. Neither of her sisters ran. Mirabella scarcely could, surrounded by priestesses and

Westwoods, and of course Katharine would not. The little poisoner has been waiting for her chance, hatching a plan all on her own.

"Arsinoe!"

It is Luke, with Hank flapping on his shoulder.

"I can't wait!" she shouts. She has to make it to the orchard and into the woods before her sisters or it will be over before it begins. Katharine said that Arsinoe was to lead the hunt. But all that means is that Arsinoe will be the quarry.

"Luke, stay out of the woods! Find Jules! Find Jules and Joseph!"

The Westwoods and Luca stop Mirabella just west of the square. They form a wall of robes, and Bree, Sara, and Elizabeth take her out of her Midsummer dress and put her into her hunting clothes: leggings and light boots, a warm tunic and cloak.

"Quickly, quickly," Luca orders breathlessly.

"I need my crossbow," Bree says. "And one for Elizabeth."

"Bree, you cannot interfere."

"I know that. But this is a hunt. Do you think the poisoner queen is going to charge into those woods by herself? She will have an entire Arron guard!"

"She is right," says Elizabeth. One of the priestesses hands her a weapon, and she hoists it in her good hand. "We will not interfere. But we won't let you face this alone."

Mirabella looks at Luca, but the High Priestess says nothing. Instead, Luca takes Bree and Elizabeth by the shoulders.

"You good girls," she says. "You loyal friends. Do not let

our queen fall to treachery. If death finds her, it must come from a queen and a queen only."

"Wait," Mirabella protests. "Arsinoe does not know that she may have a guard! I saw her run off alone, and the Milones have not gone after her!"

"Good," says Sara. "An advantage."

"But that is not fair!"

"Mira," Luca says as gently as she can. "This was never going to be fair. Now, to the woods. Over the hill to the orchard. Follow the Wolf Spring priestesses."

"Katharine, what have you done?" Pietyr asks. He puts his hands on both sides of his head as servants help Katharine out of her gown and into hunting clothes.

"She is doing what she is meant to do," says Nicolas as he watches her change. Pietyr looks like he would break him in half.

"You stay out of this," Pietyr barks. "I have had enough of your mainlander ideas. You are a suitor and not even her chosen one. You are not an Arron."

Katharine lets them bicker. The tension between them must overflow eventually. She just hopes she is there to see it when it does.

"If he has put ideas into my head, Pietyr, they are nowhere near as many as you have." Pietyr quiets. He glares at Nicolas. It is a good thing she is taking them with her on the hunt.

Katharine slides her throwing knives into their sheaths and buckles them about her waist as Natalia sweeps into her room.

"My sweet Kat. You continue to surprise me."

"This will be easier, Natalia. You will see." She slides a longer knife into her boot. "It would have been chaos trying to poison at the dinner. So much sleight of hand and changing plates. You know I have never been good at that."

"You are a skilled archer, Kat, but I have never known you to be good at hunting. This is more risk than the Council cares to take."

"Be that as it may, they cannot stop it now." Katharine gestures to a servant. "Crossbow. And bolts dipped in Winter Rose," she orders, referring to the Arrons' favorite hunting poison.

"No, we cannot," Natalia agrees. "The wait for your return will be long, with my sister and Renata in my ear. Do not tarry. You must promise."

Katharine pauses. No one else can see what she can in Natalia's eyes. Natalia will never show fear or doubt. But they are there. *Be careful and return to her* is what she means.

"I promise, Natalia."

"Good." Natalia blinks, and the moment is gone. "Horseback, I think, is the best way. I have had Half Moon saddled, along with Pietyr's and Nicolas's horses. Bertrand Roman will join you, as well as Margaret Beaulin."

"Margaret Beaulin?" Pietyr asks, checking his own crossbow. "From the Council?"

"The same," Natalia replies. "She is war gifted. She will be useful."

WOLF SPRING

*ules wakes slowly in the warm bed, beneath the pleasant weight of Joseph's arm across her chest. His eyes open when he feels her begin to stir, and he kisses her shoulder.

"Hello, my Jules," he says, and her cheeks go hot. Joseph laughs. "Now you decide to blush? After all this?"

"It's new to me," she whispers.

"And to me."

"You know what I mean."

"I do," he says, and moves atop her again to kiss her. "But it's true. The first time with you was always going to be special. No matter how many ways I imagined it."

"Joseph." She giggles and squirms away toward the window.

Sealhead Cove is full of floating lit lanterns.

"Joseph," Jules says, and grips the sill. They had fallen asleep, and slept too long.

THE QUEENS' HUNT

❦

*A*rsinoe stumbles farther and farther into the woods.

"Where do we go, Braddock?" She is already breathless from kicking through the heavy summer undergrowth. She looks around. The bent-over tree? Perhaps it would grant her luck. But it is not far enough. And besides, it has no loyalty, no reason to favor her above either of her sisters.

"There's a thicket," she pants. "Where the deer go." Jules has taken her there. She turns right and left and momentarily panics, thinking she has somehow managed to get herself lost in her own trees.

A while ago, the hunting horn blew from Wolf Spring, the townsfolk's way of telling her that at least one of her sisters has entered the woods. It is all the help she can hope for, and it seems an age has passed since the horn sounded.

Somewhere in the distance, leaves rustle and twigs crack underfoot. The sounds are far away but not quiet, chasing sounds rather than stalking. Arsinoe crouches and backs up, behind a large trunk. She motions for Braddock, and he comes to sniff her hands and see what she has.

"Stupid bear. You have to run, don't you see? They'll kill you if you don't." He blinks at her with calm bear eyes. As a great brown, he has not had to fear much, and though he can sense the fear in her, without the familiar-bond she cannot make him understand.

If only Jules would come. She must know, by now, what has happened. Unless they got to her. That thought settles like ice in Arsinoe's stomach. If anyone has hurt Jules, Arsinoe will find a way to tear them to pieces.

"We can't rest long, boy," she says, and pats Braddock's broad head. "We have to keep moving."

"Up that tree," Bree says, and points. The tree is tall, with many sprawling, climbable branches, and it is heavy with leaves. They mean to put Mirabella up it so she might see her sisters coming and burn them up with fire or bolts of lightning as they approach.

"They may never pass by this way," Mirabella objects.

"Give me your cloak." Elizabeth holds her hand out, and Mirabella takes it off so that Bree can help Elizabeth into it. "I will run decoy. I will find them and bring them right beneath you."

"No! That is too dangerous. You cannot outrun a bear or dodge a poisoned arrow. We should stay together."

"How long do you want to stay up in that tree?" Elizabeth asks. "This hunt will end only when one queen is dead." She squares her shoulders. "Don't worry about me, Mira. I may have only one hand, but my legs have never been stronger."

"Take Bree with you, at least."

Her friends look at each other reluctantly, but they know they will never get her to agree otherwise.

"All right, then," Mirabella says. She turns and looks up. "I will need some help onto the first branches."

Katharine and her riders are the last into the woods, but that does not bother her. She always intended to be the hunter, chasing her prey.

"The other queens have a strong lead," Margaret Beaulin says, scanning the trees.

"We should have brought hounds," says Bertrand Roman.

Katharine laughs.

"That would not have been very sporting." Let her sisters run. They cannot run forever. And they cannot have gotten far on foot. She turns Half Moon in a prancing circle. He is as eager to be off as she is.

"Is it a waste of words to ask you to keep to the middle?" Pietyr asks, and Nicolas grins.

"Of course it is," Katharine replies.

"A great brown bear can disembowel a running horse. Think of Half Moon, if you will not think of yourself."

Katharine strokes the black gelding's frothy neck.

"That bear will not touch us. And if you see it, try to take it alive." She puts her heels to Half Moon's sides and takes off down the path, not waiting to hear them argue. They act like taking the bear alive is an impossible task. But she had their weapons tipped specially with sleeping draught. A few cuts and arrows, and the beast should fall serenely to the ground.

"But it will not be that easy for you, sister," Katharine whispers, and leans forward excitedly in the saddle.

WOLF SPRING

*J*ules and Joseph hurry past the docks toward the market with Camden running ahead, jumping onto crates and piles of rope, frustrated that they cannot leap and bound like she can.

"It's practically dark." Jules moans. "The feast'll have started!"

"Arsinoe will understand." Joseph falls behind, trying to button his shirt. Jules did not give him much time to dress before leaving the house. "And she's safe. Everyone is with her. Madrigal and Ellis."

"Madrigal! What good is she? None on a good day, and now less than that when she's doubled over with baby sickness."

"That baby is your little sister or brother."

Jules looks back at him grudgingly. But Arsinoe is who matters now. Jules can just imagine how she will scowl when they slide in beside her at the feasting table. 'What took you so long?' she will say. 'I didn't have anyone to plug my ears during the Council speeches.'

They walk quickly through the market, past the empty stalls, and through the alley that leads to the square. Except the sliver of the square that Jules can see is empty. There is no one at the tables and no laughter carrying down the streets. She looks back out to the harbor. Maybe she was mistaken, and the lanterns she saw from Joseph's window were an illusion or a dream. But there they are, burning, bobbing on the water. The ceremony is over.

"Where is everyone?" Joseph asks.

Camden whines and swings her dark-tipped tail back and forth. Something is wrong.

"We'll try the docks and the shore?" Jules suggests. She can think of nowhere else to go.

"Juillenne! Joseph!"

Luke comes running with Hank fluttering and clucking on his heels. "Where have you been?"

"We fell asleep," Jules replies honestly, too distracted to feel shy. "What's happened? Where is everyone?"

"They're in the orchard," Luke spits. "Waiting on the edges of the forest. The poisoners and the queen, Queen Katharine, she challenged them to a hunt!"

"A hunt?" Joseph repeats, and his brow furrows. "Luke, where is Arsinoe?"

"I don't know! She went into the woods first with Braddock. Both of them are after her now. Especially that poisoner. She kept staring at Queen Arsinoe the whole time!"

"Where?" Jules demands, and when Luke starts to sputter, she reaches out and shakes him. "Where?"

"The southern edge, near the creek. But she could have gone anywhere. Where were you, Jules? Why weren't you here?"

Jules does not answer. She runs for the forest, not near the orchard where the crowd would see her, but up the hill and off the road to follow the stream. Camden sprints ahead, her pink nose twitching and scenting the air. In her panic and haste, Arsinoe may have gone anywhere. But she will not have left Braddock behind, and the scent of the bear will be easy for Camden to pick up.

"Jules, wait," Joseph calls out. He is right on her heels, but even his long stride is no match for her short one when her blood is up.

"Wait for what?" she snaps, frustrated. She pauses for one step and turns. "I know that we can't interfere. But I can't let her be hunted out there alone, Joseph. Can you?"

"No." He grabs her arm and they start to run again. "We have to find her."

THE QUEENS' HUNT

❧

*T*he poisoners see Braddock first. His enormous, shaggy form is impossible to hide. Arsinoe hears the cries and then the hoofbeats. She looks at her bear.

"Run!"

But a great brown's instinct is not to run. It is to fight. He turns toward their pursuers, still far off in the trees. He sniffs the air curiously and stands up on his hind legs.

"No," Arsinoe pleads. She pats his side desperately and motions with her hands toward where they must go, deeper into the trees, into the dense growth where the horses will not have speed. "Please, Braddock, please come! They'll kill you!"

They cannot kill him. The big sweet bear. The poisoners will remember the havoc he wreaked the night of the Quickening. They will not take any chances. They will not give Arsinoe any time to tell them that he is not mean-tempered; that it was all her fault.

"Come on, Braddock, come on!" Her feet move in place, and her eyes dart between him and the approaching riders. Katharine is in the lead, her crossbow raised.

"Please!" Arsinoe hisses, and then cries out with relief when he drops to all fours and follows her into the underbrush.

Mirabella stiffens at the sound of running horses. They are close, but she is safe enough, high in her tree. She presses against the trunk and braces her legs, her feet stuck firmly into the V of a branch. Bree and Elizabeth left to run decoy only a short time ago. She lost track of them almost immediately. Will she see them run past with Katharine on their heels? Or a bear? She clenches and unclenches her fists. Her lightning is stronger than her fire, but the fire is faster. And more accurate.

The shouting and hoofbeats grow louder, and she twists to see whether she can spot movement. The noises are violent. Crashing. But Elizabeth and Bree set off in the opposite direction. They should be safe unless they have circled back.

It is terrible, waiting there, listening to her sisters hunting each other. Wondering what is happening. Not knowing what to hope for. The clever thing to do would be to remain right where she is. To wait for it to be over and for Bree and Elizabeth to return.

Mirabella climbs down from her tree and drops to the ground.

* * *

Her sister and her bear have heard them coming and darted into the foliage like frightened rabbits, but it will not save them. The distance covered by Half Moon's legs is much greater than the distance covered by Arsinoe's. If Arsinoe were smart, she would ride the bear. Or perhaps there are limits to even what a familiar will allow.

"Don't lose them!" Nicolas calls, exhilarated, his eyes bright. Even Pietyr has gotten into the spirit of things and rides as focused as a diving hawk.

The bear comes into view, and Katharine holds her crossbow at the ready. But she is not after it. The others, with their weapons edged with sleeping draught, may have their fun with him. She wants only Arsinoe. It was always going to be Arsinoe she hunted, the one from Wolf Spring, the one who would die here, in front of her own city. It seems only fitting.

Half Moon thunders through the ferns and shrubs, and the bear grows larger ahead, dwarfing the black-dressed queen running by its side. Katharine should have painted poison onto Half Moon's shoes so she could simply ride Arsinoe into the ground. Oh well. Perhaps she will save that for Mirabella.

She smiles until the bear turns to fight.

"No, Braddock, no!" Arsinoe shouts, and stomps her feet, but he will not obey. He is tired of running. The hoofbeats and unfamiliar voices coming closer and closer make him angry. He stands on his hind legs and roars so they will go away. He will not swat them unless he has to.

Arsinoe does not know what to do. They cannot stop, but he will not come. She shakes her head and turns to run on alone but stops after only a few strides. He is her bear. She cannot leave him.

"Go!" Mirabella shouts.

Arsinoe freezes. She searches the trees and sees Mirabella ducked behind a fat trunk, her hood pulled over her hair.

"Go!" Mirabella orders again, eyes wild. "Go now! Run, Arsinoe! You must run!"

"I can't!" she cries as Braddock drops to his feet and charges the horses. She can only stand and watch as the knives and arrows fly. She can only listen to him bellow as they sink deep into his soft, brown coat.

She looks at Mirabella through blurry eyes.

"You run," Arsinoe says. "Save yourself. They have already caught me." She turns and cups her hands to yell. "Come and get me, you poisoner cowards! If you're brave enough to go where your horses can't follow!"

She does not wait to see if they will take the bait. She knows that they will. And she knows where she is. It is not far to the deer thicket, where she can drop to the ground and hide. If she is lucky, Katharine will pass by unaware. Perhaps even close enough that Arsinoe can grab her and slit her throat.

"Stay here!" Katharine orders. She bares her teeth and urges Half Moon past the stumbling, wounded bear, into the bushes after Arsinoe. When Half Moon breaks through the undergrowth, they are well within range, and Katharine takes aim.

"Where do you think you are running to?" she whispers, and then fires her shot. The bolt catches Arsinoe squarely in the back. She falls with a small gasp, a sound Katharine will relish for many nights afterward. Katharine shouts her victory, then whirls Half Moon around in a circle. She could have sworn that she heard another scream come from somewhere in the trees.

Bree claps her hands over Mirabella's mouth, stopping her screams. Mirabella jerks and struggles, but Elizabeth is there as well, and together they wrestle her to the ground.

Arsinoe fell. Katharine shot her in the back, and she fell. It is over.

Hot tears slide down Mirabella's cheeks as she watches Katharine dismount. From where they lie hidden in the ferns, Arsinoe's body is nothing but a limp pile of black clothes.

Katharine kicks Arsinoe in the ribs, turning her over, and Arsinoe yelps like a dog.

"What will kill you first," Katharine wonders, "my poison or my crossbow bolt?" She cocks her head. "No last words? No last retort?" She bends to listen. Then she laughs.

"Let me go," Mirabella whispers furiously.

"No, Mira," Bree whispers back. "Please. It is over. The bolt was poisoned. Let it be over."

"No," Mirabella says, but Bree is right. Whatever she could have done for Arsinoe, she did not do it in time.

Katharine twirls Arsinoe's red-streaked mask around her finger.

"What a monster that bear made of you," Katharine says, studying Arsinoe's exposed scarred face. "You should be glad that we killed it."

Arsinoe coughs. Her breathing is ragged and wet.

"And what a monster they have made of *you*, little Katharine. Scars or no scars."

What happens next happens so quickly that Mirabella almost does not see. Juillenne Milone bursts out from the trees behind Katharine.

"Get away from her!" she screams, and Katharine flies backward and lands with a grunt. Jules's hand is out as though to push, but she was too far away to have touched her. Mirabella watches, unblinking, as Jules races to Arsinoe's side, and when Katharine regains her footing, Jules does it again, knocking Katharine back through the air with an unseen force, to roll where she lands.

"Arsinoe, put your arm around my neck. Help me, Arsinoe, hurry!"

Jules calls Katharine's horse and makes it kneel and heaves herself and Arsinoe into the saddle. They gallop away with Juillenne's mountain cat loping behind on three legs, and all Katharine can do is scream and pound her fists against the ground.

Mirabella, Elizabeth, and Bree duck low as Katharine's hunting party catches up to her.

"Queen Katharine! Are you hurt?"

"No." Katharine stands up and brushes dirt and grass from her skirt. "I got her. I got Arsinoe. But that naturalist stole the body." She stalks forward and jumps nimbly into the saddle behind a boy with ice-blond hair. One of the Arrons. "Ride, Pietyr! I will not lose my sister's corpse!" She kicks the horse and it takes off, and the rest of the poisoners follow.

"What was that?" Bree asks after the hoofbeats fade. "Though I have never seen it, I would swear that was the war gift."

"But how?" Elizabeth asks. "Jules Milone is a naturalist."

"I do not know." Mirabella begins to sob. "And I do not care." She leans against her friends and they wrap her in their arms. They are safe. She is safe. She should be grateful, but she cannot be when Arsinoe is dead.

WOLF SPRING

*J*oseph lost track of Jules and Camden almost the moment that the mountain cat caught Braddock's scent. They were far too fast for him, and though he tried to catch up, there was no chance. So he backtracked through the forest toward the orchard, where at least he will not have to worry alone.

He exits the wood and joins the silent, gathered crowd, slipping through people until he finds Billy beside the Milones and Matthew.

"Someone comes!"

"Is it Arsinoe?" Billy asks, neck stretched.

"It's so soon," Cait says quietly. "Too soon."

And she is right. The queen who emerges from the trees is not Arsinoe but Mirabella.

"Mira," Billy says. "Is she all right? Is Katharine dead?"

Joseph looks into Mirabella's eyes and goes cold all over.

"I am sorry," Mirabella says. "But Queen Katharine shot her in the back."

The gathered people barely react. No raucous celebration by the poisoners. No relief from the elementals. They will save their prayers and toasts for later when they are alone. As for the naturalists, they are an iron lot to begin with and have braced themselves for this news since Arsinoe was born.

"No. No!" Billy elbows his way toward Mirabella, who is being held up by Bree Westwood and one of the priestesses. She looks at Billy regretfully. She cannot even meet Joseph's eyes.

"Mira, you're lying!" Billy shouts. "I don't believe it. I won't believe it until I see her!"

Matthew reaches for Billy's arm, but he twists loose. Joseph takes him by the shoulders, and Billy grabs him back, shaking so hard that they almost fall.

"What's the matter with them? Why aren't they doing anything?" He turns to the Milones and screams into their grim, silent faces. "What's wrong with you? Go in there and find her!"

"Easy, Billy," Joseph says into his ear. "It might not be true. It can't be. Jules and Camden had her scent."

Joseph's heart thuds at his own words. If Jules and Camden were killed, he will lose his mind.

"I'm going in there," Billy says, and pulls free.

"Billy." Mirabella holds up her hands. "You will not find her. She is gone."

"She's not gone!"

"No. I mean that her . . ." Her eyes shift to Joseph. "Jules tried to save her. And afterward . . . she took Arsinoe away."

Joseph's eyes fill. Madrigal grasps her stomach and falls to her knees.

I am sorry, Mirabella mouths.

"I know," Joseph whispers. "I know."

The crowd straightens at the sounds of hoofbeats and rustling leaves. The Arrons step to the fore with their ever loyal Black Council. So far, they have wisely kept to the edges, but their queen is returning. And a queen returning in victory is to be honored, regardless of where that victory took place.

Margaret Beaulin rides out of the trees first. She slows her horse and trots directly to Natalia Arron, so close that Natalia must move her head to the side to avoid the horse's tired blowing.

"It is done."

"They could still be wrong," Billy says, and Joseph keeps an arm across his foster brother's chest as Natalia questions every rider, even the gold-haired suitor. And then Queen Katharine emerges, riding tandem behind the Arron boy.

"She took my horse," Katharine fumes. "She stole Half Moon!"

"Who?" Cait Milone demands. "Arsinoe?"

Katharine looks positively furious, but when she sees who is asking, her face calms, and she lowers her eyes respectfully.

"Queen Arsinoe, my sister, is dead, Mistress Milone. I shot her with a poisoned bolt from my crossbow. The 'she' who I speak of is your granddaughter, Juillenne. She stole my horse and fled with the body."

"If that is so," Cait says, her voice strained, "then she acted out of grief and will soon return to her senses."

"I am sure you are right, Cait," says Natalia. "But the queen's body must be returned. Queen Arsinoe is deserving of her burial rites."

Joseph's eyes narrow as Katharine covers her face, perhaps to hide a sneer. When she lowers her hands, her face is solemn.

"But there is more," she says. "When the Milone girl attacked me, it was not with her familiar. It was with the war gift."

Silence. Then shouts of disbelief. Katharine's voice rises above the noise.

"Think what you will, Wolf Spring. But I have seen it. Juillenne Milone is legion cursed."

THE NORTHEAST WOODS

*J*ules slows the horse when they come to the banks of the River Calder. The night air is chilled, and the water rushes by black in the moonlight. Arsinoe lies across the pommel of her saddle. Dead? Jules refuses to think so, but is too afraid to check. She calls Camden and holds the horse steady as the cat jumps onto its hindquarters to ford the river.

"I'll say one thing for the poisoners," Jules says. "They breed fine horses. This fellow is faster than any of the saddle horses in Wolf Spring by half. And stronger." He has carried Camden's considerable weight for at least a third of the distance, and Jules has not even used her gift to press him.

"Arsinoe? Can you hear me?"

There is no response. Jules grits her teeth as the horse hops the last few steps onto the opposite bank, jostling Arsinoe in the saddle. Arsinoe has not spoken since they fled from Katharine. She has not even moaned. But Jules will keep going. She will keep running as long as she feels warmth in Arsinoe's body.

"Please, Arsinoe. Don't be dead."

The bolt sticks out from Arsinoe's back and presses against Jules's leg whenever the horse moves. Something has to be done about it. Every time it shifts it does more damage. She lifts Arsinoe's shoulder gently to look.

"Don't touch it," Arsinoe gasps, and Jules is so startled she almost screams. "Don't touch the bolt. You don't know what she used on it."

Jules leans down and covers Arsinoe's head with kisses. She is alive. She is even feisty.

"So I'll wrap my hand first," Jules says, grinning over tears of relief. "It has to come out."

"No." Arsinoe grimaces, her teeth white in the moonlight. "Just let it stay."

Jules slides her arm around Arsinoe's neck. She is no healer, and no one will help an injured queen now that the Ascension has started. She can only think of one place and one person. But the journey seems so far.

"It's all right, Jules," Arsinoe whispers.

She looks down at Arsinoe's pale face. She is weak, but the bleeding has slowed.

Camden slides off the back of the horse, and they pick up their pace again, heading ever farther north.

WOLF SPRING TEMPLE

"Mira, take some warm cider." Elizabeth puts a cup into her hands, but Mirabella barely looks at it. "Even at Midsummer, the nights grow so cool here beside the sea."

"Is that from the barrels outside? She cannot have that, you little fool!" One of the Rolanth priestesses grabs the cup so roughly that cider sloshes over the edge. "That has not been inspected."

"Do not call her a little fool," Bree says, seething. "And if the queen cannot have that cider, then go and warm her some that she *can* have."

The priestess scowls, but she leaves to do as she is told. After she turns her back, Bree mimes a kicking motion into her backside. She turns to Elizabeth.

"You should leave this order if they treat you this way."

"I'm an initiate, Bree. We exist to be kicked around."

"You are one of the queen's best friends."

"The Goddess doesn't give preferential treatment. Neither do her priestesses."

Bree blows a stray lock of hair away from her face and mutters under her breath. Mirabella thinks she catches the word "malarkey."

Elizabeth and Bree have not left her side since the Queens' Hunt. They steady her as the rest of their party flutters about like worried birds, confused and ineffectual, running into one another. Luca is at the Milone house with the members of the Black Council, discussing punishments for Jules. She assaulted one queen, and absconded with the body of another. But her most grievous offense lies with what she is: legion cursed.

Mirabella closes her eyes. Poor Jules. Poor Joseph. There should be no punishment. There should be commendation. Honor. She did what Mirabella was too afraid to do. Mirabella could have tossed Katharine just as easily with a gust of wind. She could have felled her and her horse together with a bolt of lightning.

The door of the temple opens and the High Priestess walks inside. Sara steps up to greet her and takes her by the hands.

"Luca," she says. "Have they found Queen Arsinoe's body?"

"No, and they are not likely to," Luca replies. "The Milone girl knows these forests, and now that night has fallen, there is little chance of picking up her trail before morning. By then, she will be too far ahead of us."

"What is the punishment?" Mirabella calls out, and the

room quiets. It is obvious from her tone that she does not think there should be one.

"There is no punishment for taking the body, Mira," Luca says gently. "The Council is satisfied well enough with a dead queen. And they do not wish to anger the people of Wolf Spring by executing one of their favorite daughters." She raises her eyebrows and cocks her head. "I was frankly impressed. Surprised but impressed. However, there is still the question of the legion curse. When Juillienne Milone returns, she will need to go to the capital for questioning."

"'Favorite daughters,'" a Rolanth priestess scoffs. "Wolf Spring will turn her out on her ear, now that they know she is legion cursed. They may execute her themselves." Murmurs of agreement ripple through the room. The priestesses from Rolanth and Wolf Spring glare, one side daring the other to say any different.

"Luca, you know that is a lie," Mirabella says. "They will not question her. They will lock her up and put her to death as soon as the crown is decided."

"That may be," says Luca. "Goddess knows, it is dangerous for one so strong to bear the curse. If she were to go mad . . . but it is their decision." She looks at Mirabella calmly. "Unless you are queen. Then it would be up to your Council."

Mirabella could save Jules. Of course. She must save her, for Arsinoe's sake.

The door opens again, and Rho stalks inside.

"Some of the Arron party went back into the woods with a

large litter and a wagon," she says. "Ropes. Lanterns."

"For what?" Mirabella asks.

"A victory rug, I am thinking. They were after the body of Arsinoe's bear."

"How terrible." Elizabeth shrinks at the thought. "To defile a familiar that way. A queen's familiar!"

"Katharine is wicked," Mirabella whispers. "I am so sorry, Arsinoe, that I did not take care of her a long time ago."

THE SEAWATCH MOUNTAINS

*T*he horse has finally begun to drag his hooves. Jules pats his froth-covered neck.

"Good, brave boy," she says. She pushed him hard, only easing the pace when they came to the rocky paths in the foothills of the mountains.

In her arms, Arsinoe begins to cough. Her whole body convulses and stiffens like a plank, threatening to tip all the way off the saddle.

"Arsinoe, be still!"

Jules stops the horse and dismounts, her legs aching so badly that they barely work. She curses the poisoners under her breath, but truthfully the pain might be just from so many hours in the saddle.

"Camden, help me."

She eases Arsinoe down, and Camden slides underneath her, helping to soften the landing. She purrs and licks worriedly at the queen's clammy cheek.

Arsinoe shouts when the crossbow bolt sticking out of her back bends against the earth, and Jules quickly rolls her onto her side.

In the pale light of the moon and stars, Arsinoe looks dead already.

"I hear a stream nearby," Jules says with forced cheer. "Though weak as I am now, I couldn't convince a fish to splash me in the face, let alone convince one to let us eat it."

"No fish," Arsinoe murmurs. "Water."

Jules leads the horse toward the sound of the stream and she and Camden bend with him to drink. In the horse's saddle-bags, she finds a silver flask and dumps out whatever poison Katharine had stored inside, tipping it into the rushing current to dissipate. She rinses it three times and fills it with cold, clear water.

"Here." Jules kneels and tugs Arsinoe's head into her lap, pressing the flask to her lips. Arsinoe can only manage a mouthful before she starts to cough again, and when she is through, dark blood is dotted across her chin.

"You shouldn't have done this, Jules. You'll get into trouble."

"Since when have we cared about trouble?" Jules studies Arsinoe's scarred face fondly and traces the lines of the cuts with her thumb.

"She took . . . my mask."

"I'll get it back," Jules promises. "I'll get it back, and her head besides."

"No." Arsinoe starts to cough again. More blood coats her chin. "Not your job. Let . . . Mirabella . . ."

"You shouldn't have had to try to run," Jules says. "You shouldn't have been on your own. I'm so sorry! I am never there when you need me."

"You're always there."

"Not today. I was with Joseph and we fell asleep! I was supposed to be with you and I was with him! Asleep!"

Arsinoe grins.

"Finally."

Jules wipes her face. "He is not more important than you! He's faithless. Untrustworthy. Not worth this!"

"Well, who is?" Arsinoe quips. "But he is better than you think. It was my fault, Jules. What happened between him and Mirabella."

"What are you talking about?"

"I did a spell. It went wrong. It was early on, before I knew what low magic could do. But I never wanted it to hurt you." She coughs again, her fingers hooked like claws. When she quiets, a sheen of sweat coats her forehead.

"I can't breathe," she says. "Jules. I can't breathe." Her eyes slip shut.

"Arsinoe?" Jules leans over her and shakes her gently. "Arsinoe, no!"

Panicked, she looks into the trees for someone, anyone to shout to. Camden pads close. She nuzzles Arsinoe's face, and the queen's head falls loosely away.

"Let's go. Camden, let's go!"

Jules heaves Arsinoe's body up and calls for the horse to kneel. They are so tired. But Arsinoe is dying. So they have to ride.

THE INN OF THE
CROOKED TAIL CAT

———————————— ⚜ ————————————

*T*he poisoners only make it as far as Highgate before they stop to celebrate. Under the direction of Genevieve and Cousin Lucian from the Council, they take over the entirety of the first inn that they find: the Inn of the Crooked Tail Cat. Despite its dubious name, the inn is clean and well-kept, the kitchen stocked with enough fine pots and knives to prepare an impromptu poisoner's feast. All afternoon and into the evening, Queen Katharine's party toasts her and listens to the story of the hunt told over and over again.

They even drag the bear inside, tied down in the back of a wagon. Poisoned and unconscious.

"What will happen to him now?" Nicolas asks, looking at the bear. "What happens to a familiar after its naturalist is dead?"

Katharine leans back in her chair and studies the great brown with a cocked head. It is still large and intimidating, even strapped into a wagon with its tongue out between its teeth. There is something so satisfying about seeing it at her mercy, its shining brown coat cut through and bleeding from blades and arrows coated with her poisons.

"It would go back to the woods, I suppose."

"But in Wolf Spring, I learned that familiars are granted unnatural long life," Nicolas goes on. "Will it still? Or without the link to its naturalist, will it age and die as any other bear?"

Pietyr, seated beside Katharine, finishes his cup of May wine and slams it down on the table. "These are questions best posed to a naturalist," he says. "Perhaps you would like to go back and ask them. Then they could take you on to Rolanth. You should be beginning your suit of Queen Mirabella soon, yes?"

Nicolas smiles and shrugs.

"Soon," he says. "Unless my queen will kill her first." He dips his head and kisses Katharine's gloved hand, then gets up from the table. He approaches the bear, and Katharine watches as he dumps his cup of wine over its head.

"You cannot really like him," Pietyr snaps.

"Why not? There is plenty about him to like. I have never seen his eyes on anyone but me, for example. And I have not found daisies in his hair, put there by lusty priestesses."

"I have not had another girl since you, Kat," Pietyr says quietly. "You have ruined me for them." His eyes turn back to Nicolas, who is laughing and clinking cups with giftless Renata

Hargrove from the Council. "He does not love you like I do. He cannot."

"And how do you know, Pietyr?" Katharine asks, leaning so close that he must feel her breath against his ear. "What must he do to prove that he does? Must he throw me down into the Breccia Domain?"

Pietyr stiffens, and Katharine sits back and happily tosses a handful of poison berries into her mouth.

"You eat too much. You will be sick tonight."

"Sick, perhaps," she says, and eats another handful. "But I will not die. I have been poisoned and poisoned again since I was a child, Pietyr. I know what I am doing. You must relax and try to enjoy yourself."

He settles into his chair, and crosses his arms, the only dismal spot in the room. The music from the country musicians is not refined, and the inn is plain and without a single chandelier. But the poisoners, so elated by the victory in Wolf Spring, do not seem to mind. Even Natalia dances, her back straight, smiling softly in the arms of her younger brother Antonin.

"Play louder!" Genevieve orders. "So if the elemental's coaches pass by they will hear it!"

Everyone raises a cheer, and the musicians play harder. Katharine wishes that Mirabella could hear all this. See all this. But though coaches from Rolanth may pass by carrying priestesses, Mirabella will not be with them. The elemental queen and her Westwoods traveled to Wolf Spring by sea, where they can control the currents and shifting winds, and, of course, where they were sure not to run into any poisoners.

Margaret Beaulin approaches the table and bows. Then she leans against it, so drunk that her left eye has begun to wander in its socket.

"An inspired move, bringing the bear inside," she says. "The only thing better would be if it were Arsinoe's body lying strapped in the wagon."

Katharine's eyes narrow.

"A vanquished queen is deserving of her burial rites, Margaret," she growls in a different voice. "She is worthy of the people's love and affection."

Candles have burned in the windows of every town they passed through, in honor of Queen Arsinoe. And that is the way it should be.

Margaret waves her hand, oblivious to Katharine's grave tone.

"Let them mourn and be done with it. Her name will not be spoken after your crowning. It will be lost in time. Like a pebble in a river."

Katharine's gloved fingers grip the wood of her chair so tightly that it squeaks.

"Katharine?" Pietyr asks. "Are you all right?"

Katharine snatches up her cup of tainted wine. She wants to throw it into Margaret Beaulin's face, leap upon her, and pour it down her war-gifted throat.

Perhaps someday. But not now. She stands, and the musicians stop playing. The poisoners stop dancing midstep.

"A toast. To my sister Queen Arsinoe."

Jaws drop slightly. They titter as if expecting a joke. But Katharine is not joking, and eventually, Natalia walks to her wine cup and holds it aloft. After a moment, the others follow suit.

"It would be easy to hate her," Katharine says, thinking of her sister, her eyes losing focus on the crowd. "Another queen standing in the way. But Queen Arsinoe was an innocent in this. Just as much an innocent as I. Before that bear"—she gestures toward it—"before Beltane, the people felt about her what they felt about me. That we were weak. Born to die. Sacrifices to the chosen queen's legend. So let us not forget the queen we truly hate. The darling of Rolanth and the temple."

Katharine holds her cup high.

"So I toast to Queen Arsinoe, my sister, whom I killed with mercy. It will not be so when I kill Queen Mirabella. Queen Mirabella will suffer."

THE BLACK COTTAGE

B y the time Jules reaches the Black Cottage, she is too exhausted to be cautious. She pushes the spent horse the last strides through the trees; in the stream, he nearly stumbles and falls. She has to jerk up hard on his poor head to keep him on his feet.

"Caragh!"

She trots across the dirt path through the edging of waxed-leaf shrubs. Her voice is strained and odd-sounding. It seems like forever since she heard any voice at all. For hours it has been nothing but hoofbeats and rustling trees.

"Caragh!"

The front door of the cottage opens, and her aunt Caragh steps cautiously outside.

"Juillenne?"

"Yes," Jules says. Her shoulders sag. They ache beneath Arsinoe's weight. "It's me."

Caragh does not speak, but her chocolate hound bounds through the door and down the stone steps to jump at the horse and bay happily.

"Aunt Caragh, help us!" The words come out thin as air as she slides sideways out of the saddle, dragging Arsinoe's body with her. But she does not hit the ground. Caragh's arms are there to catch her.

"Jules," Caragh says. She cups Jules's face between her hands and then feels all up and down her bones. Beside them, her hound sniffs excitedly all over Camden, collapsed in the grass. Finally, Caragh pushes Arsinoe's short black hair away from her face. Her lips tremble when she sees the scars.

"I didn't know where else to go," Jules whispers.

Footsteps shuffle through the cottage door onto the porch, and Jules looks up at an old woman dressed all in black and stout as a small ox. Stark white hair falls over her right shoulder in a long braid.

"Caragh," she says. "They cannot stay here."

"Who is she?" Jules asks. "I thought you were alone. I thought your banishment . . . your punishment was to be alone here until the new queens come."

"That's Willa," Caragh explains. "The old Midwife. Someone had to teach me." She looks toward the old woman. "I won't turn my niece away."

"It is not her I care about." Willa nods toward Arsinoe. "That is a dead queen. And no queen may return here once she has grown. Not unless she is carrying her triplets."

"She's not dead!" Jules shouts. "And you will help her!"

Willa snorts.

"Such orders," she grumbles as she walks down the steps. "I see the resemblance now between you and your aunt."

"Turn her, Jules," Caragh says. "Let me see."

"Be careful. Don't touch it. It's a poisoned bolt."

Caragh's hand stops in midair.

"A poisoned bolt? Jules, there's nothing to be done about that."

"No, you—" Jules hesitates. But what does it matter if Caragh knows their secret? Everyone on the island thinks Arsinoe is dead. That she is really a poisoner makes no difference now.

Jules opens her mouth to speak, but stops when she sees Willa's unsurprised expression.

"You knew," says Jules. "You knew all along."

Willa reaches down and grasps one of Arsinoe's arms.

"Get her inside," she says gruffly. "She is barely alive, but we will see what can be done. I am a poisoner as well. I can handle the bolt."

Jules jerks awake in an unfamiliar bed. It is full dark out, and she reaches across the blankets to Camden so the big cat can soothe her with a purr. Then she remembers. They are at the Black Cottage. With Arsinoe. And Caragh.

Removing the poisoned bolt, cleaning and sewing the wound closed went easier than Jules had expected, mostly because Arsinoe never regained consciousness. Willa's sure hands twisted and pulled, rubbed and tugged until the queen lay beneath a soft blanket, looking as calm and serene as if it were no more than a well-earned nap. Afterward, Caragh helped Jules down the hall to another room, where she and Camden were asleep as soon as they closed their eyes.

Jules slides out of bed, still in her clothes and shoes, and Camden stretches and jumps to the floor. There are lights casting shadows in the hall. Caragh or Willa must still be up somewhere.

Jules slips softly to the room where they put Arsinoe and peeks inside. The queen's breathing is shallow but visible in the steady light of the candle on the bedside table. Jules watches for a few moments, but Arsinoe will not wake tonight. So she tiptoes farther toward the other source of light, hoping to find her aunt.

The Black Cottage is no small place. It is larger than the Milone house and full of fine things: silver candelabras, glorious oil paintings, and rugs so plush that she cannot resist wriggling her toes in them. She pauses briefly to peer up a long, dark staircase and then follows the light and sounds through the sitting room to the kitchen.

The chocolate hound hears them coming and trots out. She dances a happy, sniffing circle around Camden before leaning her long body against Jules.

"You're awake," Caragh says when Jules enters the kitchen, which is brightly lit by several yellow lamps. "How is Arsinoe?"

Jules sits down at the table opposite her. "Still resting. Still breathing."

"From the look of you when you arrived, you should still

be sleeping as well. That poor horse of yours is snoring in the barn, you can be sure."

"He's not mine," she says, though she supposes that he is, now. "I stole him. From Queen Katharine."

"Hmph," says Willa, who had crept up behind her very quietly for someone using a cane. "What in the world is happening with this Ascension Year?" She sets down bundles of goldenrod and yarrow beside Caragh as she grinds oils and herbs with a mortar and pestle. "It is a good thing she came when she did. These are all in bloom."

"We have more," Caragh says. "Jarred and hanging dried in the storeroom."

"Fresh is better," Willa says, and taps her on the chin.

Jules watches silently as the two women talk. There is an easy fondness between them that is strange to see. Jules is glad that Caragh has not been lonely. She is glad to see her smile. But it is not how she imagined her over the last five years.

"Do you know nothing about the Ascension, then?" Jules asks. "Don't you get any news?"

"Worcester brings us supplies every month," says Willa. "In his little cart, pulled by his good shaggy pony. Sometimes he brings us news."

"And sometimes he comes twice," says Caragh. "When Willa is looking particularly fetching." She chuckles, and Willa makes a face.

"What is that?" Jules asks. She points to the mortar and pestle.

"An ointment for Arsinoe."

"And make it thicker than you did the last time." Willa stretches her back. "I am going to get some sleep before the queen wakes. *If* she wakes. She lost a lot of blood, and she is weak. It was a very long ride for you, I gather."

Jules went as fast as she could. Maybe she should have gone somewhere else. Somewhere closer.

Willa walks past and grasps her shoulder firmly.

"Do not worry too much. She was always the toughest of them, even when she was a girl."

"You . . . remember her, then?"

"Of course I do. I remember all of them. Until they were six, they were mine."

And then she leaves, and Jules and Caragh are alone.

Caragh studies Jules, her head cocked as she separates leaves from flowers and drops them into the bowl of the mortar.

"You have grown up so well, Jules. So pretty."

"I have barely grown *up* at all," Jules mumbles. "I'm shorter than everyone at home."

"Tiny," Caragh says, "but fierce."

Camden's ears flicker back and forth as if to agree. Camden has always taken compliments better than she has.

"I knew you were strong when you were a girl. But I never imagined a mountain cat." She looks down. "How are Mum and Dad?"

"They're fine. They miss you." Jules holds her hand out to the hound, who comes to rest her chin on Jules's knee. "They miss you, too, Juniper," she says, and the dog pants happily. "Jake especially."

"And how is Madrigal?"

Jules hesitates. How to tell Caragh about Madrigal and Matthew? About their baby? And should she tell her, when it is not her place, and when it will make no difference, with Caragh banished to the cottage?

"Madrigal is Madrigal. I've long since stopped waiting for her to be anything different."

"That's probably wise," says Caragh. "But she does love you, Jules. She always has."

Not like you did, Jules wants to say.

"I never thought I'd see you again, Aunt Caragh."

Caragh grinds harder on the mixture of ointment. Her time at the cottage has put more muscle on her arms, and more thickness to her waist. Her brown-gold hair is long and unstyled. She is still beautiful. Jules has always thought Caragh was just as beautiful as Madrigal, only in a different way.

"They're bound to let me out of here someday," Caragh says. "And replace me with some good priestess. Someone like Willa. Not long after the new queen is crowned, I should think."

"Why would they do that?"

"Because this punishment was an Arron grudge against the Milones. And the next queen won't be an Arron queen. Willa seems certain of it, and having raised the young girls, she must know."

"She must," says Jules darkly. "Though maybe she's not so certain now."

THE WESTERN SEA

The journey from Wolf Spring to Rolanth by sea is fast. Faster than traveling by wagon by several days. That morning, Mirabella watched priestesses release birds from the deck, back to Rolanth to announce the return of the queen.

She wonders whether word of Arsinoe's death will beat them there. Whether she will return to candles in the windows and her people dressed for mourning in crimson and black. She hopes so. Then she will not have to be the one to tell them.

When the ship passed around Cape Horn, many lights were visible from the shore. But Cape Horn is much farther south than Rolanth.

Mirabella stares at the dark, wood walls of her cabin. She has not been much use on this journey, letting other elementals guide the ship. She has lacked the will, since Arsinoe's death. They do not need her, anyway, with so many able to control the winds. And Sara is strong enough with water to handle the currents by herself.

Someone knocks.

"Yes?"

The door opens, and Billy pokes his head inside. She has not seen much of him since leaving port. The one time she approached his quarters, she heard him weeping through the door, and turned away.

"Care for some company?"

"Please." She gestures for him to come inside and sit.

"My room is too quiet," he says. "I miss Harriet and her clucking."

Mirabella sets aside the book she had been paging through. She ought to sit properly, swing her legs off her bed and move their visit to a table. It is improper for her to recline, with Billy seated beside her feet. But what does she care? They are not strangers. And she does not have the energy to worry about impropriety anyhow.

"Harriet will be well, with Joseph's family?" she asks.

"She'd better be. If I return to find her in a stew pot . . ." Billy trails off. His cheeks are gray. Ashen. He has not looked at her since coming inside. Only past her. He meant to use her as a distraction from his grief, and she is failing him.

"It is not much longer until we reach Rolanth," Mirabella says, lifting her voice.

"I know. You're all cheaters, you elementals. Calling the winds and pushing the waves. This barely qualifies as sailing." He smiles, but it looks wrong without touching his eyes.

"At least you saw her again," Mirabella says gently. "At least you had time with her. I hope that your last moments were good ones."

"I should have told her. I never told her."

"I am sure that she knew."

"How could she? All I did was tell her that she was unfit. Unsuitable. Infuriating, with none of the makings a man looks for in a wife." He laughs hollowly. "And that was true. But I would have overlooked all that."

Mirabella exhales. She meant to chuckle.

Billy reaches onto the side table and picks up a couple bits of jewelry that Bree left lying there. "This is such a strange stateroom. Things left out. Nothing nailed down."

"No need for that on an elemental ship."

He curls the black-and-silver bracelet in his fingers and drops his hand into his lap.

"What will you do now?" he asks. "Will you forget her too?"

Mirabella turns to her wall as though she can see through it to the tossing ocean outside. As she always does, she feels the elements all around her. The lightning she could crackle through the clear sky. The wind that would scream for her. The soft hum of the flame atop her candle. She could reach out with her gift and use the sea like her fist. Topple the ship and press it with waves until it cracked. All the elementals on board could not stop her.

But Billy is there, whom Arsinoe loved. And somewhere is Jules, who is still being hunted. And Kat. She must not forget about Kat.

Still so much work to be done.

"I will not forget her if you stay and help me to remember," Mirabella says. "If you stay and help me to avenge her."

"Stay," he says.

"Yes. And rule with me, for her."

They regard each other in the quiet, dim light. He seems as surprised to hear it as she is surprised to ask. Since she was a child, Luca tried to convince her that she was an important queen. It was a lesson she neither believed nor wanted. But she believes it now.

"You would choose me as your king," he says.

"King-consort," she corrects him. "But yes."

"Is that what she would want?"

"I do not know. But we must marry someone. And the ones we would have . . . we cannot have."

Billy stares at her hard.

"So we are a good match." Then he shakes his head. "I can't do this. So soon after. It feels wrong."

"You want to avenge her, do you not? Or would you give up now and go back to the mainland? Will you go and pay court to Katharine, her murderer?"

"No," Billy barks, and his expression turns dark. "Never."

"Then stay and be a part of it." Mirabella holds out her hand. She needs him to say yes. She suddenly cannot bear the thought of him leaving. He—the only suitor who loved her sister—he must be king.

"I wanted her to have everything," he says, staring at her hand. "I wanted to have everything with her." Mirabella waits.

She lets him wipe his eyes and take his deep breaths. Billy Chatworth has a good heart. He is smart, and strong, and loyal.

"Will we seal this bargain with a handshake, then?" he asks.

"Is that how it is done on the mainland?"

"Only between men of honor," he says, and slides his hand into hers.

It is not the first time they have touched. But this touch is charged with the knowledge that one day they will exchange much more than a handshake. Billy's fingers slip out of hers, and he looks away, guilty. But Arsinoe and Joseph are not there to judge.

"So what now?" he asks.

"Now we take the fight to Katharine."

The ship reaches port in Rolanth not long after, and Bree and Elizabeth come to take Mirabella above. They are surprised to find Billy already there, fastening her light summer cape about her shoulders.

"You're wearing all black," Elizabeth says to him.

"Black is the color of mourning where I come from."

"Well, here it is the color of queens," Bree says. She unties the gauzy crimson scarf at her throat and reties it onto his. "There. For your Arsinoe."

He touches it and looks at Mirabella.

"Or should I be in all black? For you?" he asks, but she shakes her head.

"No," Mirabella says. "That is fitting."

Bree and Elizabeth exchange a glance. Not even they know about the betrothal agreement. Word would spread too fast, and Mirabella did not want Luca's questions, or Sara's worries.

Mirabella and Billy step up onto the deck together to face the massive crowd gathered at the Rolanth docks. All around the port, candles burn in the proud, white buildings, and the people are dressed in black and crimson to mourn a queen. Their eyes are somber and chins high. The only sound is the cawing of seabirds fighting over fish scraps.

Sara and Luca stand on the deck already, but Mirabella walks quickly past them, tugging Billy behind her before either has a chance to speak. This is her crowd. Her moment. She opens her mouth with every eye upon her.

"No doubt you have heard what happened in Wolf Spring," she says, loudly. "The death of my sister, the naturalist Queen Arsinoe, at the hands of the poisoner Queen Katharine." She pauses to let the grumbling build, the disdainful whispers about the poisoners. "Now she thinks to come to Rolanth for the festival of the Reaping Moon. To have her triumph before all of you."

The people start to shout, and she lets them, talking louder over the tops of their furrowed brows and shaking fists.

"She thinks to parade into our city—*my* city—and kill me as if it is sport. But she will not!"

Mirabella feels the whisper of robes at her shoulder, and Luca's calm voice cuts through the noise.

"Mira," she says. "What are you up to?"

Mirabella reaches back and takes Billy by the hand.

"Today I choose my king-consort! And he chooses me, uniting Wolf Spring and Rolanth under one crown!

"And today I challenge Queen Katharine to a duel!" she shouts. "A duel in Indrid Down! I would have you join me there, and we will put an end to this poisoner at last!"

Her people cheer. She raises Billy's hand in hers, and the people cheer louder. This is what they have wanted. To see their chosen queen rise up and seize her throne.

"Mirabella," Luca says. "This is not wise."

"Perhaps not, but it is done," says Mirabella. "Katharine thinks she will celebrate the Reaping Moon here. But by the time the Reaping Moon comes, she will already be dead."

WOLF SPRING

*J*oseph wrings his rag out in his soap bucket and wrinkles his nose. Someone has thrown eggs against the windows of Gillespie's Bookshop. A whole clutch of them it seems. And in the midday heat, the sticky, running yolks have already started to smell.

Joseph starts at the top and wipes down, the cloth and water not doing much but smearing the whole mess together. He should have brought a brush. And more buckets.

"Such a waste of good eggs."

Joseph looks up and sees Madge, hawker of the best fried clams in the market, reflected in the window, a basket covered in blue cloth hooked over her arm. He nods to her, and her wizened eyes squint in disgust.

"If they had any brains in their head," she says, "they'd have used rotten eggs. Then the smell'd be bad enough to have you throwing up on your own shoes."

"Do you know who it was?"

"Could have been anybody."

Joseph dunks his rag again and goes back to cleaning. It could have been anybody. Barely a week has passed since Jules disappeared with Arsinoe's body. Since the town learned about her legion curse. But how quickly they have turned on her. Her and everyone who loves her.

"He might not have even heard the eggs," Madge says, her eyes on the black cloth Luke hung up inside to cover the windows. Black and crimson, for his queen. "It's not like he's peeked out here or left that house since it happened. He hasn't even left his bed except to piss."

"How would you know?" Joseph asks, and Madge flips back the cloth over her basket to reveal fried oysters and fresh baked bread. A little bottle of ale.

"Not up except to piss, I said, so who do you think's been feeding him?"

Joseph smiles at the basket. Good old Madge.

"Maybe you shouldn't," he says. "They'll see. My family's had boats pulled out of slips at night, people too cowardly to revoke business face-to-face. They might stop coming to your stand."

"Let them. Who needs them." She pauses and sneers over her shoulder at anyone who might be watching. "The cursed deserve compassion. Understanding. Not to be pecked to death like a chicken with a dark spot." She points a finger at the smearing of eggs. "And not the sentence the Council's going to give her when she returns."

Joseph scrapes eggshell from the window and says nothing. After a moment, Madge squeezes his shoulder and steps past him into the shop, quieting the cheerful brass bell with one hand.

It takes him nearly two hours to scrub the mess from the windows. When he is finished, his rag is ruined, mostly slime, and the water in his bucket is foul-smelling sludge. No matter how many times he rinses it, Gillespie's will still smell slightly on very hot days. But it is better.

Joseph is stretching the knots out of his back and shoulders when a pretty black crow lands beside his bucket and peers inside.

"Aria," he says, and she caws.

He looks around for Madrigal and finds her walking calmly toward him from the square. Her white shirtsleeves are rolled against the heat, and her black skirt is tied with a crimson sash.

"Still no word from Jules?" he asks, even though he knows the answer.

"Nothing."

"I thought she would be back by now."

Madrigal shrugs.

"Digging a grave or building a pyre takes time," she says. "Our Jules is all right. She'll come back when it's done."

"And what if it isn't done? What if Arsinoe is alive?"

"The Arrons took Braddock. Arsinoe never would have let them if she were alive. And they found her blood. Right where

Queen Katharine said they would."

"I didn't say she wasn't shot," Joseph says, trying to explain without having to tell Madrigal the truth about Arsinoe's poisoner gift. "I just don't know where Jules would go. If she needed someplace safe."

"There's nowhere Jules feels safe," says Madrigal. "Not since the Ascension started. Or maybe ever. She's always been watchful. Ready. That was the war gift, even then." Madrigal takes a breath, and her face falls. "Only some*ones* have ever made Jules feel safe. You used to, Joseph. And my sister, Caragh."

"Caragh," Joseph whispers, and Madrigal's eyes brighten as she realizes what he means.

"The Black Cottage. But that's so far."

"You know our Jules. She would have tried."

Flustered, Joseph picks up his bucket and sloshes filth across his shoes. He feels like a fool for not thinking of the cottage before. He wants to run for it immediately, so sure that he will find her there.

"We have to be careful," Madrigal says. "The Council has spies here now. They will be watching. We have to wait for cover of dark."

GREAVESDRAKE MANOR

❖

*T*he Arrons hold a grand party at Greavesdrake Manor in honor of Katharine's victory. Small celebrations along the road from Wolf Spring were not enough. Nor was the parade back into the capital, with Katharine riding point before the revived and roaring bear.

"The beast was such a spectacle," Renata Hargrove comments to several gathered guests. "Thrashing against the ropes and swinging its head back and forth. Even though it had just been poisoned and badly bled!"

"Where is it now?"

"Caged in the courtyard of the Volroy. I can barely look at it without shivering."

"Wait until I parade it into Rolanth for the Reaping Moon," Katharine says. She reaches for a flute of champagne and does not bother to sniff for toxin before draining nearly half. "Poor Mirabella will probably faint."

Nicolas slips his hand around Katharine's waist and pulls her onto the dance floor. He holds her very close and whispers things that make her heart pound. And Pietyr watches from their table, clenching his jaw so hard his face looks like it is about to shatter.

"Why do you look at him?" Nicolas asks.

"At who?"

"At Pietyr Renard. There has been something between the two of you. I can see it in the way he watches us."

"If there was before, it is over now." But even as she says so, Katharine's eyes flicker toward Pietyr. Nicolas is handsome. He is bold, and he wants her. But he has not replaced Pietyr, and she fears bitterly that he never will.

"Send him away," Nicolas whispers.

"No."

"Send him away," he says again. "Soon I will be in your bed, and I don't want to look over my shoulder and find him standing there."

Katharine pulls back. She gazes at him coolly. It was a request. But it sounded like an order.

"Pietyr will stay as long as he likes," she says. "He is an Arron. He is family."

Nicolas shrugs, and his voice returns to its normal softness.

"As you wish. But will he take part in the Hunt of the Stags?"

"He may."

"And will he try to poison me there? Cut me with a poisoned blade?"

"Will you try to put your knife in his back?" Katharine counters, but Nicolas only laughs.

"Of course not, my sweet," he says. "When I kill a man, I look into his eyes."

Katharine forces a smile. Of course he is joking. He must be. No one must ever be allowed to harm Pietyr. No one but her.

Something across the room catches Nicolas's attention, and he steps away.

"One moment, Queen Katharine. I have a gift for you, and it has just arrived." He excuses himself and cuts through the guests toward the main doors, where Natalia's butler, Edmund, is waiting.

Pietyr approaches her from behind.

"He leaves you in the middle of a song?"

"He says he has a gift for me."

He turns her into his arms, and they begin to dance. It is easier and more natural feeling than with Nicolas. She and Pietyr are matched. When she looks into his eyes, she sees herself. Her better self reflected back at her.

"Whatever gift it is, it will not be worthy of you. He does not know how to treat a poisoner queen."

Nicolas returns, with Edmund following and carrying a silver tray. A vase at its center holds a small bundle of greens capped with tiny white blossoms, and along the outside edge several cups stand filled with a white liquid.

Nicolas leads them off the dance floor to Natalia's table, where Natalia sits talking with Genevieve, their brother

Antonin, Cousin Lucian, and other members of the Black Council.

"If you will permit me," he says, and they look up. "I have brought a gift, in honor of Queen Katharine's victory." He sets a glass before every poisoner at the table, even shoving a cup into Pietyr's hand, before serving Natalia and Katharine last. "I hope you don't mind my use of your staff, but . . . I wanted it to be a surprise."

Natalia looks at the plants in the vase.

"White snakeroot," she says.

"I don't believe you have it here," says Nicolas.

"We do not." She adjusts her heavy black mamba as its drugged head slides down her arm. "But I know it well. Grazing on as little as a small bundle can toxify an entire mother cow, rendering the meat, and the milk, completely poisonous."

"Serving a poison known to cause milk-sickness in a glass of milk," Pietyr says, and sniffs his glass. "You are quite a student, Nicolas. Soon you will be an expert in it."

"Renard," Nicolas replies, "what talent you have for making a compliment sound like a threat."

Katharine glances between them, and Natalia lifts her milk, knowing as usual when to diffuse a situation.

"A truly exotic poison," she says. "A fine gift. We will savor it, slowly." Her eyes find Katharine's. Slowly and in a minute amount. Katharine has been exposed to white snakeroot only two or three times.

Katharine raises her glass and drains it. She wipes her lips with the back of her hand and listens to the gasps.

Natalia's eyes tremble above the rim of her cup, but she sips. "You will be drunk on that, Queen Katharine," she says. "It is too potent. You should retire now to your rooms."

But Katharine is not brought to her rooms. She is brought into Natalia's study. By the time she reaches it, the poison is already breaking into her body. She barely has time to remove Sweetheart from her wrist and hand her off to Pietyr before she falls to the rug.

The convulsions are violent. Painful. Her teeth clench, and she bites her tongue. The blood tastes of the poisoned milk.

She listens to the fear in Natalia's and Pietyr's voices as they scurry to invoke the other side of their gift, the healer's side, combing their memories over old lessons. Remedies. Antidotes. Bottles rattle on Natalia's shelves as she fingers through them. Drawers squeak open and slam shut.

"Put your hand down her throat," Natalia orders. "Make her void her stomach."

Pietyr kneels at her head. He tries.

"I cannot get past her teeth!"

"Katharine!" Natalia looms over her. Her only mother, and her face is full of fear. "Kat, throw it up now!"

The convulsions ease, and she relaxes, though the pain remains. It feels as though someone has reached through her ribs to squeeze her heart.

Pietyr gathers her into his lap. He kisses her forehead and pushes damp black hair from her cheeks.

"Katharine, please," he whispers. "You will kill yourself if you keep on this way."

Katharine's head swivels loosely on her neck. When she speaks, her voice is rasping and strange, hardly her own.

"Do not be ridiculous, boy. You cannot kill what is already dead."

THE BLACK COTTAGE

※

When Arsinoe wakes, her first sight is Jules and Camden sharing a chair. She smiles weakly and blinks against the brightness, every muscle in her body groaning and stiff. But she is warm, and alive, and the bed she is in would be comfortable were it not for the throbbing sewn-up hole in her back. She has no idea where they are, but there is something very familiar about this room.

"Jules?"

"Arsinoe!" Jules and Camden jump up from the chair. Camden leaps onto her feet, purring, her tail winging back and forth.

"Water," Arsinoe croaks, and swallows for what feels like forever after Jules pours her a cup. Her mouth tastes terrible. Like old blood.

"Aunt Caragh!" Jules shouts. "Willa! She's awake!"

"Willa?" Arsinoe rubs her eyes. She knows where they are now. The Black Cottage, where she was born.

259

Caragh walks into the room with Juniper, her dark brown hound, and immediately comes to kiss Arsinoe on the cheek. Arsinoe can only stare. Then old Willa pushes Caragh out of the way to press the back of her hand against Arsinoe's forehead.

"No fever," Willa says. "Your luck is holding."

"She has more luck than anyone I've ever heard of," Jules says. "How many times have you almost died? Three? Four?"

"Try ten or eleven." Arsinoe pushes up off her pillow. Caragh and Jules inhale, but Willa quickly stuffs another behind her back.

"Let her sit up," she says gruffly. "It is good for her lungs. And her poisoner gift will let her heal faster than you would."

"Poisoner gift," Arsinoe says. "My secret's less of a secret."

"She already knew," says Jules.

Arsinoe reaches out and strokes Juniper's brown head. Looking into the dog's sweet, dark eyes, she almost wants to cry. She has missed them so much.

"You must be surprised to be here," says Caragh.

"I'm surprised to be anywhere." She pauses as she remembers the Queens' Hunt. The vicious look on Katharine's face. "Braddock?"

Jules shakes her head.

"I don't know, Arsinoe. We had to run so fast. . . ." She says no more, but Arsinoe knows that the poisoners would not have left the bear alive. They could not have, as angry as he was. Poor Braddock. She had been a fool to think she could protect him.

"Billy," she says suddenly. "He must think I'm dead. Everyone must."

"Everyone does," says Jules. "Or at least no one has come looking."

"I am going out for more yarrow." Willa trudges around the bed and heads for the door. "And now that she is awake, there are vegetables that need picking. I have not forgotten what it took to feed her when she was a child. I can only imagine what she will eat now. Come, Caragh."

Caragh nods. But before she goes, she touches Arsinoe's scarred cheek.

"I'm sorry you took an arrow to the back," she says. "But I'm still glad to see you."

She smiles, closed lipped and almost grim as she rolls up her sleeves. Nothing about Caragh is free and easy like her sister, Madrigal. But there is more in a single gesture than a dozen of Madrigal's embraces.

"The way she looks at me," Arsinoe says when she and Jules are alone, "it's like she doesn't see any scars at all."

"She hasn't changed," Jules says. "Not in that way, anyhow."

"In what way, then?"

Jules leans her head back.

"It's just strange to see her here. So calm. Like she's at home. I know, she is at home, but—"

"I know what you mean," says Arsinoe. "I want her home again, too."

Jules grasps the tip of Camden's tail and rubs the fur until

Camden swats at her. "Tell me what happened. I only remember being shot in the back. And then you, pulling me into the saddle."

"I used the war gift," Jules replies. "I pushed Katharine right through the air. She must've rolled three times."

"Wish I could've seen that."

"I don't know how I did it. The curse is bound. The war gift isn't that strong. I just . . . did it. Because I had to."

"Could you do it again?" Arsinoe asks.

"Not for all the cakes in Luke's oven."

Arsinoe almost asks how Jules feels. If the curse is taking its toll on her mind. But she does not. Jules is fine. Safe. The question would only add to her worry.

"Jules." Arsinoe squints one eye. "When I was drifting in and out . . . did I confess to you that I used low magic on you and Joseph?"

"You did."

"Did I tell you how sorry I am? How I didn't know what my low magic could do?"

"You did. And it doesn't matter. We'll never really know whether it was your magic, or Mirabella's beauty, or Joseph being half-dead and easily aroused."

Arsinoe chuckles.

"Besides. I've forgiven him."

"Truly?"

"Truly." Jules says, and nods.

Camden's ears prick.

"What is it?" Arsinoe asks. They listen. Hoofbeats, from the direction of the mountains. Jules springs for the window. If it is riders from the Black Council, there is no time to run.

Arsinoe throws back her quilt and winces as she dangles her leg over the side of the bed.

Jules turns and frowns.

"Arsinoe, you dolt! Stay in bed!"

"Dolt? What a thing to say when I've almost died."

But Jules is no longer listening. Her eyes widen, her knuckles white as she grips onto the curtains.

"Stay there," she says, and bolts for the door. "It's Joseph!"

"Joseph? Camden, stay and help me!"

But the cat scrambles off the bed and dashes after Jules, as excited to see him as she is.

"Stupid, love-sick cat," Arsinoe grumbles. She uses the bedside table to brace and reaches for the arm of the chair. Somehow she manages to get to the window and holds fast to the sash.

Just past the cottage steps, Jules and Joseph have their arms wrapped around each other. His reins are still looped over his elbow, so Jules probably dragged him bodily off his horse. Madrigal is there too, sitting very upright, staring directly at Caragh.

Arsinoe turns and limps out of the room, sliding against the wall as she goes down the hallway. When she gets to the door, Joseph is so buried in Jules that at first he does not even see her. But when he does, he shouts.

"Arsinoe!"

"Arsinoe." Madrigal's mouth hangs open, and Arsinoe nods to her before Joseph gently scoops her into his arms, squeezing a bit too tightly.

"Careful," she says. "I really was shot by a crossbow."

He kisses her cheek and turns to Jules.

"You did it, Jules. You saved her."

"Yes, she is alive." Willa steps up onto the porch, carrying two plucked chickens. "And so popular. You are all welcome at our table tonight. But tomorrow you go. Contrary to its size, the Black Cottage was not intended to house guests."

GREAVESDRAKE MANOR

*G*enevieve lies stretched across the silk brocade chaise in Natalia's study, eating figs glazed in sugar and cantarella. Ever since Midsummer, it is as though she is on a great holiday, humming and buying lavish gowns and dresses from her favorite shops in the capital. She is acting as if killing Arsinoe has won them the crown, and it is beginning to get on Natalia's nerves.

"Why are you not at the Volroy, sister?" Natalia asks.

"I am not needed today," Genevieve replies. "They are discussing a request from Rolanth for funds to restore the Vaulted Theatre."

"You should be there to advise."

"They already know what I would advise. Our eyes in Rolanth say they are overextended in renovating the central district. They will bankrupt themselves and ask the crown to bail them out." She eats another fig and licks poison from her fingers. "Only Lucian Marlowe will argue their side. Saying that the crown's coffers are for all queens, not just ours. Can you imagine?"

Natalia stares past Genevieve through the windows that overlook the drive. Katharine is somewhere out there, riding the bridle paths with her suitor and Pietyr. She alone deserves a moment to celebrate. Not the Council. They must keep working in preparation for the journey to Rolanth at the Reaping Moon.

"If I were to die," Natalia says suddenly, "you would be the head of the family."

Genevieve puts down her figs.

"Sister? Are you unwell?"

"I am fine." Natalia walks to the window, hoping to catch a glimpse of Katharine on horseback. She has gifted her a flashy new stallion, all black, with long, lean legs and a smooth stride. He will not replace Half Moon, but she hopes that they will get along.

"Then what are you thinking of?"

Genevieve rises to a seated position and sets her sticky plate to one side.

"I suppose I am thinking of our mother," Natalia replies. "And what she would say if she were alive to see us now."

"Mother," Genevieve says, and shudders.

Yes. Mother was terrifying. She held the Council, and Queen Camille, in a clenched fist. When she controlled the Arrons, the whole island feared them. The only thing the Arrons had to fear was her.

Natalia, though she has tried, has never been her mother's match. And Genevieve is even less so. Genevieve inherited all their mother's cruelty but none of her initiative, and so she is cutthroat but unreliable. She never knows where to strike.

"And what would mother say?" Genevieve wonders aloud.

Natalia crosses her arms.

"She would certainly say that we are horrible breeders. No children for me and none for you. Only a boy for Christophe."

"But Antonin has two girls and will have more."

Genevieve says nothing of children for herself. She has never shown much romantic inclination, and of the lovers she has had, those that lasted the longest were women. As for Natalia, the Goddess sent her Katharine, and she is more than enough.

She smiles, watching Katharine and Pietyr ride side by side out of the trees. The new stallion rises up on his hind legs when Katharine tries to slow him. She looks so delicate on his massive back, but soon she has him prancing docilely in a circle.

Natalia sighs.

"Enough of this. Has there been any word of the Milone girl? Any word of Arsinoe's body?"

"None. And no one expects any. The naturalist knows her woods. If she hides the corpse away or buries it, no one will find it except for the bugs." Genevieve raises an eyebrow. "It is the Milone girl who is the real problem. So strong and legion cursed? And with the war gift of all things. Something must be done."

"Something will be done," Natalia says. "But not yet. The

legion curse is an abomination. It is my guess that the temple will take care of her for us. Which will give us a chance to keep our hands clean with Wolf Spring."

Natalia presses her forefingers to the bridge of her nose.

"You will not be able to do this for much longer, sister," Genevieve says.

"Do what?"

"Hide away in your hilltop manor. Soon, Katharine will be living in the east tower with her king-consort, and you will have no more excuses to avoid your Council seat."

"Do not remind me." Natalia narrows her eyes at a rider approaching up the long, tree-lined drive. A messenger. Riding fast. Katharine intercepts the letter, and tears it open. Natalia tenses. She rushes from the room when Katharine begins to scream.

Katharine pats her new stallion's neck. Together they led Pietyr and Nicolas on a merry chase through the woods, and the stallion does not want it to end. But she keeps her hands firm on the reins until he quiets.

"Shall we go in for tea?" she asks the boys. "And later to the city, to buy sardines to feed my poor sister's bear?"

"I do not like you so near that thing," Pietyr says, and she rolls her eyes. During the parade back to the city, Pietyr flinched every time it fought against its ropes. "It is not happy with you, Kat, for what you did to its mistress."

"Truly, Pietyr, I thought the same at first. But I have fed the bear many times since, and whatever anger it had is gone. It is as if it does not care at all."

"Perhaps it's no longer a familiar, now that she is dead," Nicolas adds. "In any case, I enjoy seeing it, Queen Katharine. And perhaps hunting it, at this year's Beltane Festival?"

She smiles, a little nervously. "Perhaps."

Hoofbeats make them pause. They stop their mounts and wait for the messenger to canter up the drive.

"Good afternoon, Queen Katharine," the girl says, breathless from her ride. She bows as deep as she can in the saddle. "I have a message for Mistress Arron."

"I will take it." Katharine holds out a gloved hand, and the messenger gives it over. She salutes them before riding away.

Katharine breaks the Black Council's wax seal and opens the letter. Another letter is folded inside and falls out onto the ground. She dismounts to collect it, and Pietyr takes her stallion's reins. When she turns the letter over, it reveals the blue-and-black wax of Rolanth. Of her sister Mirabella.

Katharine reads it and starts to scream.

"Kat!" Pietyr quickly dismounts. "Kat, what is it?"

She crumples the letter from Rolanth in her fist. It was not addressed to her. It was not addressed to anyone. It was a notice, found tacked to the gates of the Volroy.

Pietyr takes her by the shoulders, but she breaks free, screaming so loud she spooks the horses, and her new stallion bolts for the safety of the stables. Nicolas struggles to keep his mare still, his expression confused.

"Katharine!" she hears Natalia calling, running to her across the courtyard. "Kat! Are you all right?"

"How many of these are there?" Katharine shouts. She stalks toward Natalia and Genevieve and holds up the crumpled paper in her fist. "How many? You must have known! When were you going to tell me?"

"Tell you what?" Genevieve squeaks as Natalia pries the letter from Katharine's fingers and reads.

"It is a challenge," Natalia says. "Mirabella has challenged Katharine to a duel, to be held at the great arena in Indrid Down."

"What?" Pietyr asks. "When?"

"At the next full moon."

Genevieve moans. That is less than two weeks away.

Natalia grabs for the accompanying letter from the Council.

"It says they are everywhere," Katharine says. "Tacked to every board and signpost in Indrid Down."

"How did she manage it?" Genevieve asks shrilly. "It must have taken a small army to pull off such a stunt!"

"Then she must have used a small army," Natalia replies.

Katharine grits her teeth. She recites the challenge from memory in a bitter voice.

"A duel. To be held the day of July's full moon, in the arena in our great capital of Indrid Down. All are welcome to bear witness to the end of the Ascension and the beginning of a new elemental reign . . . !'" Katharine grabs at her hair and shrieks, tearing it loose of its bun. "Who has seen these?"

"There is no way to know," says Natalia. "But if it were me, I would dispatch riders to every corner. I would make sure that the entire island hears of the challenge."

"Must everyone be here to witness this?" Genevieve hisses. She throws her hand up at Pietyr's mare, who has fled only a few paces away. "Even the horses? Shall I call the kitchen staff and the maids?"

"This is not the way." Katharine begins to pace, biting at her nails and muttering to herself. "It is not what we planned. Not what we hoped. We would see her disgraced in her own city." She spins angrily and points to the letter. "'All are welcome to bear witness.' Bear! Is that some slight against me and the way I dispatched Arsinoe?"

"If it is, I do not see how."

Katharine takes a deep breath. She smooths her mussed hair. Mirabella will not get away with this. The supreme brat will live only long enough to regret ever coming to the capital.

"Kat," Pietyr says gently, "a triumph is still a triumph, whether in Rolanth or Indrid Down. This will be even more gratifying in many ways, as it will be before all of those in the city who have watched you grow from a child. Mirabella's boldness will only make it easier. And sweeter when she loses."

Katharine pauses. Then she exhales, and the shoulders of everyone around her relax slightly.

"Perhaps you are right. Either way, she will be dead. Here we can arrange things the way we like. And I will not have to disturb the bear by making him travel." She grabs the notice from Natalia and tears it down the center, smiling sweetly as the halves float to the gravel drive. "I will hold a ball, the night before. To welcome her."

"Yes," says Natalia. "That is a fine idea."

Katharine nods, and blinks at them. They look terrified.

"Natalia, I am so sorry! I did not mean to carry on so!"

"It is all right, Kat. Though you must control your temper. What has come over you? You are behaving like an elemental."

Katharine lowers her head. She curtsies to Natalia and walks alone toward the house. But it is not long before Pietyr catches up to her.

"A duel," he says. "Katharine. What will we do? I cannot believe that the temple would allow it! The risk is too great, on both sides."

"She thinks she can win," Katharine says as they enter the manor, cool darkness enveloping them and making her skin prickle. "That the Goddess is on her side." She reaches for belladonna berries piled high in a gold bowl on a foyer table and stuffs a handful into her mouth.

"She *may* win," Pietyr cautions. "In the open space of the arena, she will have the advantage."

"She will have no advantage."

"Katharine. That is plenty of berries." He takes her arm, but she wrenches away and eats still more, the juices running down her chin. "Kat, you will sicken!"

Katharine laughs.

"And what if Mirabella is right?" Pietyr asks. "What if the Goddess is on her side?"

Katharine turns on him, grinning with teeth full of poison, and for a moment her vision blacks out and makes his face a void, dark and bottomless as the pit of the Breccia Domain.

"It does not matter. *They* are on mine."

ROLANTH

*T*he notice that Bree prepared in swirling black ink challenging Katharine to a duel in the Indrid Down Arena is absolutely perfect. It bears Mirabella's signature, re-created at the printer's. But she made sure to send the original to tack to the Volroy gates.

"They are everywhere?" Mirabella asks.

"Everywhere," Bree replies. "From here to Bastian City and even northwest to Sunpool."

"And to Wolf Spring?"

"Of course."

"Good," Mirabella says. "I would have Arsinoe's family there to see the poisoner fall." She chuckles slightly.

"You are jovial?"

"Only when I imagine Katharine's face when she reads this," Mirabella says, but her smile does not last. It is easy to think of killing Katharine when she is angry. But when the anger fades . . . she must not let the anger fade.

Beside them, Elizabeth worries at the stump of her left wrist.

"Are you all right, Elizabeth?" Mirabella asks. "Does it still pain you?"

"Not often," Elizabeth replies. She looks down at the skin, pulled taut over the nub of bone. The scars from the stitches have faded to a deep pink. "I'm only wondering about the tattooed bracelet. It will feel strange to adorn an eyesore such as this."

Elizabeth turns her wrists over, toying with her one bracelet of ribbon and beads. Soon they will perform the ritual and ink the black bands into her skin, and she will be a full priestess, belonging to the temple forever.

"Your arm is not ugly, Elizabeth," Bree says hotly. "It was an ugly thing that was done to you."

"When do they want to hold the ceremony?" Mirabella asks.

"As soon as I will consent. It's past time. . . . I've been an initiate for almost three years."

"And will you do it?" asks Bree. "You should not. You should throw off those robes and stay with us. You will always be welcome at Westwood House." Bree's voice is forceful. Determined. She does not understand why Elizabeth stays after what they did to her. Bree is not suited to serve like Elizabeth is.

"I haven't decided," Elizabeth says. "I wouldn't mind staying an initiate for a little while longer. Perhaps a few years. Perhaps forever. Then I could keep Pepper, and still have the choice to stay or go."

Mirabella looks ahead to their white-robed escort. They have drifted quite a distance away, but she is sure they are still listening. She squeezes Elizabeth's elbow.

"You will tell us? So we can be there?"

Elizabeth nods, and Mirabella kisses both her friends on the cheeks before parting company to go and see Luca.

She finds the High Priestess in her rooms high in the temple, soaking up a spilled cup of tea with one of her silk pillows.

"Perhaps a towel?" Mirabella suggests, and Luca startles.

"Mira, you frightened me." She holds up the soiled pillow and makes a regretful face, then drops it beside her desk, ruined. "You have just missed Rho."

"Oh," Mirabella raises her brows, unable to feign disappointment. "Are the two of you hatching plans again?"

"I do not know what you mean."

"Of course you do. I have heard the whispers about Beltane. Your idea to sacrifice my sisters into the fires and make me a White-Handed Queen." She pauses to watch Luca try to maintain a passive expression. "Your priestesses forget I have ears. They grow careless when they speak. But with all of your scheming, I cannot believe that you disapprove of the duel."

"Whether or not I disapprove does not matter. You announced it before the city."

"You think we should let her come to Rolanth?"

"At least we would have the advantage of having her attack be here, at home, where she would feel unfamiliar and off balance."

"Yes," says Mirabella. "And how did that work for Arsinoe?

Coming here is what Katharine wants. She wants me cut down in Rolanth. Humiliated in front of my people. I was never her target in the Wolf Spring woods! It was always Arsinoe. It was always going to be Arsinoe."

Luca studies her quietly from beneath her white hood.

"Perhaps we have missed our chance," Luca says, "Once, you were the chosen queen. Now all is uncertain. Now our fortunes have reversed."

"A duel in the arena favors me," Mirabella presses. "Elemental queens have fared well before—"

Luca turns back to her spilled tea and pours again in the remains of the first cup. When she drinks, it drips onto her robes.

"I feel the Goddess's hand in this, Luca. You must trust in me."

"Her hand, perhaps," the High Priestess says softly. "But the Goddess is not always kind, Mira. We cannot know her will. Even in those moments when I have felt most close to her . . . that I thought I saw a hint of her plans . . ." She gestures with a trembling hand. "One moment it is clear and the next it is gone."

"Then how do we know we are doing the right thing?"

"We do not. We do our best, knowing that there is no choice and that she will have her way, in the end."

THE BLACK COTTAGE

***

Willa walks past Arsinoe on the way to the kitchen.

"Goose and onion pie tonight." Willa holds up a small yellow onion and chucks Arsinoe beneath the chin with it.

"Mmm," Arsinoe replies uncertainly. "Was that . . . one of my favorites?"

"You do not remember?"

"I don't." Arsinoe follows her through the sitting room, looking at the paintings and the furniture. It would not have changed much, but nothing feels familiar. "Mirabella remembers everything. If she were here, the sentimental goof would be hugging that chair."

"Even when she was a girl, Mirabella had far too much dignity to go about hugging chairs. Unlike you. How are you healing?"

Arsinoe follows her into the kitchen and rolls her shoulder.

The wound from the crossbow bolt has closed. Before long, it will be no more than a fresh, deep scar. She can feel the new dead spot forming in her back, like the dead spots in her face. Another wound, another ruin.

"I'm all right."

"Good. Then you can leave." Willa takes down a bowl filled with dough she prepared that morning, and Arsinoe snorts.

"Were you always this affectionate? Or did you put us on swaddle boards and hang us off doors?"

Willa scoffs.

"We have not swaddled queens in seven ages." Then she pauses in her kneading, and fixes Arsinoe with a sharp eye. "It isn't that I want you to go. I never imagined I would see you again, after the day they took you. But if the Black Council finds you here, they will have my old neck and Caragh's as well."

"Not for long," Arsinoe says. "Once Mirabella is crowned and replaces the Arrons on the Council with Westwoods, everything will change. They might even let Caragh go."

"Perhaps." Willa presses her lips together, but cannot quite hide her smile.

Arsinoe cocks her head.

"Is that what you want to happen? Why you did it? Why you switched us as babies?"

The old woman slaps the dough onto the counter and shakes flour down over it.

"What makes you think *I* was the one who switched you?"

"Who else?"

"Who else was here?" Willa asks. "The Queen. Your mother. I was only the Midwife, and the Midwife does as she is told."

"But why would she?"

"Do you wish she had not?" Willa looks at Arsinoe sharply. "And in any case, she did not say. I gather that the Arrons were not kind. And during her rule, I do not think she liked what she saw within the poisoner Council. Besides, in Mirabella she saw the queen to come, and the queen always knows what she has. So there was little harm in sabotaging the other two."

"Sabotaging the other two," Arsinoe repeats, and her lips twist wryly.

"Queen Camille was a sweet girl. But the only one who ever loved her was her king-consort. She was glad to leave. She was glad to have done with her duty."

"Hmph," Arsinoe says. "It should sting, hearing that. But it doesn't."

"It does not because you are a queen. You are not like other mothers or other daughters. You are not like other people."

Arsinoe takes up a knife and begins slicing onions. Seeing Willa work the dough has started to make her hungry.

"Did she go, then?" Arsinoe asks. "With her king-consort, to live happily off the island?"

"How should I know? Perhaps. It is what she wanted. Though they say that the weak ones do not live long after their triplets are born.

"A queen's life is glorious and short. Whether she rules or dies in her Ascension Year. This is the way things are. Being put out by it will not change it."

"The weak ones," Arsinoe says, and stabs a mushroom. "But Mirabella will be a queen who rules into her fiftieth year. She'll have her triplets and leave and die somewhere grand, an old woman."

"Don't crush me between your buttocks," Caragh says gruffly, and slaps the rump of one of the chestnut saddle horses that Joseph and Madrigal rode in on. He and the other horse have had to share a stall in the small stable, and the close quarters have made them pushy.

"You used to use your gift instead of your hands. Or have you lost it, being here so long?"

Caragh sets her jaw and looks up at her pretty sister.

"I've never used my gift for something as frivolous as cleaning a stall."

She opens the stall door and leaves, resting the pitchfork against the wall before moving down the line. She places a measure of grain into the black horse's bucket and strokes his nose.

"Frivolous," Madrigal says. She sucks her cheek indignantly. "No, I suppose you wouldn't. Frivolity is strictly my domain, is that it?"

"I didn't say that."

"Of course you didn't. You never say what you mean."

Caragh clenches her jaw. She looks back at the black horse and smells the savory scent of his breath as he chews the grain.

"I haven't seen a horse this well-bred in a long time. And those saddle horses, did you borrow them from Addie Lane? They aren't bad at all."

Madrigal puts her hands on her hips. She taps her foot. She has barely been at the cottage for a week and already she has climbed on Caragh's last nerve.

"What do you want, Madrigal?"

"To look after my daughter."

"That isn't what I meant. I meant right now. Is there something you want to say?" Her eyes drift down to Madrigal's belly. "If it's that you're pregnant, I can see that already."

Madrigal glances toward her waist. It is early yet, but on her slight frame it shows enough for Caragh to know.

"Jules must be glad to be a big sister," Caragh goes on. "I'm so proud to see her grown up strong and happy. And Joseph . . . He looks so much like Matthew. For a moment, I almost ran and jumped into his arms."

Madrigal swallows. She murmurs something under her breath.

"Maddie, speak up."

"Don't call me Maddie," Madrigal snaps.

But there is something that Madrigal wants to tell her. Some unpleasant thing, from the way she stands there, toeing annoying patterns into the dirt.

"The baby," Madrigal says. "It's Matthew's."

Caragh's fingers grip the stall door. Every horse in the barn stops eating and looks at her, even Willa's mean brown mule. Matthew. Her Matthew. But he is not her Matthew anymore.

"I just wanted to be the one to tell you," Madrigal says, her voice uncertain. "I didn't want Jules or Joseph to blurt it out." She steps closer, soft, hesitant steps in the dust and straw. "Caragh?"

"What?"

"Say something."

"What do you want me to say? That I've been waiting here like a fool, when I knew there was no hope in waiting? That things change out there, but nothing changes here? You don't need me to tell you those things. I'll leave here old and bent, like Willa. And you don't need my blessing if you want to live my life for me."

"That's not what I'm doing," Madrigal says as Caragh's brown hound starts to howl.

"Quiet. The howl means company. And company means you have to hide."

The old man and his pony cart take their time coming down the path to the Black Cottage. It is a good thing, for it gives Arsinoe plenty of time to get comfortable in her hiding spot, seated beneath a window. Peering out, she sees Jules and Joseph dart into the stables. Who knows where Madrigal is.

When old Worcester reaches the house, Willa helps him to unload his sacks of grain and jugs of wine, along with three or four wrapped parcels. They talk for what feels like an eternity before he finally turns his cart back down the path. Much of what they discussed seems to be about a letter he gave to her. She stands in the middle of the supplies and reads it again and again until Arsinoe loses her patience. She gets to her feet and throws up the sash.

"Willa! What is that?"

Willa walks the letter back into the cottage. The others emerge from the stable like squirrels from their burrows.

Arsinoe takes the letter and reads.

"What is it?" asks Jules as she comes inside.

"It's an announcement," Arsinoe says. "Mirabella is challenging Katharine to a duel."

"Is that wise?" Madrigal asks. "A hunt is a risk, but a duel is riskier still. A show of frontal assaults. Both could die."

"The Goddess will not allow both to die," says Willa.

"How do you know?" Joseph asks.

"Because in all our long history, she has never allowed all of her queens to die. And I should know. Half of our library here is volumes of queen history."

"But all of her queens *wouldn't be* dead," Jules says. "If both Mirabella and Katharine die in the duel, Arsinoe will still be alive."

Every eye turns to her, and Arsinoe steps back.

"Maybe that is the plan," Jules says. "The Goddess's plan."

But Willa waves her hand.

"No. Mirabella will be the Queen Crowned. Queen Camille

knew it. The entire island has known it, until recently. Arsinoe has been granted her life, a fugitive life in secret. Nothing more."

"You haven't seen how many times she's saved her," Joseph says. "And brought her back. Just to live as a fugitive? I don't believe it."

Arsinoe scoffs. They have all gone mad, looking at her like that. Eyes big as dinner plates and twice as sparkly.

She stares past them, at a large woven tapestry hanging on the wall. It depicts the Hunt of the Stags, the ritual performed by suitors during the Beltane of a crowning year. The tapestry shows young men with bared teeth and shining knives. One lies disemboweled in the foreground, and the stag they hunted has fallen onto its knees. There is so much blood, it is a wonder the weaver did not run out of red thread. And that could be Billy, bleeding to death on the sacred ground of Innisfuil.

"All these brutal traditions," Arsinoe says quietly.

"Arsinoe?" Madrigal asks.

For a long time, Arsinoe dreamed of a chance like this one. To run away. To disappear. But always the Goddess moved her about like a game piece, placing her where she wanted her. She even gave her Jules, legion-cursed Jules, who Luke had always said was put nearby for a reason. But what was that reason? To win her freedom? Or to win the crown?

Either way, Arsinoe is tired of wondering. She swallows hard and feels her scars, every one of them from her cheek to her ribs. From now on, she will do what she wants.

"We have to go to Indrid Down," she says.

"Yes," Jules says, and claps her hands. "Mirabella and Katharine will make their last stand, and when they fall, you will be there, waiting."

"No, Jules. Willa is right. Mirabella is the chosen queen. And I think I was spared so I could help her." She grasps Jules by the shoulders, crumpling the duel challenge in her fist. "I'm going to the capital, and I'm going to help Mirabella put down that poisoner queen."

THE QUEENS' DUEL

ROLANTH

§

$\mathcal{M}$irabella's coaches are outfitted with silver fastenings and black plumes. The blue elemental insignia flies on flags beside the queen's black ones. And there are white coaches too, white coaches pulled by white horses and filled with priestesses so that all of Indrid Down will know that the temple stands with her.

"Are you sure you would not rather go by sea?" Sara asks as they pack the last of Mirabella's things into trunks. "It would be safer."

"She would parade into my city," Mirabella says. "So I will parade into hers."

Sara holds up a gown.

"This, for the ball?"

Mirabella barely glances at it. It is some shiny, satin thing with a fitted bodice and wide straps.

"That is fine." She turns about the room. Her room at

Westwood House since she was taken from the Black Cottage. It is not bare; she has not overpacked. But it still feels emptied, like if she speaks too loud her voice will echo.

"And for the jewels?"

"Anything but black pearls," she says. "I have heard that Katharine favors black pearls, and I do not want us to look alike."

"You could never look alike," says Billy.

Mirabella and Sara turn. Billy stands just inside the door. Sara cocks an eyebrow at his crimson shirt. He should not wear it when they go to the capital, still mourning for a fallen queen when he has declared for Mirabella. But no one will ask him to take it off. And the crimson will win them more favor from the naturalists.

Sara curtsies and leaves to give them privacy.

"How much longer will the mourning last?" Billy asks.

"Not long," Mirabella replies.

Soon the candles and the crimson will be gone. The prayers said for Arsinoe at altars will cease. Vanquished queens are not spoken of past the Ascension Year. There is no hall in the Volroy that houses their portraits. No one even remembers their names.

"Are you ready?" she asks. "Do you have attire for the ball?"

"I do. Though I can't believe we're going to dance and feast with them the night before you kill her."

"The ball is nothing more than Katharine's way of regaining control. I set the duel, so she sets the ball. It is all quite transparent. And it will not work."

Billy holds up a long, rectangular box. "I brought something for you."

He opens it and takes out a choker of black gems cut into faceted ovals and set in silver. They sparkle as he turns them in the light, and she wonders how long ago he bought them, and if they were meant for someone else. But she will not ruin the moment by asking.

"Here," he says, and Mirabella holds up her hair to let him place them around her neck.

"They are beautiful."

"Far more beautiful than anything the poisoner has," he says. "They can dress that little witch up any way they like. But she'll still be a monster."

"Do not say that word," Mirabella cautions. "We do not say 'witch' here. No matter what we feel about Katharine, you must be careful when we are in the capital. I would have you be a popular king-consort among the people."

Billy grits his teeth.

"Of course. It's just what she did. . . ."

"I know."

"I hate her. Don't you? She took her from me. From us."

Billy's hand lingers on her shoulder, from fastening the choker, and Mirabella lays hers atop it.

"I met Katharine before Beltane," he says. "My father wanted me introduced to all of you, before the other suitors."

"You never came to me."

"I chose Arsinoe before I could. But it's the strangest thing. When I met Katharine, she seemed so sweet. Harmless, even. I actually pitied her. The girl I met was nothing like the one in Wolf Spring. But I suppose I only saw what she wanted me to see."

"I suppose," says Mirabella. "Billy, before we depart, I would have you pen a letter to precede us into the capital."

"A letter? Saying what?"

"Saying that you will be my king-consort and will not pay court to Katharine. Phrase it as meanly as you like. But I would have one more blow to her ego before she sees me at the ball."

INDRID DOWN

❧

*N*atalia and Genevieve walk briskly through the bustling streets of the capital after overseeing the improvements being made to the arena: repairs to the stands and extra risers built, a fresh coat of paint on the gallery rail, and all the vast competition ground tilled through and made soft, the tufts of long, hard grass and field stones removed by hand. It has been a long time since the arena was used for anything but fairs and carnivals. A long time since the island has seen a duel or even since it had a war queen who enjoyed watching battle sport.

"The hotels will run out of rooms," Genevieve grumbles. "There will be tents set up along the roadsides. People will sleep on the streets."

"Only for a few days. And while they are here, they will spend their money."

Up and down the main thoroughfare on High Street, shop

windows are filled with fresh displays of goods. Carts laden with golden smoked ducks and baskets of fruit travel down back alleys to be unloaded into storerooms. It is a chance for non-poisoner merchants to show their best, and they have been down at the Bardon Harbor docks since before dawn, fighting with the poisoner shops over the choice sea catch before it is laced with henbane and nightshade.

"They will spend money and make money," says Genevieve. "The elemental merchants will set up stalls to sell their paintings and weavings and glass trinkets."

Natalia watches her sister pout. After the duel is over, Genevieve is sure to be wearing an elemental jewel or two and parading about in a new silk scarf. Everyone knows that the finest ones come from Rolanth.

"May we stop for a bite to eat?" Genevieve asks, craning her neck toward her favorite cheese shop.

"We will take tea at the Highbern. Since we must go there anyway to finalize the ball." Natalia takes a high step over a gutter and tugs on Genevieve's sleeve to hurry her along. "Smile. We should not be seen with troubled frowns on our faces."

"But we are troubled," Genevieve says as she brightens her expression. "The duel is a disaster. They will be face-to-face, trapped there together until one lies dead. It will be just as if the Ascension were to end with them locked in the east tower. It is just what we have been trying to avoid!"

"Well, perhaps we did not need to. Kat is not the weak queen she once was. I do not know what has changed, but it is like she has woken up."

"You do know what has changed. Even if you will not tell me. You know what happened when she went missing after Beltane. You must."

"I do not."

"She is so strange now." Genevieve's eyes narrow. "With those knives she throws and that mad laugh that comes out of her sometimes. Eating so much poison . . . and practically enjoying the sickness that follows!"

"Do not speak of her like that. Kat is not strange."

"She is not your daughter either; she is a queen. So stop calling her 'Kat.'"

Natalia stops midstride, and clenches her fists. Were they not in the middle of a busy public street, she would strike her sister across the face.

Genevieve clears her throat and lowers her eyes.

"Forgive me. It is the strain of the duel."

Natalia resumes walking. They are not far now from the Highbern. She can see its flags rising above the other buildings ahead.

"Do not worry so much, Genevieve," Natalia says quietly. "Katharine was clever enough to give us the opportunity of a ball. Tomorrow night, Mirabella will be there amid food and crowds, and by the time it is over, she will be no threat in the duel."

"You intend to poison her?" Genevieve asks, hurrying to keep pace.

"Not to death. Just to weaken, so that Katharine will have an easy time of it in the arena. She will be able to slaughter her in front of the entire island, at her leisure."

"How will you manage that? Your sleight of hand is good, but they will not allow us near her. You will not be able to get close enough."

"I do not need to," Natalia says. "Why do you think I have maintained the alliance with Chatworth all this time? Why do you think he has insinuated himself into the Westwoods' trust?" She rolls her shoulders back. "He will do it."

"We cannot trust a mainlander with this! And what if old Luca has turned him?"

"Impossible. The temple is not rich enough. Mirabella thinks to charge into the capital like a thundercloud. But when I am through, she will not even be able to make it rain."

THE HIGHBERN HOTEL

───────────── ✦ ─────────────

The Highbern Hotel is a grand place, larger and more finely built than anything in Rolanth. The hotel's ceilings stretch high overhead, checkered in black and gold. The columns in the ballrooms are gilded and the chandelier is the biggest Mirabella has ever seen. In her rooms, they find large beds stuffed with down, the coverlets embroidered with gold and red thread.

"What a pleasant place to stay in," Mirabella muses. "Were I not here to kill or die."

Mirabella takes a seat beside her window and looks out across the rooftops. Indrid Down is very pretty, and the strong smells of the crowded city do not rise that high, so the breeze is fresh and warm. The Highbern is directly across from the west tower of the Volroy, separated only by a wide street and the long, hedge-lined courtyard of rosebushes and lilacs. Closer to the fortress, she can just make out the shape of a cage mostly obscured by topiary shrubs. Inside is a brown, motionless hill of fur. Arsinoe's bear. It survived after all and is now the prisoner of their poisoner sister. Well, that will end, too, after Katharine is dead. Though Mirabella does not quite know what she will do with the big familiar.

Someone knocks at the door that separates her room from the sitting room, and she tears her eyes away.

"Mirabella, come out now and keep your strength up," Billy says, his voice muffled through the wood. "I've brought a platter of food that required practically no cooking."

Practically no cooking. It really is a wonder that he has gotten no better at it. No better at all.

Mirabella joins him in the sitting room, where he has cut a loaf of his bread and spread it with butter. There are also some jarred apples and a wedge of blue-veined cheese.

"I miss your apron," she says, and he laughs.

They eat for a few moments in silence. It is quiet on the top floor, but downstairs must be loud with people preparing for the ball tomorrow night. Sara, Bree, and Elizabeth are there, and Luca with her gaggle of priestesses, intent on observing every move the Arrons make.

"Have you seen the bear?" Mirabella asks quietly.

"His name is Braddock," Billy replies, his voice grave. "And I have. I walked through the courtyard and snuck him some sugared walnuts from a street vendor."

"No one tried to stop you?"

"They don't even have a fence around the cage. I suppose

they don't think anyone would be stupid enough to stick their arms between the bars. Maybe even I shouldn't have."

"Do not be silly. He is still her familiar, even if she is gone. He remembers those she loved."

Billy's bite of bread stalls between his plate and his mouth. "Will we let him go after it's over?" he asks. "Back to the woods at Innisfuil, where she found him?"

"Is that what she would want?"

"I don't know. I think so. Or maybe she would want Jules to have him." Billy runs his hand roughly across his face.

Mirabella takes a deep breath and looks around the room. It is calm and elegant, the windows closed against the noisy streets and armed priestesses set in pairs in the hall.

"It will all be over soon," she says. "One sleepless night. Then the ball. And then the duel."

"And then you are queen," says Billy.

Mirabella quiets. Up to now, it has all been haste and resolve. Quickly mobilizing the priestesses and the Westwoods and thinking of ways to antagonize Katharine. But now she is here, with only hours to fill before their fate, and her certainty is beginning to fade. What was it Luca said about knowing the Goddess's will? Clear one moment and gone the next.

"Mirabella? Are you all right?"

"Not quite," she says.

"What?"

"After the duel, I will be the presumptive queen. I will not be crowned officially until Beltane in the spring. So you will have fall and a long winter to wait before you are a king."

Billy wipes at the corners of his mouth with a napkin. He would rather wait longer. Before she can be crowned, he may come to resent this bargain they struck.

"We are friends, are we not, Billy? And friendship in marriage is a strong foundation."

Hesitantly, he slides his hand across the table and turns it palm up. Equally hesitant, she places her hand atop it.

She feels no spark. No quickening of her pulse. Looking into his eyes is not like looking into Joseph's. She squeezes his hand.

"But I am not her," she says, and sighs. "I am not Arsinoe, and if come Beltane, you do not wish to take part in the Hunt of the Stags and do not wish to become king—"

He shakes her hand lightly. "Don't think of this now. There's plenty of time. Only . . . I didn't think there would still be a hunt. Since we've declared for each other."

"It will only be a formality. Nicolas Martel may still take part, and he may try to kill you and take the crown. But we will have priestesses on the hunt to guard you."

"Well, that's good, then," he says sarcastically. He turns toward the windows. "What is that sound? Sounds like chanting."

They go to the window and look down. A crowd has gathered, big enough to block the street between the Highbern and the Volroy, which is causing some shouting on both sides as carts try to make their way past. Those in the center stare up at her floor. Cursing her. Telling her to go back to Rolanth.

"Mira," Billy says. "You're smiling."

"Am I?" She gazes down and chuckles. "To hear Luca tell it, the whole island is sick of the poisoners, and I am the savior they wait for. What a tale."

"It is true, to some. To many."

She draws on her gift. Below, dark shadows form on the upturned faces of the crowd as her thunderclouds gather over the hotel. The people stop shouting. She cracks lightning through the air, and they duck and hold on to each other.

"What are you doing?" Billy asks.

"Nothing," she replies. "Only making sure that they know that the elemental queen is here."

GREAVESDRAKE MANOR

*P*ietyr glares out the window at Nicolas practicing his archery, this time from horseback. Every time Nicolas gallops past, Katharine can see Pietyr wishing for him to fall. And every time Nicolas shoots, she flinches, expecting the bolt to break through the window and pierce Pietyr's chest.

"There is something off about him, Katharine," Pietyr says. "And not just for a mainlander."

"Pietyr. Come away from the window."

"You should get rid of him. He will never be your king-consort anyway; you know Natalia intends to choose the Chatworth boy."

Katharine makes a face. Chatworth is with Mirabella now. Before that he was with Arsinoe.

"I do not know what she can be thinking," Katharine says. "What will that look like, to accept my sisters' cast-offs? And besides, I do not like him."

"But you like Nicolas?" And when Katharine does not answer, "That is ridiculous. You cannot like Nicolas."

At first, it was good fun to make Pietyr jealous. To make him suffer. He had it coming and worse, after all. But the joke is not a joke anymore. He seethes at Nicolas, and Nicolas's cool response unnerves her. The moment Nicolas gets a whiff of power, he will find a way to hurt Pietyr. Whether to humiliate him or kill him she is not sure, but she senses he is capable of either.

They are in the billiards room, but neither is focused enough to play. She shoots and listens to the balls clack together, not watching where they go. Instead she watches Pietyr pout. Even pouting, he is handsome.

"I do not like the ideas he puts into your head. He encourages you to be reckless!" Pietyr breaks away from the window and comes to roll the cue ball across the table, angrily stuffing it into a pocket.

"Perhaps it is you I should send away," she whispers. But he only scoffs and crosses his arms as if she cannot mean it. "Nicolas is a better match for me now, in many ways. Even better than you."

His eyes raise to hers.

"Kat. That is not true."

"Our goals are more aligned. We have similar minds. And if I decide to defy Natalia, he will make a strong king-consort." She inclines her head and tries to be kind. "It is not fair, this game that I have made you play. Thinking we could be together again. That there was hope for us." Once, she thought that she would keep Pietyr as her lover, no matter which suitor she married. But that is a dream from a long time ago and dreamed by a different Katharine.

"Pietyr, I want you to go."

"Go?" he asks. "Go where?"

"I do not care. Away from here. Back to the country. But you must go and go now."

His bright blue eyes swim with something like regret. Will he weep? If he weeps, she will not have the heart to send him off. She will take him in her arms instead.

"Why are you saying this?"

When she does not respond, he shakes his head adamantly.

"I cannot go now. You are to fight a duel in two days. You do not know what you are saying. This Ascension . . . it has made you volatile. When you return to your senses, you will thank me for staying."

He talks to her as if she is a child, and whispers break into her mind. Angry, sweet whispers, and her fingers move to her ankle, to the poisoned blade she always keeps there. She slides it from its sheath almost without realizing what she is doing.

Pietyr has turned his back on her. A mistake. But he turns around at the last instant, and the knife slices through the air instead of his skin.

"Katharine!"

"I said go, so you go," she says.

"Kat, stop!"

She strikes again and catches his sleeve; the dark gray fabric begins to stain red. He backpedals around the billiard table and into the bar, knocking over a tray and a decanter of Natalia's favorite tainted brandy.

"It is for your own good," she says miserably. "There is danger for you here."

"I do not care. I will not leave you, Kat. And you still love me, I know that you do."

Katharine stops short.

"Whatever is left in me that can love," she says, "loves you."

Before he can speak, she raises the knife and carves into her own face, along the hairline and her ear as though cutting off a mask. Her blood runs bright red down her neck and into her bodice.

"Katharine," he whispers. "Oh, my Katharine."

"Pietyr Renard," she says in a gravelly voice. "We have not been your Katharine since you threw me down the Breccia Domain."

Pietyr stumbles out of Greavedrake in a daze. Katharine told him to go. But he did not gather any of his belongings. Instead, he rushes to the stable and saddles the best horse he can find. His hands tremble as he tightens the cinch. All he can see is the image of her cutting into herself.

"It is not her fault." He leads the horse quickly out of its stall and mounts. "It is my fault, and I will find a way to make it right."

Pietyr puts heels to the horse and gallops down the drive, hurrying for the road that curves north around the capital and on to Prynn. He will ride all day and into the night, then rest and change horses in the morning.

He will ride all the way to Innisfuil Valley. Back to the cold, dark heart of the island: the Breccia Domain.

THE ROAD TO INDRID DOWN

*J*ules," Arsinoe says. "You've been staring at that map for hours."

They are traveling through the quiet roads in the shadow of the mountain, all on horseback, except for Arsinoe, who had to borrow Willa's ill-tempered brown mule. It is sticky hot, even riding in the shade, but Jules and Caragh both insist that everyone keep their cloak hoods up in case anyone passes.

"Jules! It's a good thing you're a naturalist, else your horse would've run face first into a tree with all the attention you're paying."

Jules responds with a grunt but keeps on studying the map of the capital.

"Let her be, Arsinoe," Joseph says, riding up beside her. "If she studies now, by the time we reach Indrid Down, she'll be able to pass through the city like water in a stream. And we won't have to study as much."

"You should still study it," Jules mutters.

"Give it here, then," he says, and holds his hand out. But she will not relinquish the map. "That's what I thought."

"Is that the war gift?" Arsinoe asks him quietly. "The strategy? The preparation?"

Joseph shrugs. And in the saddle, Jules frowns. No one knows. There is so much about the war gift that none of them understands.

Arsinoe shoves her hood down and tosses her short hair.

"I miss the breeze off the cove," she says.

"Put your hood back up," says Caragh, riding behind on her stout chestnut mountain mare.

"Let her keep it down," Madrigal objects. She takes down her own and leans her head back to catch the wind. "We haven't seen anyone since we left the cottage. These roads are practically deserted; you said so yourself."

"It doesn't mean we shouldn't be cautious."

"You never should have come, anyway. You'll get us into trouble if we're caught with you away from the Black Cottage."

"Madrigal," says Caragh mildly, "we are traveling with a presumed dead queen and a legion-cursed fugitive. If we're caught, my being away from the cottage will be the least of our offenses."

Madrigal scowls. She twists in the saddle, back toward Jules.

"How much farther until we reach Indrid Down?"

"Tomorrow. Afternoon, maybe. Or just before nightfall."

"Good," Arsinoe says. "I want to go and see Braddock."

Jules lowers the map. The notice of the duel was not the

only news that Worcester brought with him. He also told tales of Katharine's victorious return to the capital, and the parade of the vanquished naturalist's bear familiar.

"I know that you do," Jules says. "But we can't risk it. When everyone is distracted by the duel, Caragh and Madrigal will sneak in and free him. Then you can see him afterward."

"But I left him for dead," says Arsinoe. "I need to explain to him why I just left him there, for her to put in a cage."

From the ground, Camden stands and puts her paws up onto Arsinoe's knee before jumping into the saddle to provide heavy cougar comfort.

"Thanks, Cam," Arsinoe says around the cat's licks. "But you're angering the mule."

Camden yawns, unbothered by the mule's grunting and ineffectual bucks, occasionally whapping the mule in the face with her tail.

"Camden, be nice to that mule," Jules says, and then looks at Arsinoe. "Braddock is a good bear. He'll forgive you."

Arsinoe quiets, and lets Jules concentrate on the map. It is she who will have the most to do when they arrive in the capital. It will be up to her to use her war gift, to sabotage Katharine's poisoned weapons and guide them safely off course. It makes Arsinoe's stomach tighten just to think of it.

Joseph sees the look on her face. He rides close and nudges her with his knee.

"It'll be fine," he says.

BARDON HARBOR

❧

A shining, mainland boat is docked in a private Arron slip on the northern shore of Bardon Harbor. Inside, Natalia lies in William Chatworth's arms, the soft rocking of the water threatening to lull her to sleep.

"I'm surprised," he says, and puffs cigar smoke. "I didn't think you would be able to sneak away for so long. Not with the ball tonight."

"For so long." Natalia chuckles, watching the smoke swirl patterns in the air. It was not really so long. But it was pleasant. They have not been together for months, and she is surprised to find she has missed it. Missed him, in a way.

Chatworth tugs his arm from beneath her head and stubs out his cigar.

"Do you have it, then?" he asks.

"Of course I do. It is the main reason I came."

She hands him a small bottle, and he holds it gingerly between two fingers.

"Stop being afraid of it," she says. "You could drink it all and it would not kill you. Nor will it hurt if it gets on your hands."

She sits up in the small bed and reaches for her clothes: a servant's uniform that she changed into on the carriage ride from Greavesdrake.

"If it's so weak," he wonders, "why bother?"

"Insurance. I would take the wind out of that elemental. My Katharine wants the chance to humiliate her. So she shall have it." Natalia stands and fastens the last of her buttons. Chatworth remains on the bed, languorous and confident. Perhaps over-confident, and it occurs to her that, aside from having bluster and money, he has never shown any particular skill.

"If you are caught . . . ," she says, and pauses. "Do not get caught."

"Don't worry. Everyone in that camp trusts my son. And Sara Westwood has come to trust me."

"Has she? Then she is an even bigger fool than I thought."

"Don't be jealous," he says, but he means the opposite. He is such a vain and beautiful man. She wonders whether that son of his will grow to be just as vain, just as arrogant. Whether he will be difficult to manage when he is Katharine's king-consort.

"Come back to bed."

"There is no time."

"But I like you so much in that outfit." He tries to grab her, but she steps away and whips his arms with her cotton apron.

"Just poison that elemental brat, will you, and stop playing about!" She turns and leaves amid his laughter, to sneak back onto the docks and return home unnoticed.

THE QUEENS' BALL

*J*ules spins out of the way as a servant with a tray of wine nearly crashes into her. He calls her an imbecile, and she grits her teeth and curtsies. She must keep her head bowed. Joseph's orders, as he said her two-colored eyes made her far too easy to notice, even with Camden safely hidden away in a nearby stable.

"There's a bounty on your head," he said. "And the city is crawling with guards. You shouldn't go at all!"

But Arsinoe could not rest easy without at least one set of eyes on Mirabella, so here Jules is.

Jules lowers her chin and walks through the corridors bordering the kitchen nearest the northern ballroom. Many guests are already inside, and more rustle through the doors every minute. Close to the entrance, there are too many searching glances gawking at the finery and hoping for a glimpse of the queens. But those will lessen once Mirabella and Katharine make their entrances and draw away all of the attention.

Jules turns down a hall, the heels of her boots loud against the floor. The stone of the Highbern Hotel amplifies everything, and though the passageways are wide and well-aired by the opening and closing front doors, to Jules they are suffocating. Nothing in the capital is open enough, and she misses the fields and docks of home.

She turns and pretends to move a vase as another servant passes by.

"Nothing will happen here, anyway, with all these people and priestesses milling about," she mutters before realizing Camden is not there to mutter to. She should have stayed with Joseph and Arsinoe or gone with Aunt Caragh and Madrigal to the dueling arena. She is about to do just that, when a black cloak catches her eye, passing the kitchens.

"What's this now?" she whispers, before following it down the corridor.

Mirabella and Billy wait on the staircase outside of the ballroom's eastern entrance, two still statues in the midst of chaos as attendants put finishing touches on Mirabella's makeup and straighten the fall of her gown and Billy's coattails. Mirabella's fingers rest in the crook of Billy's arm. On some other staircase, she does not doubt that Katharine's rest similarly in Nicolas Martel's.

Billy looks over at her. His choker of black gems sparkles at her throat, and he smiles. Her future king-consort. Her suitor now, for real.

On the other side of the large wooden door, sounds of the

ball grow quiet and she hears Luca's muffled voice announce her entrance.

"It is time," Sara whispers over her shoulder, and the door opens.

"Are we supposed to smile and nod?" Billy asks. "How do we play to the crowd when more than half of them want you dead?"

Mirabella laughs. It breaks the spell of silence, and the guests begin to whisper among themselves. They murmur about her dress. About her jewels. About how lovely she and the suitor look together. Billy helps her up the steps to the Westwood table, and they stand behind their chairs to wait for Katharine.

They do not have to wait long. When she appears, the guests muffle, poisoners and non-poisoners alike. Katharine's skirt flares out with her long strides, her hair in shining curls. She does not seem small anymore. She does not seem at all like the pale, pinned-tight girl she was atop the cliffs when Mirabella was first reunited with her at the Disembarking.

"The Undead Queen," they whisper. But she has never seemed more alive.

"She wants it more than I do," Mirabella says, watching Katharine's lips curl as she turns to whisper into Nicolas's ear.

"It doesn't matter," Billy replies stiffly. "She still won't get it."

Before Katharine and her suitor take their place amid the Arrons, dazzling in their snakes and scorpions, Katharine cocks her head at Mirabella and winks. Nicolas smiles at Billy and discreetly spits onto the floor.

Billy's jaw tightens.

"You are right; it does not matter," Mirabella says, and squeezes his hand.

"Fine," he says as they sit. "But if he takes part in the Hunt of the Stags this year, he'll find my boot in his back in the middle of the woods."

She has no doubt that is true. Billy is so like Arsinoe was. What a fine match they would have made had she lived. Thinking of Arsinoe, she watches Katharine intently until the Highbern is rattled by a great, cold gust of wind. Inside, the guests shudder and duck.

"Tomorrow," Bree says out of the side of her mouth. "Save it for the duel!" She stretches her long leg past Sara's skirts to kick Mirabella beneath the table, and Mirabella tears her eyes away from her sister so the wind will quiet.

Yes. Tomorrow.

The musicians begin to play. Servants circulate small bunches of dark purple grapes and cups of wine. There is excitement in the air. The people are joyous, celebrating, and if there is any undercurrent at all, it is of relief. One queen has been killed, and two stand ready to claim the crown. Things are as they should be.

Bree pushes away from the long table and takes both Mirabella and Billy by the hands.

"Come, let us dance!"

They step onto the floor, and the crowd parts to make room, priestess guards gathering around the edge. Bree stays only a moment, smiling and twirling in circles before she wanders away to find her own partner. She will not have much trouble. Bree is luminous as always, and her festival gown is easily the most beautiful: strapless and black, with silver beads sewn into the fabric.

Billy turns Mirabella about, keeping close to the Westwood table.

"You are a very fine dancer," Mirabella says.

"I ought to be, after six years of forced lessons. I can do most any dance you would require, for any formal occasion."

"You probably know dances that I have never heard of."

"Possibly. But don't worry. I'm also a very fine teacher." His eyes are warm. Charming and wrinkled at the corners. For a moment, it seems as if Arsinoe's eyes are boring into her back, and Billy misses his step.

"What is wrong?" she asks.

"Nothing," he says quickly. "Nothing. I only thought I saw . . . Never mind."

She tugs Billy close and squeezes him.

"I think I can feel her, too," she whispers.

They keep dancing but on stiff legs. When he turns her toward the poisoner table, she glares at Katharine and hopes her little sister can feel the hatred from them both. "Look," Billy says when they turn back to the Westwoods. "My father is here."

William Chatworth is leaning across her table, talking to Sara. He is leaning so far that his sleeves are nearly dipping into their wine cups.

"He didn't tell me he was going to be here." Billy spins her faster. "He's probably angry that I didn't tell him about our betrothal." He pulls her sharply around.

"Ouch!"

"Oh! I'm sorry," he says. His eyes narrow at his father walking around the table now to take Mirabella's empty seat beside Sara. "Nothing distracts me quite like he does. Did I hurt you?"

"No. You—" She stops. For a moment, she thinks she is imagining it, but there is Joseph. Watching them from the crowd. "What are you . . . ?" she whispers.

Joseph shakes his head. He steps back to disappear into the other guests, but Bree has seen him too, and grabs him and drags him into a dance, chattering furiously into his ear.

"Bree," Mirabella calls, and Bree presses her lips together in a very serious, un-Bree-like line. She dances Joseph closer.

"He should not be here," Bree hisses, holding on to him with a grip like iron.

"Why not?" Billy asks. "He's my foster brother, isn't he?"

"Billy," Joseph says. He glances around furtively. His dark hair is brushed back, and those storm-blue eyes of his can take Mirabella to the ground with one look. "Jules is here somewhere."

"Oh." Billy pulls Mirabella slightly away. "What is she doing here? When did she get back?"

"I can't explain now," Joseph says. "And I can't stay. I'll find you later." He spins Bree out and lets go to slip smoothly into the crowd.

"That was strange," says Mirabella.

"I am going to tell the priestesses he is here," Bree whispers, but Mirabella stops her.

"No, Bree. It was nothing. It is harmless."

Bree seems unsure, but eventually she nods, and goes off to find another dancing partner.

"I would know what happened to Arsinoe," Billy says. "I want to know where Jules took her. I want to know. . . ."

"So do I," says Mirabella, and turns to glare again at Katharine.

Jules catches the black-cloaked figure when they have stopped to watch the dancing from behind the folds of a curtained doorway. She grasps the figure from behind and covers their mouth, lifting them up so that, despite Jules's shorter size, the cloaked figure's legs kick uselessly in the air.

"What do you think you're doing?" she asks, tearing down the hood and depositing Arsinoe in a corner.

"Stop grabbing at me," Arsinoe whispers, arms slapping at Jules's shoulders. "You'll get us both caught!" She pulls her hood back up to hide her face. "I only wanted to see."

"I told you to stay back and that I would watch out for her. Didn't you trust me? And how did you slip away from Joseph?"

"Oh, like it was hard," Arsinoe says sarcastically. "Ditching Camden was the real challenge."

"Where are they now?"

"Here, probably. Looking for me."

Jules purses her lips. She takes Arsinoe by the shoulder and begins to haul her out, down the quiet corridor, toward one of the servants' side exits to the street.

"You are reckless," Jules says.

"I know, but—" Arsinoe struggles out of her grip.

"Don't make me use my war gift to throw you out of here."

"You would never," Arsinoe says, and grins. But the smile slides off her face. "Did you see the way they were dancing? Mirabella and Billy?"

Jules puts an arm around her. When she shoves her toward the door now, it is much more gently.

"You say Mirabella loves you. Well, so does Billy. They think you're dead, Arsinoe. They're probably missing you together."

"But he'll be her king-consort, won't he? And if I stay dead, I won't be able to . . . run away with him . . . anywhere." She looks down. "I was supposed to be able to let him know, Jules."

"I know it's hard. But you can't be seen. What good would it do? We just have to get Mirabella through the duel and then we can decide what to do next."

"All right," Arsinoe says, and lets Jules lead her through the dark streets of the capital.

Katharine's eyes narrow as she watches Mirabella. Her pretty sister, so easily beloved by the island. So easily gifted. Everything for her so easy but never earned. Never deserved.

Beside her, Nicolas keeps feeding her bits of this and that and commenting on some of the stranger fashions. He is a fly, buzzing in her ear. Katharine crushes a grape in her gloved hand. But the cloth is so thick to cover her poisoning scars that she cannot even feel the juice.

"Make her look at me again," Katharine whispers. "Make her care."

But Mirabella does not. She goes on dancing with the Chatworth boy, as rigid as if she were strapped to a pole.

"What did you say, Queen Katharine?" Nicolas asks.

"Nothing," she replies. The entire ballroom is focused on Mirabella. The Arrons have never seen so many turned backs.

"Traitors," she whispers.

Katharine pushes her chair away from the table and stands. She is of so little consequence to the crowd that she could move across the floor unnoticed.

So she does.

Katharine appears out of nowhere and slips in between Mirabella and Billy like a snake, so fast that neither can think to act. Everything stops. Bows drag to a halt on musicians' strings.

"Play," Katharine commands. She wraps her gloved hands around Mirabella's wrists and drags her to the middle of the emptying floor.

The music is an awkward plucking.

"What are you doing?" Mirabella asks, her eyes wide.

"Dancing with my sister," replies Katharine. "Though I

would not call your movements dancing, exactly. Are your legs made of wood?"

Mirabella clenches her jaw. She grabs on to Katharine's gloved wrists.

"You are so afraid." Katharine smiles prettily. "The chosen queen would not be so afraid."

"I am not afraid. I am angry."

Katharine draws Mirabella in close as they spin slowly past the tables, past the gaping mouths of the guests and servants frozen with trays raised in the air. After they pass the Westwood table, Luca stands and walks quickly toward Natalia's chair.

"This is not done, Katharine."

"Then how are we doing it?" Katharine grins. She tilts her head to consider Mirabella's face and hair.

"You are beautiful, sister. Hair so carefully brushed. Cheeks so flawless and free of paint and powder. No scars and no rashes, even after all the presents I sent. Tell me, has even one found its way to you?"

"It found its way to a priestess."

Katharine clucks her tongue.

"The poor girl. But that is your fault, for letting them intervene in our business."

She steps back and whirls Mirabella around. Theirs is the only movement in the room, and the music plays clumsily, as even the violinists are staring.

"Do you know what I think?" Katharine asks. "I think you

are a shame. I think you are a waste."

Her fingers trace Mirabella's veins, envying her unblemished skin.

"You are the strongest," she says. "You could be the one. But up close, you are such a disappointment. Your eyes are wary as a kicked dog's, when you and I both know you have never been kicked in your life. Not like me, who has been kicked down with poisons and popped blisters and made to vomit until I weep.

"That is why I am going to win," she goes on as they twirl. "I may be the weakest, but I am a queen, through and through. All the way down to my dead blood and bones."

"Katharine, stop this now." Mirabella's voice is pitiful. And she shudders when Katharine leans close.

"Do you know what they do with the dead queens, sister?" Katharine asks. "Do you know what they do with their bodies?"

She stops the farce of a dance to stand still in the center of the floor and jerks Mirabella toward her until they are chest to chest and eye to eye.

"They throw them into the Breccia for the island to eat. And may I tell you a secret?"

Katharine's lips press to Mirabella's ear, almost like a kiss.

"They are tired of it."

THE BRECCIA DOMAIN

———————————— ⚜ ————————————

$\mathcal{P}$ ietyr walks his mare slowly through Innisfuil Valley. She is tired. So is he. He traded his silver armband for her at the last coach stop before the mountain pass and has not slept since getting out of the coach. Nearly two solid days of fast travel, by coach and on three horses, but he made it. Or at least he thinks so. He has only come to Innisfuil for Beltane, and without the glut of black and white tents, the place looks completely unfamiliar.

Pietyr rides along the edge of the southern trees. He is hesitant to plunge in. Despite sunlight so bright it is near blinding, the valley does not feel safe or peaceful. It feels watchful, and overeager for visitors.

When they enter the trees, the mare shies and he dismounts. If she were to spook when they reach the Breccia, she could send them both plummeting over the edge. He leads her slowly and pats her muzzle. She does not like these trees empty of birds, these woods empty of sound, any better than he does.

Soon enough the ground changes, and his mare's hooves ring off small half-submerged stones. Pietyr lifts his head and sees the Breccia, though he would swear it had not been visible a moment before.

The Breccia Domain. A deep, dark cut into the heart of the island. It is blacker than a crow's wing, blacker than night. It is where they once threw the bodies of the vanquished queens, and where he threw his Kat when he thought the priestesses were going to behead her.

Pietyr tosses the mare's reins across a low branch. The long, knotted rope in his saddlebag was purchased from a trusted merchant in Prynn. Coil after coil of thick, sturdy knots that weighed the mare down on one side as they rode. Coil after coil, and still he is not sure whether he purchased enough.

He studies the trees, but none seems strong enough to tie off on. Not even the ones as thick as his waist, when the Breccia Domain is leering over his shoulder. He would prefer a trunk as thick as his horse. He considers rigging an additional safety line to her saddle, but if she were to run she would drag him back up over the side. And besides, the extra line would cost too much rope.

"Get on with it," he growls, loudly, to break the silence and bolster his courage. "I did not ride all this way for nothing." He holds his mare's cheeks between his hands. "If I am lucky," he says to her, "I will see what Kat saw."

The horse blinks. It does not take a naturalist to see she

knows he is lying. If Pietyr is lucky, he will not see, or feel, anything at all.

He chooses a tree and ties his rope, then lets out slack all the way to the mouth of the fissure. Sweat dots his forehead. His hands shake. He is terrified of a hole in the ground. How Nicolas Martel would laugh at him if he were there.

Pietyr throws the loose end of the rope over the side of the rocks, and it unfurls for many long seconds. He does not hear it strike the bottom. It only comes to an end, tugging against his fists.

Perhaps the rumors are true, and there is no bottom.

With the rope in place, he walks back to his horse, and takes a small lamp out of his saddlebag. He ties it to his belt, and stuffs extra matches into every pocket. Then he breathes in deep, goes to the edge, and lowers himself over the side.

The knotted rope makes for easy enough going. His feet do not slip, and his hands are strong and sure. Even so, he keeps his eyes on the patch of blue-and-white sky overhead. When the patch is dishearteningly small and his legs have begun to tire, he finally looks around, resting against the side of the crevasse. The sides are sheer, steep rock. He does not know how Katharine was able to stop her fall.

He continues on, deeper and deeper into the dark. Until his feet search for the next knot, and it is not there.

Pietyr's hands clench tight as he tries to catch his previous foothold. It is hard not to panic thinking of how far it is to climb back up and how far he may yet have to fall. And it is so dark now that he cannot see the rope in front of his face.

A sudden wind moves across his shoulders. He jerks, and his hip strikes painfully against the stone. But it is only wind, sneaking down from the surface. Never mind that the wind somehow smells like death and rot. Or that when he laughs at his foolishness, there is no echo.

There is nothing here, he thinks as the back of his neck prickles. *There is no one down here, no one watching. This was a waste.*

He reaches for the lantern at his belt. He will light it just to be sure, to get a look at the darkness and nothing below his feet. But when his fingers find a match, he does not want to strike it. What if he is near the bottom? Will he see everything that they have discarded? Long-dead queens lying in piles of bones and ragged black dresses, staring up at him with empty, accusing eye sockets and bare, yawning jaws.

Or will he see Katharine, his Katharine, rotting where he threw her, and the claw marks on the stones of whatever scratched its way out to take her place?

No, he thinks. *That is foolishness. A flight of frightened fancy.*

He strikes the match.

It struggles to light, and he touches it quickly to the lamp. Yellow-orange flame casts against his clothes, against his rope and the stone it hangs beside. Carefully, he unties the lantern and holds it out, looking down, past his feet.

There is nothing. No bones of dead queens. No cavern

bottom of rocky growths. It is only a void, and that is a wonder in itself considering how far he has descended. The length of rope he would need to reach the bottom would have been too much for his horse to carry. All he can do now is drop the lamp, and try to see something in the moment that it lands.

Before he can let go, something scrapes against the rock. The sound was not subtle. It sounded close, but he cannot see a thing.

I imagined it, he thinks, and then, *a lizard. Or a natural shifting of the ground.*

Foul-smelling wind ruffles his hair. It curls into his collar like a bundle of clammy fingers.

"Who is there?"

A silly question, and no one replies. But in Pietyr's mind, he sees teeth and a grin stretched wide in the dark.

He swings his lamp out to all sides. There are more noises now: scraping and the clacking of bones.

"It is not possible!" he shouts, foregoing all restraint. "There is nothing here!"

But everyone knows that the Breccia Domain is more than an empty hole in the earth. Who knows what happened to the queens who were thrown down into the dark? Into the heart of the island, where the Goddess's eye is always open. Who knows how she kept those queens or what she turned them into.

Pietyr tries to steady his rapid breath.

"What did you do to her? What did you do to my Katharine?"

At the mention of her name, the air warms. Katharine was one of them. One of the fallen. There are centuries of sisters here, ready to listen to her woes and cradle her with skeletal hands.

But that was a lie. Whatever help they gave was not for her. It was for them, and they have twisted through Katharine like ivy.

"Who are you?" he shouts, but he already knows, and so the queens who dwell in the Breccia do not bother to tell him. What remains of them is uglier than bones and gray, withered skin. It is crushed hopes. The air reeks of their bitterness.

Pietyr scrambles back up the rope. He has to get back to Katharine.

"It is my fault," he says, and drops the lamp to use both hands to climb. As the light flashes through the dark, it flashes past an upturned face. It is just for an instant but it makes him scream, and the image of its empty eyes lingers in the dark. Pietyr climbs as fast as he can. It is not until he feels the bones brush against his ankle that he realizes that Katharine is a queen, and though she was able to survive the Breccia, he, in fact, may not.

INDRID DOWN

❦

*T*he great round arena of Indrid Down sits on the outskirts of the city, at the center of a large open field, easy to be spotted in. But it was simple enough for Jules and Arsinoe to sneak into it and meet Caragh and Madrigal after dark, creeping along the southern side, full of scaffolds and building materials.

"Do you think anyone saw us?" Arsinoe wonders, out of breath.

"Shush," says Jules, and stares out into the night for any sign of movement.

"Don't be so worried," says Madrigal, and both Jules and Arsinoe jump. "The guards are few and posted up high. Or patrolling below in the staging rooms. Come," she says. "I'll take you to Caragh."

They pass beneath the scaffolding, and Arsinoe stares up in wonder. The arena is enormous, a grand spectacle even though several sections have fallen into disrepair. Part of the northern wall has crumbled away entirely, and the age of the structure is visible in cracks and weather-worn edges.

"Where's Aunt Caragh?" Jules asks.

"Below the extra seating, near one of the entrances to the competition ground. It will be a good place."

Jules senses something and stops short, causing Arsinoe to run into her back just as Camden collides with their fronts, purring and butting her head into their faces.

"Blegh," Arsinoe says, plucking fur from her mouth. "I thought she was stashed at the stable."

"Try telling her that," Caragh says. She stands leaning against a beam, arms crossed loosely. "Better to sneak her in under cover of dark, anyway. Tomorrow we'd have had to bring her in a cart, hide her under a pile of something."

Arsinoe looks over their hiding place and grasps one of the supports beneath the hastily repaired section overhead.

"Why here?" she asks. "The visibility would be better from the western side."

"That is exactly why here," Jules says. "No one will want to sneak in and watch from underneath the worst seats in the house."

Arsinoe pushes against the beam. Tomorrow the arena will fill to capacity. People will pack in on top of one another.

"I hope they don't fall through."

"I hope Jules can do what she says." Madrigal looks out at the arena ground and sighs. "We never should have bound you.

If you'd had all these years to develop your skill, this would be easy."

Arsinoe says nothing, but she sees the way Caragh purses her lips. The binding on the legion curse may have been the only thing that kept Jules sane. It may be the only thing keeping her sane now.

"If you don't think you can," says Arsinoe, "or if you don't want to, we can find another way."

"No," says Jules. "I can do it. I can guide Katharine's poisoned weapons off course long enough for Mirabella to kill her. This was my idea, the way least likely to get you caught. We can't change plans now."

Arsinoe's stomach flutters with nerves. There is no time to change plans, anyway. The night is late. So late it is nearly dawn. Jules has not used her war gift much, but it has been there when it mattered most. And besides, Mirabella is so strong. The duel will be over with one lightning bolt.

THE HIGHBERN HOTEL

*M*irabella eases out of her ball gown and shivers. "Is there a chill?" she asks.

"Here, Mira." Elizabeth drags the coverlet from the bed and uses her good arm to wrap Mirabella up tight. "Is that better?"

"Yes." But in truth, the blanket feels like it came from a snowbank rather than a down-stuffed bed. And it hurts, like pinpricks against her skin. She takes a breath, and that hurts too.

"You are so pale." Elizabeth presses her hand to Mirabella's cheeks and Mirabella gasps. A freshly tattooed black bracelet encircles Elizabeth's wrist. Bree sees it as well and takes hold of Elizabeth's arms. They have even tattooed her left, just above the end of the stump. She has taken the oaths and become a full priestess.

"You were supposed to tell us," Bree says. "We would have been there."

"Where is Pepper?" Mirabella searches Elizabeth's hood and her long dark hair. She had not realized how long it had been since she had seen the plucky woodpecker. She had just assumed he was staying in the trees outside the hotel.

"He's gone," Elizabeth whispers. "Rho made me choose. She had him in her fist." A tear slides down her cheek. "I guess she knew about him all along."

Mirabella trembles, partly from rage, and the anger quickens her for a moment and makes it easier to breathe.

"I could have stopped her," she says. "I will still stop her."

"No." Elizabeth wipes her face with the back of her sleeve. "I would have chosen this, anyway. To be a priestess."

Sara and Luca enter the room, Sara with a tray of tea. She sets it on a small circular table.

"You must be shaken to the core after that dance," Sara says, and pours a steaming cup. "What a spectacle. Queen Katharine has nerve to spare."

"Yes," says Luca. "I am sure that Natalia never imagined she and I would need to separate the two of you like children fighting over toys."

"It was not a fight," says Mirabella. "It was not anything."

"She is only trying to scare you." Bree curls her lip. "As if she could."

But Katharine did scare her. And judging by their taut, pale faces, she had scared them all.

Mirabella blinks. The room is spinning. And blacking in and out. Sara hands her a cup of tea.

"I must sit," she murmurs. The teacup falls and shatters at her feet, and she crumples to the floor.

"Mira!" Elizabeth shouts.

Sara draws back, her hands to her face.

"It is poison!" she gasps. "Where is the taster? Where is he?"

"It was not his fault," Mirabella whispers.

Luca kneels at her side and barks for Rho. It takes less than a minute for the war-gifted priestess to secure the room, shuttering windows and ordering guards.

"How?" Rho asks.

"It must have been Katharine," Luca says. "She must have had something on her gloves."

Luca holds Mirabella's hand and studies her skin everywhere that Katharine touched her during their dance. There is no redness or blisters. No sign of irritation.

"Where is Billy?"

"He stayed behind," Bree says. "With Joseph Sandrin."

"He should have been watching her." Sara grinds her teeth. "Protecting her!"

"So should we all," Luca says. "But it does not matter now."

"I have sent for healers," Rho calls from the door.

"There is no pain," Mirabella says. "I am only weak. Perhaps it is not . . ." Her voice trails off. "Perhaps it is not poison at all."

Sara touches her cheek. Bree and Elizabeth are both crying. She wishes she could tell them to stop. That she is fine.

When the healers arrive, they lift her into bed. They take

blood from her arm and sniff her breath. They poke and prod and pull back her eyelids to see how her eyes move.

"She is getting no worse," they murmur after a time. "Whatever it is, it is not progressing."

"Why would they poison her if not to kill her?" Bree asks.

"Because they have killed her," Luca says softly.

Sara kneels beside the bed and takes Mirabella's hand. The poison does not race through her body. She does not break out in spasms or labor to breathe.

"Cowards," Rho growls from the door, and Mirabella hears something break as the war priestess loses her temper.

"Can the duel be postponed?" Sara asks.

Luca shakes her head. There is no rule against this. A poisoner is allowed to poison, as they will. As they can. No matter how Mirabella survives the night, she will still be too weak to fight in the morning. She will walk into the arena as good as giftless.

"This was my fault, child," Luca says sadly. "I let down my guard."

THE ARENA

he arena grounds fill quickly. The vendors come first, right before dawn, to prepare food to sell from their stands: skewers of chicken and plums, sweet roasted nuts, barrels of cooled wine and cider. Many foods Arsinoe had not tried. Her stomach rumbles. She sent Madrigal out as soon as the crowds were heavy enough to hide her, with plenty of coin to procure samples of everything. But she is not back yet.

"So many people," Arsinoe muses as the makeshift stands creak over their heads. "Dressed in their best. Hair pinned and faces painted, to watch a queen die."

"Don't think of that," Jules says, lurking in shadow with Camden. "It must be done. And when it's over, the island will have a new elemental queen. And we'll be free to go."

"I should go alone," says Arsinoe. "You shouldn't have to give up everything too."

"What am I giving up?" Jules asks. "A town that will hunt

me for my war gift? There's no peace for me either, now that my curse is known."

"Not everyone would be that way. Not Cait or Ellis. What about Madrigal and your new baby sister or brother?"

Jules lowers her eyes, and Arsinoe holds her breath. She does not know what she will do if Jules goes back to Wolf Spring. She does not know how to be without her.

"I've never had any path but yours," Jules says. "So I'll stay with you, until the end." She smiles impishly. "Or until the curse drives me mad."

At the sound of approaching footsteps, they tuck back into the shadows, and Arsinoe pulls the hood of her light cloak down over her eyes. But it is only Madrigal and Caragh. And Joseph as well, found wandering out on the arena grounds.

Madrigal hands Arsinoe several skewers of different meats.

"Don't share," she warns her as Arsinoe takes first bites. "Some are poisoned."

"Were you followed?" Jules asks Joseph.

"No," he replies. "I meant to come last night, but by the time I realized you had left the ball, it was so late that I slept in the stables. Then I snuck in with the morning crowds." He looks out at the throngs of people. "Honestly, we needn't have bothered sneaking. Only one thing's on people's minds today, and it is not us."

Caragh ducks below the beams and peers out into the stands.

"There are so many poisoners," she says. "So many elementals."

"Almost no naturalists," Madrigal adds. "Not that I would've expected them to make the journey."

"Jules," Caragh says. "Look there." She points. On the western side of the arena sits a serious-faced group wearing cloaks lined with bright red wool. They are so still that they stand out, calm in the midst of chaos.

"Who are they?" Jules asks.

"I think they are warriors. From Bastian City."

"Are there oracles too?" Arsinoe asks. "Can they tell us what's going to happen and relieve us of the suspense?"

The corner of Caragh's mouth twists upward. She turns to Madrigal and says, "We should go. Back to the Volroy to be ready to free the bear. We'll guide him out to the riverbank while the city is mostly empty."

Madrigal frowns. It is clear she would rather stay and watch the action. But eventually she nods and goes without complaint.

"Do you think they'll manage to do it without killing each other first?" Arsinoe wonders aloud, and Joseph comes to stand between her and Jules. He slips an arm about the shoulders of each of them.

"Where will we go?" he asks. "After this?"

"Sunpool, maybe," says Jules. "I've always wanted to see it. And with so many oracles, they'll already know we're coming."

"Not the ending we hoped for," says Joseph, "but far better than the ending we feared. The only thing missing will be Billy."

Arsinoe tries to smile. To enjoy the daydream of the three

of them together at last. But a daydream is all it is. In Sunpool or anywhere else they will be hunted. Their lives will be in disguise and in secret, on the move and on the run, and what kind of a life is that? Better than no life at all, Jules would say, but Arsinoe is not so sure.

A rumble passes overhead when the gallery begins to fill with the duel's most illustrious guests: Council members and Arrons.

"It won't be long now, Jules," Arsinoe says. "Are you ready?"

Jules cracks her knuckles.

"As I'll ever be."

Katharine tightens her leather armguard. Her bow has been restrung and her quiver filled with poisoned arrows made with fancy black and white feathers. At her belt, her slim, sharp throwing knives have been edged with enough curare to fell a horse. She also has a short-bladed sword. Though she does not intend to get close enough to use it, it would make for a fine and showy finishing strike.

"Will you take the crossbow?" Natalia asks as she buttons Katharine's black silk vest and smooths the sleeves of her shirt.

"No. I have already used it on Arsinoe. Each of my sisters deserves her own special send-off."

Natalia holds up Katharine's tall, light boots. Her skirt of soft black leather will just touch the tops of them, and her maid Giselle has braided her hair into a knotted bun. There will be no long tresses to pull, nothing to get into her eyes.

"You seem so calm, Natalia," Katharine notes. "So confident."

"I am always calm and confident." Natalia kneels to lace the boots. When she starts to hum, Katharine narrows her eyes. Before the ball, Natalia had been terrified. Snapping at the guards and asking where Pietyr was a hundred times. Such a change, between the ball and today.

A servant enters carrying a tray of edible poisons: belladonna berries and a savory tart of jack-o-lantern mushrooms. Fresh milk laced with more of Nicolas's white snakeroot.

"Katharine," Natalia cautions. "Is that wise?"

"I would not go into a duel hungry."

"Then let me send for something else."

Katharine cuts a large slice of tart and swallows half of the milk.

"The pain is nothing," Katharine assures her, wiping her chin. "I have endured much worse." She pops a berry into her mouth as her stomach starts to churn, and looks at her reflection in the mirror. She is no little girl who would turn into Natalia's skirts and weep. She is no weak queen to be thrown down the Breccia Domain. She is outfitted for battle. And after today, she will be the next Queen Crowned.

Mirabella recovers from the poison faster than anyone dared hope, and the priestesses pray thanks to the Goddess. But it is still not fast enough.

When she holds her hand out to a candle, she can light it, but she cannot make it flare. Water is a waste of time. She has not dared to test her lightning, and Luca says that she should not, that it would give the Arrons too much satisfaction to see only a rain shower form above the arena.

"I feel like I failed you," Billy says, standing behind her. "Now I have failed you both."

"You did not fail anyone. Not me. Certainly not Arsinoe." The sadness in her loved ones' eyes is hard for Mirabella to take. No one imagined that she could lose the duel before it even started. "Sooner or later, Billy, the poison always finds its target. This was not your fault."

The priestess fastening her light dress of black wool begins to weep. Rho cuffs her on the back of the head and steps forward to finish what she started, tugging Mirabella's bodice tight.

"Avoid her," the red-haired priestess whispers. "Use your shield and avoid her as long as you can. Save your gift for one good shot."

THE QUEENS' DUEL

$\pmb{\delta}$

When the duel begins, everyone in attendance is on their feet, screaming regardless of their affiliation. None of them have ever seen a duel. The air is abuzz with excitement, even stronger than the scent of cinnamon-spiced sweets and roasted meat on sticks.

Mirabella walks to the center of the arena. Wind blows her hair off her shoulders, and she pretends that it is *her* wind even as fear drenches her heart like cold water. Before the ball, her greatest fear was that her will would fail when she looked into Katharine's eyes. How foolish she had been.

She nods to the Westwoods and to Luca in the gallery. She would raise her arm, but the shining silver shield feels like it weighs more than she does.

"When I was a child, I asked to play here," Katharine says as she and Natalia stand at the entrance to the competition ground.

"But you would never let me. Do you remember?"

"I remember," Natalia replies. "But this is no game, Kat."

Katharine taps the throwing knives at her belt and feels the sway of the sword strapped to her back. The crowd roars for Mirabella as she makes her entrance, but that is all right. It is the last time that anyone will ever cheer for her.

"Poor Mirabella," Katharine says. "So brash and impulsive. Coming to my city to challenge me. After it is over, they will call her a fool."

But that will not be fair. Mirabella did not know who Katharine really was. How could she? Not even Natalia knows that, and Katharine always thought that Natalia knew everything.

"Go and sit in the gallery," Katharine says. "I would walk in alone." Natalia's mouth tightens, so Katharine softens her voice. "I do not want you to miss it."

Natalia touches Katharine's hair. Her eyes move over every inch: her face, her hands, the laces of her boots, as if she is trying to commit them to memory.

Katharine almost shrugs her off. She wants to begin. She wants the crowd to roar for *her*.

Natalia leaves, and Katharine waits until she sees her ice-blond head in the gallery before walking out with her arms raised.

The crowd screams. From the oldest woman in the stands to the children watching from window seats in nearby buildings, they all scream. Only the priestesses remain still and silent. But of course they would; they are priestesses.

The noise fills Katharine with pleasure, but it does not compare to the feeling she gets when she looks at Mirabella. Her pretty, regal sister is glaring at her. Yet underneath the glare is fear so thick that Katharine can almost smell it.

"That is a very fine shield," she calls out, and the crowd quiets. "You are going to need it."

Across the arena, Mirabella cringes as Katharine unslings her bow and nocks an arrow. She fires it and rolls to dodge any counter of lightning. But none comes. There is only the crowd's moan when her arrow bounces off the shield. She nocks another and lets it fly, and Mirabella dives clumsily to the ground. Katharine dodges again, anticipating a counterattack. But again there is nothing.

Something is not right.

"What is this, Sister?" she shouts. "Is the great elemental afraid to fight?"

Mirabella peeks out from behind her shield.

"That would be a strange thing indeed," she shouts back, though her voice is high and weak, "when it was I who issued the challenge!"

Suspicious, Katharine advances until she is close enough to see the sweat dotting Mirabella's forehead and to note the rapid rise and fall of her rib cage, too labored for so early in the fight. Her eyes are the eyes of a cornered dog.

And it is plain to see that she has been poisoned.

Katharine turns toward the gallery, where Natalia watches confidently beside the rest of the Black Council.

"So this is why you were not worried." It does not matter what she has done in the months since Beltane. To Natalia, she will always be a failure.

Katharine drops her bow and quiver of arrows into the freshly tilled dirt. She pulls a throwing knife from her belt and takes careful aim. Mirabella cannot cover every inch of herself with that shield.

With her sister crouched and poison-slowed, it will not be the glorious victory Katharine planned. But the end result will be the same.

She throws the knife.

It is not until her blade curves unexpectedly to the right that Katharine suspects the fight may yet be interesting.

Mirabella dodges another knife. The boards creak and dirt settles onto Arsinoe's head as the crowd above twists in their seats to get a better view.

"Was that you?" Arsinoe asks Jules. "Or a bad throw?"

"I don't know," Jules replies irritably. "I haven't done much of this."

In the arena, Mirabella rolls and nearly loses her hold on the shield.

"What is the matter with her?" Joseph asks from over Arsinoe's shoulder. "Why doesn't she strike?"

"I don't know," Arsinoe says. But something is wrong. The crowd senses it too, murmuring in confusion every time Mirabella dodges an attack and does not counter.

"Why won't she do anything?" Jules growls, using her war gift to push another of Katharine's knives wide. Her cheeks are red from exertion and her brown hair damp at the roots. "This won't work if she refuses to kill! Legion cursed or not, I can't spark fire!"

"Good Goddess," Arsinoe whispers as Katharine goes back to her bow. She shoots an arrow and pinions Mirabella's trailing skirt to the boards of the arena wall. "Mirabella's been poisoned."

Mirabella felt the feather of the poisoned arrow graze her leg when it passed. That is how close it came to being over. The sound of it sinking deep into the wood chilled her to the bone. She thought it was the sound of it burying itself in her thigh.

She drops her shield to yank at her skirt, trying to rip it loose. But it is stuck fast. The material is too thick to tear through.

Mirabella panics. She cries out and calls the wind to send Katharine flying halfway across the arena. But nothing more comes than a strong gust. It wobbles Katharine and sends her sideways onto her knee, but it does not even knock her over.

Katharine laughs and draws the sword from the hilt on her back.

"This was not the way it was meant to be," Mirabella says.

"Poor sister," says Katharine. "You have heard those priestesses say you were chosen so many times that you actually came to believe it."

"Luca!" Mirabella screams. "Bree! Elizabeth!" She stops

and takes deep, frightened breaths. "Turn away! Turn away and do not watch."

Overhead, the summer sky is cloudless and free of storms. The last she will see as her sister raises the sword. How strange, how humiliating, that this is how the poisoner will kill her, in a way where the poison on the blade does not even matter.

"Katharine! Get away from her!"

Mirabella flinches as Katharine is jerked backward, tossed toppling into the dirt. The shout came from the side of the arena opposite, and Mirabella cannot believe her eyes.

It is Arsinoe. Arsinoe and Juillenne Milone.

When Arsinoe saw the sword ready to swing down and sever Mirabella's head, she did not think. She just bolted into the arena, and Jules followed. Jules followed like always, and used her war gift to send Katharine flying.

The crowd screams at the sight of Arsinoe returned from the dead, and she realizes what she has done.

Katharine rolls up onto her knee, her lips pulled back in a grimace of disbelief.

"You!" she yells, and points at the two of them. "You, again!"

"Yes, me again," Jules growls. She steps in front of Arsinoe. Joseph and Camden run to Mirabella.

And then the crowd finds its voice.

"That is the naturalist!"

"It cannot be; she is dead!"

Arsinoe shifts her weight. There is no mistaking her, unmasked before the city. They see her scars, slashed across her cheek.

"You are dead!" Katharine shrieks. "I killed you!"

"You should have checked," Arsinoe yells back. "The poisoned bolt never pierced my leather armor." The stands rumble with shocked whispers.

"I saw the blood!" Katharine screeches, and braces when Jules clenches her fists.

"You saw what we wanted you to see."

"Arsinoe?" Mirabella asks. "Arsinoe, you are alive?"

Arsinoe keeps one eye on Katharine as she walks to her sister. She stretches her hand out, and Mirabella's fingers wrap around it.

"But I saw you fall . . . in the forest . . ."

"I'm a good actress. Born for the stage." The lie is a gamble; all Katharine need do is ask her to show her back or even to raise her right arm quickly, and her poisoner secret will be out. But Katharine has not dared to make a move, and she will not, for as long as Jules is there.

"Let me help you." With Joseph's help, Arsinoe tears the last of Mirabella's skirt loose from the arrow to hang ragged at her knees. "I've never seen you look so awful," Arsinoe says, and Mirabella laughs. "And you're so tall. But you were always the tallest."

Mirabella's eyes soften as Arsinoe's words sink in. She knows that Arsinoe remembers her.

"That is because I am the oldest," Mirabella says, and lifts her chin.

"By less than five minutes, to hear Willa tell it."

Jules whistles from the center of the ring. She motions with her head toward Katharine, then again to the crowd. There is no quick escape. Camden's ears flicker back and forth, betraying Jules's fear. Joseph steps up beside Arsinoe.

"Well?" he asks. "What's the plan now?"

"You knew what the plan was," she says out of the side of her mouth. "The plan didn't work. Why do you think we had to run out here?"

"Fantastic." Joseph sighs.

"Guards!" Genevieve Arron yells from the gallery, leaning so far over the railing that it looks like she might fall over it. Even from the distance of half the arena, Arsinoe can see how white her knuckles are.

"Take the fugitive queen and the naturalists to the cells!"

Arsinoe, Jules, Joseph, and Mirabella form a tight circle as the Volroy guards flood into the arena. Even with Jules and Camden, they cannot fight their way out. And they cannot run, except perhaps to go up and over the stands, and Mirabella could never manage it, still so weak.

"Arsinoe," Mirabella says. "You could have gotten away. You should not have tried to save me."

"I don't think there was ever any saving us," Arsinoe replies grimly. "I just didn't want to be what they thought I was."

"Stop!" Katharine waves her arms at the guards and the

Council. "This is not over! I can still kill them! I can kill them both if you will remove that"—she points at Jules and sputters with rage—"that cursed naturalist girl!"

"Don't you touch her!" Joseph and Arsinoe bark together.

"This is over!" Arsinoe shouts up to the gallery. "She can't kill me, no matter what she thinks. And I refuse to kill anyone."

"Nor will I," adds Mirabella, and the High Priestess, on her feet beside Natalia Arron, closes her eyes. Luca inclines her head as Natalia murmurs to her and nods. Then Natalia whispers to the Council. At once, guards and priestesses run into the arena, separating Arsinoe and Mirabella from Katharine. Jules punches the first in the eye and knocks back another three.

"Don't fight," Arsinoe says. "It's over, Jules. But I will find a way to get you out of this."

"What about you?" Jules asks as the guards place nervous hands on her. She glares at them and jerks back and forth, not hard enough to free herself but hard enough that they know she could. "Arsinoe, what about you?"

Arsinoe stares after her as Jules is taken away with Joseph and Camden. But she has no answer.

THE VOLROY

*he guards take them to the Volroy, as Arsinoe expected. But instead of hauling them into the Council chamber to be thrown at the feet of Natalia Arron and High Priestess Luca, they are brought quickly and quietly underground and put into the cells deep beneath the castle.

"You can't leave us here," Arsinoe argues as the door closes. "We would speak to the Council! Mirabella, call for priestesses!" She turns, but Mirabella lowers herself quietly onto one of the wooden benches. They have locked them up together at least, and in one of the nicer cells, with four walls and a door with a barred window, and plenty of straw on the floor.

Shouts and scuffling ring out in the corridor, and Arsinoe looks and sees Jules and Joseph being dragged past. Jules slams her escort hard against the stones when Camden yowls. They have the poor cougar choked between two long poles, attached to ropes around her neck.

"Let the cat go," Arsinoe says, "and you'll have an easier time of it."

They frown but release their poles. Arsinoe's throat burns with anger watching poor Camden scramble fearfully behind Jules's legs.

"It'll be all right, Jules," she calls. "Joseph, take care! We won't be down here long!" There is no reply. Just the sound of their scraping shoes growing fainter and fainter.

"We are a curse on the ones we love," Mirabella says.

"Yes. But what were we supposed to do? Die like we were told?" Arsinoe turns away from the door and sits down on the bench beside her sister. "How do you feel?"

"Poisoned. But I suppose you know what that is like."

"Actually . . . ," Arsinoe starts, but stops when she hears Billy's voice.

"Let me pass," he barks. "She's my betrothed. I will see her!"

"Is he talking about you?" asks Arsinoe.

Mirabella chuckles. "No, you fool. Of course not."

Arsinoe rushes to the cell door and slaps her palms against the wood, her face to the bars.

"Stand aside," she orders the guards, and is surprised when they do. It seems that in the Volroy queens are queens, even fugitive ones.

"Arsinoe!"

Billy runs to her. His fingers twist around the bars, and he shakes the door. He kicks at it.

"Damn these bars!"

"Never mind them." Arsinoe puts her hands over his, and he stares at them like he cannot believe the touch is real.

"You're alive," he whispers, his smile a flash in the shadowy hall. "I should wring your neck."

"Good luck reaching far enough in here to do it," she says, and he laughs. "I'm sorry. I wanted to find a way to tell you, but I didn't know how."

"It doesn't matter." He slides his hand through to touch her face.

"I think I've gotten us into a mess."

"As usual. But we'll get out of it. Everything will be all right. Now that you're alive."

"I'm still sorry that you thought I wasn't."

"I'm sorry I agreed to marry your sister," he says, and nods to Mirabella over Arsinoe's shoulder. "How are you, Mira? Holding steady?"

"Just fine," Mirabella says, and Arsinoe blushes. All her words to Billy have been overheard. But what does it matter? She cannot hold back, and Mirabella is apparently thrilled, leaning toward them with her knees tucked up like a child hearing a bedtime story.

"Billy," Arsinoe whispers, her voice so low that even he can hardly hear, "Jules's aunt Caragh and Madrigal are in the city. Look for them at the stables across from the Highbern or in the southern forest by the riverbank. They'll be waiting for us, with Braddock. Get word to Cait and Ellis. They have to come to help Jules and Joseph, if nothing else."

"I will," he promises. He hurries away, and Arsinoe wants to scream. She grabs the bars, teeth clenched so she cannot beg him to stay. But Billy stops and comes back.

"I love you," he says suddenly. "I should have told you. Maybe I never knew. But I do. And you love me, too. Say it."

For a moment, Arsinoe just blinks. Then she laughs.

"Mainlander. You can't make me say it."

"Then say it when I get you out of here. Promise."

"I promise." Her eyes flicker toward the ceiling. "What's happening up there, in the Council chamber?"

Billy's eyes flicker toward the ceiling as well.

"No news yet. Maybe that's a good thing." He lingers. "I don't want to leave you here. Neither of you."

"I know. But you have to, for now. Find out what you can about Jules and Joseph," Arsinoe says. "Don't leave them without help."

"I won't." He slips his fingers through the bars to touch her cheek again. "You will be out before the end of the day."

Natalia stands carefully still in the Council chamber, waiting for the High Priestess to arrive. Carefully still so as not to resemble a confused and stupid bird, like Sara Westwood.

"Queen Mirabella should be placed in a secured room in the East Tower," Sara says. Her voice is shrill, and it is not the first time she has suggested the move. "She does not belong in the cells!"

"The queens are safe and well-guarded," Lucian Marlowe

replies. "The sooner we sit down calmly, the sooner a resolu-
tion may be made." He looks to Natalia for help, and she stares
him down. What a fool to try to reason with a Westwood. He
ought to grab Sara and shove her through the door.

And where is Luca? High Priestess Luca, who takes forever
to get anywhere and uses her old legs as an excuse. But everyone knows she is fast and smooth as a snake when she wishes
to be.

It seems another age passes before they hear the swishing
of Luca's robes, and she arrives flanked by the red-headed
giantess.

"Finally," Genevieve whispers as she ushers the priestesses
into the chamber. "All are here, and the queens in their cells."
She somehow manages to sound as if they have gotten their
way. As if any of this has gone their way.

Natalia is the last to be seated, and she does so with grace,
though everyone in this room she would gleefully throw out a
window.

"This is unthinkable," Antonin says, staring down at his
hands. "So many in the arena heard their words today. As if
there were not enough whispers about these queens already."

"Whispers?" Margaret Beaulin interjects. "The whispers
have risen to a roar. And long before this. The whispers started
over little undead Katharine. They are not proper queens, the
people say. There is something wrong with them."

"Do not speak this way about the queens," Sara Westwood
hisses. "They are sacred!"

"Enough words." Cousin Lucian rubs his temples with long

fingers. "The only thing that matters is what we do. And whatever is done must be done publicly. Katharine must execute them herself. With no interference seen from us."

"Executed? That has not been decided! Queen Mirabella has committed no crime. She was not part of this naturalist stunt!"

"It does not matter," snarls Genevieve. "You heard her. She refuses to kill Arsinoe. And a queen who refuses to kill has committed treason."

"Against who?"

"Against the island!"

Sara looks to the High Priestess for help. But Luca looks only at Natalia and Natalia back at her, as if they are the only ones who matter. Because they are.

"I would speak to the High Priestess alone," Natalia says.

Apprehension flutters through the Council. It passes back and forth between her relatives in furtive glances until Genevieve is forced to speak.

"Sister. This decision is for us all."

"Indeed. And after Luca and I have finished talking, you will all agree with what we decide. Now go."

Genevieve closes her mouth. She shoves herself away from the table and voices her displeasure by loudly ruffling her skirt. She leaves, and the others follow her out.

"Council members," Luca says before they close the doors, "do remember to quiet your voices in the halls. The guards and servants still have ears."

Renata Hargrove scowls, and the heavy black doors thump shut.

"How is it possible that Genevieve and I share the same blood?" Natalia asks, and sighs heavily. "Shall I call for tea?"

"No. But I would not mind a glass of that." Luca peers over Natalia's shoulder into the corner of the room where there is a small stock of liquor. "Unless it is all poisoned?"

Natalia walks to it and pours two glasses.

"Not with Renata and Margaret on the Council." She hands a glass to Luca, and they sit together at the long, oiled wood table of the chamber. Side by side, they look at the relief sculpture that wraps around the room in black-and-white marble, scenes depicting all of the island's gifts, joined together as one.

"You know that crowning Mirabella has become impossible," Natalia says quietly.

"Not impossible," Luca says, but her eyes fall to her glass. "We will give them until Beltane, as is their right. And if they still will not, then we will put them in the tower."

Natalia drains her drink. When she returns from refilling it, she brings back the decanter.

"You know that will not be allowed. Not when there is one willing queen."

"Yes," says Luca. "Your undead girl. How happy you must be."

The old woman's eyes bore into her. What steel there is in this High Priestess. But not even steel can guard against the love for a queen.

"I know you do not want Mirabella to die. I know she is more to you than the temple's ambition." Natalia sets her glass down and stares into it. "We both know to what lengths we have gone to ensure that Katharine and Mirabella survived."

"All of our plans," Luca whispers. "All of our preparations. All failed."

"These queens are uncontrollable. Unpredictable. They have taken the choice out of our hands, perhaps without even knowing they were doing it." She watches Luca drink. The High Priestess knows all this. She is no fool. "This is not the way that I would have Katharine take the crown."

Luca's response is quick. "But you do mean for her to take it."

"Genevieve was right when she called their actions treason," says Natalia. "And Antonin was right when he said the people will doubt us, no matter the outcome. So I would have your voice again in this chamber. And someone of your choosing placed on Katharine's new Council. If the crown is to weather this storm, it will need the backing of the temple."

"You are bribing me," Luca says. "For Mirabella's life!"

"Not a bribe. Never a bribe. None of us has won here, Luca. If we do not come together, we will lose what is left."

She sits very still and lets Luca study her. Lets her try to discern whether she is honest or plotting. In the end, the High Priestess will accept. Natalia only extended the offer as a courtesy anyway. Mirabella will die, whether Luca agrees to benefit from it or not.

Finally, Luca nods.

"We should not let Arsinoe's execution be in front of the people," she says. "She has caused too much trouble already. Who knows what else she might try if given the chance."

"I agree," says Natalia. "Though I also agree with the Council, that Katharine must execute at least one of them in the square."

Luca's face goes slack thinking of how it will be, to preside over Mirabella's execution.

"The people were robbed of a duel," Natalia presses. "And what they saw instead was not the image we would leave them with."

"It will not be easy for Sara and the Westwoods to accept this."

"I know," Natalia replies. "But you can convince them."

Natalia pours into Luca's cup and pushes it toward her. Luca takes up the cup and drains it. When she sets it down, her hand shakes.

"Three seats on the Council," she says. "Three seats, of my choosing."

"Done." Natalia strikes her hand against the tabletop.

Poor old Luca. Her eyes wobble with doubt, as though that was too easy. As though she should have asked for more in exchange for her queen.

"Order the executions," the High Priestess murmurs. "And in the morning Katharine shall be crowned. I will do it myself."

Natalia exhales. It could have gone worse. The infighting,

the roundtable discussions dragging into the night. Sara West-wood wailing.

"It is a relief," she says, gentler now, "to have a High Priestess of your fortitude."

"Oh," Luca replies. "Natalia, do shut up."

INDRID DOWN

———————— ◊ ————————

$\mathcal{M}$adrigal and Jules's aunt Caragh were not at the
stables opposite the Highbern Hotel. He should
have known that they would not be, after passing Braddock's
empty cage in the Volroy courtyard. But Billy started his search
there anyway, hoping, knowing how much harder it would be to
find them in the woods.

The southern woods, Arsinoe said. By the riverbank. He
asks a nut vendor which way to go and makes his way there,
alternately creeping through the trees and then being noisy so
they might find him instead. He wanders for most of the afternoon. Until he is sweaty and tired.

"I can't stay out here in the dark," he says to himself, and
punches his way through a shrub.

Braddock greets him by standing up on his hind legs, and
Billy screams.

"Shush! Shush!" Madrigal hisses. She slaps his shoulder as

his heart pounds, and the bear lowers to sniff at his pockets. "What's the matter with you? And what's taken so long? Where is Jules?"

"I couldn't get in to see Jules," he says quickly. "I have a message from Arsinoe." He tells them of the duel and the queens locked in the Volroy cells. Their faces fill with terror.

"I don't know what's happened with Jules and Joseph after they were locked away," he says. "But I think they're safe. For now."

Madrigal begins to pace.

"They will never let her go. They will never let my Jules go, now that they have her. Now that they know about her legion curse. They'll put her to death!"

The woman who must be Jules's aunt Caragh looks up toward the sunset and the fading light. She looks a little like Madrigal, he supposes, around the eyes and the shape of her face. But the rest is all Grandma Cait. The same hardness and the same firm lines. He feels like he is looking at a photo of Cait from twenty years ago.

"I need to return to the city," Madrigal says. "To see what's happening."

"Stay," says Caragh. "I don't want to have to search the capital for you, too." She puts a hand on Braddock's back as he snuffles Billy's clothes. It is sad to see the bear so diminished. The days in the cage have lessened him. The poisoners' arrows have lessened him. Fear is not a lesson that most great browns ever learn.

"I'm sorry, boy," Billy says. "I didn't bring you anything."

"It's not that." Caragh pats the bear fondly. "He's looking for Arsinoe. He knows you've been near her. He may not be her familiar, but whatever low magic she used to bind him is strong." She looks at Madrigal and at her crow. "We must get word to our parents. Send Aria."

"We have to do more than that," Madrigal protests.

"We will."

"Well, what?" But Madrigal takes up her bird and whispers to her before tossing her into the air.

"I'll speak with my father," says Billy. "He can press his friends here to release Joseph and Jules. And Luca and the temple will have Arsinoe and Mirabella released by nightfall, surely."

"Funny," Madrigal says without stopping her movement. "You never struck me as an idiot. We are in Indrid Down now, Billy. Where the poisoners rule. And if you think they aren't going to take this opportunity to get rid of Arsinoe *and* the legion-cursed naturalist, you're fooling yourself."

"You don't know that."

"No. She's right," Caragh says, and Madrigal blinks. "We need backing here. Natalia Arron will try to get away with something if she can."

"Even if we ride straight through," says Madrigal, "switch for fresh horses. Nobody in Wolf Spring will make it back in time. Not even if Matthew takes them on the *Whistler.*"

"I'm not thinking of Wolf Spring. I'm thinking of Bastian

City. The warriors we saw in the stands today. They may still be here. We may be able to find them before they leave the capital."

"Why would they help us?" Billy asks.

"Because of Jules," Madrigal exclaims excitedly. "She is not only one of ours. She is one of theirs."

"I still say it's unnecessary," Billy says. "My father has clout here. Friends within the Westwoods and the Arrons. He won't leave Joseph to rot. I'm going to wait with him at the Highbern for news. He'll get it sorted. You'll see."

"And when he doesn't," says Caragh, "you come back to help. We'll be here with the warriors in red-lined cloaks."

THE VOLROY CELLS

*ules presses her cheek against the bars of the small cold cell. A nice change from pressing her cheek against the hard, stone walls. She does not know exactly where inside the Volroy they are, but they are down deep. Much deeper than Arsinoe and Mirabella. The trip they took to get here was full of stairs. And full of thrown elbows.

Camden rests her big heavy head on Jules's leg. Jules scratches her ears. They have only slept a little, with no sense of how much time has passed. They have moved past tired to restless and back again.

"How is Cam doing?" Joseph asks from his cell one down from hers.

"She's nervous," Jules replies. "We should have been dragged back up before the Council by now."

"Maybe they mean to forget about us." Joseph's voice is deliberately light. "And keep us down here forever."

365

A hot ball rises in Jules's throat. Let them try. Cait would never allow it. Nor would Joseph's mother. And between the two families they could cause more than enough loud trouble to rattle the Arrons.

"Joseph," Jules whispers. "I'm sorry I got you into all this."

"There's nowhere else I'd rather be. Except for maybe in that cell with you."

Jules smiles softly. Their one afternoon together in Joseph's bed feels like years ago, and it makes her sad, as if the memory belongs to another time, before the Queens' Hunt and Arsinoe almost dying, before everything went so horribly wrong.

"I'm sorry I left you that day, after we . . . after the Queens' Hunt. I'm sorry I disappeared to the Black Cottage."

"You had to. You had to save Arsinoe. I'd have told you to do it if you hadn't done it yourself."

"I know. But I was thinking of you, Joseph."

"It's all right. Arsinoe comes first." He chuckles. "I stopped being jealous about that when we were eight."

"You were jealous for two years?"

"Just about. I guess it took that long for me to love her, too. And because . . . you have always been the most important person to me. Everybody has that, I think. And for me, it will always be you." He sighs. "At least for these last forty-eight hours."

"Don't say that," she says fiercely. "We will get out of here. That day in your bedroom . . . It won't be our only day."

"Best day of my life," he whispers, and she hears him shift in his cell. "Jules?"

"Yeah?"

"If something does go wrong . . . if we can't save Arsinoe . . . I want you to come away with me. Off Fennbirn. I could make a life for us out there, someplace we won't see her ghost every time we look outside."

Jules swallows. If she cannot save Arsinoe, she will see her ghost every day. No matter where she is.

"Arsinoe will find a way out of this. She always does."

"I know," says Joseph. "But if she doesn't . . . if she can't . . . will you go with me?"

Jules looks down at Camden, who blinks up at her with hopeful, yellow-green eyes.

"Yes, Joseph. I'll go with you."

THE HIGHBERN HOTEL

❧

*B*illy waits with his father at the Highbern, staring out the window with his arms crossed over his chest. They have been waiting for so long he could burst. He wants to pace, but his father would only give him that disappointed look. So instead he stares at the Volroy, thinking about Arsinoe trapped inside. Hoping she is giving the guards a hard time.

Perhaps Jules's aunt Caragh was right and he should have stayed with them and helped them mobilize the warriors. It has been too long with no word from the Council, and as outsiders, he and his father will be among the last to receive news. The sky outside has darkened to gray. The woods in the distance are visible only as a blurry smudge. Caragh will not have waited this long. Their plan will have already begun, and he will be left out of it.

Caragh. She was not at all what he expected after hearing Joseph's and Jules's fond remembrances of her. In his mind, she was a nurturer, kind and comforting, a woman who would give up her freedom for the love of a child even when the child was not hers. But the woman he met was hard and decisive. Perhaps the Black Cottage had changed her. Or perhaps there were more sides to a woman than he had ever understood.

The knock at the door surprises him. It is the Volroy messenger, but he did not see him ride up. The young boy hands Billy's father a sealed letter and bows before leaving.

"What does it say?" Billy asks as his father reads. He knew Arsinoe would not have to stay in the cells long. Perhaps they have already been released.

William stuffs the letter into his jacket pocket. His face betrays no feeling, no interest one way or the other. It almost never does, and that has kept Billy off-balance for most of his life.

"The crowning is tomorrow," his father says.

"What crowning?"

"The queen's," William says impatiently. "Queen Katharine. Your future bride."

Billy blinks. He cannot comprehend this news. Not his future bride. Never his future bride.

"But what of Arsinoe? What of Mirabella?"

William shrugs.

"According to the letter, the Wolf Spring girl has probably been executed already. The other one will survive until after the crowning—and after your wedding—to be executed publicly."

"You have to stop it," Billy says. His father raises his eyes, and Billy backs up a step. "Make a deal with the Arrons. Keep Arsinoe and Mirabella alive in secret. I know that you can. I know that you've been working with them since before this started!"

"Stay calm. You knew what would happen."

"It's different now."

"It is. We've won."

His father turns away. Billy can practically see him forget that his son is there, as visions of expansion roll through his head. Plans for their new stream of assets. Exclusive trade with the island for the next generation. And the backing of the poisoners to silence any competitor who does not like it.

"You've done well," his father murmurs distractedly. "I'm proud of you, son."

"And I have long wanted that," Billy whispers. "But why are you proud, Father, when I have done nothing but try to undermine you? I fell in love with the wrong queen. And I wouldn't poison Mirabella, so you had to poison her yourself. I hadn't figured that part out, to be honest. I didn't until Luca said that Katharine hadn't done it by touch. Then I remembered you lingering by our table that night."

"It didn't kill her. And it kept the alliance. It made you a king."

"If I accept."

His father stares.

"And I will accept," Billy goes on. "As long as you go to the

Arrons now and stop Arsinoe's execution."

"Let her go. She's as good as dead. She probably is already."

"It won't hurt to try."

"Billy," William says firmly. "You'll do as I say."

"I won't."

"You will."

"I won't!" Billy shouts, and his father draws his hand back as if to strike him. But he stops short when Billy does not flinch. Billy has never noticed before, that his father is not as large as he once was. That as the years passed, Billy has actually grown to be the taller.

William looks down in disgust and searches his coat for a cigar.

"You won't throw away everything for one girl," he mutters.

"You're wrong, Father," Billy says, right before he turns and walks out the door.

THE QUEEN
CROWNED

THE CROWNING

***

*K*atharine stands on the wooden block, studying her reflection in the mirror as Natalia straightens the skirt of her gown.

"Some naturalist sympathizer has freed the bear," Natalia says. "We are searching the city but have not yet found him."

"Let him go," says Katharine. The bear does not matter anymore. All that matters now is the black satin against her skin. And the guests gathering in the inner chamber of the Volroy.

"When you dressed me last year for my birthday, did you think that we would ever be here? Moments before my crowning?"

"Of course I did, Kat," Natalia says. But Katharine knows the truth. She has surprised them all.

Natalia helps her down from the block, and Katharine twirls once. The gown is simple but elegant. She wears no jewels, and her hair is loose and similarly unadorned. She looks strangely innocent. Almost like the girl she used to be.

"You are beautiful, Queen Katharine." Natalia slides Katharine's hair back over her shoulder. "I wonder that Pietyr is not here to see this. It seems a shame."

Katharine frowns. "Oh well," she says. "I will not miss one guest amongst so many." And she refuses to think of Pietyr on a day like today. Soon she will be crowned. Then she will murder her sister Arsinoe, for real this time, with no escaping. And then she will be married.

She adjusts the fingers of her simple black gloves and smiles.

"So you are not disappointed?" Natalia asks. "That all of this must be done in such haste?"

"Not at all," replies Katharine. "I only care that it is done."

Katharine's crowning is small by crowning standards. The public is not allowed to attend. Only the Black Council, and the temple priestesses, and members of the Arron family. It is a solemn affair with no joy on the faces of the priestesses. No joy on the faces of the Arrons either. Only nervousness. At her ceremonial crowning during next spring's Beltane Festival, they will do better.

High Priestess Luca presides over the affair, straight-backed and imposing in her formal robes, especially for someone so old. She begins by reading the Council and the temple's joint decree: Katharine would be crowned and Arsinoe and Mirabella executed by her. The decree does not mention her sisters by name. After today, they will never be mentioned by name again.

The air inside the chamber is cool and stale as Katharine kneels before the High Priestess. Luca will set the crown upon Katharine's head herself, symbolically uniting the Council and the temple once more.

Katharine tries not to smirk. It cannot be easy for the proud woman to admit that she was wrong.

As Luca bends her head to pray, Katharine glances at her guests. Nicolas, with his secret smile. William Chatworth, the father of the suitor Natalia says she must choose. Genevieve, with steely, violet eyes. And Natalia herself.

The prayers end, and the attending priestesses rise. They offer Katharine water from a silver pitcher. They say it was collected from the River Cro, which runs down from the peak of Mount Horn. Though if it is, she does not know how they managed to get it there so quickly. Perhaps they always keep a pitcher on hand. But no matter. She drinks and it runs down her chin, ice cold, and Katharine is surprised to see that it is Cora, the head priestess of Indrid Down Temple, who holds the pitcher.

"Rise, Queen Katharine," Luca says, and opens her palms. "Daughter of the Goddess. Daughter of the island." Her hands have been anointed with scented oil, and a little blood. At a normal crowning, the blood would have been taken from the stag killed during the Hunt. Katharine wonders whose blood it is now. She would have offered to cut the throat of Arsinoe's bear had someone not turned it loose.

Except for Luca's few words, the crowning is largely silent. They do not ask her for vows or oaths. A queen is made of the island as the island is made of her. They have no right and no need to ask her to swear.

The High Priestess reaches for the wooden tattoo tool, simply carved, its tip a short bundle of needles.

The tattooed crown has not been done for generations. It was Natalia's idea. Perhaps a bad one, Katharine thinks, as she watches Luca's hands shake. She will be lucky if her crown does not zig and zag across her forehead.

"Do not worry," Luca whispers as if reading Katharine's mind. "I still put bracelets on many of my own priestesses." She places the tool to Katharine's brow.

The first strike is a shock. And there is no time to recover before the next, and the next, a seemingly never-ending sequence of pain as Luca taps the needles and black ink into Katharine's skin just below her hairline.

It takes a long time. A lot of time and pain, but it is a crown that will not fade and cannot be taken from her head to give to another.

"Rise, Katharine," Luca says. "The Queen Crowned of Fenn-birn Island."

Katharine stands, and the assembled guests clap until she holds up her hand.

"I would choose my consort," she says.

"As you will," Luca replies. "Whom do you choose?"

"I choose . . . ," Katharine looks at William Chatworth. He seems to her a piggish man and too smug and confident when his son has not even bothered to be present. Natalia must be mad to recommend him. But Natalia is not the queen.

"I choose the suitor Nicolas Martel."

THE VOLROY CELLS

*A*rsinoe has been banging her head against the stone wall for what seems like hours. But there is no way to tell for sure. The only way to gauge the passage of time is by the guard changes.

"Are you feeling any better?" she asks Mirabella.

Mirabella draws her leg up beneath her torn black skirt and braces her heel on the edge of the wooden bench.

"I feel almost well, actually. Whatever I was poisoned with, it seems to have run its course. It seems it was not meant to kill me."

"Of course not," Arsinoe says. "*She* was meant to kill you." She sighs and leans back. Flicks her hand toward the wooden door. "Can you burn us a way out of here, then?"

"No. The wood is too thick. I would have to call fire so hot it would burn you up with it. If the smoke did not kill us first."

Arsinoe glances at her sister. Mirabella has sloughed her

light overlaid jacket to sit in a corseted bodice with wide black straps. It must be true what they say, and elementals do not feel the drafts or the damp.

"Why did they put you in a skirt?" Arsinoe asks. "Didn't they know they were dressing you for a duel?"

"I am wearing boots," Mirabella replies. "And no slip or petticoat." She rolls her head toward Arsinoe and smiles tiredly. "Appearances, appearances."

Arsinoe chuckles.

"At least when we're dead, there'll be no more of that."

"You think we are to die, then?" Mirabella asks, and Arsinoe cocks her eyebrow. She has to remind herself that her sister was not raised like she was. Mirabella was treated as the queen. Death must seem impossible.

Arsinoe sighs. "I don't think they'll let me out to cause any more trouble. But you have the High Priestess. And the Westwoods. They're shrewd; maybe they can barter you for me. Though I don't like to think about what they'll do to Jules and Joseph."

"They will not do anything," Mirabella says, and the air in the cell begins to crackle. Arsinoe stares down at her arm in wonder as the hairs rise and stand on end.

"Do you promise?" Arsinoe asks. "If you get out of here, do you promise to take care of them?"

"Of course I will."

Arsinoe stands and stretches her back.

"Good. Because it's my fault, you know. Joseph being

banished five years ago. Jules being poisoned after Beltane. Even Cam getting mauled by that sick, old bear."

"They do not see it like that."

"Of course they don't. They're too good."

Footsteps sound in the corridor. It could be Billy, coming back to tell her that they will be released, free to kill another day. Even to be locked together in the tower would be preferable to this.

But the footsteps are too light and accompanied by too many other footsteps. And there is too much rustling.

Katharine's face appears at the barred opening of the wooden door.

"Sisters," Katharine says. Her pretty, dark-lashed eyes flicker between Arsinoe and Mirabella, who stands up quickly and brushes dust and straw from her dress.

Arsinoe waits for Katharine to say more. But she just stands before their cell, smiling. Like she is waiting for something. Mirabella gasps.

"What?" Arsinoe asks.

"Her forehead," Mirabella whispers. "Look at her forehead."

Arsinoe squints and peers through the bars. A thin, black line has been etched across Katharine's brow, just below her hairline.

"I wanted to show you," Katharine says brightly. "So there would be no confusion. So that no one could tell you lies. I wanted you to see my crown for yourselves."

Arsinoe swallows. "Is that what that is?" she asks. "I thought you must've rolled across a piece of coal."

Katharine laughs. "Joke all you want. But it is done. And I owe it to you, in part. Thanks to your grand pronouncements of mercy for each other, the Council and the temple felt they had no choice. Your refusal to kill made them finally see that I am the only true queen born of this cycle."

Arsinoe scoffs. She should probably be afraid, but instead she is irritated. Almost angry. Poor Mirabella looks as though she might be sick, seeing that crown painted on Katharine's forehead.

"The only true queen," Arsinoe spits. "The only killer."

"But she was not always," Mirabella says. "You were not always, Katharine. You were sweet once. We used to—"

"Do not try to make me guilty," Katharine interrupts. "It had to be one of us. That is the way the game is played. That is what we are."

"Have it your way, then," says Arsinoe. "Take us out of this cell and back to the arena. See which of us walks out."

Katharine clucks her tongue. "I am afraid not, Sister. You both had plenty of chances."

"Have you come only to gloat?" Mirabella asks. "Where is the High Priestess? Or Sara Westwood? Where are the Milones, for Arsinoe? We would see them if this will truly come to pass."

"Yes," Arsinoe says, and waves her hand. "Let them come and tell us this news. You should go, Queen Katharine. And if you return"—Arsinoe rises onto her tiptoes to look farther down on her smaller sister—"bring a box to stand on."

Such darkness comes into Katharine's eyes that Arsinoe sinks back onto flat feet. Again she thinks that there is something not right about Katharine. Something off. And she does not know why, but she is certain that the Arrons do not know what it is.

"Open the door," Katharine orders. Keys jangle and the door opens, and the new queen steps inside.

"You misunderstand," she says, and Arsinoe and Mirabella step back as guards spill into the cell. They herd Mirabella to the wall and grab Arsinoe's arms and hold her fast. "I have not come to tell you news! I have come to deliver your fate."

"What are you talking about?" Arsinoe jerks in the guards' grip.

"On the island, only queens kill queens," Katharine says sweetly. "That will not change just because two are traitors to their birthright. You, Arsinoe, are a queen. So you may not be executed by any other than one of your own." She reaches into her sleeve and draws out a stoppered glass vial of amber liquid. "Guards, restrain Queen Mirabella."

Mirabella bares her teeth. Every torch lining the corridor of the prison flares nearly to the ceiling.

"Tell her to be still," Katharine says to Arsinoe. "Unless you want me to return later with the heads of the legion-cursed girl and her mountain cat."

The torch flames lower, and the heat vanishes as Mirabella ceases to struggle.

"Fighting will not change this," Katharine continues. "But the fates of your friends have not yet been decided."

"You mean to poison us," Arsinoe says calmly.

"Yes. But only you, for now. Queen Mirabella will be executed tomorrow morning in the square." Katharine smiles meanly. "For that is what the High Priestess wishes."

"No," Mirabella cries. "You are lying!"

Katharine may not be lying, but she is certainly cruel. Arsinoe glances through the open door, and into the hall. Jules and Joseph cannot have been taken that far. There are only so many floors of cells to take them to. Still, there are plenty of guards. Strong, armed guards. She can only hope that Mirabella is even stronger. They will not get another chance.

"Come now, let us get on with this," Katharine says. "I am still to be married this evening."

"Don't fight," Arsinoe says to Mirabella. "For Jules's and Joseph's sakes."

"No! Arsinoe, no!" Mirabella protests, but the guards back her up against the wall.

Arsinoe stares at the poison in Katharine's hand. She forces her eyes to widen. She takes a deep breath and another. Faster and faster. It is not hard to seem frightened. She is frightened. Just not of what is inside of the vial.

Katharine removes the stopper and Arsinoe pretends to lose her nerve, twisting, trying to pull free, her heels digging into the straw-lined floor. The look in Katharine's eyes is wickedly mirthful, and Arsinoe is tempted to forgo her plan. It would almost be worth it just to see Katharine's face when she drinks the poison and does not die.

"Lower her onto her back," Katharine orders.

Arsinoe kicks and screeches. She presses her lips together when Katharine bends over to pour the poison in, so that Katharine must force her mouth open, squeezing her cheeks with gloved fingers.

The poison is oily. Bitter-tasting. It smells sharply of vegetation. It runs into her mouth and down her throat, so much of it that she nearly chokes and coughs it up onto her face, making the guards reel backward. She hears Mirabella screaming on the other side of the cell, and feels the floor tremble as a great crack of lightning strikes the fortress above.

Katharine cries out. She pushes away from Arsinoe and runs for the door, covering her head.

"You," she says, and points at Mirabella. "You will have to be weakened before your execution. I will not have any shows of lightning diverting the people's attention."

"Are you so afraid?" Mirabella shouts, with tears in her voice. She shoves past the guards and falls to her knees at Arsinoe's side, and Arsinoe coughs and convulses.

Katharine watches until Arsinoe begins to grow still. As Mirabella's weight presses down on her chest, Arsinoe lets her eyes drift shut.

"I am not afraid," Katharine says. "And I am not without mercy." She turns to the guards. "Let her cry awhile over the corpse before you take it away. And then prepare it for viewing.

I would have it on display at the execution. So afterward they can lie side by side."

Mirabella pulls Arsinoe's limp form onto her lap. She weeps so loudly that it is hard to hear when the sounds of Katharine's escort fade into the corridor.

And even then, Arsinoe waits until the only sound she hears is Mirabella before she finally reopens her eyes.

THE WEDDING

*A*s Nicolas takes his oaths before the High Priestess, Katharine's mind wanders. It is not that she is not excited to be marrying him. She is. But it feels almost like the denouement, after the thrill of the crown inked into her skin. After the joy of pouring poison down her sister's frightened throat. She had waited so long for that. She could almost spin in place remembering how Arsinoe struggled and how Mirabella *screamed*.

She slumps, sees Natalia watching, and straightens up again. It is just that there are so many oaths. Nicolas is not a queen, and he must swear, and swear, and swear his allegiance.

Only Natalia and the Black Council are present for the wedding, with Luca and a few priestesses. The small dark room in the East Tower is lit by three tall candelabras. Someone should have opened a window. The reek of the sacred incense is making her want to cough.

"Drink and be anointed," Luca says.

They make him drink from her crowning cup and dab him with blood and oil. Poor Nicolas. He tries hard to look like he belongs there. But he keeps looking at her, like she might come to him instead of standing to one side. No one told him that the wedding of a king-consort is more to the Goddess than it is to the queen. That she will not even touch him. That they will not even kiss.

Katharine studies him in the candlelight. He is so handsome and a good match for her. But he is not Pietyr.

A tight, cold ball settles in the pit of her stomach. Pietyr tried to kill her. But only because he thought she would be killed anyway and killed horribly, by serrated knives and strangers pulling her apart.

Of course he could have hidden her instead. But that is not the Arron way. Arrons win, or they lose. All or nothing. And Katharine never expected him to be any different.

Finally, Nicolas finishes his vows and is allowed to face the queen. The priestesses bow to her. Even Luca. Then they file out of the room, followed by the Council. Natalia leaves without looking her in the eye, still angry about her choice of suitor. But Natalia is as a mother to her and will not stay angry forever.

Nicolas takes her gloved hands.

"That is it?" he asks. "I thought they would take my blood or burn their symbol into my chest. I thought we would be bound together by lengths of cord."

"Is that what they do in your country?"

"No. In my country, we would both take vows. And my bride would wear white."

"She would not if she were a queen," Katharine says.

Nicolas lifts her hand to his mouth. He kisses it so greedily that his teeth graze the fabric. He has been respectful in his courtship. He has not even kissed her properly on the mouth. But when he pulls her forward and crushes her to his chest, his hands slide into her hair and cup the back of her head. He is not gentle or shy.

Katharine raises her elbows and pushes out of his grip.

"Not now," she says.

"What do you mean, 'not now'? We are married. You are mine."

"We are each other's," she corrects him. He reaches for her again, but she moves away, her gown rustling like a rattlesnake's tail. "I would see Natalia. I do not like it when she is angry with me."

"See her later, Katharine. I don't want to wait. I would have you out of those clothes. Skin to skin." His eyes move over her hungrily. "I have been patient, and we are here, in our castle."

"You have been patient," she says. "But our wedding night will not be here. With everything so rushed and sudden there was no time to prepare even a bedchamber in the West Tower. It is all covered over in dust sheets. Full of coughing priestesses chasing away cobwebs."

"Where, then? And when?"

"My rooms at Greavesdrake. Natalia has arranged a carriage to take us there."

* * *

When someone opens the door to Natalia's study high in the East Tower, she expects a servant. Some good and thoughtful boy come to bring her a hot cup of poisoned tea. But it is not. It is William Chatworth.

"Some other time, William," she says, and returns to the letter she has been scribbling, another letter to her brother Christophe seeking the whereabouts of Pietyr, as well as to tell him what has transpired. Perhaps the news will finally jolt her brother out from underneath that wife of his, away from her country estate and back to the capital where he belongs.

"Not some other time. Now." William strides into the room and helps himself to a pour of her brandy, so fast that she can barely slap it out of his hand.

"It is tainted," she says as they stare at the shattered wet mess upon the floor. "With nightshade and fresh elderberry."

Chatworth exhales. He flexes his fist and releases it. Then he swings back hard and slaps Natalia across the face.

Her head turns. She takes a step back, mostly from shock. It is shock more than the pain that makes her eyes water.

"Perhaps I should have let you drink it," she says. The impact has driven her teeth into her cheek, and she spits a little blood down at his shoes. "But then again, I see that you are drunk already."

"You married your brat to the Martel boy."

"There was nothing I could do. You were there. She made her choice in front of everyone. Perhaps if your son had bothered to show up—"

"So say she changed her mind. That she was angry at him for not being at the crowning."

"I cannot," Natalia says calmly. "She is the queen. And we had to proceed quickly. We are in a precarious place—"

"Undo it."

"I said I cannot." Natalia grimaces, tired of his breath and his mainland concerns. His normally clear, handsome eyes are squinted and swollen. She does not like him like this. Though perhaps this is what he truly is underneath. Angry, and ugly, and small. "They are wed. He is on his way to her bedchamber now."

"What does it matter? She can sleep with him and then marry Billy later. Your queens are not ladies. None of you are fit to be true wives. My son will have to teach her."

"He will not teach her anything," Natalia snaps. "Now leave, William. You are drunk."

But Chatworth does not leave. His face turns red and spittle flies from his lips.

"I've spent years feeding Joseph Sandrin to get Billy a place on Fennbirn. To get him a crown. I poisoned the elemental. And before that, the girl in Wolf Spring."

"We will not forget it." Natalia turns her back. A mistake, perhaps, but she cannot bear to look at him any longer. "You will have as much of our trade as I can manage; I do not think Nicolas's family will be overly diligent. All that you lack is the title, and for that, you get to keep your son. That must please you, surely."

He falls quiet, and Natalia begins scribbling on her letter again. His hands wrapping around her neck from behind are such a surprise that she does not even cry out.

He is strong and so angry that it is only moments before Natalia's vision swims. Her hands claw at his fingers and then at her table for anything to help her. All she has is a glass paperweight, a pretty, lilac thing, rounded and not very large. A gift from Genevieve. She picks it up and twists as far as she can to smash it against the side of his head.

The blow is glancing but makes him stumble, and she falls to the ground, gasping. She tries to call for help, but her voice comes out a croak. Then William kicks her in the stomach, and every muscle in her body clenches tight.

He hits her. And hits her. Without a sound. She stares into his drunken, bloodshot eyes, hearing nothing but her heartbeat and his labored breathing.

I cannot end like this, she thinks. *I am Natalia Arron.*

She puts her arms up to fight, clawing wildly.

"Kat," she gasps. "Katharine."

And then Chatworth's hands close around her throat again, and Natalia's world goes dark.

Rho steps into the threshold to find the mainlander standing over Natalia.

"This is your fault," he is muttering, and spits at the motionless body. "You should have done what you were to—"

His words cut off abruptly when Rho enters. She sweeps

past him in her white robes and kneels to feel for Natalia's pulse even though she knows she will not find one. Her neck is crushed. Her eyes are red with burst blood vessels.

"Clean it up," the mainlander says. "Clean it up, and find me someone else to deal with."

Rho stands. She looks him in the eyes. And without a word, she draws her serrated knife and sinks the blade deep between his ribs. The expression on his face as she carves him up from lungs to heart is delicious to her old war gift. Were it not for the vows she took to the temple to leave her gift behind, she would push him with her mind. Throw him up against the wall so hard he bounced.

"You . . . ," he gasps. "You . . ."

"You should not have touched her, mainlander."

She yanks her knife free. He staggers backward, his hand fluttering at the blood pouring from his side. Then he drops to the rug, dead even before he lands.

Rho cleans the blade on the black band of her robes. The blood can remain there for who knows how long, invisible, her secret badge. She calls out for aid, and two initiates come running.

They moan and clap their hands over their mouths when they reach the door.

"Roll him up in a rug," Rho says. "And dispose of him in the river."

It takes them too long to respond for her liking, but they are new, so she tries to be patient.

"What about . . . Mistress Arron?" asks the taller when she finds her voice.

Rho stares down at Natalia's body. So much trouble she has caused them over the years. But Natalia was of the island. Of the Goddess, like Rho herself is. And at the end, she died an ally.

"Go and find her sister. Bring her here and tell her what has happened. Tell her gently."

THE VOLROY CELLS

I still do not understand," Mirabella whispers. "So Katharine really did shoot you with the poisoned bolt?"

"Right," Arsinoe says, lying on the floor of their cell, still pretending to be poisoned and dead.

"But you did not die of poison because you *cannot* die of poison. . . . Were you really wearing thick leather armor underneath your clothes?"

"No."

"Then how did you not die of the bolt wound?"

"Just be glad I didn't," Arsinoe whispers. "Now go on weeping."

Mirabella glances over her shoulder. Unlike Arsinoe, Mirabella was not born for the stage. Her fake cry sounds like a harbor seal Arsinoe and Jules found beside the cove once, with a bellyache and horrible gas.

"Not so loud," Arsinoe hisses. "We don't want them to give you all night to mourn! Just enough so they can hear you. And believe that I'm dead."

Mirabella pretends to sniffle this time, much more softly, and Arsinoe closes her eyes. She must try to be patient. After all, Mirabella's first tears were real, before she looked down and realized that Arsinoe was grinning.

Mirabella quiets, and Arsinoe opens one eye.

"They crowned her," Mirabella murmurs. "I cannot believe they crowned her."

"And ordered your execution," Arsinoe adds. "Good Goddess. They really made you want to be queen, didn't they? They held that crown out for you like a prize."

"I am angry about being executed," Mirabella says, and scowls. "But there must have been some reason . . . why Luca would let them. . . ."

"Because we gave them no choice." Arsinoe squeezes her sister's hand. "But you have to be brave now. I can't get out of here without you."

"Get out of here to what?" Mirabella asks bitterly. "I will not go back to Rolanth, to a temple who would see me killed. Not even if they imprisoned Katharine instead. Not even if they said you could live."

"Which they would never say," Arsinoe mutters.

They are fugitives now. Exiles. Arsinoe cannot go back to Wolf Spring any more than Mirabella can return to Rolanth. She cannot go back to the Milones and get them in worse trouble than they may already face.

"The island crowned its queen," Arsinoe says. "Another poisoner, and not even the strongest poisoner of the litter." She humphs. "I don't know about you, but I don't want anything more to do with them."

"Nor do I," Mirabella agrees. "So what do we do? Stand side by side united tomorrow as we are executed?"

"No. You have a terrible sense of rebellion." Arsinoe swats her. Then she lies back and knocks her head against the straw-covered floor.

"The island crowned its queen," Mirabella murmurs. "You are right. So perhaps it is not that we are done with it, but that it is done with us. Perhaps it will let us go."

Arsinoe looks up hopefully. But the hope is fleeting.

"I've tried that. Twice."

"You have not tried with me."

That is true. Mirabella's gift is so strong, it could tear a hole through the mist. And dying at sea would be better anyway, than dying at the hands of the Arrons.

Mirabella holds her hand out.

"All right," Arsinoe says, and takes it.

She grins until footsteps sound down the corridor. Then she goes limp. So much must go their way for their escape to work. But this is their only chance.

The key turns in the lock. The door swings open. Guards shuffle inside, murmuring apologies. To them and every other guard they will encounter, Arsinoe and Mirabella are still queens, and the sisters will use that to their advantage.

"Forgive us, Queen Mirabella. But we have to take her."

"No!" Mirabella throws herself across Arsinoe's chest. "A few moments more!"

Arsinoe wishes she could open her eyes to see how many guards there are. From their footsteps, she would guess no more than three.

"Come now. Any longer will only make it harder."

Mirabella pitches such a fit that Arsinoe almost laughs. But her acting is much better now.

"Take Queen Mirabella aside," the guard says, and Mirabella shouts and struggles and makes a general ruckus. They lift Arsinoe by the arms, and she lets her head fall back. She waits until they have her hoisted high enough that she can get her feet underneath her, and then she takes her chance.

She jerks her right arm loose and punches the guard straight across the face. The poor girl crumples like a dropped sack of potatoes. Jules would be proud. Arsinoe twists her left arm, prepared to pull and pull, but her luck holds. The shock of seeing her come back to life has loosened the other guard's fingers. So Arsinoe draws back and hits her, too.

The last guard holding Mirabella stares at Arsinoe in wonder. He is a skinny thing, not much older than Joseph's little brother, Jonah.

"What—" he stammers. "How?" He lets go of Mirabella and takes a few disoriented steps.

Arsinoe squares herself to fight before he can collect his wits and alert the rest of the prison.

But to her surprise, Mirabella threads her fingers together

and swings down hard to club him at the back of the neck. His eyes cross as he falls to the floor.

"Oh!" Mirabella exclaims softly.

"'Oh' is right," Arsinoe says. She reaches down and relieves the lead guard of her keys, then takes up the lantern they set near the door. "Now tear that skirt of yours to use for gags, and let's get out of here."

Jules's and Joseph's last meal was a good one. Their guards were kind and brought them roasted duck and bread and soft cheese. Even a bag of sugared nuts from a street vendor.

"I can't eat this," Jules says, and listens to Joseph toss his metal plate down.

"Nor can I," Joseph replies. "What's roasted duck when we're going to be dead in the morning? I can toss some to you. For Cam."

Jules nudges her plate toward the cougar, who lies with her head on Jules's knee. Camden will not even sniff at it.

"She won't take it either." She strokes the cat's broad, golden head. She cannot believe that they will pass their last hours like this. She is numb. Not even afraid. She has not been able to feel anything since the guard came to tell them that Arsinoe had been executed. And that they would be tied to posts in the morning and executed as well, their bodies left out for Mirabella to see.

She hears Joseph moving in his cell, turning against the bars.

"I keep thinking of what we should have done," he says. "What we could have done differently. But maybe there was nothing." He snorts. "Sometimes you just lose. After all, someone has to."

"I want Cait," Jules says, her throat tightening with tears. "And Ellis." She wants Aunt Caragh and even Madrigal.

"I know," Joseph says. "I want them too. I wish we were anywhere else but in the belly of this castle. But Camden's here. And I'm here. Don't cry, Jules."

"I have to tell you something." She wipes at her cheeks. "I have to tell you what Arsinoe told me. About the low magic."

"What low magic?"

"The night you came back, she did a love spell for us. But she did it wrong. She ruined it, and she thinks that's why . . . why you and Mirabella . . ." She stops. Joseph is quiet for a long time.

"Joseph? Don't you have anything to say?"

"Like what, Jules?" he asks softly.

"Well . . . do you think that's why it happened? Arsinoe's low magic is so strong. It could've been. It really could have been."

"I know what you're doing."

"What?"

"Trying to forgive me," he says, and she can hear the smile in his voice. "You don't want to go out there tomorrow still hating me."

"I don't hate you."

"I hope you don't. But what happened with Mirabella was my fault. Maybe the magic put us in each other's path, maybe it even helped us along, but that doesn't make me blameless, Jules. I made a mistake. I wish I hadn't, but it doesn't change what I did."

Jules knew all that, deep down. But she feels freer somehow now that he has said it.

"Well, anyway," she says cheekily. "I was just trying to make you feel better about it, since we're about to die."

Joseph laughs.

"How I love you, Jules."

Footsteps echo down the hall, and Jules wipes her tears on her sleeve. No guard on patrol will see tear streaks on her face. Not ever.

"What now?" Joseph asks.

Jules stiffens when she hears a sound like a body falling. Camden's ears prick, and she gets to her feet, tail ticking back and forth.

"Jules!" Arsinoe hisses. "Jules, are you down here?"

"Arsinoe!" Jules and Camden scramble up to the bars as Arsinoe runs to them. They embrace her as well as they can with hands and paws. Camden purrs and licks her face.

"Camden, blegh." Arsinoe grins and wipes her cheek.

"I might have licked you as well, I'm so happy to see you." Jules gasps. "I thought you were dead. I thought they killed you."

"Aye, they tried. But they tried the wrong way. They sent

that sister of mine to poison me." Arsinoe fumbles with a ring of keys until she finds the one that opens the door. Then she tosses the ring to Mirabella to open Joseph's. "Are you and Cam all right?"

Jules steps out of the cell just as Joseph collides with them and kisses them each in turn: girl, girl, cougar.

"We're okay."

"Good. We have to get out of here now. Are you strong enough? Can you fight?"

Jules clenches her fists.

"That's a silly question."

She looks across the corridor, at Mirabella, and nods to her. Then she slips out of her friends' arms and lets Arsinoe lead the way out.

GREAVESDRAKE MANOR

❦

$\mathcal{N}$icolas helps her out of the carriage, and Katharine looks up nervously at the light from her bedroom windows. Her maids will have prepared the room, setting out vases of poisonous flowers and lighting candles with perfumed wax. They will have turned down the bed.

Katharine takes a deep breath. No carriage ride from the city has ever been over so quickly.

Nicolas pulls her up the path to the house, and Natalia's butler opens the door.

"Edmund," she says. "Is Natalia at home?"

"She has not yet returned from the Volroy, my queen," he replies. "But all has been made ready according to her specifications."

"That is good." Katharine stalls a little as he takes her cloak. The air on her shoulders makes her feel very bare. "Though I expected that she would be here . . . or if not her, then Genevieve . . . Yet I suppose I should be glad that *she* is not here. . . ."

"Enough," says Nicolas, and pulls her close to kiss her neck. He takes up a lamp from the foyer table and leads her quickly down the hall.

As they pass by the rooms, Katharine is gripped by an unexpected sadness. Soon she will say good-bye to Greavesdrake, to its ancient, creaky floors and sunless rooms full of cold spots. After tonight, she will not return. Not as she does now. Greavesdrake will no longer be home.

"Nicolas, slow down. I will turn my ankle!"

"You will not." He laughs.

The house seems so empty. Where are the tittering maids, the spying servants? There is not so much as a rustling skirt darting out of their way. They reach her bedroom, and Nicolas tugs her through the doorway so hard that she nearly falls.

Inside, the space is lit softly with candles. The carpets and bed are strewn with red flower petals. She has imagined this night before. But it was never Nicolas she imagined beside her.

Nicolas turns her to face him. Her breath is already fast.

"I do not know why I am so nervous," she says.

"Do not be."

He kisses her.

It is not like Pietyr's kisses. Not like a dam breaking. It will take some getting used to, but at least his lips are soft. He strips her of her gloves.

"These scars." He stares at her hands. "Will they fade?"

"I do not know," she says, and tries to pull her hands away. But instead of being disgusted, the sight of the scars only seems to arouse him further. He bites them and traces them with his tongue. He kisses her neck and her collarbone, and his touch is rough, as though their wedding has made him bold. She has heard it is like that sometimes with mainland men. Though she does not remember where she heard it. From Pietyr, perhaps, during her education. Or from Genevieve, meaning to frighten her.

Nicolas takes himself out of his shirt and works his fingers into the fastenings of her gown.

Katharine turns away.

"Stop. Wait." She walks through the anteroom and into her bedchamber. It has all happened so fast. The duel, her crowning, poisoning Arsinoe. She has had barely a moment to breathe, and now she feels all those missed breaths clawing at her throat.

"Wait for what?" Nicolas asks. He follows her and kisses her shoulder. Gentler now. She closes her eyes.

In the morning, it will be over. She will execute Mirabella, and the hum in her blood will quiet. The dead queens of the Breccia Domain satisfied. But even as she leans into her king-consort's arms, she feels the dead queens picking at her, surging through her. They make her strong and never leave her alone.

Pietyr, I should never have sent you away, she thinks as she flinches from wetness left on her neck by Nicolas's kisses.

Nicolas stops. He pulls her up, holds her chin so she must look him in the eye.

"Are you thinking of him?" he asks.

"No," she lies.

"Good." He picks her up and carries her to the bed. "Because he is not here."

THE VOLROY

$\mathcal{A}$rsinoe's blood pounds in her ears as they head up and up the Volroy steps. She feels safer now that Jules is there, even though she is still in the lead. Part of her thought that when they freed Jules and Joseph, Jules would take over the escape. But they will get out either way.

They reach the next floor, and Arsinoe presses flat to the wall. This is the last gate. She remembers the ornate iron brazier in the center of the room from when they were being dragged down to the cells. She leans forward by a fraction and quickly leans back. There are so many guards. No less than ten. A few are seated around the rectangular table. Others lean against the walls. Three stand directly beside the passageway through the gate. All are armed with clubs and knives. Two carry crossbows.

Arsinoe turns and holds up ten fingers. Jules nods. Joseph's and Mirabella's faces pale. But there is no way out but through.

Arsinoe takes a deep breath. She hopes that everyone knows what to do. And that they are able to do it.

She barrels into the room and runs headlong into the nearest guard, dropping her shoulder into his chest so hard that she hears a crack. That must be good, because he folds up and hits the floor without throwing so much as a punch.

"The scarred queen! The queens!" The guard by the gate shouts. Chairs tip over as the guards at the table rise. They hesitate to raise weapons against queens. Especially one who seems able to come back from the dead.

Jules darts out from the shadow of the corridor and levels one of them holding a crossbow. Camden, snarling, quickly pins the other, and Joseph rips the weapon from his hands.

"Quiet! No one move!" Arsinoe commands, hands out. "Get to the middle of the floor. Lie on your bellies!"

A guard wearing a black captain's sash shakes her head.

"We can't let you out of here, my queen," she says.

"You can, and you will," says Arsinoe.

But the captain's hand goes to her short-bladed sword. She draws it and spins away from Arsinoe, aiming for Joseph. It is a fool's move. Jules's war gift stops the sword from ever coming down, and Joseph reflexively fires the crossbow. The bolt sinks deep into the captain's chest.

The sight of their captain spitting red sends the rest into a frenzy. Arsinoe is immediately shoved and has to duck fast to avoid the swing of a black-lacquered club. The sound of it ringing off the stones makes her dizzy. That could have been her head, split wide open. Ducked low, she grabs for the knife at the guard's belt and sinks it into his leg, then into his shoulder as he falls.

Someone else's club catches her in the back. Her vision swims bright and dark, and she collapses onto the floor.

There is so much noise. So much struggle. Someone steps on her hand and crushes it. Mirabella is screaming.

"Jules?" Arsinoe groans. "Where is Jules?"

Bones pop, and the guard who hit Arsinoe falls dead to the ground. Someone reaches underneath her and pulls her up.

"I've got you, Arsinoe," Jules says. "I've got you."

Arsinoe turns to look at her, and her eyes widen.

"Jules, look out!"

But before the knife can swing down, the attacking guard bursts into flames. Mirabella's face is furious, her fire so hot that the guard only shrieks for a moment. She lowers the fire as the stench of burned flesh spreads heavily through the air. Jules coughs amid the smoke and fires a crossbow bolt into the dying body, to put him out of his misery.

"I had to," Mirabella says. "I—" Camden, who must have been guarding her, wrinkles her muzzle and slinks away to curl behind Jules's legs.

Arsinoe looks around. It happened so quickly. Every guard is dead or unconscious. The room is full of sick-smelling smoke. Joseph is on one knee, panting from the exertion of the fight.

"Let's get out of here," Arsinoe mutters.

Joseph stands, his right side dark with blood.

"Joseph!"

Jules slips out from beneath Arsinoe's arm and goes to him, pressing hard against the wound.

"Here." Mirabella tears more strips from her skirt to bind it.

"I'm fine," he says. "It's just a cut. It's not even that deep."

Jules lifts his shirt. She and Mirabella wrap him up tight, using so much of the skirt that Mirabella's legs are visible over the tops of her boots.

"I'm all right, Jules." Joseph touches her face. His hand trembles.

"I know," she replies. "You'll be perfectly fine, as soon as we get out of here." She puts his arm over her shoulders and nods to Arsinoe.

"Right," Arsinoe says. But she swallows hard, looking at him. There will be plenty more guards to get through when they make it upstairs and into the Volroy proper.

She grabs a torch off the wall and takes up one of the fallen guard's clubs.

"Mirabella, stay behind me," says Jules. "You don't need to be out front to use your gift, do you?"

Mirabella shakes her head.

As quickly as they can, they move through the last gate and creep up the stairs to the ground level. Near the top, Arsinoe sets down the torch before the light can give them away.

There are bound to be many guards here. Probably priestesses too. It will take all of them and the Goddess besides to get clear of the Volroy, and even then, they will probably be instantly stopped in the courtyard.

They turn the corner, ready to fight. But there is no one

there. Only faintly burning candles in the sconces on the walls. And then they see the bodies.

Bodies of guards are littered across the ground. Arms and legs stick out from beneath tables and from behind half-closed doors.

"What happened here?" Joseph asks, and Jules crouches as a dozen cloaked figures run into view with weapons drawn.

The wind quickens through the windows as Mirabella gathers her elements. "Wait, wait!"

The cloaked leader pushes back his hood, and Arsinoe drops her club.

"Billy!" she cries, and runs into his arms.

"Arsinoe!"

He lifts her off the ground. He squeezes so tight that she can barely breathe and kisses her hair and the scars upon her face.

"Are you all right?" he asks. "I was terrified we would be too late."

"I'm fine," Arsinoe says, beaming. "But who is 'we'?"

A girl steps forward wearing a red-lined cloak.

"I remember you," Arsinoe says. "From the arena. You were at the duel." She looks over the rest of them, barely a dozen in total, who have laid waste to every guard on the main floor of the fortress. "What are you doing here?"

The girl regards her with respect and bows slightly.

"We are warriors from Bastian City," she says, and nods toward Jules. "And we came for her."

GREAVESDRAKE MANOR

⚜

*K*atharine wakes in the dark to Nicolas thrashing, jerking, caught in the net of some horrible dream. She reaches out and touches his shoulder, and he eases back to sleep.

The room is full of shadows. The candles and lamps have gone out or been put out; she cannot remember. What she does remember sends heat to her cheeks. Nicolas was so different from Pietyr. But he is no less passionate. Afterward, he held her tightly, pressed together skin to skin.

She rolls toward him and slips her hand beneath the blankets.

"Nicolas? Are you awake?"

He does not stir. Her king-consort is exhausted. She walks her fingers up his chest, playfully.

Her finger slides in warm liquid. At first she cringes, thinking it is drool. But then she recognizes the scent in the air. The smell of so much warm and sudden blood.

Katharine sits up. She leans across to her bedside table for the candle and long matches. Her hands tremble as she lights it, even though she knows what she will see.

Nicolas lies dead, covered in blood. It pools atop his chest and in the wrinkles of the fabric, staining the sheet bright red. It has run from his mouth and from his nose. Even from his eyes. His veins are a swollen, angry purple beneath his skin, nearly everywhere she touched him.

Katharine sits back on her knees and stares down at her new husband. Poor Nicolas. Poor mainland boy, with no gift to help him withstand the toxins. She looks down at her skin, at her hands, at her whole body where the poison resides. The poison inside her must be strong indeed if it can produce such an effect so quickly.

Poor Nicolas. He lay with a queen, and he died for it.

Hoofbeats ring across the stones of the drive. Katharine gets quickly out of bed and stuffs her arms into her dressing gown.

"Natalia. Natalia will help me."

She smooths and folds the tangled, blood-soaked bedclothes, breathing hard, beginning to weep. She touches Nicolas's cooling cheek, and then pulls the sheet over his face. Natalia cannot arrive and see him that way.

"I am sorry," she whispers as footsteps sound in the hall.

"Kat?" Pietyr says, and knocks. "I saw your candle from outside. Are you awake?"

"Pietyr!" Katharine cries. She runs to him and crushes

herself to his chest as he comes through the door.

"You are trembling. What is—?"

She closes her eyes. He has seen it. Seen what she has done. He draws away to look at her. In the faint, shadowed light, he can only barely make out the crown of ink across her forehead. He touches it with his thumb.

"So you have done it," he says sadly. "Tell me what has happened."

It falls out of her mouth in a torrent. The farce of a duel. The crowning. The assassination of Arsinoe. Her wedding night, and the dead king-consort in her bed. When she is finished, she waits, sure that he will shove her away.

"My sweet Katharine," he says, and wipes the tears from her cheek.

"How can you say that?" Her fingers have left streaks of red on his shirt. She tears free and returns to her bedroom, where the shape of Nicolas lies, what is left of his blood pooling in his back and legs.

"I killed him. Just by touching him. There is something wrong with me!"

Pietyr steps around her. He takes up a lamp from the table and pulls back the sheet. Katharine turns away when she sees how gray Nicolas's skin has turned and how sunken his eyes. Pietyr picks up an arm and inspects the fingers.

"So much poison," he whispers.

She is practically made of it. She is like they said she was, the Undead Queen.

She claws at her own face, disgusted, rubbing the fresh scab of her crown until it smears across her forehead, bloody and black.

Pietyr sets down the lamp and comes to her. He pins her arms to her sides.

"Stop. You are a queen. You are crowned. And none of this was your fault."

"You are not surprised," Katharine says. "Why?"

Pietyr looks deep into her eyes for a long time. Almost as if he expects to find someone else there.

"Because after you sent me away, I went to the Breccia Domain. I went down into it."

His fingers dig into her skin, and she notices that they are cold.

"What do you really remember, Kat? From when you fell?"

"From when you pushed me," Katharine says, and jerks loose. She lowers her eyes. "And I remember nothing."

"Nothing," Pietyr repeats. "Perhaps not. Or perhaps you are lying. What I saw there, or what I thought I saw there, made me scream like I have not screamed since I was a child."

She looks up. *He knows.*

The dead queens had gnawed on the bones of their injustices for centuries before he had dropped Katharine right into their laps. That they were able to pour their wishes into her, filling her up with ambition and twisted strength, was his fault.

"At least I was not afraid for you anymore," he says quietly. "The old sisters would never have let you be killed. Not when you were their way into the crown. Out of that hole."

"But it was all for nothing." She stares helplessly at Nicolas graying beneath the sheet. She has become poison. No mainland king may lie with her and survive. No mainland-fathered children could survive the long months in her belly.

"I cannot bear the triplets," she whispers. "I cannot be the queen."

She begins to weep, and Pietyr gathers her to him. "Natalia. How disappointed she will be. How disappointed you must be . . . how disgusted. . . ."

"Never." Pietyr kisses her smeared crown. He kisses her cheeks and kisses away the tears that slip down them.

"Pietyr, I am poison."

"And I am a poisoner. And you have never been more precious to me than you are right now." He raises his head at the sound of an approaching carriage and wraps his arms around her tighter.

"I failed you once. I betrayed you once. But I will not again. From now on, I will protect you, Kat, whatever happens."

INDRID DOWN

$\mathcal{T}$he warriors in the red-lined cloaks are led by a girl named Emilia Vatros and her father. She has the quick, dispassionate eyes of a hunting bird, and Jules likes her immediately.

"Why are you really helping us?" Jules asks.

"It is like I said," Emilia replies, and Madrigal seconds her.

"It wasn't hard to get them to come. You were the whole reason they were in the capital."

"She should have been sent to us anyway," says Emilia's father, eyeing Madrigal. "You should have let her choose, to be yours or to be ours."

"She was mine," Madrigal says. "She was born to me."

"The Goddess feels different."

"How do you know what the Goddess feels?" Madrigal snaps, but Jules shushes her. Emilia's father stands as straight as Cait, his hair dark brown and face lightly lined. And if Madrigal engages him in debate, they will stand in the shadows bickering until the sun comes up and their entire party is discovered.

"Let's get moving, then," Arsinoe says. Two warriors come to take Joseph from Jules's shoulders. Jules looks to Arsinoe, and she nods. They will accept help now, and ask questions later.

Quickly and quietly, they slip through the main level of the Volroy, running and ducking through the castle keep and the inner cloister until they reach the arched, exterior gateway and hunch in the shadows.

Jules swallows nervously. Emilia has dragged her to the fore, and she cannot help but feel as though her war gift is being tested.

"There they are," Emilia whispers, and Jules pushes away from the stone wall of the arch to see what she sees: four fast flashes in the dark, from their compatriots scouting ahead.

"Four flashes," Jules says. "Four guards between us and the edge of the courtyard."

"Yes. Do you see them?"

Jules creeps forward and looks up to the battlements. She sees two. "Where?"

"The other two are along the hedge. Too close together to take separately. Whichever died last would shout, raise an alarm."

Emilia unslings her bow.

"Can't we wait until they leave?" Jules asks. "And then slip out toward the forest?" Once they are in the nighttime streets, it will be easy. Jules still remembers the map of Indrid Down.

It is not more than a twenty-minute run before they find the meadow and then the trees for good cover.

"We have waited too long as it is. It is a wonder someone has not awoken the entire guard already." Emilia nocks an arrow and whistles. Across the corridor, another warrior does the same. Both take aim at the guards, chatting near the hedge.

"Guide my arrow," Emilia whispers.

"What? I can't!"

Emilia grins. "Yes you can," she says. "But it's all right. I can make the shot without you."

Another whistle and the arrows fly. Both guards fall with nary a sound.

"Hey," Jules growls, and grabs Emilia's arm. "Don't do that. We have queens here. Don't waste time by messing about with me!"

Emilia cocks her head. Then her eyes dart to the battlements when another warrior whistles.

"The battlements! They've seen us!"

Jules looks up just as one of the guards fires a crossbow. She flinches and pushes her mind hard, and the bolt bounces off the stones to Emilia's right.

"Go, now!" Jules waves for Arsinoe to come. They dash through the courtyard. Guards at the battlements have alerted others, and arrows strike the ground, too close for Jules's liking. She turns back and pushes out, out, sending as many as she can off course. Even with the blood pounding in her ears, the effort is exhausting.

A warrior fires an arrow beside her, and she watches a guard tumble down the wall.

"Jules!" Arsinoe calls. "Come on!"

Jules and Emilia turn to run, helped by the cover of the other warriors. As they pass the guards fallen by the hedge, an arm shoots out and grasps Jules's ankle. She flies face first onto the path and rolls to kick, but Emilia leaps over the top of him. She takes his head in the crook of her arm and twists.

"Dead now," she says. "Let's go!"

The fleeing queens and their rescue party dissolve into the streets, some going one way, some another. The layout of the city memorized, they meet in alleys to cross paths, running breathless and silent until they break into the meadow in twos and threes to dissipate like drops of ink into water.

"You were good back there." Emilia grins. "I do not like to think of how many poisoned arrows your executioner would have needed to pierce your gift."

"How can you say that to her and smile?" Arsinoe asks.

"How can you talk at all?" Billy asks, panting. He has taken over helping Joseph and struggles beneath the extra weight.

Jules reaches out, but Joseph waves his hand.

"I'm fine, Jules, I'm fine." She steps close and kisses his face. It is cool to the touch and drenched in sweat.

"We have to get him to a healer."

"We came on a barge," says Emilia's father. "It will carry you wherever you wish to go."

GREAVESDRAKE MANOR

⚜

*K*atharine's door opens, but the person who bursts in is not who they expect. It is not Natalia. It is Genevieve.

"Forgive me, Queen Katharine. I do not wish to interrupt but I felt you should know—"

Genevieve stops when she sees Pietyr with Katharine in his arms. Then her mouth drops open at the sight of Nicolas lying dead in the bed.

"What . . . ?"

Genevieve rushes past Katharine and Pietyr and stares down at the body. She does not ask whether someone else could have poisoned him. She is enough of a poisoner herself to see what has happened.

"Katharine, what have you done?"

"I did not mean it!" Katharine cries.

"It will be all right," Pietyr whispers into her hair.

"How will it be all right?" Genevieve asks, her lilac eyes wild. "We have made her into poison!"

"We have made her a Queen Crowned," says Pietyr.

"No," Katharine says. "How can I be, Pietyr, if I can take no king-consort? If I cannot bear the triplets?"

"The poison may fade in time," says Pietyr, but his voice is doubtful.

Genevieve slumps against the bed. Her hand slides in a puddle of cooling blood, and she shakes it off, splattering the sheets. As she leans toward the lamp for something to wipe herself clean with, the light shows her face, swollen from crying.

"Genevieve," Katharine says. "What is wrong?"

Genevieve's arms fall to her lap. She seems to shrink right in front of them.

"Natalia is dead. Murdered."

Katharine freezes. That cannot be right. Natalia, murdered? No one would dare. No one *could.*

"There must be some mistake," says Pietyr. "Who? Who did it?"

"It does not matter who. We are over. Finished." Genevieve's fingers wrap around the corner of the bedsheets, shaking. "Look at this dead king! The temple will not have this . . . nor the Council. . . ." She looks around desperately as if she will find Natalia there somewhere, hiding. "What are we to do? We will have to stop Mirabella's execution! Give her the crown instead! How those Westwoods are going to laugh—"

"Stop it!" Pietyr storms across the room. He grabs Genevieve by the arm and drags her to her feet. "Tell us what happened to Natalia. Tell us now."

"William Chatworth strangled her," Genevieve says. "The war priestess found him and put her knife into his chest. But by then, it was too late."

A fat tear rolls down Katharine's face. Too late. And the murderer dead as well, so she cannot have her vengeance, cannot poison him for days, for weeks, like he deserved. She would have crafted something for him to make him spasm so hard he broke his own back.

Katharine clutches at her stomach. Such pain, such anger boils up inside of her that she can feel even the dead queens cower.

"Natalia," she whispers. "My mother."

"Where is she?" Pietyr asks. "We would see her."

"She is at the Volroy, being guarded by priestesses. Perhaps they will let you in." Genevieve wipes at her own tears. "Before they execute Katharine as an abomination."

"You are a disgrace," Pietyr says suddenly. He had been staring out the window toward the Volroy as they spoke. Now he shoves Genevieve down onto the bed beside the dead king-consort. "No one is going to execute our queen. No true Arron would allow it."

Genevieve jumps to her feet, fists trembling. "Natalia is dead!" she shouts. "Do you not hear what I am saying?"

Outside, below the window, the sound of hoofbeats

announces another rider. It is a messenger. "They have escaped!" he calls up to the house. "The queens! They have escaped the cells and are gone!"

"Queens?" Katharine asks. "How is it 'queens'? I poisoned Arsinoe myself."

"What are we to do?" Genevieve moans. "I am not Natalia. . . . I do not—"

"Be silent, Genevieve, and listen to me," Pietyr says. "Kat, listen. No one can be allowed inside here, do you understand? No one can see this body."

"What will we do with it?" Katharine asks. "With him?"

"We will make up a tale." Pietyr takes her face in his hands. "And you will be the Queen Crowned like we planned." He looks at Genevieve. "Like we promised."

He straightens his clothes and smooths his hair. He goes to bar the door.

"We will find Mirabella. And Arsinoe if she indeed still lives. And we will kill them. With no queens left, the temple will have no choice."

"I do not understand," Genevieve says. "If she still cannot bear the triplets . . ."

"That does not matter." Pietyr closes the door and turns the key in the lock.

"Katharine will be the Queen Crowned," he says. "It is just that she will be the last."

THE INDRID DOWN WOODS

❧

---

*A*rsinoe's bear greets their running party by standing on his hind legs. He hardly knows these fast people in red-lined cloaks and swats at them defensively as they pass. Arsinoe stops below his chest. She is too out of breath to say his name, but his nose sniffs the air eagerly, and he lowers onto her shoulders, smothering her in bear fur and rolling her roughly around on the ground.

"Braddock," she says when she is able. "You're safe."

He is safe but not the same. He is fur and bones. Those poisoners had not known how to feed him properly.

"We should not tarry here long," says Emilia, and looks meaningfully at the queens. She is far more used to giving orders than taking them, Arsinoe could tell that at first glance.

"Jules!"

"Caragh!"

Jules and her aunt embrace beneath the weight of Joseph's arm. It took Jules and Billy both to support him and help him through the forest.

"Can you help him?" Jules asks, but Joseph tugs free.

"I'm all right," he says. "Just bind it tighter."

Arsinoe gets to her feet. She turns Joseph into the moonlight and slaps his hands away when he tries to stop her. She lifts the bandage. Caragh leans down and looks for only a moment before straightening again.

"You see?" Joseph smiles. "It's nothing. A scratch."

Caragh's eyes are wide and soft.

"Good," Jules says, but she kisses Joseph very hard. One sob escapes her as she takes his hand and holds him up. But one sob only. She presses her forehead to his.

Arsinoe turns to Mirabella. Of course she has been listening. Her knuckles are pressed to her lips.

"What if we took him back into the city?" Arsinoe asks. "It's Indrid Down. They have the best healers there. They must."

"No," says Joseph. "I'm fine. I'm going with you, wherever that is. So where is it?"

Arsinoe touches his face. He will be all right. He must be. Joseph Sandrin is one half of Jules.

"There are doctors on the mainland," Billy suggests. "Good ones. Surgeons, far better than here. And it's a short sail through the mist. We can come back and find you," he adds when Joseph starts to protest.

"No," Arsinoe says. "That's good. That's where we're going anyway."

Everyone stops and stares at her. Even Mirabella.

"You could return to your cities," Madrigal suggests. "And gather support there. Not everyone will back the Council's decision to execute you."

"We could take you," says Emilia. "Hide you in Bastian City. We would welcome you, Juillenne. You and anyone whom you wished us to protect."

Jules looks from Emilia to Arsinoe. Then she looks down.

Before the Ascension began, Arsinoe always thought she would find her way back to Wolf Spring. That the madness of the year would pass, and everything would return to normal. Days spent with Jules at the Milone house. Nights beside a warm fire inside the Lion's Head with Billy and Joseph. With Cait and Ellis. Luke and his handsome rooster, Hank. But that life—that good, familiar, and precious time—is over.

The alliance between queens might hold long enough to topple Katharine. But afterward, the people would want them to start all over again. It would be Mirabella or herself. One to kill the other. That is how it has always been.

"Are you sure you want to do this?" Arsinoe asks her sister.

"I will not go back," Mirabella says solemnly. "The Council ordered my death, and they went along with it. Luca went along with it."

Arsinoe takes a deep breath. A queen sits upon the throne.

The island has no more need of them. She *must* let them go. She has to.

"So we make for Bardon Harbor," says Arsinoe. "Let's steal a boat big enough to get us off this Goddess-forsaken island."

BARDON HARBOR

❧

*J*ules helped the warriors call the small river barge that took them into Bardon Harbor. It was not much, barely large enough to fit them all, and nowhere near sturdy enough to brave the rough waters of the sea, but they climbed aboard. Now Jules stands beside the warriors, pushing it with her mind. Joseph chuckles watching Camden at Jules's knee, training all her cougar-focus on the barge as well.

"Look at our girl," he says to Arsinoe, sitting beside him on the barge with her hand pressed hard to the wound in his side. "She's outgrowing us."

"That's not true." But she supposes that it is. She and Joseph have both been chasing after Jules since they were children.

He chuckles again and winces.

"Here," she says. "Let me bind that tighter."

"No, Arsinoe. It's fine."

"Joseph, you have bled through the bandage. You should have stayed behind with Aunt Caragh. Found a healer."

"And miss the adventure?" He smiles his lopsided Joseph smile.

"You're wincing."

"Yes. My side is sore because there's a hole in it. Once we reach the mainland, Billy'll take me to a doctor. And they'll sew me up right and proper."

The barge continues through the moonlight, skimming across the dark surface of the river. Arsinoe looks back. Warriors stayed behind, to run decoy in case of pursuit. Caragh and Braddock stayed behind as well.

"There was no getting the bear on the barge, Arsinoe," Joseph says, reading her thoughts.

"I know."

"You did save him. And Caragh will take good care of him at the Black Cottage."

Stream-caught fish and berries for the rest of his days. And he will be safe. But she will never see him again.

Jules leaves the warriors and comes to squat beside them. She touches Joseph's cheek and Camden climbs atop his legs to keep him warm. "Is he all right?"

"*He* is still conscious and can answer for himself," he says.

"It's not much longer now," Jules says, and as she looks out worriedly at the river, the small barge seems to move faster. If the warriors notice, they do not acknowledge it, but Madrigal, Mirabella, and Billy all look over their shoulders.

"Good," Joseph says. "Fishers are up early. If we want to steal a boat, we won't have much time."

They reach the mouth of the river, and Bardon Harbor slides

into view. The boats docked at the port are much larger than the vessels in Sealhead Cove. Their masts rise through the predawn fog. These are far-ranging ships, built to chase frothbacks across the open sea, with smaller whale boats lashed to their sides. They are too big to be sailed with such a skeleton crew, but that is what Mirabella is for. And they will need a large vessel if the sea decides to put up any kind of fight.

The barge nudges silently up against the nearest dock, disturbing nothing but a couple of roosting gulls.

"Slowly, slowly," Madrigal says as she helps Mirabella off the barge. "These docks are unfamiliar, and the moon gives us only so much light."

Billy helps Arsinoe and Jules to lift Joseph, and grimaces at all the blood. Arsinoe flashes a bracing smile.

"It'll be all right," she says.

"I hope so. You queens do have a way of working things out. All right, Joseph. Don't dawdle. You weigh more than your slender frame would suggest." He takes Joseph off their hands and aids him as he limps down the dock.

"Are you ready, Jules?" Arsinoe asks. But Jules turns back to Madrigal, and to Emilia and the warriors.

"I'm right behind you," she says.

Jules watches her friends creep along the docks. In the thick morning mist, they look like magic, like fairies, stealing in and out of view.

"You won't really go, will you, Jules?" Madrigal asks. Her

hand is on her belly; she is always so worried about her unborn baby. Jules reaches out and touches her mother's stomach.

"Try to make peace with Aunt Caragh. She's your sister. And a midwife now. She can help you with this."

"Peace. There may be no peace, but I will have this baby at the Black Cottage, if you will go there with me," Madrigal says, but Jules does not reply. It will be better if she leaves. Better for Wolf Spring. Without her, the Black Council might decide to leave well enough alone. Goddess knows, they will have enough to deal with, after this debacle of an Ascension.

"You should stay with us," Emilia says fiercely. "Let the queens and the mainlanders go."

"I am her guardian." Jules's eyes follow Arsinoe through the harbor. "And I will remain her guardian. Until the end."

"This *is* where it ends," says Emilia. "Though not for you. I sense a great destiny for you, Juillenne Milone." She offers her hand, steady as stone. The warriors came to her aid for no other reason than she was one of theirs. They would take her, and even Camden. And Jules would very much like to see the halls of Bastian City.

"Looking after her will be a great destiny."

On the docks, Arsinoe leads Mirabella by the hand. The affection between them is easy and natural, and it makes Jules's chest ache. Her place beside Arsinoe is less now that Mirabella is there. She does not need Jules like she used to.

"I can't let her go alone," Jules says. "There are still battles to fight." She turns to face the warriors and her mother. "And I can't let Joseph go either."

Emilia's eyes flash. But she holds her tongue, and Jules and Camden step off the barge. It rocks as their weight leaves it.

"When your battle is over," Emilia says, "we will be here. Until then, be well. Take care of your queen." She smiles down at Camden in the moonlight. "And your cat."

Emilia pushes off, and the barge slides quietly through the water, returning to rejoin the rest of the warriors. Madrigal paces along the edge, but there is no danger of her jumping. She presses a kiss to her palm and raises it in a wave. Perhaps she is crying, but if she is, through the fog, Jules cannot see it.

Mirabella waits nervously as Billy and Arsinoe loose their ship from its moorings. There is a sadness in her and an uneasiness, but underneath she hums with excitement. Preparing to face the open waves, and the mists, and the Goddess who would see them dead; it is like Luca told her that day. It is clear, and she is right where she belongs.

"Are you sure it's not too big for you?" Joseph asks doubtfully. She has Joseph's arm slung across her shoulders.

"They have not crafted a ship that is too big for me."

Footfalls and paw steps sound across the dock, and Jules slides in under Joseph's other arm. "Let me help," she says, and she and Mirabella take him across the gangplank. They ease him down beside the portside rail on the main deck.

"Can you secure him?" Mirabella asks.

"Can you break us through the mist?" Jules asks back, and

begins to lash him down with ropes. Mirabella pushes the wind, and the current, and the boat rocks forward. Jules nearly loses her footing and looks up at her sourly. But then she smiles.

Billy and Arsinoe ready the sails, and Mirabella goes to the foredeck. She looks back at the shore, at the island. Even had she won the crown and ruled, she would have left the island eventually. But she never thought it would be like this. A fugitive queen and without even saying good-bye to her dearest Bree and Elizabeth.

"Are you ready?" Arsinoe asks, a bit breathless from tugging ropes. Billy is at the helm, to help her steer. But he will not need to help much.

"The people we leave behind," says Mirabella. "They will take care of one another?"

"I hope so," Arsinoe replies. "I think so."

Mirabella turns to face the gray morning sea.

"Then yes. I am ready."

THE VOLROY

❦

*H*igh in the West Tower, Katharine and Pietyr await news of the escaped queens. The High Priestess is there as well, and the Black Council, not to mention a gaggle of priestesses and Sara Westwood. They would have admitted Cait or Madrigal Milone too, had either of them bothered to come to the city for the duel.

"Where is your king-consort?" High Priestess Luca asks, and Genevieve's eyes dart around wildly. Pietyr is going to have to glue her eyes shut to keep from giving them away.

"At Greavesdrake, High Priestess," Katharine replies. "Resting."

They are surprisingly sedate, this group. Waiting calmly and with something that looks like patience. But it is not truly patience. It is shock. Their fugitive queens have broken out of their cells, and every person in the room feels the space where Natalia Arron should be.

"This should never have happened," Antonin says, seated at a dark, oval table with his head in his hands. "Two poisoner queens in the same cycle. Queen Arsinoe should have come to us. She should have been ours to raise."

"Along with you, Queen Katharine," Genevieve says quickly, and Antonin looks up.

"Of course along with her."

Katharine smiles through closed lips. Of course. But Arsinoe seems to have been the stronger poisoner. Had they been raised together, Katharine would have lived only until Mirabella was killed. Then she would have found herself at the sharp end of a knife. Possibly held by an Arron.

Katharine turns toward the door. A messenger is arriving, and the gathered people rise from their chairs.

"What news of Mirabella?" Luca asks sharply. "What news of the queens?"

"We were too late," the boy says, breathless. "They escaped on a ship."

"And you did not give chase?" Pietyr snaps, but the poor messenger looks at the ground.

"There would have been little point with Mirabella at the helm," Luca answers for him. "With her wind and her currents, no one was going to catch them."

"A gift as strong as hers, she might have sunk them for trying," Sara adds, and Katharine narrows her eyes.

"What direction did they sail?" Luca asks.

Katharine drifts through the room, to the eastward-facing

windows. From there, she can see clear past the port and on to the sea. But there is no tiny ship fleeing up the coast to Rolanth. There is no tiny ship anywhere that she can see.

"They sailed straight out, High Priestess," the boy says. "Straight out and away to the east."

"They must be found," Pietyr says. "Stopped." When no one hurries to move, he turns on them angrily. "It was you who decreed their fates! Will none of you now enforce the decree?"

Katharine places her hands atop the cold, stone sill of the window. On her forehead, her scabbed crown has been wiped and made clean, once again a fine, black band. She stares into the distance and feels the muttering of the dead queens deep in her bones. She has done what they wanted. Become what they intended.

Across her city, the dawn grows bright. It shines off the black buildings and cobblestone streets, hueing them orange and pink. Katharine looks past the island and over the shimmering water. In the distance, the sky has remained dark. Storm clouds are gathering, and when she listens closely, she hears lightning crackling softly over faraway water.

"Do not worry, Pietyr," Katharine says, and their bickering stops. She turns and smiles a queen's smile, with a queen's confidence. Then she looks back at the sea and the confrontation that is about to take place there.

"Neither of my sisters will be returning to the island. The crown and the throne are mine."

THE SEA

*A*rsinoe steps up to the railing and watches the shore move farther and farther away. If they manage to pass through the net of mist, they will watch the whole island grow smaller, until it is only a shape, and then a dot, and then gone.

Something furry brushes her shoulder. Camden, paws on the rail beside her, growling down at the waves. Arsinoe ruffles the big cat's scruff and pulls her down to take her back to Jules.

Joseph smiles up at her from Jules's arms. "Here we are again," he says. "The three of us, in a boat."

Arsinoe tries to laugh. But he is so pale. The makeshift bandages are soaked through with blood.

"We should put Cam below," she says to Jules. "Somewhere soft, or in a crate, before the journey turns rough."

"Will you put her there for me?" Jules asks. She will not leave Joseph. Not until they find a healer on the mainland.

Arsinoe takes the cougar below to find a space for her.

"Put her in a cabin," Billy says, following her down. "That will be the safest spot."

They find the best one together, and Arsinoe kisses Camden's head before shutting her inside.

"How soon can we get to the mainland?"

"I think that depends on Mirabella, doesn't it? And the mist? I mean, I don't like to think about what happened the last time—"

Before he can say anything foolish, Arsinoe throws her arms around him and kisses him. He is surprised, and stiff, but it is better this time, without a mouthful of poison. She leans into his chest, and he holds her tightly. It is better than a great number of things.

"We'd better get back up," she says after she lets him go.

"Right. Back up," he mumbles, and follows her up the stairs.

They have left Bardon Harbor behind. The guards from the wakened city were too late, and their horses' hooves skidded to a stop on the shore. No one bothered to unmoor a ship to give chase, knowing that they could not catch up to Mirabella. And now, the dawn spills across the water in a thousand yellow sparkles, and the sea is calm.

Perhaps they have truly been let go and the mist will part like a drawn-back curtain.

The winds ruffle their collars at first and whip a little hair into their eyes. For as long as the skies remain clear they pretend it is only wind. A good sailing wind, to help them along. When the first of the mist slithers across the waves they try to pretend it is only fog, or froth. But soon enough the mist is a wall, and the storm is a gale. It is the Goddess, bearing down.

"Do you think she still wants to keep us?" Arsinoe shouts as she stands beside Mirabella on the foredeck.

Mirabella keeps her arms thrust down at her sides as she concentrates. "Perhaps it is one last test."

No one says that they should turn back. But every one of them is afraid. The net of mist lies heavily atop the water, white and so very thick.

"Do not fear it!" Mirabella shouts.

"Easy for you to say! You don't know what it's like to try to pass through! How it chokes you and turns you around!"

Mirabella takes Arsinoe by the hand. "Are you ready, Sister?" she asks.

"I am. We go through! Or we sink!"

Mirabella pushes wind into the sails so hard that the entire ship jumps forward like a horse breaking its harness. The storm is as fine a storm as Mirabella has ever seen. She would be in love with it were it not trying to stand in their way.

"Go back with them," she says to Arsinoe.

"Are you sure?"

"Yes. Go back with them and hold tight to something." She looks at her little sister's terrified face as seawater slams over the rail. She smiles. "Hold tight to Billy, perhaps."

Arsinoe's eyes shift away from the storm and she manages a laugh.

"If you say so."

Mirabella watches her go. Jules has her arms wrapped

around Joseph and gripping tight to ropes, soaked and miserable-looking already. Arsinoe joins Billy at the helm, and they cling to the wheel as the ship rises and falls.

Mirabella turns back to the storm. The electricity in the air hums in her elemental veins. The dawn is gone. All is dark. The waves raise them up only to send them crashing back down, and the first of the lightning crackles across the sky.

The net of mist swallows the boat to curl around the port side in thick, white fingers. Mirabella sends them surging ahead; she uses the wind to push the mist away. She calls more rain, more lightning to dance with the storm of the island.

If the Goddess truly wanted to keep her, then she should not have chosen a storm as the means to try.

Beneath the warring storms, it is dark as midnight. Only lightning illuminates their way, and it is terrifying: near constant. Arsinoe has never seen lightning strike lightning before, and after this is over, she has no care to again.

Together, she and Billy fight to keep the wheel steady, half steering and half holding on to keep from being washed overboard. Joseph and Jules huddle together near the railing, arms wrapped around ropes. Mirabella stands alone on the foredeck, using one storm to fight the other.

"I don't know how much longer we can do this," Billy shouts between the thunder. "I don't know how much longer *she* can!"

Arsinoe's teeth chatter in the wet and the wind, her jaw clacking too hard to reply.

They crest a wave and slam down. She bites her lip and tastes warm salt, but cannot tell whether it is blood or the sea. A wave tilts the deck hard to starboard, and for one frozen moment, it seems they will not come back upright. But they do. She barely has time to sigh with relief before another wave hits, with so much force it feels like being slammed into a wall.

"Are you all right?" Billy shouts, and she nods, coughing. There is so much water and cold. She wipes salt from her eyes. Mirabella is still upright amid everything, and Arsinoe smiles. She does not know how anyone ever expected that she or Katharine could stand against *that*.

Jules grabs Joseph by the arm and hauls him to her chest as the waves batter them against the railing. "Joseph, hold on to me! Hold on to me, and don't let go!"

"I will never," he says, his voice soft and clear so close to her neck. His breathing is shallow, and he no longer shivers. She draws back to look into his eyes. There is too much seawater for tears.

"What will we do," she asks gently, "when we reach the mainland?"

"Anything we want." His eyes drift shut. "There is a great school there, and bells that ring like music. . . . We can learn anything we like."

"Anything," she says. "And everything. And we will be together."

"We will be. Just like I planned." He smiles that Joseph smile, and Jules kisses him and kisses him, even after she no longer feels him kissing back.

The storm pitches them back and forth in the mist, but Mirabella clings to the rail like a barnacle, even though she is panting, and the strength is leaving her legs.

The mist still holds them like a net.

"I've got you, Sister," Arsinoe says. "I'll help you."

Mirabella blinks. Somehow Arsinoe fought her way across the deck. Somehow she is standing and pulling Mirabella back onto her feet. She slips her fingers into Mirabella's hand and squeezes.

"I'm no elemental," Arsinoe says. "But I am still a queen."

Mirabella laughs. She screams. And they face down the storm one more time as wind pushes the sails taut and the waves strike hard enough to tear at their clothes.

Perhaps if Katharine were there and they were three together it would have all gone easier. But as it is, they are only two, and the Goddess takes that much more convincing.

When the storm dies, it dies so quickly that Mirabella's storm continues to rage for long moments before she realizes. She trembles, and Arsinoe catches her when she seems about to fall.

Around them, the white mist swirls and parts, revealing sunlight on the water, and in the distance, the dark shape of land.

* * *

"That's it!" Billy shouts. "That's home. I'd know it anywhere!"

Home. His home. Arsinoe throws her arms around Mirabella, and they huddle on the foredeck, so tired that their laughter sounds nearly like tears.

"I was afraid it was the island," Arsinoe says. "Like it was on Beltane. But we made it! Jules! Jules, look!"

Jules is seated beside the rail with Joseph pulled across her lap. He is not moving.

Billy leaps down from the helm and rushes below to let Camden up; they can hear the poor cat butting against the door. In moments, she leaps onto the deck, lashing her tail angrily, and bounds to Jules. But when she sniffs at Joseph, she lets out a long, low moan.

"No." Arsinoe runs to them. "No!"

She kneels and touches his cold face.

Billy turns away and curses. He grips the rail and shouts at no one.

"But we're here," Arsinoe says. "We made it!"

Jules grasps her, and they hold each other tight.

Mirabella approaches quietly, her ragged, torn skirt rustling and soaked with salt water.

"Oh, Joseph," she whispers, and begins to weep.

"I'm sorry," Arsinoe says as Jules struggles up from underneath them. Joseph's face is peaceful. But he cannot really be gone. Not their Joseph.

Jules wanders across the deck. "Will you have a funeral for

him?" she asks. "Billy, will you?"

"Of . . . of course we will," he says.

"Jules?" Arsinoe asks. "What are you doing?"

Jules is faced back toward the mist that shrouds the ghost of the island.

"All that sailing," she whispers. "Yet it's still not far. I won't even need to row long to reach a port."

"Jules!" Arsinoe scrambles up. She goes to her and takes her by the arm. "What are you talking about? You are not going back."

Jules shakes her off, and Arsinoe's mouth drops open.

"I can't go," Jules says. "You know I can't. I belong in one place, and that's there." She nods to the island. But she cannot really want to return. She must just be afraid. And sad. But they are all sad.

Jules reaches out and looses one of the small whaling boats from the starboard side.

"No." Arsinoe slaps her hands. "I'm sorry about Joseph. I know you loved him. I loved him, too! But you can't go!"

"You don't need me anymore," Jules says, and actually smiles. "You've fought, and you've won."

"*We* have won. Don't you see?" Arsinoe turns around and points to the mainland.

"There's everything, right there! There's freedom, and choices, and a life spent together! No one to tell us we weren't meant to be. No crown. No Council. No killing. We get to decide who we are now, outside of all that."

The boat rocks gently, and the mainland shines green under summer sun. There is no mist. No one waiting to kill her or tell her to kill.

The whaling boat splashes into the water. Jules and Camden are already inside it.

"Wait," Arsinoe says. She reaches for the rigging, but Jules casts off. "Wait, I said!"

They look up at her sadly.

"I don't want to go without you," Arsinoe whispers.

"I know. But you have to."

The moment Jules's oars touch the water, the island's mist creeps out. It swirls around the boat greedily with something that almost seems like relief. Like affection. As if it was Jules, truly, who the island was trying to keep.

"Look after them for me," Jules calls to Billy and Mirabella.

"Jules, get back on this ship!" Arsinoe takes a deep breath, about to jump over the rail, but Billy grabs her by the shoulders. He pulls her to his chest, and she shouts and struggles, watching Jules grow smaller until the mist thickens and Arsinoe can no longer see her face.

"It will be all right," Billy says. He squeezes her, hard. Mirabella comes closer and takes her hand.

"It will be," Arsinoe whispers as tears drip from her chin.

She turns her head to look into the sun, toward an unknown country. An unknown future. Anything could await them there, and the possibilities cloud her mind. She does not remember what it was like not to live in fear or in resentment, of being killed or of having to. She hears Jules's voice calling to her across the water.

"I love you, Arsinoe."

"Jules, come back!" She turns around. "It'll be different, you'll see!"

But when she looks, Jules and the island are gone. The mist of Fennbirn has disappeared, and where it was only moments ago there is only the sea, clear and sparkling.

The queens of Fennbirn will return.

ACKNOWLEDGMENTS

You would think that the more of these you write the easier it would become, like eventually it would just be a laundry list of thank you, thank you, check, check. Alas, it isn't, because with each new one, the folks you have to thank have done so much more even than they did the last time and any acknowledgment feels inadequate. This whole page should have jazz hands all over it is what I'm saying.

Thank you to my amazing editor, Alexandra Cooper, for cracking the pacing whip and the detail whip and the art of subtlety whip (which is a hard whip to wield), and all the other myriad whips you seem to own to get this book into shape. Thank you to my agent, Adriann Ranta-Zurhellen, who is, I'll just say it, the best agent who has ever agented or will ever agent on this or any other planet. Thanks to Olivia Russo for wrangling publicity with such a deft and organized hand.

Thanks to the entire team at HarperTeen: Jon Howard,

Aurora Parlagreco, Erin Fitzsimmons, Alyssa Miele, Bess Braswell, and Audrey Diestelkamp. I know I'm missing people here and it pains me. Thanks to Robin Roy, whose name I see in copyediting comment bubbles.

Thanks to Morgan Rath and Crystal Patriarche at Book-Sparks, for being amazing to work with and also for the fried chicken.

Thanks to Allison Devereux and Kirsten Wolf at Wolf Literary.

Thanks to my mom, who is pleased with anything I write; to my dad, who actually hasn't started reading this series yet; and to my brother, Ryan, who *gasp* actually has. Thanks to Susan Murray for being excited about every new thing I tell her about the queens. Thanks to the wonderful novelist April Genevieve Tucholke for support and wise counsel through the art of tarot.

And to Dylan Zoerb, for luck.

TURN THE PAGE FOR AN
EXCLUSIVE *ONE DARK THRONE*
BONUS CHAPTER.

THE BODY OF THE
KING-CONSORT

⚜

*B*y the time Katharine is able to return to Greaves-drake, it is past dusk. It was a long day, waiting for some sailor to return with the drowned bodies of Mirabella and Arsinoe, and listening to the Black Council worry and grumble and snipe at one another. A long day, with nothing at all to show for it. No one returned with her dead sisters, to lay them at her feet. And without Natalia to lead them, the Black Council is rudderless. Though it is painful to think about, someone will have to take Natalia's place. The most obvious choice would be Genevieve, now matriarch of the Arron family. But Katharine does not know if she could stand that. Or if Natalia would even have wanted it.

All in all, it was not the first day she would have wished for. Tainted by uncertainty and surrounded by pesky priestesses. High Priestess Luca judged her every move, her every sigh, her every sign of fatigue. Even above the jolting sounds of the

3

carriage, Luca's mocking words still ring in Katharine's ears.

"How do you like it? Is it all you and the Arrons hoped?"

Yes, Katharine wanted to snap. *We hoped for missing queens and Natalia dead. Do our plans not dazzle?*

But instead she had bowed her head. She had won, after all. She was queen, and as queen she would have to work with the temple, and all the cities of the island. So she let Luca go on and on about the difficulties that lay before them. Convincing the people of the "rightness" of Katharine's crown, and the unfortunate distraction of planning Natalia's funeral.

The casual mention of Natalia's funeral stopped Katharine in her tracks.

"It would be much easier if she were here," Katharine had said. "For there is no one left on the island who is half the leader that she was."

Thinking on it now brings her anger back afresh, and she knocks against the carriage roof.

"Driver," she calls out. "A little faster, if you please."

"Eager to return to your king-consort, my queen?" the coachman asks, and laughs heartily. "We'll get you to him soon enough, don't worry."

The carriage jolts forward, and Katharine sinks against the cushions. Let them think so. It is not as though they are wrong, even if her eagerness is for an entirely different reason.

Nicolas's dead body has been untended all day. Wrapped in a sheet and stuffed unceremoniously into her closet. When she, Pietyr, and Genevieve were summoned to the Volroy, she spread the tale to the Black Council that she had let her king-consort rest on account of the early hour. But as the day dragged on, they started to wonder. She had to send Genevieve with a personal message to him, with Katharine's regrets that her business was keeping her from him for so long and her wish that he remain at Greavesdrake in comfort. She hopes that Genevieve was smart enough to order some food brought for show so the servants would not wonder. And she hopes that she stayed with him a few moments afterward and pretended to converse. It is silly, since he is dead, but Katharine hopes that he was not always alone.

Edmund bows deep as she strides through the doors, and Katharine clasps her hands before her so he will not see them shake.

"Has he not been down?" she asks, walking toward the stairs and turning around again.

"He has not. Mistress Genevieve lunched with him, as you must know. He left instruction with her that he was not to be disturbed by anyone other than yourself."

"He is sweet," Katharine says in a voice like wood. "Edmund?"

"Yes, madam?"

"Will you stay on here now that Natalia is gone?"

"I will serve the Arrons, Queen Katharine. As I have these many years."

"Good." She nearly kisses his cheek before she remembers

that her touch is poisoned and may give him a rash. "Natalia was very fond of you, you know. She always spoke so highly of you."

"Thank you, Queen Katharine. She was a very fine mistress."

She looks at him more carefully in the candlelight, trying to detect signs of sadness or redness in his eyes. But she is unsurprised to find none. Whatever he feels, he keeps to himself. He does not even make eye contact. He never has, not even long ago, when she was a child and would have found it comforting.

"Genevieve will be a good mistress to you as well," she says as she goes down the hall toward her staircase. "Or she will hear about it from me."

When she reaches her rooms, she takes a deep breath. She is no stranger to the scent of decay. But the summer sun shone hot from dawn to dusk, and who knows whether Genevieve remembered to open the windows. She places her gloved hand over the doorknob and twists it open.

"My queen!"

Katharine yanks the door shut.

"Giselle!" She exhales, and turns to take her maid's hands, pulling her up from where she had dropped to her knee. "You startled me!"

"Forgive me, Queen Katharine. . . . I—"

"Here at Greavesdrake, you may still call me Kat. Like always."

Giselle smiles as though relieved, but Katharine knows that

she will never call her "Kat" again.

"I'm so glad to see you returned," says Giselle. "That you and your king-consort will remain with us another night. I tried to be of use to him this morning, to see whether he had need of anything, but he didn't reply."

"I am sure he was sleeping. He is a deep sleeper."

"Of course." Giselle smiles like they are sharing a saucy secret, and Katharine feels sick to her stomach. "Will you stay with us much longer?"

"Perhaps. The West Tower is nowhere near ready. But who knows how fast the servants work within the Volroy walls. Now, if you will excuse me."

Giselle curtsies deeply. Katharine waits until she is gone, out of sight, before opening the door again and slipping inside.

The smell is not so bad. Nowhere near as bad as she feared. A week's worth of fresh cut flowers and open windows will put the rooms to rights again, if they can get Nicolas's body out before another day passes.

She walks quietly through the dark rooms that she knows so well. She lights candles, for herself and for Sweetheart, coiled in her cage on Katharine's desk.

"Such a long day," she says. "To be followed by many, many more long days." She picks up a candelabra and walks into her bedchamber. She throws open the closet door.

Nicolas is there, stuffed upright and wrapped round and round in so many layers that none of the blood has managed to soak through. The shape of his head and shoulders are barely visible. He might be a package to be tied up with a bow. He might be a rug.

Katharine sets the candles down and reaches out to touch the sheet.

"Hello, husband," she says.

When Pietyr arrives much later, he finds her still sitting beside the open closet door, chatting with Nicolas.

"Katharine, come away from there," he says, and holds out his hands. She stands and he folds her into warm arms. "I am sorry." He kisses her cheeks and the top of her head. "I am sorry it took me so long. But look at you. You are not bothered at all! My fierce little Kat."

"Not bothered. But I was wondering." She cuffs him lightly on the shoulder. "What kept you? I thought you would be behind me in the next carriage!"

"Tangled up in Volroy business," he says vaguely. "Making sure your new quarters were being properly prepared. And I had a room made up there for me to stay in. Then it took time to sneak out. Given what we are to do tonight, it would be better if people thought I was nowhere near here. I only hope it will prove as simple to sneak back in again before morning. Now"—he looks at Nicolas's body—"what to do with that fellow?"

"Do not talk about him that way. 'That fellow.' He was your king!"

"And now he is dead, my queen. However you wish to frame it, something must be done with him. Unless"—Pietyr pulls away from her with wide, teasing eyes—"unless you intend to keep him? Prop him up beside you at the Volroy as he goes green? I know you are the undead queen, my pet, but people will still look at you strangely."

"You!" she exclaims, and the dead queens roil in her blood. But their whispers are not angry. They like Pietyr. They know Pietyr. "How can you joke now? This is a disaster. Not one day crowned and my king-consort is dead and I killed him."

"Not on purpose, my love."

No. Not on purpose. But she does not think that Nicolas would care one way or the other. She would look to Nicolas's corpse for an imagined nod of forgiveness, but since Pietyr has arrived, she cannot bring herself to face him.

"I am sorry, Kat. I should not joke. I was only trying to provide relief. I was there with you today. I know the weight of this on your shoulders."

"I know that, Pietyr. And I cannot do this without you."

He takes her hand and kisses her fingertips, drawing her away from the closet to sit with him upon the bed. He is tired. But she also senses an energy in him. Much has changed with the victory of the Ascension and the loss of Natalia. The death of the king-consort. And Pietyr knows how to take advantage of perceived failures. He did it when he came to Greavesdrake, after the failure of her birthday *Gave Noir*.

"Tomorrow will be just as hard," he says. "Perhaps harder. Tomorrow Natalia will be ready for viewing in Indrid Down Square."

"Criers and notices must go out early. I would have the

entire capital wear crimson for her. I do not know how I will face it, Pietyr. To see her lying there . . . She will not even look like herself. You heard the undertakers: they will have to paint her face to cover the popped blood vessels, rouge her cheeks to hide the swelling. . . . Natalia has not been rosy-cheeked a day in her life."

"No she has not. But perhaps that will make it easier. I know that I will need to see it if only to believe it. And so will the people. That is what it will take for them to believe that Natalia Arron, the giant, is dead."

A tear slides down Katharine's cheek. It does not seem possible that Natalia would leave her now.

"You will never leave me, Pietyr. Will you?"

"Never. I will be here like I promised."

"And you will be, even if I do not place you on the Black Council?"

Pietyr smiles slightly. Katharine has not awarded him Natalia's vacant seat on the Council yet, but everyone knows that it will not be long.

He touches her face. With his ice-blue eyes and pale blond hair, he is so like Natalia. He leans close and kisses her softly.

"I am here because I love you, Kat. Because I fell in love with you when I was not supposed to. And that will never change." He exhales and leans back, listening to the silence of Greavesdrake at night. Even the chirping of the insects outside seems more muted here than in other places.

"Now we ought to go," he says, and pulls her up off the bed.

"I have a plan for him"—he nods toward Nicolas—"and if it is to succeed, it must be carried out before morning."

Moving Nicolas's body is the least queenly experience of Katharine's life. It was a disgusting, disturbing chore to get him into his riding clothes and wrap him up again in a dark blanket. Now they must smuggle him quietly out of the manor. It is not easy. He is heavy and smells unpleasant, and she keeps tripping over the ill-fitting trousers that Pietyr made her change into. On top of that, the quiet night amplifies their every move, and the lack of breeze makes the summer heat more stifling. By the time they get him inside the stable, both she and Pietyr are drenched in sweat.

Quickly, Pietyr goes to saddle two black horses.

"Not that one," Katharine whispers when he goes toward the wrong stall. "She shies too easily. We do not need her dumping Nicolas in the dirt."

Pietyr nods, and soon enough, they are heaving the body over the new horse's pommel. Even this steady one does not like the way the corpse collapses over its shoulder, and both horses dislike the smell of rotting flesh. They blow their nostrils wide and paw the ground, but Katharine holds them fast as Pietyr mounts behind Nicolas's draped body. Then she quickly leaps into her own saddle.

"A lucky thing Mirabella challenged you to a duel on the full moon," Pietyr says as they pick their way slowly along the bridle paths, going farther and farther into wooded land. "Or we would likely have met with a true accident." He looks back at her, but she cannot make out his expression. "This is dangerous work as it is. I should not have brought you, Kat, but I needed your help."

They ride for a long time before Pietyr finally decides they have gone far enough and begins to look for the right place. There are plenty of choices. Riding in the hills is known to be treacherous, and some of the paths are not well-kept. Nicolas, as a Mainlander, would not have known which to avoid.

"Here," Pietyr says, and Katharine pulls her horse to a halt behind his. The moonlight casts silver onto the path, and down through the trees she can see a deep ravine, just off the trail. She dismounts and helps Pietyr take the body down off his pommel.

"What do we do?" she asks.

"Throw him," he replies. And when her eyes widen, he touches her shoulder and says, "Any scrapes and damage from the tumble down the hill will make it look more like a fall. And he will not feel it, I promise you. But we must unwrap him first."

They unroll Nicolas as gently as they can, despite being about to throw him into a ravine, and Katharine cannot help but recoil when the blanket is gone and his dead arms thump against the ground, his dead face staring up at the night sky.

"I am sorry," she says as she quickly grasps onto his wrists.

"I am sorry, too," says Pietyr, hoisting Nicolas by the ankles. "Even though I never liked you."

"On 'three,' Kat," he says, and they swing back once, and harder, and on the third let him fly. The sounds he makes crashing down the hill, through underbrush and saplings and against the trunks of trees, are ghastly. She is glad of the darkness now, so she will not have to carry a clear picture of it in her memory.

"I have to go down after him," Pietyr says grimly. "To make sure the wounds appear to be mortal. Stay here."

"Be careful." She watches as Pietyr slowly descends, holding her breath until he reaches the body. When he leans over to lift Nicolas's corpse and smash the skull against a rock, she turns away and presses her forehead to her horse's neck. "Forgive me, Nicolas," she whispers. "I never intended you harm."

Pietyr returns to the path and wipes his hands on the dark blanket.

"We will burn this," he says. "And near dawn, I will ride out on his horse, in more of his riding clothes and a yellow wig. I will let myself be glimpsed by people on the roads but pass by too quickly to be recognized. And then I'll leave the horse in these woods before slipping into my makeshift bedchamber in the Volroy."

Katharine nods.

"When the mare returns without her rider, you and I will lead the searches," Pietyr goes on. "We ought to keep them away from here for several days."

Katharine glances down into the ravine, toward her fallen consort, as already her regret fades. "Long enough for the state of the body to truly defy examination."

13

Pietyr pulls her close and kisses her, harder than he has since before Beltane. Her Pietyr, who knows her like no one else knows her.

"Are we going to be all right, Pietyr? Even without Natalia to guide us?"

"We will," he says, and strokes her hair. "You have come so far, my little Kat. And I could not be prouder."

Katharine smiles, but she is not his little Kat, not anymore. Now she is Queen Katharine, the Undead. And all of Fennbirn will come to know her legend.